THE SHEPHERD'S HEART · BOOK 3

FAIR ★ VALLEY
Refuge

Ps. 46:1

Lynnett

What Readers Think About
The Shepherd's Heart Series

Rocky Mountain Oasis is a delightful step back into the Wild West. Ms. Bonner draws her characters in bold and wonderful strokes that give a portrait of them so tender and convincing you cannot help loving them. I really enjoyed this novel. It is touching and fulfilling. It also includes a very strong message of redemption. I look forward to her next novel.
—Lionel D. Alford
Author of *Aegypt*, and *The Second Mission.*

I love *Rocky Mountain Oasis*. I just couldn't put it down. I kept it in my hands until I was done. The story line was well written and the use of historical facts made the story all the more fascinating for me. Thanks for such a great book! I can't wait for the next one!
—Krista
Amazon Reviewer

Rocky Mountain Oasis is very well written, I really enjoyed every word of it! I really related to Brooke's feelings and emotions. Lynette does an excellent job making you feel each aspect of her life. Plus the suspense part, just really keeps you on the edge of your seat!!! This is a great historical, mail order bride read... I highly recommend it!
—Martha
Amazon Reviewer

Lynnette Bonner has outdone herself with *High Desert Haven*. This action-packed story of life in the Old West just begs to be turned into a movie. It's a powerful tale of hardship and happiness, of loss and love, and most of all, of the power of faith. If you enjoy stories of the way life really was in the nineteenth century, don't miss *High Desert Haven*.
—AMANDA CABOT - Author of *Tomorrow's Garden*

Set in a time when men killed for land and beautiful women, *High Desert Haven* is a sweet romance with enough flying bullets to please any Western fans. The blazing hearts and guns blend well with the faith message, which the author beautifully weaves into the characters' lives. If you're looking for a novel to get you through a sleepless night, this is the one. Then again, it's probably the reason you're still awake.

—April Gardner
Award-winning author of *Wounded Spirits*

High Desert Haven has more than enough action to keep readers' lamps burning into the night. Bonner has shaped a lively romance that shoots straight from the heart.

—Sharon McAnear-
Author of the Jemma series and the Stars in My Crown series

Brimming with endearing flesh-and-blood characters amidst the beautiful high desert mountains, Lynnette Bonner has crafted a heart-tugging story interwoven with enough romance and suspense and spiritual gems to keep readers turning pages far into the night. This second book in The Shepherd's Heart series is worth the wait!

—Laura Frantz
Author of *The Frontiersman's Daughter*, *Courting Morrow Little*, and *The Colonel's Lady*

Bonner has consistently wowed us with her attention to detail, heart touching characters and hair raising danger. It's a fun ride, one that will make you laugh out loud and then weep. You will never regret the time spent or the sleep lost in reading these books. I have re-read them many times now, and each time is like the first. Her love for Christ shows through every page. I have enjoyed them all immensely and I can't wait for more.

—Anndra
Amazon Reviewer

THE SHEPHERD'S HEART BOOK 3

FAIR VALLEY Refuge

Lynnette BONNER

Pacific Lights

Fair Valley Refuge
THE SHEPHERD'S HEART SERIES, Book 3

Published by Pacific Lights Publishing
Copyright © 2012, 2015 by Lynnette Bonner. All rights reserved.

Cover design by Lynnette Bonner, Indie Cover Design, images ©
  www.bigstock.com, File: #2460720
  www.bigstock.com, File: #78680417

Author photo © Emily Hinderman, EMH Photography

Scripture taken from the New King James Version®. Copyright © 1982 by
Thomas Nelson, Inc. Used by permission. All rights reserved.

ISBN: 978-1-942982-03-6

Printed in the U.S.A.

TO TO MY GRANDPARENTS:

CLAY & ONA STEWART
&
LIONEL & ELTHA FURMAN

Each has gone on to their eternal reward, but they left a Godly legacy and a lasting impression on this world, and I'm proud to have known and loved them.

Acknowledgments

Behind every successful author is a supportive spouse. And I've truly been blessed with one of the best!

There have been many times when he's held down the fort at home, so I could either go somewhere quiet to write, or pursue one or another of the myriad things that crop up in a writer's life (like the ever-so-important coffee with a critique partner.)

Honey, I'm so thankful for all you do!

Αγαπο σε!

Psalm 23

The Lord is my shepherd; I shall not want.
He makes me to lie down in green pastures;
He leads me beside the still waters.
He restores my soul;
He leads me in the paths of righteousness For His name's sake.
Yea, though I walk through the valley of the shadow of death,
I will fear no evil;
For You are with me;
Your rod and Your staff, they comfort me.
You prepare a table before me in the presence of my enemies;
You anoint my head with oil; My cup runs over.
Surely goodness and mercy shall follow me
All the days of my life;
And I will dwell in the house of the Lord Forever.

★

PROLOGUE

New York City, July 21, 1867

Thick black clouds covered the moon and stars, blocking out even the pretense of light. God had, at least, granted that favor. Ignoring the pain that emanated from every pore of her body, the woman clutched the baby to her chest and took Zeb's hand, allowing him to help her from the coach. "I'll only be a moment."

"Yes'm."

Darting a look around, she scuttled across the cobblestone street.

The Foundling Hospital lay just ahead now, all its lights extinguished. Hannah had told her to expect that. She trembled as she stepped onto the walk. Pausing, she swiped the tears from her cheeks and glanced both ways, and then behind her, straining to glimpse any movement or change of shadow. No one was there, as it should be at this hour of night.

Clutching her precious bundle tightly, she hurried on towards the hospital. Mercifully, the babe slept. At least her last memory of the child would be one of peace and contentment.

The door loomed ahead, its pointed arch only a lighter shadow outlining a darker center. Her steps faltered, now that safety was so near.

Easing back into the dark shadows next to the door of the hospital, she pressed against the wall and lifted the baby touching her damp cheek to the child's small soft one. A silent sob parted her lips, shook her shoulders, and stole the strength from her legs. Sliding down, she laid the babe across her lap and wrapped the blanket tightly around her so she wouldn't get cold in the night. She dashed more tears from her cheeks with quick, angry swipes and tucked the note carefully into the folds of the blanket making sure the rag doll was there too. It was not right, this travesty.

Yet love compelled her. One last time, she trailed the back of her first finger over her daughter's soft cheek. "Ahh Lambkin, the good Lord He be knowin' I'm only tryin' ta save ye. 'Tis His forgiveness I'll rest on. I ken not another path to take."

The baby took a soft shuddering breath and turned her face towards the finger, searching even in her sleep for something to latch onto.

Quickly now, lest she change her mind, the woman opened the outer door of the hospital and stepped into the vestibule. Standing still, she let her vision adjust to the soft candlelight, searching first for anyone who might be lurking in the room. It was empty. She sighed in relief even as her heart sank at being so close to this oh-so-final act.

There across the room, tucked into a small alcove she could see the candle-lit niche holding a white-swathed cradle. A crucifix hung above it, Christ's arms stretched wide to welcome the children placed below him, a reminder that loving sacrifice had been made before.

She swallowed, looked down, pressed her lips together and closed her eyes, instinctively pulling the child tighter to her breast. *I'm so unlike Ye, dear Father. I ken only make this sacrifice kickin' and screamin' on the inside. I didna know he was such a bad'n. Give me strength, Father of Grace.*

The baby bleated a soft cry of protest and the woman's heart skittered. The last thing she needed was for one of the nuns to hear and come to see what was going on. Quickly she brought the babe's hand to her tiny mouth so she could find her thumb. A smile softened her face as the wee child spurned her thumb and settled for slurping on her two middle fingers.

Tears blurred her vision again, shattering the candle flames into glittering, twinkling, haloed-stars. Slowly, she stepped towards the cradle and laid the bundle of blessing inside. Trembling, she clasped the heart-shaped silver locket at her neck and slid it back and forth on the chain. *She's a right to be free from me mistakes.* The metal against metal zinged softly as she stared down at the babe, indecision furrowing her brow. *She's also the right to know.* After only a moment's hesitation she lifted the chain from around her neck and tucked it into the babe's blanket next to the note and the rag doll.

Looking up at the crucifix, she folded her barren arms. "Ye brought this child safe from me womb into this world. I give her back to Ye." The broken whisper sounded loud in the room. A sob caught in her throat as she touched the baby's cheek for the last time. "The Lord bless ye and keep ye, chil'. May He cause His face to shine upon ye. And give ye rest."

Turning she stumbled out into the darkness, leaving the babe behind.

Sister Josephine Claremont stepped into the vestibule the next morning, her hands tucked carefully into her sleeves. A slight rustling sound was her first clue that they had a new little one. Leaning over the side of the cradle, she peered down at the tiny babe. Lying on its stomach, eyes open, two fingers captured in its little mouth, the baby couldn't have been more than a day or two old.

"My, my, tiny one." She reached for the baby and snuggled it into the crook of her neck. "What hardships has our Good Lord rescued you from, eh?"

The baby shifted a wobbly head and slobbered all over its fist trying to find something to suck on.

"Now, now. That's not going to do you a bit of good, that fist is not. What say we get you a yummy meal of milk, hmmm?" Sister Josephine calmly walked upstairs to the nursery, even though her heart was pounding like the choir-boy who got carried away with his drum last Christmas. It never ceased to surprise her when a child was left here for them.

Sister Rose tsked when she entered the nursery. "Oh my, another one? Is it a boy or a girl?" Rose slipped a clean shirt over little Francy's head.

Five-year-old Anna stopped tracing on the slate and scampered over to see the baby. "Who's baby?"

"The Good Lord's, child."

Josephine laid the baby on its back and unwound the blanket around it. A thin onion-skin paper fluttered to the floor and Anna bent and picked it up. A silver locket and a small rag doll were the only other items with the child.

At the feel of the cool air on its body the little mite balled up its fists and howled.

"Hmmm! Good lungs!" Rose commented, handing Francy two wooden blocks.

Josephine reached for a dry diaper. "Girl," she pronounced in the middle of the procedure. "There now!" She cooed as she wrapped the blanket tightly around the little tike once more. "All done, and we'll get you a nice warm bottle of milk. How will that be? Hmmm?"

"Here's her letter." Anna held the paper up to Sister Josephine.

"I'll go get Mother Superior while you get her a bottle," Rose said.

Josephine looked down at Anna. "Thank you, child. I'm going to the kitchen for just a moment. I'll be right back and you can help me feed the baby. Mean time, watch Francy like a big girl."

Mother Superior and Sister Rose entered the nursery just as she was settling back down with the new little one and showing Anna how to hold the bottle.

Smoothing one palm down her habit, Mother Superior held out her hand for the letter. She scanned it and then lifted her head, eyes rounding. "We need to get this child on the next Baby Train. That's in two days. See to the task of outfitting her. I will look through our records for a suitable family."

CHAPTER ONE

Shiloh, Oregon. April, 1887

Victoria Snyder gasped and snatched the newspaper closer to her face. "Oh! Today of all days!" How had she missed seeing the ad until just now?

Mama rushed into the dining room, her hair still in rag curls. "What is it, Victoria? I thought I heard you talking to someone?"

Victoria schooled her features, carefully folded the paper and set it aside. *Wedding planning. That's what's kept me from noticing it.* The last thing Mama needed to worry about on her wedding day was a couple more needy children. "It'll keep, Mama."

She stood and placed a kiss on Mama's cheek, hoping the wild pounding of her heart could not be heard. In her own ears it sounded like the thunder of a wild stampede. Her mind rushed over today's schedule. Would she make it to the train station on time? It would be tight, but she could make it. She *had* to make it.

She patted Mama's shoulders forcing her thoughts back to the present task. "You are going to be the most beautiful bride in Oregon today!"

Mama chuckled. "Well, not with these things in my hair! Come help me take them out, would you? My arms get dreadfully tired, trying to untie them all."

Victoria grinned, delighted by her mother's excitement. She would think about getting to the train station, after the wedding. Right now she wanted to revel in Mama's giddiness. "Dr. Martin will be happy to take you as his wife any way he can get you! I think you should walk down the aisle with all those rags in your hair, just to see if he really loves you, or not!"

"Oh, Posh!" Mama waved away her joke with a flick of her wrist.

Victoria covered her mouth as Mama grinned and rushed

from the room in a flurry of frilled petticoats. She couldn't stop a little giggle at the thought of Mama actually showing up at the church with all her rag curls still in. *Wouldn't that give Julia Nickerson something to talk about at the next quilting bee!*

Lifting the skirt of her new golden-yellow gown, she followed Mama to help her finish getting ready. Entering the room, she glanced around and smoothed a hand down the front of her dress. Everywhere she looked Mama's touch was evident. From the colorful, hand-appliquéd floral quilt they'd sewn the year Victoria turned thirteen, to the braided rugs they'd just finished last summer – everything in this room would be a reminder of Mama. She fiddled with the pendant at her throat, unanticipated dread threatening to rob her of today's joy. After the wedding, Mama and Dr. Martin were going on a wedding tour to San Francisco, California. And when Mama got back she would move into Dr. Martin's little home above his office. Mama's trunks were already packed and waiting by the door.

Mama caught her eye in the mirror. "I'll just be across town, Ria."

Victoria forced a smile. "Of course you will. It'll just be different. I'll get used to it. And," she shook her finger, "don't think you are getting away from me, because I plan to visit you! Often!"

Mama chuckled. "You'd better, or I will come after you with my rolling pin! Now," she patted her hair and arched her dark eyebrows.

Victoria stepped up behind her and deftly began pulling the rags from her hair. She glanced up and compared their reflections. They were about as different as any two women could be. Mama's dark hair and coffee colored eyes graced a heart-shaped face with a smooth, clear complexion. It amazed her that anyone in this town actually believed she was Clarice Snyder's daughter. Even Papa had been blessed with dark hair and bronze skin.

Before Mama and Papa had moved to Shiloh they had lived in Nebraska. She could still vividly remember the taunts the children at school used to hurl at her. She swallowed and pressed away the memories. That was in the past. Still, she often wondered if she really did have vile blood running through her veins. Who were her people? Where had she come from?

"What are you thinking, honey?"

Victoria wrinkled her freckled nose at her red hair. "It's amazing that anyone in this town believes I'm really your daughter."

Mama's features softened. She reached up and patted Victoria's hand, meeting her gaze in the mirror. "You are as much my daughter as anyone of my own flesh and blood could ever have been, darling. The day the Good Lord brought you to Papa and me was the best day of our lives, and don't you be forgetting it. Just because I'm marrying again and moving over to the doctor's house, doesn't mean I don't love you."

"I know." Victoria made an effort to lift her shoulders and put a smile on her face. She would get through this. Mama certainly deserved this bit of happiness after all she'd been through.

Mama spun around on the stool and captured Victoria's hands. "Honey, I know I've told you this before, but I want to remind you again. You are special. Just because your parents gave you up, doesn't mean the Lord doesn't have great plans for you. I can't tell you the number of times that I've thanked the Lord for sending you to Papa and me." Tears pooled in her eyes. "When Jesus took Papa home, I thought I wouldn't be able to bear it, and you were such a source of strength to me."

Victoria pressed a handkerchief into Mama's hands, blinking back tears of her own. "Now, Mama. We can't have you looking all puffy-eyed on your wedding day."

Mama chuckled and dabbed at her tears. "Honey, I just don't want you to feel like I'm abandoning you."

Pulling her into a hug, Victoria rested her cheek atop the dark curls. "I know you aren't. Things are just going to be different. It'll just take a little while to adjust, is all. I'm so happy for you. And I'm really glad you are feeling so much better, lately. I don't know what I would do if I lost you, too." And that was the truth of it.

Mama patted her arm. "I'm not planning on skipping through

the pearly gates anytime soon, dear. I'm afraid you are stuck with me for a good long while yet."

Victoria chuckled. "Good! Now," she set Mama away from her and spun her back towards the mirror, "we need to finish getting you ready. Sky Jordan said he would be here to get you at ten and it's already a quarter past nine. We can't have you late to your own wedding!" She removed the last few rags from Mama's hair.

Grinning, Mama clasped a pearl necklace about her throat. "Doc said he'd come for me himself, if I was even one minute late."

"I can see him doing it, too." Victoria plucked the wedding dress off the bed and gestured for Mama to stand. Settling the gorgeous champagne satin over Mama's head, Victoria fluffed and fussed with the skirt until it lay in disciplined pleats over the voluminous petticoats. Stepping back she admired the ecru lace and pearls that graced the fitted bodice of the gown. "Oh Mama! You are so beautiful! Here." She gestured to the stool in front of the dressing table again and Mama sat. Victoria bent and began fastening the tiny satin-covered buttons that lined the back of the dress.

Mama cleared her throat and fiddled with something on the dresser top. "Rocky got back home this week."

Victoria's fingers stilled, her heart shying like a stung mare. Resuming the buttoning, she carefully kept any hint of emotion from her voice. "I heard."

"He stopped by Doc's last night while Hannah and I were there. Doc asked him to walk me down the aisle. I was hoping he'd get back in time."

"Before she went back to the orphanage last night, Hannah told me he was shot trying to help Jason apprehend a criminal."

"Mmmm, but Doc says he's going to be fine. It will just take a few weeks for him to fully recover the use of his arm."

Victoria fastened the last button and stood. Her lips pressed together, she reached for the brush and styled Mama's hair for the beautiful pearl combs. Nothing she said would keep the morning peaceful. Mama loved Rocky and had been gently pressuring Victoria in his direction for years – ever since Victoria had innocently proclaimed on her thirteenth birthday that she thought she loved him.

"Honey." Mama waited until Victoria met her gaze in the mirror. "I would much rather have had the few years I had with Robert, than to have never known what it was like to love him at all. Only the Lord knows the future. Don't rob yourself of happiness because you are afraid of what the future holds."

Victoria snugged the last comb into a wave of dark hair and rested the circlet of the veil on Mama's head, then bent and kissed Mama's warm cheek. "Alright, I promise not to rob myself of future happiness."

Mama arched a slim, dark brow.

Victoria gave her a cheeky smile, knowing she hadn't promised what Mama really wanted to hear.

"Ria, you know good and well what I mean."

Victoria sighed. "Mama, Rocky has not so much as ever even hinted that he thinks of me as more than a friend. But if he does, I promise you I will seriously consider him."

A gleam of satisfaction leapt into Mama's eyes and she nodded her acquiescence to Victoria's promise.

There. Now Mama could go through the day with a light heart.

And it wasn't like she was in any danger of having to follow through on her promise. Rocky was never going to pay attention to her in that way. So she would never have to worry about having a lawman for a husband – A lawman who could be killed in the line of duty anytime he went to work, or even stepped out his door to call in the dog.

And that would definitely ensure her future happiness.

ChristyAnne glared daggers at Jimmy Horn across the swaying train aisle. *Big bully!* She pressed her own half of an apple into Damera's tiny hands and sat back, folding her arms. This time she would watch and make sure Mera got to eat it. Jimmy smirked, stuffed a huge bite of apple in his mouth and turned to look out the train window. *Hope he chokes on it!*

Mera tapped her arm. "Sissy, you can have yer apple. 'Sokay."

ChristyAnne smiled and used the sleeve of her dress to wipe away Mera's tears. "You eat it, Mera. 'S good for ya." Her tummy rumbled and she coughed, hoping Mera hadn't heard it. Raymond Thornton had taken Mera's biscuit at breakfast, so she'd given hers to her. *Least dumb 'ol Ray got picked at the last stop. Don't havta worry none 'bout him no more.*

She carefully wrapped the biscuit from tonight's meal in a scrap of cloth she'd saved and stuffed it into the top of her small valise. She and Mera could share it later. There wouldn't be any more food today and Mera always got hungry right before bedtime. A small snack usually helped her settle down and go to sleep. If they didn't get picked today, they'd at least have a bit of something to calm Mera's hungry tummy.

Since Jimmy was now busy drawing pictures in the dust on the seat in front of him she looked out her window. The train chuffed into a forest of tall trees that blocked out the sun and she could see her reflection pretty good in the dirty glass. She practiced her smile, the rhythmic chug of the engine in the background a monotonous reminder that they were moving farther and farther away from all they'd ever known. She adjusted her lips. Not too big a smile, but not too timid either. She'd tried big and timid both already. Those hadn't worked for her. Well… She sighed. Maybe they had. Someone at every stop had wanted to take her home with them, but no one, so far, had wanted Mera too. And she refused to be separated from her sister.

Miss Nickerson, the woman who worked for The Children's Aid Society, was getting desperate to find homes for the rest of them that were left. At the last stop, she'd made ChristyAnne go with an old woman and her husband who wanted a maid. ChristyAnne shuddered at the memory of that old woman dragging her out of the church by one arm while Mera screamed for her from Miss Nickerson's arms. Mama had always told her if she couldn't say anything nice not to say it at all, but the look on that woman's face when she'd told her she would break all of her fine dishes, rub dirt into her floor and even poison her well if she didn't take her little sister too, had almost been worth the whole ordeal.

ChristyAnne suppressed a giggle.

The woman's expression had reminded her of the time Raymond Thornton put that big ol' toad in the top of the lunch basket and it jumped out into Miss Nickerson's lap, because she looked just like Miss Nickerson had that day. Her mouth had dropped open and she'd sputtered several indecipherable phrases, then promptly marched ChristyAnne back inside the church to announce that she'd changed her mind about taking her. Miss Nickerson had been beside herself, but ChristyAnne had never been more relieved than at that moment. She had simply pulled the distraught Mera into her arms and rested her cheek atop her head, holding on tight.

The train lurched over a rough section of track and the whistle sounded. ChristyAnne reached over and clasped Mera's little hand. *No one is going to separate us!* Mera was all the family she had left in the whole wide world and nobody was going to take that from her.

The next stop was going to be the last on this trip. And if nobody picked them, ChristyAnne had determined that she and Mera would run away rather than go all the way back to New York. *I'm big for ten. Lotsa people think I'm older. I can get a job and take care of us.* She closed her eyes and rested her forehead against the glass. "I'm trying, Mama," she whispered. *I'm trying to take care of Damera like I promised you. But I miss you lots.* Hot tears pressed at the backs of her lids, but she didn't let them fall. She didn't want Mera to see how worried she was, and Miss Nickerson would just tell her to toughen up if she saw the tears.

Maybe at the next stop there would be a family that would want them both. Maybe.

Rocky gingerly slipped his arm into his Sunday-best, black coat.

Pain sizzled in jagged shards through his shoulder and down into his torso. He winced, closed his eyes and waited for the pain to pass. *Thank you, Lord that I'm still here to feel this pain.* It was the prayer he'd been repeating daily since his accident two weeks ago.

The scent of bacon and coffee wafted through his room. His stomach let loose with a rumble that could probably be heard in the next county.

Downstairs, someone knocked at the door and Dad answered it. "'Morning, Dad." That was Sky's voice – probably dropping off Brooke and Sierra, so Brooke could visit with Ma while Sky picked up the bride. Dad would be on his way out the door to head for the Sheriff's office. With all of them busy with the wedding today, Dad had said he would cover things down at the jail and to give Clarice and Doc his best wishes.

Rocky pulled a deep breath in through his nose and eased it out through his mouth. His tense muscles gave up some of their pull. So long as he didn't move his right arm the pain was tolerable. Thankfully Ma had pressed his shirt and suit last night, so he hadn't had to deal with ironing them this morning.

Using his left hand, he flipped his string-tie over one shoulder and fumbled to pull it around so he could tie it at the front.

Today he would have the honor of giving away Victoria's mother. Doc Martin had asked him yesterday, as he'd examined his arm, if he would be willing to do it. Rocky had never felt so privileged. Clarice Snyder was pure gold – one of his favorite people ever.

Her daughter's not so bad either. He grinned at that thought as he made an X from the two sides of the tie and tried to loop them together. His heart felt as light as Hannah Johnston's biscuits. Yesterday, Clarice had granted him permission to call on her daughter. Victoria hadn't been far from his thoughts recently – but especially since the accident. Yet the very reason for her occupying his thoughts, the fact that he'd almost lost his life, was the reason Victoria wouldn't want anything to do with him. He was a lawman. And her father had been a lawman. One killed in the line of duty.

He sighed and gave up on the tie, heading downstairs to where Ma could help him with it. All he could do was lay his heart bare before Victoria and hope she didn't trample it under her tiny booted heels. The irony in it all was that if he could get his hands on some nice horse-flesh and find suitable property in the area, he'd walk away from his tin star in a heartbeat. But he didn't see that happening any time soon. His savings would just have to sit in the bank a little longer.

Ma was in the front parlor, snuggling Sierra and cooing like only a granny could. "How is Grammy's baby, huh? Is Grammy's baby just getting to be *such a big girl*? Oh yes you are!" She smooched the baby's cheek loudly. Sierra slobbered happily on one fist, her gaze fixed on Ma's face. She didn't look too impressed with all Ma's commotion.

Rocky grinned at Brooke seated in the armchair to his right. "I see Ma's hands are full. Can you help me with this?" He gestured to the tie. "One handed bows are not something I've been practicing, lately. I'm bad enough when I have two."

Brooke smiled tiredly. "Sure." She started to rise.

Rocky reached out to stop her. "Just sit." Quickly, before she could protest, he bent down to a level that she could reach. "Sky tells me Sierra prefers to sleep during daylight hours."

"Yes. And last night was no exception." She grinned and deftly gave the tie one last adjustment. "There, you're all set. You look great."

Rocky gave a small bow. "Thank you. You don't look too bad yourself. I'd say green is definitely your color."

"Oh, yes. He's right, Honey," Ma pitched in. "Your red-blonde hair looks stunning with that green."

"Thank you. Sky picked this material out for me and had Mrs. Chandler sew it as a gift after Sierra was born. I thought that was very sweet of him."

Ma turned back to Sierra. "You have one smart Daddy. Yes you do!"

Rocky adjusted the sleeves on his coat. "Well, I better get on over to the church. Is Sky coming back for you ladies, or would you like me to walk you over now?"

Ma waved him on. "We have a few minutes yet. Sky said he would be back for us. Don't forget to grab yourself some bacon and eggs in the kitchen on your way out. Everything is made ready and waiting."

He grinned. "Thanks, Ma. My stomach could have been mistaken for T. Edgerton Hogg's Southern Pacific Railroad when I first smelled that bacon this morning."

Ma chuckled. "See you over there."

With a wave of his hand, Rocky headed for the kitchen, hastily sandwiched bacon and eggs between slices of bread, then hurried out the back door as he stuffed a huge bite in his mouth.

Bright sunshine warmed Shiloh. It was a good day for a wedding. A good day to start wooing Victoria's heart.

★

Chapter Two

In the small back room of the church Victoria sat with her mother. Mrs. Hollybough was playing the music Mama had picked out for the time before the ceremony, so the ushers must be seating people. Victoria glanced at Mama who sat on her chair, hands folded in her lap, eyes closed. *Probably praying. Which I should be doing myself. Lord, bless Mama and Doc Martin as they join their lives today. Keep them safe while they travel to California and back and help me with all the adjustments I'm going to need to make in the near future.* Her mind turned to the article she had read in that morning's paper. *And help me know what to do about those children, Lord.*

A tap at the door interrupted her prayer. Mama opened excited eyes as Victoria stood. They smiled at each other.

"Ready?" Victoria asked.

Mama laughed. "I've been ready since we walked in here and sat down."

Victoria opened the door. Rocky stood on the other side, looking more than handsome in his black Sunday-best suit.

She swallowed and glanced behind him towards the sanctuary. "Everything set?"

"They're ready for you." His gaze slid past her so that the words were directed straight to Mama.

A small sadness enveloped her and she bit her lip. This was the first time she'd seen him since he'd come home. And he'd spoken only to Mama. Barely even looked at her.

She brushed the disappointment aside. Right now she had to concentrate on making Mama's day the best it could be and she had no business being disappointed in anything Rocky did anyhow. She stooped and placed a kiss on Mama's cheek. "I'll be waiting for you up there. I love you so much!"

Mama returned the kiss and then Victoria pressed the bouquet of white daisies into her hand and brushed past Rocky, her own single daisy clutched against her like a lifeline.

Rocky stopped her with a touch to her elbow.

She turned towards him.

"Be sure and save me a dance, today." He smiled, his deep brown eyes softening.

Her heart forgot to beat, then suddenly remembered and set to beating extra fast as though to make up for lost time. She looked down at the Daisy. "Alright." *He's a lawman. He's a lawman. He's a lawman.* She glanced back up, forcing herself to meet his gaze.

For one moment they stood, transfixed, simply gazing at each other. Then Rocky ran his left hand down the front of his coat and focused on the floor. "Better get going." He looked back into her eyes.

"Yes. See you out there." His right arm, bent at the elbow, pressed slightly into his torso, as though to protect it from being jostled. "Is your arm okay?" Her gaze flickered to his shoulder.

He waved away her concern, again using only his left hand. "I'm fine. Don't worry about me."

Mama stepped out into the church entry and took Rocky's arm.

Quickly, Victoria fluffed out mama's train and then, stepping back around in front of her, preceded them to the aisle. Mama's best friend, Miz Hannah Johnston who ran the town orphanage, motioned to Mrs. Hollybough on the organ and the music changed. Clasping the daisy in front of her, Victoria started down the aisle, her steps deliberate and slow.

Doc Martin, who would soon be her third father but only the second one she'd ever known, stood at the head of the aisle nervously adjusting his cuffs. Pastor Hollybough smiled reassuringly as Victoria took her place and turned to face the family and friends gathered in the sanctuary.

Julia Nickerson's mother and father had managed to secure the seats right next to the one reserved for Rocky after he gave Mama away. *Where is Julia, I wonder?* Come to think of it, she hadn't seen Julia around town for several weeks. She scanned the sanctuary surreptitiously and her brows arched in surprise. Julia never missed any social events in their small little town, but she wasn't here today.

Victoria pressed her lips together and fixed her attention on the door as the bridal processional started and everyone stood. Why should it bother her that Julia's parents were obviously scheming to get Rocky to marry their daughter? *It's not like you're planning on marrying him.* Still, whoever he *did* marry, she hoped he was wise enough to stay away from the likes of the Nickersons, Julia in particular. With determination, she turned her thoughts elsewhere.

Mama radiated joy as she came down the aisle on Rocky's arm, creamy satin rustling and her gaze fixed solely on Doc.

Doc took an involuntary step towards Mama as she and Rocky stopped at the front of the church and Victoria bit the inside of her cheek to smother the giggle that wanted to burst forth. He looked like a little boy on Christmas who'd been told he had to wait to open his presents for a few more minutes.

Rocky caught her eye and by the gleam in his own, she could tell he found it amusing, as well.

As she stood and watched Mama and Doc exchange vows her heart grew lighter and lighter. This was so right for Mama. After Papa's death, Victoria had feared she would lose Mama to poor health, but Doc had come by faithfully with a little of this powder and that herb. Probably his company, more than his medicines, was what had restored her health.

"I now pronounce you man and wife," Pastor Hollybough declared. "Doc, you may kiss your bride." Doc did so with relish and to the cheers of the audience.

Victoria grinned. She felt like she might burst forth into song as she headed back down the aisle. *Lord, you are so good. Thanks for helping me see once again to how wonderful this is for Mama.*

Rocky gritted his teeth and fisted his left hand. If Jay Olson asked

Ria to dance one more time he might just have to go out there and cut in, pain be hanged. Couldn't she see what kind of a man Jay was? His arm encircled her waist far too tightly. Obviously the guy had only one thing on his mind! Ria laughed at something Jay said and Rocky stomped over to the punch bowl and snatched up one of the prefilled cut crystal glasses. He was going to have to have a talk with her about that man. Rocky took a big gulp of his punch. Even if she didn't want anything to do with him, the man she did marry needed to be four times the man Jay was!

Sky strolled up to him, Sierra tucked into the crook of his arm with her downy head lolling on his shoulder.

Rocky nodded a greeting, and tossed back another gulp of punch.

"Rock, you look like you did that time the big ol' bull stepped on your foot and then refused to budge."

The memory brought a pained smile to Rocky's face. "That bad, huh?"

Silently they watched Victoria and Jay twirl around the dance floor. "Why don't you ask her to dance?"

Rocky drained his cup and plunked it down on the table next to him. "Maybe another time." His shoulder felt like it was on fire. He pressed his lips together, refusing to admit that he was up and about too soon.

Jay leaned forward and said something into Victoria's ear. Her face burned scarlet and her jaw dropped for one second before it hardened and she stiffened in his arms.

Sky said, "Yeah. You're probably right. You should just stand back and let Jay woo her. That'd be best."

Rocky's whole body trembled with the self control it took not to march out onto the dance floor and lay Jay out with one well-placed fist. He reached for a chair and leaned his good arm into the back of it with a white-knuckled grip. What had Jay said to her?

The song ended and Victoria abruptly pushed back from Jay, said something to him, then lifted her skirts and stalked away. Jay leaned back into his heels, slid his hands into his pockets and scanned Ria from head to toe as she stormed off. Turning with a smirk on his face, he met Rocky's gaze and stilled.

Rocky deliberately narrowed his eyes and stood erect.

Jay's smile faltered, then broadened. He gave Rocky a two-fingered salute and then headed jauntily for the door, disappearing into the sunlight outside.

Sharyah stepped up beside Rocky. "What was that all about?"

Startled, he looked at his sister's worried frown.

Sky chuckled and adjusted Sierra on his shoulder. "Just a couple dogs struttin' around a tasty bone, Sharyah. Don't let it worry you. Rocky's gonna see any day now that if he wants that bone, he'd better stand up and start fighting for it." Sky pierced him with a look and arched a meaningful eyebrow.

"Really! Men!" Sharyah picked up her skirts and started off in a huff, tossing over her shoulder, "Victoria is much more than just a tasty bone and if Rocky can't see that then he doesn't deserve her!"

Rocky rubbed his jaw, angled Sky a glare, and headed over to say his congratulations to the new bride and groom. His shoulder had had enough of this day. He would have to talk to Victoria another time.

Clarice and Doc were talking with Miz Hannah Johnston. All three looked up as he approached.

Doc stood to his feet. "Well, speak of the devil!"

"Now, Dale! More like an angel, wouldn't you say?" Clarice pulled Rocky into a motherly embrace.

Rocky gritted his teeth against the shards of pain jostled loose by her squeeze and hoped his face looked normal as he stepped back.

"Well now, yes, I think you're right," Doc replied. But his attention never left Clarice.

Putting both her hands on Rocky's cheeks, Clarice looked up at him. "Honey, thank you for honoring me by walking me down the aisle. It means a great deal to me."

"Sure, anytime. The honor was all mine."

"Now," she stepped back, "we were just talking about you

before you walked up. Would you mind helping Victoria get my trunks from the house into Hannah's buggy and then bringing them over to Doc's place?"

"Sure." He winced inwardly at the thought of having to lift anything heavier than a coffee mug, but the smile on his face never faltered. *So much for some rest.* "I'll head over there right now. You two have a good trip."

"I'll jus' go on with him," Miz Hannah said. "That way my buggy'll be right there an' he won't have to do no waitin'." She pulled Clarice into her plump ebony arms. "Doll, you go on and have yourself a wonderful time."

Clarice smiled. "You know we will."

Miz Hannah turned to him. "Come on, Darlin'. Let's go move some trunks."

As they approached Hannah's buggy Rocky's footsteps slowed, an uneasy feeling settling in the pit of his stomach. He had no desire to be driven across town by a woman. But if there was one unspoken rule in the little town of Shiloh it was this: No one touched Miz Hannah's buggy but her.

He cleared his throat. "I'll just walk on over and meet you there, Hannah."

Hannah threw back her big head and let loose with a laugh loud enough to draw the attention of several people down the street. "Honey chil', ain't nobody never died from being driv around by Hannah Johnston. You jus' climb on up there. I got somethin' needs discussin'."

Reluctantly, Rocky did as he was told. And Hannah set the buggy in motion with a smart snap of the reins and her characteristic, "Come on now!" call.

Rocky clenched his jaw and closed his eyes against the shooting pain. The consistent dull throbbing was much preferable to the stabbing shards that shot through him now.

Hannah huffed. "Honey, heaven knows you ain't gonna be liftin' no trunks, as much pain as you in. You do a good job o' hiding it, but I sees it. Not much gets by Miz Hannah. No sir, not much. Clarice woulda seen it too, 'cept for her head bein' in the clouds and all. But don't you worry none, I done sent Cade over already. He's gonna meet us there."

Rocky looked over at her. "He's back in town?"

"Yes. Said he done got a right smart price for them hosses. Right smart."

"That's good. Can you just drop me at home, then? I am about done for." He gave her a sheepish smile.

"Wisht' I could. Really I does. But I'm gonna need you to talk some sense into Victoria 'fore this day is through. 'Sides," she angled him a knowing look, "I was there last night when you asked her mama for permission to call. Ain't no time like the present."

Rocky frowned, wondering why she needed him to talk some sense into Ria. "What do you mean?" His mind flashed to Jay and heat surged through his chest. "What kind of crazy thing is she doing?"

"Don't get all het up, now. She ain't doin' nothin' what she ain't been doin' for the past several years. And that's goin' to the train station in Salem to pick up the straggler orphans what don't find no home."

He relaxed, easing back into the seat. About once a year an orphan train came through Salem. The children on it were from large cities back east, usually New York. Their parents were either deceased, or unable to care for them for some reason. Since Salem was one of the last stops on the route, any orphans who did not find a home here, had to travel all the way back to New York. Several years ago, Victoria had taken it upon herself to make sure every last child left at the end of the day would find a home. She met the train, and brought any unchosen children back to Shiloh, housed them in the orphanage, and worked tirelessly until she found good stable homes for them.

"She does that every year. What's different about this time?"

"What's different is, I don't gots no more beds down to the orphanage. Any chil' she brings home, ain't gonna have a bed to sleep in. I done tol' her she needs to leave things in the Good Lawd's hands this time. Truth be tol' I was hopin' with the weddin' and all that she wouldn't notice the ad in the paper. But you know her and her obsession with helpin' them children. She's bound and determined to go."

"If she didn't listen to you, what makes you think she'd listen to me?"

Hannah bellowed a laugh and slapped her thigh. The horse twisted back his brown ears at the raucous sound and snorted, jangling the bit in his mouth. "Honey chil', she'll listen to you 'cause she cares right smart what you think."

Rocky didn't allow her words to take him down a path of hope. "Who does she have taking her to the train?"

Hannah angled him a look, chin tipped down, her widened eyes a stark white against the ebony of her face. "Usually she has Doc take her, but seein' as how he is indisposed today, she done asked Jay Olson to take her."

"Jay Olson?!" Rocky sat forward with a start.

Hannah gestured for him to calm down. "But he done somethin' she didn't like, though I don't rightly know what it was, and now she plans on goin' by herself."

"Well at least she has some sense," he muttered, settling back against the seat.

"I gots Elsa watchin' the children down to the orphanage whilst I come up to the weddin' but I cain't leave her alone long enough to run Ria down to Salem and back."

Even though it was most likely more sensible than having Jay Olson escort her, the thought of Victoria travelling the 20 miles to Salem and back by herself, sent a coil of frustration rushing through Rocky. Anything could happen to a woman alone on the trail these days. Especially with Salem growing like it was. He sighed. "I'll have a talk with her, but I can't promise you it'll do any good. You know how she gets when she has her mind set on something. Mules have nothing on her when it comes to stubbornness."

Hannah shook her head. "Ain't that the truth. Yes sir. Good Lawd's truth you just spoke."

A moment later she pulled to a stop in front of Victoria's

house and Rocky wearily climbed from the seat. Hannah got down from her side of the carriage before he'd even thought of moving to help her and he gave her an apologetic look.

Hannah's face softened. "You's about done for. Want I should look at that shoulder?"

Rocky consciously relaxed his jaw as he started for the house. "My shoulder will be fine as soon as I get some rest. Thanks, though." He knocked on the kitchen door.

Victoria answered, a look of curiosity on her face. "Oh, hello. Since Cade stopped by, I didn't expect to see you here."

Rocky tried not to frown as he removed his hat. Had Cade compromised Victoria's integrity by going into her house while she was alone? Rocky clenched his fists at the thought of what something like that could do to Victoria's good name. Cade, of all people, should know what gossip fueled by a bit of truth could do to someone's reputation. But he was so easy-going, the gossip about him and his numerous courtships generally had about as much effect on him as rain did on a well-oiled slicker. On the other hand, the girls involved weren't able to so lightly dismiss the pronged tongues of the town's busybodies. Rocky had seen that on several occasions. And he didn't want Victoria facing similar backbiting through no fault of her own. *If Cade has thoughtlessly maligned her by his careless actions....* "Cade's inside?"

Victoria nodded and stepped back, motioning him and Hannah inside. "Yes, he stopped by with Sharyah several minutes ago. Said Hannah had asked them both to come by and help move Mama's things over to Doc's place."

Rocky eased out a breath of relief as he followed Hannah through the door.

Hanging her shawl on a peg, Hannah slanted him an amused look.

He smiled softly. Good ol' Hannah. She thought of everything.

Victoria smoothed her hands down the sides of her skirt. He most definitely liked her new dress. Somehow the yellow of it drew his attention to her red curls. Right now, he wanted to reach out and wrap the one caressing her cheek around his finger.

She blushed and glanced down, and he realized he'd been staring. He rubbed the back of his neck, looking at the floor. "Got any coffee?"

Hannah huffed and flapped her hands at him. "No coffee for you, now. You jus' go sit yourself down and I'll bring you some willow bark tea." She poured water in the kettle. "Ria, I ain't gonna hide nothin' from you. I done brung Rocky over here to talk some sense into you. So you jus' go on and have a talk with him. Cade, Sharyah and I, we'll take care o' Clarice's trunks." Victoria opened her mouth to say something but Hannah held a finger in her direction as she clunked the kettle down on the stove. "I mean it now. You and I done all the talkin' we gonna do on the subject."

Rocky suppressed a grin. Victoria was none too pleased at being dismissed from her own kitchen. She had a way of holding her mouth just so when she was about to let someone have a piece of her mind. He held his hand out towards the small sitting room. "Let's sit." He nodded his head, encouraging her to let it go.

With a tiny huff, Victoria complied.

"Cade!" Hannah bellowed as they left the kitchen. "Buggy's here!"

As Rocky and Victoria headed through the small dining room of the house, Rocky could hear a low-voiced conversation between Cade and Sharyah in the sitting room. Suddenly, the sound of a resounding slap cracked through the air.

Victoria darted him a glance, her mouth dropping open in surprise.

"Don't you ever say something like that to me again, Cascade Bennett!" Looking for all the world like she was running from a fire, Sharyah stormed out of the sitting room, skirts lifted. She bolted past them, tears streaming down her cheeks.

Rocky and Victoria watched her brush past Hannah, bang through the kitchen door, and slam it behind her. The walls of the old house rattled with the force of her anger.

A moment later Cade stepped into the doorway, his serious

blue gaze fixed on the closed portal, one hand thoughtfully rubbing his cheek.

CHAPTER THREE

Victoria winced. Sharyah had been mooning over Cade Bennett for as long as she could remember. She wondered what he'd said to her to earn a slap. Sharyah wasn't the type to fly off the handle for no reason.

"Cade?" Rocky took a step towards him, anger radiating from every inch of his stance as he instinctively came to his sister's defense.

Victoria laid a hand on his arm. He glanced at her and she shook her head. Cade was still staring off after Sharyah. Maybe this would be what it took to make Cade realize how good Sharyah would be for him. Victoria sighed. Cade needed to settle down sometime, but she didn't want Rocky to lose his friend over a confrontation that could come to no resolve.

Whatever Cade had said to Sharyah, Victoria knew it couldn't have been anything inappropriate. He would never do that. Probably it was just an off handed comment that had hurt Sharyah's feelings. Cade was a good man. He would settle down, and sooner than later. But for now, she could sense he needed some space. "Cade, Mama's trunks are to the right of the door in the first room down the hall."

Cade dropped his hand to his side and headed back through the sitting room and down the hall without another word.

Rocky glared at his retreating back and spoke quietly. "If he were any other man...." A muscle in his jaw pulsed as he repeatedly clenched it.

"You know he wouldn't have said anything suggestive to her."

Rocky thought for a moment then seemed to relax. "Yeah, you're right." He pierced her with a look. "Speaking of suggestive, what did Jay Olson say to you?"

Victoria felt her cheeks flame and led the way across the sitting room, gesturing to the settee.

He didn't sit. Instead, he studied her with his dark, long-lashed eyes slightly narrowed and a look of determination firming his jaw. He slid his hat through his hands, crimping the brim, and never looking away.

She glanced at the floor and squeezed her forehead with one finger and her thumb. "It was nothing." She flipped her hand as though batting away his concerns.

"It was enough of something to make you decline his offer to escort you into town."

"It wasn't so much what he said as the way he said it."

He made no comment, only waited, brow lifted, the unanswered question still on his face.

She sighed. "All he said was that he'd be honored to escort me into town. But there was something about the way he said it that made me feel… uncomfortable." *And the way he lowered his hand from my waist.* Uncomfortable was not a strong enough word to describe how *that* had made her feel. Repulsed was more like it.

Rocky seemed to relax a little and she thanked her good fortune that he didn't seem set on pushing the issue further.

"So Hannah wants you to talk me out of going to Salem today?"

Apparently taking the cue for a change of subject, Rocky eased himself down on the settee with a soft release of breath and tilted his head back against the seat, eyes closed. "Pretty much."

He must be in a lot more pain than he wants us to know about. Fear scurried through her veins. "Rocky, are you okay?"

He met her questioning gaze. "So tell me about this trip to Salem today. What is it all about?"

Not liking the way he'd dodged her question, Victoria sank into the wing chair and dusted at an invisible fleck on the brown velvet trim of her skirt. She shrugged. "It's the normal trip I take every time the orphan train comes to Salem. I just want to make sure that any children who are left there have a shot at finding a good home out here."

Rocky sat up and she noted that he was careful to keep his right arm pressed tightly against his torso as he moved. "You have a great big heart, Ria. But Hannah tells me there are no more beds at the orphanage right now. What are you going to do with the children?"

She lifted her palms by her sides, gesturing around her. "I can bring them here. There's plenty of room here."

"Hannah tells me she's been having trouble finding homes for children through the orphanage. What are you going to do with them if you can't find a home for them?"

She shrugged, swallowing down the pain of that thought. Not because she might have to take care of some children for a really long time, but because of how the children might feel if no one wanted them. "They'd be welcome to stay here indefinitely."

Elbows planted on his knees, Rocky sighed, dropped his head down next to his left hand and squeezed the back of his neck. Just then, Hannah bustled in with a tea tray and pressed a large mug of steaming tea into Rocky's hand. By the smell it was willow bark.

Victoria took up her own cup and sniffed it, happy to find that it was regular tea and she wouldn't be forced to drink the bitter willow bark brew. She sipped quietly as Hannah hurried off calling directions to Cade on the loading of the trunks.

Rocky tasted his tea, his dark brown gaze meeting hers over the rim of his cup. "You know once you bring children into your home you're going to fall in love with them and won't want to give them to someone else."

She waved a hand. "No. I've helped lots of children find homes before. I'll be fine."

He crossed the ankle of one foot over the knee of his opposite leg. "This will be different. You bring children here and you'll be living with them day in and day out. You know you won't want to part with them."

A lump formed in her throat. "I'll just have to deal with it. I obviously can't take care of children on my own for long."

"What are you going to do if they are all fifteen-year-old boys?"

She couldn't stop the smirk that tipped the corner of her mouth. "Then I'll invite them all back here and send them over to your parent's place to board in your room."

He grinned and leaned towards her speaking softly. "If our place gets too crowded, I might just have to see if any of the single ladies in town will have me. I've had my eye on a certain pretty red-head for quite some time."

Her eyes widened and heat rushed to her face as she looked down into her lap and rubbed a pinch of golden satin between her fingers. Rocky had never once flirted with her in the past. *He's a lawman!* The quelling reminder had little effect on her racing pulse. Surely she hadn't understood him correctly. There was a way to find out. She glanced back up with feigned innocence. "Saying something like that could get you slapped."

He chuckled softly. "Just give this willow bark a chance to get into my system first." He eased back and swallowed another mouthful of tea, never taking his gaze off her face. "Have I ever told you how beautiful you are?"

Victoria's heart lurched. She nibbled at the fingernail on her first finger, the heel of one foot bouncing up and down rapidly.

She shook her head.

He couldn't be showing interest in her like this now! Not when he'd just come home badly injured and she'd decided with such finality that a lawman definitely wasn't the kind of man for her. Forget his profession! Even if it weren't for that, she simply didn't deserve a man like Rocky.

Downing the last mouthful of the brew in his cup, he leaned forward and placed it on the tray Hannah had left for them. "Ria, getting shot has made me think through my life." He cleared his throat. "I was laying there on the floor with Jason and Cade leaning over me, both of them acting like I wasn't going to live to see the next minute, and I clearly remember I had one regret."

He looked up at her. "So let me put that regret to rest." His deep brown eyes softened as they took in the lines of her face. "You are quite possibly the most beautiful woman I've ever seen."

Victoria realized she was holding her breath and let it go with a quick puff that came out on a nervous bit of laughter. She felt the burn as her face flushed crimson. She looked across the room, down into her lap, at his boots – anywhere but at his face. "Your one regret was that you'd never told me I was beautiful?" She peeked up at him, unable to resist the allure of his gaze.

"No." He shook his head. "It was that I hadn't ever courted you – gotten to know you better."

Victoria blinked. *He doesn't know that I'm adopted.* That reminder was like a douse of ice water on the flame of her beating heart. She took a calming breath. He at least needed to know that before he courted her. That might, after all, change his mind. Rocky didn't know where she really came from. *She* didn't even know her own lineage. What if she really did come from bad blood like Sarah Hollister had told her in the first grade? Rocky didn't deserve to get stuck with that.

"I asked your mother's permission last night to start courting you, and she granted it. Now I'm here asking you. Will you allow me the privilege to come calling?"

She pinched the bridge of her nose, then stood abruptly and paced the room like a corralled filly. She didn't know how to tell him. Victoria stared at the floor as she paced, arms folded, blinking back tears. Why was he doing this now? After all these years? Just when she'd promised Mama this morning that she would consider his offer? *Mama obviously knew what she was doing this morning when she extracted that promise!*

And what about her own feelings? She pressed her lips together, thinking of his shoulder wound. A few inches lower and he wouldn't be here to speak to her at all. What would she do if she agreed to allow him to court her, and then they ended up marrying? Part of her longed to agree. Oh! How she longed to agree. But life as a lawman was definitely dangerous, as proven by his recent near miss. What if later, perhaps after marriage and children, something should happen to him? She didn't know how she would live through something like that. She already cared far too much. Mama was right. It was already unbearable to think of something happening to him. She didn't want the hurt and worry to become worse. And she certainly didn't deserve a man like him.

Behind her, Rocky cleared his throat. "Ria?"

Raising one hand to stop his questioning, she said, "I can't talk about this right now. I'm going to miss the train if I stay here any longer." Picking up her skirts with a rustle of satin, she started out of the room.

He sighed. "I'm coming with you. Just let me get the buggy for you."

She spun around. "You can't come with me! You're already just about done in."

Tears still blurred her vision when he stepped towards her. "Ria." The word was a soft caress. He reached up, cupped her face, and traced her cheek with his thumb. "I know my job scares you."

She closed her eyes and forced herself not to tilt her head into his touch as she whispered, "I wouldn't be able to stand it, if... something happened and...." *If only that were all of it.*

He released a soft breath. "I don't have an answer for that except I know God is in control of the future, and I won't leave this world until it's my time to go." He paused and when she remained silent he continued. "Your words give me hope, though."

She looked at him, rolling her upper lip between her teeth.

He grinned. "I didn't know if you could care for me at all. Gives me hope that you wouldn't be able to stand it if something happened to me." He winked. "That's a start." His thumb caressed her cheek again, wiping away a tear that had spilled over. "Can you leave the future up to the Lord and at least give us a chance to get to know each other a little better?"

Silence filled the room. She didn't know how to tell him that she didn't think she could trust God with her heart. It was already in so many shattered pieces, she didn't know if even God could put it back together. "There's so much you don't know about me, Rocky."

"Mmmhmm. That's why I want to spend more time with you." He stepped back. "I'll go get the buggy and you can give me your answer when you are ready." Stopping at the door, he looked back. "I do know enough about you to know that everything I learn is only going to make me care more for you, not less."

Victoria watched him walk out of the room, then her eyes slid shut. If only she could believe that were true. Once Rocky found out her parents hadn't even wanted her, he might not want anything to do with her.

The train shuddered to a stop in the station with a huge puff of hissing sound. Miss Nickerson bustled down the aisle. "Come on children. Gather your bags. Quickly now." She clapped her hands twice.

ChristyAnne helped Mera hop off the seat and slip on her coat, then she climbed up to stand on the bench so she could reach their bags in the overhead compartment. Mera stepped out into the aisle and turned, waiting for ChristyAnne to hand her one of the small suitcases they'd each been given before the trip west.

A large man with a thick drooping mustache, barreled up the aisle. He wore a round bowler hat that looked oddly small on his large round head, and clouds of cigar smoke spewed from his mouth.

How could he stand the smell? She wrinkled her nose as a gray waft enveloped her.

Without so much as pausing, he smacked Mera's arm with his cane, pushing her aside as he hurried by, grumbling under his breath about the vile-blooded offspring of no-goods who couldn't' take care of their own children.

Mera rubbed her arm, large tears pooling in her big dark eyes as she watched him disappear out the door of the rail car. "That huht me!" Her lower lip pooched out.

ChristyAnne glared out the window as the fat man retreated and then handed Mera her little bag. "I'm sorry, Mera. I'll give it a kiss in a minute, but first we have to hurry off the train or Miss Nickerson is gonna get mad at us." She pulled her own case down. "Come on. Let's go." She hopped off the bench.

Mera toddled along in front of her, clutching her suitcase with both hands up near her chest. A kind-looking man in a cap smiled and helped Mera down the train steps.

"Much obliged," ChristyAnne mumbled as she stepped down into the gravel of the train yard and adjusted her black sweater. She swallowed, pressing down her anxiety, and squatted in front of Mera to straighten her clothes. She had to make sure they both looked especially good.

Off to her right Miss Nickerson was admonishing the children to stay together, smile, be polite, speak only when spoken to, and the rest of the list of things they'd all heard at every train stop where they had been looked over since New York.

Mera's eyes were wide as she took in the hustle and bustle of the station, her small case on the ground beside her. In front of them was the depot building. A large round clock on the wall facing them proclaimed with bold black hands that it was five o'clock. Down the platform a ways, a boy about her age hawked newspapers and another offered to shine the shoes of anyone who passed his way. A man trundled by with a big stack of trunks and boxes on a rolling cart. One wheel needed some grease. It was squealing louder than Betty-Lou from back home had the time her arm got busted when she fell off the swing. The mean fat man in the bowler pushed the boy selling newspapers aside with his cane and tapped some of the ash from his cigar into the chipped, tin, change-cup of the shoe-shine boy.

"ChristyAnne!" Miss Nickerson jerked her hand in a motion to indicate she should pay attention and hurry-up all at the same time. The rest of the children were already in the single-file line headed for a small platform she could see just inside the depot doors.

Giving Mera's jacket one last dusting, ChristyAnne bent and

kissed her little sister's arm, then captured her attention with a touch to her chin. "'Member to smile, 'kay?"

Mera nodded. "An' fold my hands." She mimicked the gesture ChristyAnne had taught her in hopes that their good behavior would win them a place to live. Together.

"Good. Now," ChristyAnne hefted both their cases, "come on."

Inside, the children all set their bags in a corner and climbed up onto the platform to stand in two rows facing a gathering crowd. ChristyAnne made sure she was standing directly behind Mera. Miss Nickerson began her remarks. She always said what wonderful hard-working children they were and that none of them would be any trouble, and if they were the Children's Aid Society would take them back, so ChristyAnne didn't pay attention to what she said. Instead, she scanned the crowd. Was there a new family waiting for her and Mera here? Off to one side of the crowd was a tall man in overalls. His wife stood beside him with a small frown on her face. They looked nice enough, but as soon as Miss Nickerson stopped talking they turned around and headed for the outside doors.

ChristyAnne sighed. That was the way of it. A lot of people just came out of curiosity to see what the orphan train was all about. Two men stepped forward. They looked like brothers. One bent and smiled at Jasper, one of the twins, while the other focused his attention on Jason. ChristyAnne swallowed. It looked like the twins were gonna be split up. But as Miss Nickerson gestured them over to the corner where her assistant would fill out the paperwork, ChristyAnne heard one of the men say, "We live on neighboring farms, so they'll be able to see each other often." She sighed. That brought some relief. At least the brothers wouldn't lose track of each other. She turned to scan the crowd once more and blinked. The fat, mean man with the mustache was talking to Miss Nickerson!

"Sure, a fine dairy ve haf as you know. I vas talking to your father, yust the other day, and he told me a yob you had taken vith the Children's Aid Society. Yes, my vife vould for some company be happy. Yust come out once you are done here. Ve vill look forward to haf you to dinner, ya!"

"Why thank you, Mr. Vandenvort." Miss Nickerson patted the hair at the back of her head and adjusted her flowery hat. "It has been an honor to help these children find homes, but I have to say it is very nice to be home! And I would be happy to come to dinner tonight."

ChristyAnne suppressed an eye-roll at her simpering tone.

The man nodded. "Good. The vife I will let know. Now, I need to vork in my dairy a strong young gal. Yust one." He blew a ring of smoke towards the ceiling and turned to scan them all with watery blue eyes.

"Well! I have just the one!"

Miss Nickerson turned and looked directly at her, and ChristyAnne's heart dropped with the speed of a stone.

CHAPTER FOUR

Rocky pulled the buggy to a stop in front of the Salem depot and Victoria climbed down without waiting for him to help her. She could still see a small crowd inside around the platform. *Oh good, we're not too late.* Rocky stepped up beside her, looking none too happy that she hadn't waited for him to help her down. But she knew that any jostling caused him pain, his face already looked pinched and pale from the drive here.

She clutched her skirts in one hand and hurried towards the door.

The minute they stepped into the dim interior of the station, Victoria could tell something was wrong. Every eye in the room was fixed on the platform where the children stood. Even the agent behind the ticket counter peered over his spectacles to the other end of the depot. There were only three children left, two girls, one about ten and the other about five, and a boy of about twelve. Both girls had hair as dark as a raven's wing, while the boy was blond and fair.

"I won't go with him!" The older girl stomped her foot. "You can't make me go with him, Miss Nickerson!" She clutched the younger girl to her.

Julia Nickerson! Victoria blinked. *So that's where she's been.*

"N-N-Now y-yust you vait vun m-minute!" Victoria recognized Mr. Vandenvort from the large dairy just outside of town. She often stopped by his place on the way home from Salem and bought fresh milk for the orphanage.

The ten-year-old girl was clutching the younger one to her and glowering at him with enough venom to obliterate an entire country. His face red, and his mustache trembling, he sputtered and stuttered.

"Well! I never!" Julia fanned herself with a lace hanky as she gaped at the girls.

Biting the inside of her cheek, Victoria shouldered her way through the mesmerized crowd. It was quite obvious that Mr. Vandenvort, Mr. V to all of the locals, wanted only one of the girls, the older one by the looks of it, and she was having nothing to do with being separated from her sister. *Dear Lord give me wisdom!* "Excuse me?"

Every eye in the room turned on her. Rocky stood right beside her, his Stetson clutched in one hand.

"I would hate to see the girls separated. I would love to take them home with me."

Tears sprang into the older girl's eyes and she turned a hopeful gaze on Julia.

"Victoria!" Julia gasped. "Of course," her attention settled on Rocky and Victoria could almost hear her purring as she continued, "I should have expected to see you here. Hello, Rocky." She cocked out one hip and sidled a step closer to him.

Rocky nodded. "Julia."

Mr. Vandenvort huffed and gestured with his cigar to the girl. "Miss Victoria, you don't vant that- that- that—. She yust told me she vould all of my cows kill if I made her come home vith me!"

The little girl glared fiery darts at Mr. V. "Just take me home and see if I don't!"

Beside her Rocky scuffed his feet, and Victoria had the distinct impression he was suppressing a laugh.

"Oh, dear Lord have mercy!" Julia tore her gaze away from Rocky and pinned the little girl with a glare. "What did you tell that woman at the last stop, young lady?" She grabbed the older girl's arm. "I thought it awfully strange that she hustled you back inside so fast after all the paperwork had been signed and everything!"

Victoria bit back a grin at that. "I'm sure the girl is just a little frightened and wants to stay with her sister. Like I said, I would be happy to take them both, Julia."

She did smile then, at the girl, hoping to reassure her that everything would be alright now. The younger child peeked up from where she clutched her sister's skirts, lifting her face just far enough to cast a quick look at Victoria. As soon as she met Victoria's glance she turned and hid her face again.

"I see I vas right! No plans I had to take home a child. Then I think to myself, maybe it vould be good to have some extra help around the place, ya?" Mr. V snorted. "These are nothing but varmints!" His glare encompassed each of the three children in turn. "Of spurious knaves, these offspring are! Those vat cannot take care of themselves, or discipline their children, yust like all along I suspected! Trouble like that, I von't have coming to vork for me!" Mr. V slapped his bowler onto his head and spun around so quickly that he had to take a sideways step to catch his balance. He stormed away muttering under his breath about how the child needed someone to teach her respect and discipline.

Victoria's face paled as she watched him stalk across the room and slam through the front doors. She had never known what an awful man he was! His wife usually helped her when she stopped by for milk.

Rocky touched her elbow and cleared his throat, bringing her focus back to the children still on the platform. The older girl had slumped with relief, her arms wrapped tightly around her younger sister and cheek resting on her head. The boy was shuffling his feet and scanning the crowd, a look of wounded hope undisguised by his big frown. Victoria had seen that, *why does no one want me?* look on too many little faces.

The crowd dispersed, and no one stepped forward to take the children home. Somewhere a luggage cart with a squeaky wheel started moving and a train whistle sounded off in the distance.

Victoria stepped towards Julia who was still fanning herself with her now limp hanky, a look of dazed befuddlement on her face as she stared across the depot. Touching her shoulder, Victoria said, "We would like to take them." Her gesture included Rocky and the three children. "You know I do this every year and I've always found good homes for the children I've taken back to Shiloh."

Julia ignored her for so long that she finally took a step back uncertainly.

Then the woman blinked and looked at her, stood erect, tucked the hanky up her sleeve and smoothed the front of her dress with trembling fingers. She glanced from the huddled girls back to Victoria and Rocky. "You're sure?"

Victoria nodded.

"Well, I'm shocked, really. Why anyone would want that child after the things she just said! It's beyond me, really. But a relief. Yes, quite a relief." Smoothing her fingers over the front of her skirt she stepped briskly over to the only four people that remained in the depot – her assistant, filling out the paperwork with a man and his wife who had a small girl clutched in her arms. Gesturing to Rocky, she said, "This woman would like to take the remaining children back to the orphanage in Shiloh. See to them as soon as you are done here."

Victoria and Rocky spoke in unison.

"Oh, we're not taking them to the orphanage—"

"—Hannah has no room. We're going to care for them at Victoria's place."

Victoria was warmed by Rocky's inclusion of himself in the care of the children. But by the look on Julia's face a small puff of wind could have knocked her over had it gusted through the depot at that moment. "Oh! My! You two aren't... you're not married are you?" She stumbled backwards and plunked herself down on the edge of the platform, once again furiously fanning her face, her worried gaze fixed directly on Rocky.

Moistening her lips, Victoria looked over at the children. All three huddled together in the middle of the stage now, looking down at her and Rocky.

Rocky cleared his throat. "We aren't married. I just drove Victoria here today and plan to help her as she needs it."

Julia narrowed her eyes. "Then why did she say, '*We* will take them?'"

"I reckon because *we* are here to get them." Rocky's tone teetered on the edge of impertinence.

Julia stood and jerked her waistcoat into place. "It's just not right, a young woman planning to care for three orphan children on her own. And one of them a boy at that. I just don't know."

Victoria shifted her feet and bit her tongue to suppress the retort that sprang to mind.

Rocky's voice vibrated with a low timbre of danger as he said, "You know that Hannah is a single woman and she does a remarkable job of taking care of the orphans. All Victoria wants to do is give these children a shot at happiness. And I just said I would be helping her, so she won't be doing it alone."

"I realize that," Julia simpered, "but I know Victoria won't have a way to support herself, especially now that her mother has married. Anything could happen. You could decide that you no longer want to help her and then she would once again be on her own, and I don't know that my conscience will let me give those poor children to you under those circumstances."

Victoria's nails bit into her palm. *Just a moment ago she was saying what a relief it would be to have the children off her hands.*

"We have regulations, you know." Julia nodded firmly and dabbed the hanky at her milk white throat. "It is our Christian duty to see that the children in our care are placed in *good* homes. Many of them come from homes where there was only one parent. Why would I want to put them back into a situation like that? Especially when I know you don't have proper income, Victoria. I mean, if you two were married, that would be one thing, I wouldn't hesitate to allow you to take the children then. But in this circumstance…" She lifted her hands to her shoulders indicating there was nothing she could do.

Victoria's eyes narrowed. Poor children, indeed. They'd had to travel across the whole country with this vixen.

"Julia, I can assure you that Miss Victoria will not lack for funds." There was a hard edge to Rocky's words.

Thankfulness welled through her. She hadn't thought about the money it would cost to take care of the children, but Julia was right on that count. She probably didn't have enough. Still they would get by. She had the garden, and the canning from last year.

And she could use the little she received from selling her baked goods to buy some cloth to sew clothes for them before school started up. They would be fine. Rocky wouldn't have to give them a red cent.

Julia pinned Rocky with a look. "So you're planning to finance her little endeavor to save the world one child at a time? What will your future wife have to say about that, hmmmm?" Julia actually had the nerve to step close to him and caress his chin with one finger.

Rocky leapt back and folded his arms even as Victoria's jaw dropped. The woman was practically throwing herself at Rocky's feet! She snapped her mouth closed before the string of most indelicate words parading through her brain popped out and sealed the children's fate with finality. *Lord, I really need a little help here. Those little children just need a home where someone can love on them. If they are meant to stay here, please work it out.* A sudden thought flashed to her mind and it was so audacious that she gasped and took a step back.

"Ria?" Rocky touched her arm.

The outer doors of the depot banged open with a clatter. Mr. V stormed towards the startled group. "My mind, I haf changed! The girl, I vill take! Respect, she vill learn! And to listen!" He held aloft one fleshy finger to emphasize his last point.

Victoria's heart hammered like a jack rabbit on the run from a fox. Her idea was now the only way to insure that those girls would be able to stay together. If she and Rocky married, Julia had said there wouldn't be any problem with them having the children. She glanced over at Rocky, but she couldn't bring herself to form the words. He stared at her for a long moment, and then something changed. His features softened and the corner of his mouth lifted almost imperceptibly.

Rocky never took his gaze from hers as he said, "Julia, you said if we were married you wouldn't hesitate to give us the children, right?"

"That's right. But under the circumstanc—"

"And you want to know what my future wife will have to

say? Well, let's find out." He lowered his voice and stepped closer. "Victoria, will you be my wife? Marry me, right here, right now."

Victoria's jaw went slack, but she snapped it shut again so quickly that she hoped no one had noticed. Had she heard him right? Or were her own thoughts jumbling with his words and making her hear things? She glanced over at the children, at Mr. V, at Julia, then to Rocky's shoulder, and finally back to his face.

Rocky swallowed, and raised his eyebrows, questioning if she was going to answer.

If she thought her heart was beating fast before, right now she was in danger of it flopping right out of her chest. She gave a firm nod. "Yes, I will marry you, Rocky."

Julia gasped and set her hanky to flapping again. Victoria suppressed a smile. Somehow she didn't think Julia had seen that coming.

ChristyAnne clutched Mera's arm so tightly that she looked up and tried to pull away. "Ow," she whispered softly.

"Sorry," ChristyAnne mumbled and let go of her arm, but she never took her attention off the pretty red-headed lady and the dark-haired man.

Waiting for Miss Nickerson to say the man and woman could have them now, she felt like she might throw up. But if she did that, maybe nobody would want her. She swallowed hard and pressed one hand to her tummy.

The man next to the red-head looked like he might fall over in surprise, but then he'd looked a little piqued since they first walked in the door. Kinda pale and tense. The way Daddy had looked after he lost his leg.

The fat man with the mustache glowered at the pretty lady, like she was standing between him and a dream come true. "The help of that girl, I need on my dairy." He jabbed a fleshy finger in ChristyAnne's direction.

Her insides churned.

The dark haired man glanced up at them, then turned to look at the dairy man. "What about the boy?"

Beside her, Jimmy clutched his hat and shuffled his feet.

"Rocky, no," the lady said.

Mean Mr. Mustache clenched his fist. "The boy is too old, a new vay to learn. Trouble I vant not. But the girl, she is young enough to learn, and strong enough to vork hard."

Miss Nickerson huffed. "Well, I won't accept some sham of a marriage. You are obviously doing this just to force me to give you these children. Mr. V has been married for several years already and would provide a good, stable home for the girl."

The dark haired man's jaw bunched up like he'd stuffed a wad of candy in his cheek. "Yes, but Victoria and I would provide a good, stable home for *all three* children. Wouldn't it be in their best interest to keep them all together?"

Miss Nickerson blinked and glanced over at the three of them. She looked at the dairy farmer long and hard, then turned her focus back to the man with the pretty lady.

"I can assure you, Julia," the dark haired man said, "that if you witness Victoria and I say our vows, the marriage will not be a sham. Both of us are God-fearing, truth-speaking people and once we make a vow, we keep it. What about you?"

There was an unmistakable challenge in his last question. ChristyAnne swallowed hard and turned to study Miss Nickerson. Would she keep her word?

"I suppose it would be in their best interest to keep them together, but…."

A trickle of hope spilled into ChristyAnne's heart.

The redheaded lady pressed her lips together like she was trying to hold back a smile.

ChristyAnne held her breath. The lady looked as if she'd won. *Oh, I hope she won!* Still, ChristyAnne wasn't sure. She bit the inside of her lip and focused on Miss Nickerson.

Miss Nickerson's voice trembled when she said, "So, I suppose if you and Victoria are willing—"

"Yes! Please?" ChristyAnne jumped off the platform. She

hadn't meant to talk but now that she was talking, she'd better make it count. "We'll be good, I promise. I'm a hard worker and Damera is little but she's real smart. I'm not sure about Jimmy." She waved her hand in Jimmy's direction, then paused. *Probably shouldn't have said that.* Quickly, she added, "He's been pretty mean the whole trip, but," she took in the muscles bulging under the dark haired man's shirt, "I'm sure *you* could handle ol' Jimmy. He'll probably polish up real nice, like an apple that's been rolling in the dirt, but when you pick it up and rub it off, it's pretty and shiny underneath." She gave an assertive nod. There, that should fix her blunder. She glanced back and forth between the man and woman expectantly. They just *had* to get married and take them home! *Please, please, please want to take us all home with you.*

"I ain't no dirty apple!" Jimmy kicked at the platform with one toe. "I'll be good too. But if we're comparin' I'd say ChristyAnne is a lot like a magpie – always chatterin'!"

ChristyAnne plunked her hands on her hips and tossed a glare over her shoulder at Jimmy, before she straightened back around towards the adults. She would deal with his magpie comment later; right now, she wanted to know what the adults would say.

The man shuffled his feet and studied the pointy toes of his boots. The pretty lady pressed the back of her hand to her mouth and stared over the top of ChristyAnne's head at nothing in particular. She knew, because she turned around to see what seemed to be so interesting, and there was nothing there. Both of them wore strange, pinched-lip looks.

She frowned, wondering what she'd said. Her eyes narrowed. Probably Jimmy's comment about the magpie! Now they had to decide if they wanted a dirty apple *and* a noisy bird living with them. Leave it to Jimmy to mess things up!

"If you are willing to have the ceremony here and now, I will agree to let the children go home with you temporarily. But I still have my reservations. You can be sure I'll be checking up on you." Miss Nickerson sounded a little defeated.

"Vel! A mistake you are making!" Mean Mr. Mustache shook

a fat finger in Miss Nickerson's face. "Sorry you vill be for not giving that girl to me for my dairy! My vife and I vithdraw our invitation for you to come to dinner!" Spinning on his heel the fat man stormed out of the building.

Miss Nickerson paled and her mouth gaped open as she watched his thunderous retreat. "Well! I never!"

ChristyAnne didn't know why Miss Nickerson looked so shocked. The man was meaner than Jackson Campbell's ol' donkey back home. It was obvious that he wouldn't treat her nice.

The man and lady hadn't noticed Mr. Meany's outburst. They looked at each other, their faces real serious-like.

ChristyAnne held her breath. They hadn't really said for sure that they'd take all of them yet. *Please, please, please.*

The lady swallowed. "Rocky, there's so much you don't know about me."

He shook his head. "I'm sure there's not a man or woman alive who didn't have a few things to learn about each other after the ceremony."

The pretty red head's face looked a little scared when she said, "I don't want you to feel pressured to—"

At the same time the man said, "I'll go fetch the minister."

Then they just stood there again and stared at each other, like they were real thirsty and the other one was a nice cool fountain.

Her lungs were about to burst but she didn't dare take a breath lest she miss a word they said.

Finally the man reached out and touched the lady's cheek ever so softly. Like papa used to do to mama, before....

"It'll be fine, Ria. I'll go get Pastor Harding." And with that he headed for the door.

ChristyAnne gasped for air, plunked down onto the cold hard floor of the station, wrapped her arms around herself, and cried. Finally, she and Mera had a home together!

"Good gracious, child! Young women do *not* sit on the floors in public places!" Miss Nickerson's voice was strident. "And you can count on that visit from me, Victoria. I mean it when I say I still have reservations about allowing you to take these children!

I won't accept some sham of a marriage just so you can have three little slaves living with you!"

The red-headed lady's shoulders jolted back and her chin tipped up. ChristyAnne thought she was about to say something, but then she sat down on the floor right next to her totally ignoring Miss Nickerson. She scooped ChristyAnne into her lap, cradling her head against her chest. "There, now," she crooned, "everything's going to be alright. Shhhhh." Pushing the hair back from her face, the lady dropped a kiss on her forehead.

Mera stepped up next to them, with her thumb planted firmly in her mouth, and the lady reached out one arm and tugged her close, too.

With a shuddering sigh, ChristyAnne closed her eyes and relaxed. Resting her cheek against the silky golden fabric of that lady's dress while she hugged Mera with her other arm, was simply the best thing she had experienced in a long time.

CHAPTER FIVE

Rocky sighed. The ceremony had been short.

While Victoria gathered up the children and collected their things, the minister pulled Rocky aside. Pastor Harding eyed him with speculative concern. "You going to be alright? You don't look so good."

Rocky ran a hand down his face and looked at him. "Got shot a couple weeks back. I was ready for this day to be done several hours ago."

"I see. Well, remember, 'What God has put together, let not man tear asunder.'"

Rocky glanced across the room at Victoria. "I meant my vows, Reverend."

"That's good son, because starting a marriage off with three half-grown children won't be a walk in the park."

"Well, we're just keeping them until good homes are found for them to go to."

There was a long silence before the Reverend said, "Sometimes God asks us to do things we wouldn't expect Him to."

Rocky thought back to this morning, and chuckled. The thought that he'd started out this day wondering how he could talk Ria into allowing him to come calling, seemed humorous, now. "Yes, that He does, Reverend."

"But I don't want to take a bath!"

Victoria sighed and glanced down at the tub of tepid water in the middle of the kitchen floor. The girls had already bathed and were asleep in Mama's old room and now she was trying to get Jimmy into the tub. Maybe it wasn't such a big deal for Jimmy to get clean tonight. She didn't know where Rocky had disappeared to, but he'd dropped her and the children off at her house and drove off without a word. Victoria felt tears of exhaustion begging for release. Rocky hadn't said more than two words to her on the way home. He was probably regretting his hasty decision to marry her.

Realizing that Jimmy still waited for her reply she looked down at him. "Well, okay how about—"

A hand dropped onto her shoulder. With a short squeal she spun around.

Rocky blinked at her.

"Oh! You startled me!" She pressed one hand to her racing heart. He must have come in through the front door.

A smile softened the corners of his mouth. "I can see that. Sorry."

"Whoa! That was great!" Jimmy chortled and imitated her squeal and spin.

Rocky composed his features, giving Jimmy a stern look. Wrapping his hand around her shoulders, he turned her to face the boy. "Jimmy you need a bath to wash off the dirt and grime both from the train and the long drive here in the wagon. From now on when Ri—ah, Mrs. Jordan, asks you to do something, I expect you to listen. Understood?"

Victoria clasped her hands, trying to ignore her cavorting pulse. 'Mrs. Jordan' made her feel slightly ill while the fact that Rocky had come to her aide gave a pleasant sensation and the pressure of his hands on her shoulders made her want to lean back into the solid strength of him. *I've gone addle-pated.*

Jimmy folded his arms and scuffed one toe. "Yessir."

Rocky released her and stepped back. "Good. You like checkers?"

The boy's eyes glinted interest for a split second before the light in them died and his shoulders sagged. "I don't know how to play. 'Sides, you didn't want me anyways."

Oh, sweet Jesus, that poor child. Victoria held her breath. How would Rocky respond to that? He *had* said something at the depot about sending Jimmy with Mr. V.

"Well, soon as you are done with your bath, come on out to the front room and I'll show you how to play checkers."

"You will?" A portion of the light returned but hesitation still laced his tone.

"Sure. I'll be waiting." With that, Rocky disappeared back down the hall.

Well, I suppose that is a start. Still, Rocky could have been a little more reassuring.

Victoria showed Jimmy the soap and towel and instructed him to put on his one extra set of clothes and bring her the dirty ones he had on now.

When she stepped into the parlor, Rocky was laid out on the settee, his stocking feet propped up on the arm. He started to get up, but she waved him back down. "You've had a long day. How's your shoulder?"

He paused a moment as though deciding how much to tell her. "Been better."

Her stomach tightened. Concern for three small children had stripped her of all defenses and now she was married to a lawman. A *wounded* lawman! "Can I get you anything?"

His warm honey-brown gaze fixed on her. "I went and told my parents."

Her heart stopped and she closed her eyes. *Mama.* She would need to tell Mama too as soon as she got back from her wedding tour.

Rocky still watched her.

"So, how did they take it?"

A sardonic smile curved his lips. "Ma said we'd better start planning a big ceremony or none of my family will speak to us ever again."

Victoria pressed a hand over her mouth. "Oh, Rocky! I'm so sorry. What did I get us into?"

He came to his feet in one swift motion. Stepping close to her, he said, "She was joking, Ria. She's been after me to court you for years."

"Really?"

He nodded.

"Why didn't you?"

Jimmy poked his head in. "Done," he announced, stuffing his dirty laundry into Victoria's hands. His wet hair stood out from his head in all directions.

Distracted, Victoria took his clothes. She wished Rocky had been able to answer her question.

Rocky held her gaze for a moment, rubbing one hand over his jaw, his eyes crinkling with humor. "I'll make sure to let you know my answer to that, later."

She swallowed, suddenly not so sure she wanted to know and thankful for the interruption. If she wasn't careful she was going to lose her heart entirely to the handsome man before her.

Finally, he looked down. "Jimmy, why don't you let Mrs. Jordan show you where that laundry should go." He eyed the boy's hair for a moment, his gaze darted to Victoria's and he winked. "Then come back here and we'll get that checkers game going."

Victoria smiled, glad he wasn't going to mention the wayward mop. The boy needed to feel welcome here – not harped on. She put a hand on Jimmy's shoulder. "I'll take care of these for you tonight. And tomorrow I can show you all around, so that next time you'll know where to take your dirty clothes. For now, just enjoy your checkers game."

"Yesssssss!" Jimmy pumped one fist by his side, then rushed for the checker board set up by the fireplace. He stopped after several strides and spun back towards her. "Thanks!"

Joy welled in Victoria's heart. When was the last time someone had taken time to show this boy special attention? "You are most welcome."

Rocky touched her elbow as she started from the room. "Where do you want him to sleep tonight?" he asked softly.

Victoria's eyes rounded. There were only three bedrooms in the house. The girls were in one, she occupied one, and the other that she'd planned for Jimmy to sleep in held only one singlewide cot. How had she not considered where Rocky would sleep? "Uh... uh... well... I thought he might sleep in the last room down the hall to the left. But…." She licked her lips, feeling heat sear her face.

Rocky scanned her face. "Don't worry about me. I'll get him settled and then head over to my place to sleep for the night."

"N-n-no!" she stammered. "She said she wouldn't accept a sham marriage – I don't want word to get back to her that you aren't… we aren't…."

"Are ya comin', mister?" Jimmy asked.

Rocky held a finger out in Jimmy's direction without taking his attention off Victoria's face. "Be right there, Jimmy." His next words were pitched much lower. "What are you saying?"

Heavens! She didn't know what she was saying! She gave a nervous laugh. "I don't know."

With a sigh he rubbed the back of his neck. "Get me a blanket and a pillow and I'll sleep out here by the fire."

"You will? But your shoulder. Oh! Maybe you *should* go back to your place tonight." She put one hand to her forehead.

"No, you're right. I should be here. I *want* to be here. But I didn't want you to…" He took her hand and gave it a squeeze. "Just get me a blanket and a pillow, alright? I'll be fine. Stop worrying."

She watched as he crossed the room to Jimmy and sat on the hearth across from him before she turned to do as he'd asked. *Lord, what have I gotten us into?*

"You done went and did *what*?" Hannah tossed her large hands into the air then settled them on her hips. "Girl! You is one muddle-headed piece o' work!" Hannah's sensible, blue, cotton dress draped over her generous frame and contrasted with the bright white of her work-day apron. The hem swirled around her ankles, showing flashes of her black boots as she stomped around the kitchen. She had braided her thick hair into a series of rows, the ends gathered into a tight bun at the back of her head.

Victoria leaned against the kitchen counter, hands pressed to her temples. She was glad Rocky had taken all the children out to show them how to gather eggs, and not so glad that Hannah had decided to show up early this morning to find out what had happened at the depot yesterday. "I know, Hannah, but she was going to give ChristyAnne to Mr. V and take Damera back to New York with her! And you know I couldn't let that happen!"

"Honey, she'd a give them babies to you if you had just worked on her a bit! I think there be another reason you gived in to the plum fool idea of marryin' Rocky on the spot!"

Victoria's face heated and she fiddled with a crumb on the sideboard, suddenly unable to meet Hannah's assessing stare. "We'll find good homes for all the children and then we can get the marriage annulled."

"Lawd, Almighty?" Hannah turned her petitioning gaze towards the ceiling. "What we gonna do with this gal?" Storming over to the sink she clunked the dish-water kettle under the pump and worked the handle furiously. "If you ain't the craziest gal this side o' the Mississippi, my name be Mark Twain! What your mama gonna say to me when she hears she left you in my care for one week and on the first day, you ups and gets yourself hitched?" She shook a finger at Victoria. "And don't you go talkin' none to me 'bout getting no annulment! There ain't no going back. But you got yourself into a doozy of a mess this time around, gal!"

"You don't think God could have sent us there at just the right time to make sure those two little girls got to stay together?"

Hannah snorted and arched her brows. "Sho' 'nuff good thing it weren't Jay Olson what took you to the depot yesterday!"

Victoria shuddered at that thought. Would she have married *him* to keep the girls together?

"I'd bet my bottom dollar you didn't stop to say a prayer, 'fore you plunged ahead." Hannah cocked her a wide-eyed look. "Honey, your problem is you don't believe the good Lawd love them babies as much as you do."

Victoria pinched the bridge of her nose. Was that true? "What kind of person would I be to let two sisters get separated from each other when I could do something to prevent it?"

Hannah paused at that. "An awful one." She sighed. "Well,

maybe my mouth is runnin' away with me. Mayhap this be the Good Lawd's way o' keeping them cuties together."

Victoria folded her arms. "I honestly don't know, Hannah."

"Aw, Honey..." Hannah slammed the kettle down onto the stove and water droplets sizzled across the hot surface. She turned and pulled Victoria into her plump embrace. "I got no call to be so hard on you when you was just doin' what you felt was right. What's done is done. You helped them babies. And you's married now. So best you make the most of it and learn to love that man with all your heart. Least ways you got yourself a good one." She nodded emphatically and turned to retrieve a mug from the cupboard. "Yes'm at least you got yourself a good one."

Victoria started to gather ingredients for flapjacks. They needed to get breakfast underway if they were going to make it to church on time. She swallowed. Church was not something she was looking forward to today. What was everyone going to think about her and Rocky's spur-of-the-moment marriage?

Hannah shooed her away from the bowl, and pressed a cup of hot coffee into her hands.

With a sigh, Victoria cupped the warmth of the mug and relinquished the flapjack ingredients to Hannah's capable hands. She inhaled a lungful of the wonderful aroma wafting from her cup.

"Now you listen to a bit of advice and you listen up good." Hannah dumped flour and a dash of salt into the bowl "I was married once. Back before my massah treat my Zeb so bad he— well," she waved a hand. "I was married once. An' mind you, Ria, men... they's different than us women. You gots to give 'em— well you know, you gots to keep 'em happy."

Heat washed down from the crown of Victoria's head into the pit of her belly. "Hannah!"

Hannah gave her a chin-tucked look. "Don't you sass me now. You ever been married afore?"

Victoria gaped at her in silence.

"I didn't think so. So you listen to me. You keep that man happy in the bedroom and your whole home will be a lot happier."

A floor-board creaked and a horrible sense of foreboding coursed through Victoria. She leaned to peer around Hannah's broad shoulders.

Rocky stood in the doorway, one hand resting on his hip, the other scrubbing at the back of his neck, a look of bemused chagrin on his face. "Ahhh... is it alright to bring the children back inside now?"

Hannah snatched the mug out of Victoria's limp hands. "You's spillin' your coffee, girl!"

Chapter Six

Simon Saunders tilted back in his chair, crossed one ankle over one knee and adjusted the belt buckle cutting into his ample mid-section. Slurping his coffee noisily, he reached for the paper and shook it open. He grunted and almost spewed the hot liquid everywhere. Plunking the cup on the table he grabbed the paper with both hands and gave it his full attention. Amazement set his heart to thumping in his ears.

All this time, she'd been so close! How had he not known?

A lazy smile split his lips. "Well, hello Darlin'. I been lookin' for you fer a long time." She looked just like Maggie. He scanned the article and then harrumphed. "So, yer a do-gooder like your ma." Married now, with three adopted children. Well, that would complicate matters slightly. He scratched his chin and angled a look towards the ceiling. No…. Maybe not. In fact, it might even help his image.

He chewed one fingernail, spitting out the bits and pieces as he contemplated how he would go about getting to know her. He frowned at his finger. He had to break that habit. His hands needed to look smooth and pampered.

It wouldn't be easy, but he hadn't come this far to fail.

Pulling over a pad of paper, he started his list. There were a lot of things he needed to do. So many little details to think through. He jotted another item down, with a chuckle. Who knew he would find her because of a wedding announcement?

"Good Lord must be watchin' out for me. Yes Sir. Things might just finally be going my way."

Victoria had never been so nervous in her life. Rocky had gone to the church earlier and asked the Reverend to announce that they were now married, so at least everyone would learn about it at once.

But as they walked into the church lot, Rocky carrying Damera on his good arm, and ChristyAnne's little hand tucked into her own, Victoria felt like she might turn and bolt for home at any moment. If ever there was a day tongues would wag in church, this was the day. She hated knowing other people were talking about her. Mama had always told her she put too much stock in what other people thought of her, but she couldn't help it. She wanted everyone to be happy and to like her. Glancing over her shoulder, she urged Jimmy to a faster walk. "Keep up please."

"Don't want to go to no church." Jimmy glowered at her.

Rocky and Victoria looked at each other and stopped.

"Son, this is not up for discussion. We are all going in there and we are going to sit quietly through the sermon. Then we are going to go home and talk about what the Pastor says today, so I expect you to listen, got it?" Rocky cocked an eyebrow at him.

ChristyAnne squeezed her hand. "Is this the same pastor that was at the train station yesterday?"

Victoria shook her head. "No, honey. That was the pastor from Salem. Pastor Hollybough is our pastor here in Shilo."

Jimmy kicked a pebble, sending it bounding across the lot. "I'm not your son!"

"That's true. But for now you are in my charge and you will listen." There was an edge of steel in Rocky's tone.

Victoria held her breath. *Please, oh please, don't make a scene right here in the church lot.*

ChristyAnne slipped her hand into Rocky's free one. "I'm happy to go into church." She blinked large brown eyes up at him.

Rocky wisely ignored her attempt at becoming his favorite and kept his gaze fixed on the boy.

"Fine." Jimmy kicked another rock. "Let's go."

Rocky's shoulders eased slightly and he started for the doors again. Victoria hurried to catch up, and they slipped into the back pew just as the first hymn started to play, Rocky on one end and Victoria on the other, with the three children in between them.

Hannah stood in the middle of a row full of orphans, her beautiful voice carrying throughout the church. "*Rock of ages, cleft for me, let me hide myself in thee.*"

Victoria hugged the hymnal close, shut her eyes and inhaled deeply. Softly, under the flow of the music, women's skirts rustled. And outside, down the street, Mr. Halvorson's dog barked from where it was tied behind the general store – like it did every Sunday. Sky and Brooke's baby, Sierra, slurped noisily on her fingers, and Mr. Bennett sang off key as usual. But the words of the song soothed her frayed nerves like a mama's hug for a scared toddler. "*Not the labors of my hands, can fulfill thy law's commands; could my zeal no respite know, could my tears forever flow, all for sin could not atone; thou must save, and thou alone.*"

Oh how she needed this reminder not to take pride in what she had done for these children. God alone could save, and that through grace – not because of anything she had done. *Father, forgive me for taking pride in anything I've done. Help me to put these children in Your hands. I really believe You sent us there yesterday to help them. Help us to know how best to do that. And if there was another way to keep these girls together and I've roped Rocky into something he regrets, please forgive me. And help him to forgive me. Help us to know where to go from here, Lord. We really need Your guidance.*

She opened her eyes, met Julia Nickerson's assessing scrutiny, and immediately lost any peace she thought she had gained. *Lord, I don't know if I can deal kindly with Julia today.*

From her pew just across the aisle from Rocky, Julia studied them openly. Her gaze raked over the three children and with a haughty arch of her brow she pressed her lips into a thin line.

How had the woman ever gotten hired on by the Children's Aid Society in the first place?

ChristyAnne shuffled her feet and glanced from Julia to Victoria, a question in her gaze. Victoria rested one hand on her head and bent down. "Don't worry about her," she whispered, "just sing the songs."

Rachel, with Sharyah by her side, glanced back, a soft smile on her face. She took in the three children between Victoria and Rocky with any entirely different expression – one of maternal pride.

Glancing down at the three children, Victoria felt a small surge of the same. They really were beautiful children.

Rocky glanced up over the top of his hymnal and Julia smiled at him, batting her lashes. Victoria bit down on her tongue so hard she almost yelped. Quickly she turned back to study her hymnal – and realized they had moved on to another song, and she hadn't turned the page.

When the songs ended and Pastor Hollybough stepped up to the pulpit, Victoria squirmed like a little kid in line to get a tooth pulled.

Pastor cleared his throat and looked over the congregation. A smile softened his features. "Well it's not often that a mother and daughter get married on the same day. But here in our little town, we now hold that distinction. I'm happy to announce that Victoria Snyder and Rocky Jordan got married yesterday in Salem."

For one moment a church mouse could have been heard breathing, and then pandemonium broke loose.

But above all the cacophony Victoria heard Julia's loud question to her mother. "You don't suppose she's in the family way, do you?"

Heat filled her face. *How could the woman even insinuate such a thing? She knew very well why they'd gotten married as they had!* She had to fix this. Lifting her skirts she stepped out into the aisle and marched toward the front of the church. Silence descended as everyone realized she was about to say something.

Words almost failed her as every eye fixed on her, but she glanced at Rocky and he gave her a nod of reassurance. That was enough to ease the stranglehold on her voice.

"Rocky and I went to the train station in Salem yesterday, like I do every year, to see if there would be any orphans who still needed homes." Victoria rubbed her hand down her skirt. She was thankful she'd only had a couple sips of coffee, or poor Mr. Taylor in the front row would be wearing her breakfast.

"There were three. Two of them are sisters. The woman from The Children's Aid Society was going to separate the girls, leaving one here and taking the other back to New York." Victoria focused her gaze on Rocky making sure not to look at Julia, but still a low murmur rippled across the congregation. Apparently many of the members knew that Julia had been the Society worker. Rocky nodded encouragement again. "Rocky and I couldn't let that happen, and the woman wouldn't allow us to take the children unless we... well... got married."

A louder murmur traversed the room.

"I have to believe," Victoria clenched her fists by her sides, "God sent me there, us there, to help them." Out of the corner of her eye, she saw Hannah shift in her pew, but Victoria kept her attention focused on the floor all the way back to her seat.

ChristyAnne slipped her small hand into Victoria's and squeezed gently. Leaning over she whispered, "I'm glad God sent you to help us. You don't know how hard I prayed that God would keep me and Mera together."

Victoria blinked back tears and studied her lap.

Pastor Hollybough cleared his throat. "I think that is an excellent example of what our Lord meant by taking care of orphans. Rocky, Victoria," he looked at them intently, "I believe our Lord will reward you for your sacrifice."

Hannah started to clap. Victoria darted her a look and Hannah smiled softly as applause filled the room.

Victoria nodded in acknowledgment, thankful that once again Hannah was giving her the benefit of the doubt.

"Speaking of sacrifice, that is the topic I've chosen for this morning's sermon...."

Victoria didn't hear much of Pastor's message; she was too busy planning how she would tell Mama this news when she got home from her wedding tour, and enjoying the feel of ChristyAnne's small hand tucked into hers.

"So, what are we gonna do tomorrow?" ChristyAnne flopped

back onto her pillow and studied Victoria with her large brown eyes.

Rocky was down the hall getting Jimmy settled for the night.

"Well," Victoria adjusted the covers around Damera's shoulders, "I suppose we will run by the general store and pick up a few things I think you girls and Jimmy will need. Then we should go down to the school and get you three introduced to your teacher. Her name is Miss Jordan. You will like her."

Damera's face lit with amazement and she popped her thumb from her mouth like a cork from a bottle. "We get ta go ta school?"

Victoria smoothed the dark curls off her forehead with a smile. "Yes, honey. And I know you will really like it there."

The little girl's eyes danced. "Is our teacher pretty?"

"Oh yes, very."

ChristyAnne huffed and dread traced the edges of her tone as she said, "It's not Miss Nickerson, is it? She kept fluttering her eyelashes at Rocky all through church!"

Victoria felt her face heat. So even ChristyAnne had noticed Julia's obvious flirtation. "No, not her. Sharyah, uh, Miss Jordan, is Rocky's sister. She's the younger lady that sat right in front of us. You remember? We talked with them some after church."

"Oh, she looked nice."

Victoria nodded. "Yes, she is."

"Well, I didn't like that other lady. She looked at us like we were something from the barnyard stuck on the bottom of her shoes."

Victoria cleared her throat and pressed her lips together, giving herself a moment to suppress a giggle. When she was sufficiently in control, she said, "Yes, well, that's no way for a young lady to talk."

"But it's true. Why do some people think we are less special, just because our Mama and Papa got sick and died?"

Tears pressed at the backs of her eyes now. How she wished she knew the answer to that question. She reached for the older girl's shoulder. "Come here and let me braid your hair while we talk. That should keep it from being so tangled in the morning."

ChristyAnne stepped over by her legs. She picked up the brush and trailed it through the girl's beautiful brown tendrils. "Honey, I don't know why some people are that way, except they've never learned to love like Jesus wants them to." Victoria plaited one long braid down the back of ChristyAnne's head, then turned the little girl to face her. "What you have to remember is that you are special to Jesus. Don't let the way other people act ever make you forget that."

"Yeah, but not even you and Rocky want us! You're just gonna give us away to someone else. I heard him tell that to the black lady that came and made pancakes this morning."

Oh Lord... She frowned and clenched her teeth together. How could he talk like that within the hearing of the children? *Heal the hurt this little girl is feeling, Father.* "Her name is Hannah, and I don't know what God has in mind for you children yet. But I won't rule out the fact that there may be a better home for you girls than with Rocky and me. For Jimmy, too."

"See? You don't really care about us. You just want to get rid of us." ChristyAnne folded her arms in a full pout now. Damera started to sniffle from her place under the covers.

Victoria reached for her and pulled her into a warm embrace. What could she say? She didn't know what the future held for these children. She certainly wouldn't have wanted them to have to worry about it so soon. But her intentions *had* been to find them a good home where they could stay together and that meant that they most likely wouldn't be staying here with her and Rocky. Only the Lord knew where the right place for them was. Perhaps it was best for them to know now. And Victoria refused to offer platitudes that might later have to be broken.

Tucking Mera closer with one arm, Victoria stroked a hand down ChristyAnne's soft braid. "Listen, now. It has nothing to do with whether we want you or not. But with what is best for you. I don't know what is going to happen, or where you and Mera will end up living. But that is not a decision for tonight. I know you want me to promise that you can stay with us, but I just can't do that right now." She rested one hand against ChristyAnne's shoulder and looked back and forth between the two girls. "I have a secret to tell you."

"You do?" ChristyAnne's expression brightened.

Mera continued sucking her thumb, but her eyebrows rose in anticipation.

Victoria chewed on her lower lip and nodded. Did she dare tell them? The last thing she wanted was for the whole town of Shiloh to find out about her. "You know what a secret is, don't you?"

Both girls nodded solemnly.

"Tell me."

"A secret is…" ChristyAnne cocked her head to one side and pursed up her lips for a long moment. "…when you don't want anyone to know something but you just have to tell *somebody*, so you make your friends promise not to tell about the something."

Victoria nodded. "That's exactly right. So I'm trusting you with my special secret, okay?"

ChristyAnne rubbed her hands together gleefully. "I just love secrets!"

Suppressing a grin, Victoria said, "I'm adopted too."

"You are?" ChristyAnne's jaw dropped nearly to her knees.

"Yes."

"But you're so beautiful, and smart!"

Victoria chuckled. *At least someone thinks so.* She tapped ChristyAnne on the nose. "You are, too. And one day you are going to find a family that will love you, just as much as my Mama and Papa did me."

Rocky poked his head in the door. "Everyone ready for a good night's sleep, in here?"

ChristyAnne rushed over to him and launched into a tale about something Jimmy had done earlier. Victoria sighed. She'd have to talk with the little girl about tattling tomorrow.

Damera tugged on her sleeve and she glanced down at the little tyke in her lap. Her thumb popped loose just long enough for her to say, "Miz Jo'dan, I'm gwad you an o'phan wike me. Den you can know how it feels," before she jammed it back into her mouth.

Compassion swelled in her heart and she pressed the little girl's head close as she rocked her back and forth. "Yes, sweet pea. I know just what you mean."

Suddenly Victoria realized that the other side of the room had grown deathly quiet. She glanced up just in time to catch the look of shock on Rocky's face before he concealed his expression.

Victoria shot to her feet, turned and tucked Mera back into bed. *Not like this!*

"Mera!" ChristyAnne stomped one small foot. "It was a secret! You aren't supposed to talk about secrets in front of other people!" She spun back towards Rocky. "You didn't know she was an orphan, did you? Well now you do, 'cause Mera spilled the beans, but you have to keep it a secret! That means you can't tell nobody!"

Slowly, Victoria turned to face him. Rocky had one hand on ChristyAnne's head, but his dark eyes were fixed solely on her. "Is that so?" There was a hint of astonishment in his voice.

ChristyAnne nodded emphatically. "Yep."

Victoria laced her hands together. "Not an orphan... exactly."

"What then?" His words were short. Clipped.

She felt the blood drain from her face. Was that anger or merely surprise in his tone? The room began to spin. She clutched for the bedpost. Pressed her forehead to the cool, smooth mahogany wood. "ChristyAnne, honey, come and I'll tuck you into bed."

Her own anger began to mount. How dare he judge her for something she couldn't help!

She felt the bed jostle as ChristyAnne crawled under the covers. Deliberately, she let go of the post, keeping her back to Rocky at the door. She bent and kissed both girls on their foreheads. "'Night, girls. See you in the morning." Lifting the lamp, she kept her concentration on the floor as she started for the door.

Rocky didn't move for a moment, but stood in her way with arms folded. She could feel his gaze boring into the top of her head and her anger mounted with each moment. If she didn't get out of here she was going to light into him right in front of the girls.

"Night, Mistew Jo'dan," Damera said, her sleepy little girl voice floating out from around her thumb.

He stepped aside. "Goodnight, girls. Sleep well."

Quickly, Victoria made her escape, but it was short lived. Rocky caught up to her in two swift strides and took her elbow just as she was about to reach the safety of her room.

She jerked away, spun to face him, and narrowly missed smashing the lamp against the wall. "Don't you dare judge me for something I have no control over, Rocky Jordan!" She launched each word with whisper-quiet precision. "And how dare you talk about getting rid of these children within their hearing as though they were some sort of burden! Don't you think they have enough to stresses already without having that added on them?"

He took the lamp from her, setting it on the low table just outside her door, and when she looked away, folding her arms, he reached out and touched her chin with a light stroke. "I don't believe in hiding anything from the children. It will only hurt them worse if they think we're going to be their family and later find out that isn't the case. There's a lot to consider before we decide whether we'd be justified in keeping them. I don't know that I can adequately provide for you and three children." He sighed. "I didn't mean for them to overhear me talking to Hannah. I'm sorry about that, but in a way it is good that they know."

She swallowed. So he was thinking the same way she was. "You don't think we could even consider keeping them?"

"I didn't say that. But I think there are probably families out there better prepared to care for two or three children and I just don't want them to be hurt."

She studied him. Like he'd been hurt just now when he found out she was adopted?

His expression gave away nothing. What was he feeling? Did he now want out of this sham of a marriage? Most likely. Maybe that was another reason he was resisting the idea of keeping the children. He had a right to be angry with her. She closed her eyes, wishing she could shut out the pain in her heart as easily as she could shut out the vision of him standing before her.

Much as she hated to, she had to let him go. "Rocky, I'm sorry you didn't know about me. We can have the marriage annulled. You're most likely right. There probably are better families out there for them. All I ask is that you give me a few days to find—"

As Rocky's hands settled firmly around her waist, her words cut off with a squeak and her eyes flew open.

She backed away, coming up against the wall. He stepped after her, a soft smile curving his mouth but an emotion in his expression that she couldn't quite read. His gaze roved across her features and then captured hers. "Are you a liar, Victoria?"

She blinked. "N-No."

"Did you mean the promises you made? Till death do us part?"

Her mouth could have rivaled a desert stone for lack of moisture. Had she? Or had she simply been doing what was needed at the time to rescue the children? She didn't have an answer to give, so she kept silent.

A muscle near his eye ticked. "Well, I meant my vows. I don't want an annulment." He leaned closer, his mouth quirking up at one corner. "I'm afraid you are stuck with me no matter what we decide is best for the children." His thumbs caressed small circles into her lower ribs.

Victoria clutched at his hands, her heart racing in betrayal of her determination to let him go. "But…" This was not the reaction she had expected. "Maybe you didn't understand what ChristyAnne said?"

"Oh yes. I heard her. She said you were an orphan, and you said, 'not an orphan exactly', so I'm assuming that means you were adopted, but your birth parents are still alive, right?"

Her brows arched. She nodded. "As far as I know."

"And you thought that would mean I would want nothing to do with you?"

She swallowed, and gave a tiny nod.

Hurt crept into his deep brown eyes and a muscle bunched along his jaw. "I see."

She bit her lip. "You are angry."

He tilted his head in thought. "A little," he whispered.

Her heart plummeted at his outright admission. Of course he was angry. He'd been duped. He married her when he thought she was one person, and now he'd found out that he didn't really know much about her at all.

Tears sprang unbidden and spilled down her cheeks. "I'm so sorry, Rocky. I should have told you. I knew it would change how you felt about me, but I just couldn't figure out—"

"Ria—" He cupped the side of her face, his thumb settling over her mouth. For several moments he stood in contemplation, softly stroking her lower lip, a jumble of emotions crossing his face. His gaze dropped to where his thumb rested and slowly he bent toward her.

A bloom of desire curled through her. If she had any sense she would turn away, but she remained rooted to the spot, even lifted her face slightly, her heart a tympani in her ears.

When he was a scant breathe away, he froze. "You want to know how I really feel about you?"

She couldn't help but give a tiny nod.

With a tilt of his head, he closed the distance between them, his lips settling on hers, soft and sure.

The kiss stole her breath. She collapsed back against the wall and he pressed closer, sliding one hand along the side of her face and curling it around the back of her head.

A shudder coursed through her and she gave in and responded with all the emotion she'd been holding at bay.

His fingers dug into her hair until the pins loosened and her curls tumbled about them.

She clutched handfuls of his shirt. She should push him away, but her grasp was more to hold him close. The kiss could be goodbye and she didn't want that – but he deserved so much more than she could give him. Her tears mingled with the taste of him and her legs trembled with weakness. But the strength of his arms held her up and the pressure of his legs kept her knees from buckling.

His kiss softened. Slowed. Enticed with an allure she'd never experienced before but longed to give in to. Finally, hands still cupping her face, he pulled back just enough to rest his forehead against hers. They both gasped for breath.

"That, Mrs. Jordan, is how I really feel about you." His thumb stroked the corner of her mouth. "I might be a little frustrated, but I would never—" He pushed back from her, glitter sparking in his eyes as he scanned her with dark appraisal. "You know what frustrates me the most?"

She made no response; only pushed her hair back from her face, not sure she wanted to know.

"The fact that you don't even know why I'm frustrated." Abruptly, he turned and walked down the hall. "I need your help, when you have a minute."

CHAPTER SEVEN

Rocky paused in the door way to the living room and turned to study Victoria. Face covered by her hands, she gave a soft moan and slid down the wall to squat near the floor, her hair falling in a red curtain around her, her shoulders shaking.

He shouldn't have been so blunt with her. Definitely shouldn't have kissed her like that. He rubbed one hand across his mouth as though he could wipe the sweet taste of her from his lips. He'd just been so frustrated when he realized that she assumed he would think less of her simply because she was adopted. What kind of a man did she think he was?

Her head fell against her raised knees and she wrapped her trembling arms tightly around them.

He clenched his fists. He should go to her. Comfort her. Apologize. But, then she might think he regretted the kiss and that wouldn't be true. He only regretted that he'd hurt her by voicing his frustration with her.

And so help him, if he went back to her now, he'd want to kiss her again, and if he kissed her again, he wouldn't want to stop. He turned, instead, for the relative safety of the parlor and sank down onto the hearth. Burying his face in his hands, elbows planted firmly on his knees, he prayed. Prayed like he hadn't prayed in a long time.

It was several moments before he heard her enter the room.

He glanced up. *Lord, show me how to reach her.*

She had plaited her hair into a braid that rested across one shoulder. Her eyes were red-rimmed, her cheeks blotchy. She didn't look at him.

I'm an idiot.

He gestured to a bottle of ointment next to him. "I need to

rebandage my shoulder. If you prefer I can head over and have Ma help me."

"No. I don't mind."

He worked at the buttons of his shirt. "I'm sorry. I shouldn't have talked to you like that. But the kiss…"

She picked up a clean bandage without saying a word.

He paused and reached for her hand. It trembled in his grasp and she closed her eyes. "Rocky, please. I know you were saying goodbye." She fumbled to find the end of the bandage. "Let's just leave it at that, and move on."

Pain sank claws into his heart. *She really knows me so little?* "I wasn't saying goodbye."

She blinked and looked at him, but her face indicated she didn't really believe him.

Aggravated, he bit the inside of his lip. Sure, the fact that her parents had given her away by choice would probably be hard to deal with. But… He frowned. God had given her a wonderful family. No girl could have asked for better parents than she'd had in Clarice and Bob Snyder. He didn't understand her. Why did she think he would want to leave her just because she wasn't their blood daughter?

He let go of her hand and carefully removed his shirt, wincing as the movement shot shards of fire through his torso. His shoulder was still painfully tender even though the wounds were nearly healed. The front wound was sealed shut completely, but along his back where the bullet had exited there was still a small open sore. Doc had said that inside, muscles had been ripped and it would take some time for them to knit back together.

"Sit down, please." Her fingers were cool, as she unwrapped the bandages, cleaned the wound and applied salve to the gash on his back. "Hold this." She pressed the end of a clean, rolled bandage to the front of his shoulder. Her fingers trembled as he reached to do what she'd asked.

He glanced up. She was blinking back tears, even as she concentrated on wrapping the bandage tight and smooth.

I'm a cad! Still, irritation coursed through him and his jaw clenched in annoyance. What would cause her to feel so inferior?

She tucked the last of the bandage under a section of the wrap and he came to his feet in one swift motion.

"Ria?" He reached for her hand. He wanted to have it out with her. Make her admit that she knew he wasn't the kind of man who would leave her simply because she was adopted.

Instead, he reached into his front pocket and pulled out a half eagle. Turning her hand over, he set the coin into her palm and curled her fingers around it. "Get the children whatever they need tomorrow."

Her shoulders relaxed perceptibly as she glanced up. "Thank you."

He clasped her small hand tightly in his and stepped closer determined to make her understand he wasn't about to leave her.

She looked away, staring over his shoulder then, tears coursing down her cheeks and doubt mixed with fear etching her expression.

He felt like someone had thrown a bucket of ice cold water on his exasperation. He couldn't bring himself to say anything.

He rolled the side of his lower lip between his teeth as he studied her. He didn't know what to tell her, he realized. Would she believe anything he said, right now? He couldn't believe she thought he'd be that selfish. How could he convince her he wasn't that kind of man?

Nothing came to mind. He released her hand and folded his arms tightly across his chest. "You don't have to thank me. It's what a man does for his family. 'Night, Ria."

Her only answer was the uncertainty reflected in her gaze and the jut of her jaw as she walked away.

He sighed as he watched her pad down the hallway. *Lord, I need a little help here.* He huffed. *Make that a lot of help.*

Rocky grimaced as Hannah threw her hands in the air pinning him with her distinctive soul-seeing stare. He looked away and glanced around the orphanage kitchen. As usual, it was spotless. Cheery yellow curtains hung at the one window. And the ever-full, bright-blue cookie jar sat in its spot on the shelf to the right of the sink. The scent of cinnamon and sugar still wafted through the kitchen, a tribute to the last batch of cookies Hannah had been placing into the jar when he arrived. How many times as children had he, Sky, Cade and Jason come over here to beg a cookie from Hannah?

Hannah was still slicing and dicing him with her eyes. He sighed and looked over at her.

"You done come out here to ask me why that gal think you gonna leave her?"

Rocky felt heat infuse his face. Again. He nodded.

"Rocky Jordan, that is probably the most selfish... Bah!" She waved a dismissive gesture. "That gal think her mama and daddy didn't love her none 'cause they give her away when she was born. She grew up in a small town back Nebraska way and the children, they was cruel to her. Told her things like how ugly she musta been for her folks to give her away. Said she probably descended from a bad lot o' folks and she wouldn't turn out none too good."

Rocky leaned back against the kitchen counter, arms folded over the pain that kicked to life just under his ribs.

"Victoria gots a soft heart. She take people's words much too serious. So her mama and daddy they brung her here and decided to let her grow up 'thout folks knowin'. But the day God took her daddy home, I saw a change take place in that gal. She turned into herself mostly. She be questioning the Good Lawd. Wonderin' if He really love her like He say he does."

"So..." he scuffed his foot across her floor, "how do I make her believe that it doesn't matter to me that she's adopted?"

Plunking her hands down on ample hips, Hannah angled a glance at the ceiling. "Lawd, you done give this one rocks 'stead o' brains?"

Rocky clenched his jaw, but bided his time. Hannah was having just a little too much fun with this.

She looked at him then and sure enough, the familiar twinkle danced in her dark gaze. "Awww, Honey." She stepped right up to him and cupped his face in her large hands. "You done got yourself one good gal. She gonna come to her senses and see what a fine catch she made, any day. And ol' Hannah is gonna help you speed things along. Just you wait and see! Now," she gestured to the kitchen table, "you plunk yourself down there whilst I get us some coffee and pie."

Rocky moved behind the table, but instead of sitting he took a moment to study the model ship that rested on a shelf high on the wall. It had sat in the same place ever since he could remember. The intricate details on the vessel had always fascinated him as a child – still did. The rigging was strung with real string and the canvas sails could be furled and unfurled with a simple tug here or loosening of the string there. Tucked inside the cabin, a small wooden man grasped the helm, another crew member bent over a coil of rope near the main-mast. *Great Happiness* was scrawled in a sloping hand across the stern of the ship. Whoever created the piece had a masterful eye.

He'd tried to ask Hannah about it once, but she'd gotten teary eyed and shooed him out of the kitchen without answering his questions. He angled her a look, once again wondering what it was about the *Great Happiness* that brought her so much pain yet made her keep it in a place where she couldn't help but see it every day.

She bustled across the kitchen and disappeared into the pantry, obviously pretending not to notice his study of the craft.

With a sigh, he turned from the ship and sat, tracing the grain of the long rough table with his finger. He had enough troubles without trying to get Hannah to open up about it again.

Hannah reappeared carrying a pitcher of cream. She set a piece of cherry pie and a steaming mug of black coffee in front of him. He inhaled appreciatively and Hannah chuckled as she added a dollop to the top of a second piece of pie and placed it before an empty chair across the table.

He savored his first bite with a grunt of satisfaction and Hannah laughed again.

"That's right. They say the way to a man's heart is through his stomach." She eased herself into the chair and slid her own pie closer. Forking off a bite she savored it before she pointed the tines in his direction. "Well if that is true, then ol' Hannah is a rich princess!" She threw back her head on a laugh, slapping her thigh at her own joke and Rocky couldn't help but smile. She lowered her chin then and pierced him with a white-eyed look. "Huh. How would you feel if alls Ria ever did was set a plate of food in front of you, never talked to you, never returned your kisses? Just the food – that's all you got."

Rocky sipped his coffee and waited knowing it was a rhetorical question.

"Course you wouldn't want that. No one would. Well, gals is even a little harder to figure than you men. See, we likes to be pampered a little." She chuckled. "Okay, make that pampered a lot! You done told her you ain't leavin'. She don't care about that! She want you to *love* her!"

Rocky opened his mouth but she waved away his attempt at a protest.

"Now, you listen to ol' Hannah. That girl jus' want to be loved the way she is. She's never felt accepted by anyone 'cept maybe her mama and her daddy afore he passed on. You can get past that but you got to show her! You got to… court that gal. Just like you planned to do 'fore you up and married her! Make her realize you think she is the most special thing in the whole wide world. Let her know that you is thinkin' of her while you work. Bring her flowers for no reason at all. Oh, and a gal likes to be told she is loved, so best you get into the practice of saying that."

Rocky shoved another bite into his mouth with a frown. He'd told her he wasn't leaving, hadn't he? What better way to express his love?

Hannah narrowed her eyes. "Don't you be frownin' at what I say, now. You come out here for advice and I'm givin' it. You do just what I say and she gonna come around before you know it.

You two got two great things on your side and that's the Lawd and the fact that you two been pinin' for each other who knows how long. God never gonna let you down, Rocky. You just turn to Him when you don't know what to do next." She savored another bite of pie, a serious contemplative look on her brow. "Ria has some… things she gonna have to overcome. But the good Lawd, well, He done sent you to her to help with just that."

Rocky shoved the last quarter of his piece of pie into his mouth and chewed thoughtfully. He washed it down with a gulp of coffee then looked up at Hannah. "I just can't believe she thinks I'd leave her just because she is adopted."

Hannah sighed and toyed with her cup. "Honey, that chil' has had her heart broke so many times I fear what might happen if the good Lawd ask her to go through one more trial. When you get to that place o' waitin' for the next bad thing to happen, life loses a lot o' its sense. She just so bruised up inside, she think the Good Lawd got it out for her. She's afraid to let you in. That's all it is, pure an' simple. Fear. Fear that you'll leave her. Fear that you be killed at work like her daddy was. Only the Good Lawd himself can help her get over that. An' I been prayin' about it for a long time." She smiled at him. "Somehow, I believe you be part of her answer."

Rocky swallowed.

"But—" Hannah slapped her palms to the table, "remember it be God's job to worry about. All's you can do is the job He give you to do, which is love that gal best you can!"

Hannah sighed. She looked up at him and folded her plump hands on the table. "You gonna do just fine by that gal, I just know it."

As Rocky stood and headed for the door, he had his doubts.

Victoria's basket, piled high with the fresh baked rolls she'd made this morning for the bakery, wafted a pleasant yeasty aroma. She eyed the three children as they ambled down the boardwalk in front of her on their way to the mercantile. A niggling bother played at the back of her mind.

What if Hannah was right? She had said Victoria didn't believe the Lord loved the children as much as she did.

Victoria longed to believe that God really loved the world as much as the Bible claimed He did. But how could God claim to love these children when, if she and Rocky hadn't been there, the girls would have been split up, probably for life? How could He claim to love them when He could have prevented their parents from dying in the first place? How could He claim to love her when her mother had taken her to the Foundling Hospital in New York when she was just two days old and dropped her off like some unwanted piece of baggage?

Victoria sighed. She'd been to church all her life. All her life she'd heard about the great love the Lord had for people. And all her life she had wondered if everyone had it right. Did God really love the world? Then why did He allow so much suffering? If she were in charge she would snuff out anyone or anything that would cause suffering.

She sighed as they came abreast of the bakery. Well she wasn't in charge and, unfortunately, the answer to her lifelong question would have to wait for more contemplation.

"Children," she called. "We need to stop here. Please sit on the bench and wait for me while I go in and talk to Mr. Jonas. I'll be right out and then we can go on down to the mercantile."

As soon as Mr. Jonas gave her the customary two bits for the rolls she and the girls and Jimmy were once again on their way to the mercantile.

Mrs. Halvorson looked up as they all entered the store and smiled widely. "Good morning!" She hurried out from behind the counter. "What can I do for you today?"

Victoria laid her hand on Jimmy's shoulder. "This young man here is in need of a new pair of boots and a pocket knife, I think."

Jimmy's eyes rounded and his jaw dropped open. "Really?"

Victoria chuckled. "Really, but boots first."

"Alright!" He gave one tremendous leap into the air, already scanning the store. Victoria turned him by one shoulder in the direction of the shoes and then looked at Mrs. Halvorson. "If you could help him try on shoes, I will take the girls back to the dress goods and see if we can't find some suitable material for a couple new dresses for them."

Mrs. Halvorson smiled, lifted her skirts and hustled after Jimmy who had already disappeared around the end of one aisle.

ChristyAnne's brows were arched when Victoria glanced down at her. "What?"

"New dresses? Really?" ChristyAnne held out the worn skirt of her faded dress. "These'll do for both of us for awhile yet."

Victoria brushed off her comments with a wave of her hand. "You can't go to school without at least one new dress a piece. It wouldn't seem right." She winked at the little girl.

ChristyAnne smiled wide and she eagerly scanned the store, searching for the materials section.

Victoria chuckled. "Right this way, ladies." She led them towards the back right corner of the store past shelves and shelves stacked above her head with all kinds of goods. The girls hustled along, right on her heels.

"How do you suppose she roped him into it?"

Victoria stopped so swiftly that ChristyAnne bumped into her from behind. The girls glanced up at her, bewildered. She held out one hand for them to be quiet and held her breath. That was Julia Nickerson's voice.

"Maybe she told him she was expecting. Maybe she *is* expecting and he just felt sorry for her and married her to protect her reputation."

Victoria's stomach clenched into a tight knot. Still Julia talking. And Victoria had no illusions over who she was talking about.

Another softer voice, "I don't know. That doesn't sound like Victoria to me. I think they've had eyes for each other for quite awhile, maybe it was just the right time? You were there weren't you?"

That was Mary Hunter's voice. Mary had moved to town with

her young husband, Harold, two years ago. Victoria had always liked her and it encouraged her a little to hear Mary standing up for her. Still, her throat burned at Julia's mean-spirited comments.

"Well, yes I was there. But I don't know whatever possessed him to propose to her like that. I think it's quite obvious that she forced him into marrying her, somehow. I mean, Rocky and I have been an item for months now. I think she was just jealous and wanted to take him away from me."

Victoria's eyes narrowed. She didn't know? And Rocky and *Julia*? An item? Maybe when pigs could fly! "Girls," she said loudly, "the dress material is just back here. I'm sure we'll find something suitable. Mrs. Halvorson always keeps a nice stock." And with that she stormed around the end of the aisle and did her best to act surprised that they were there. "Oh, Mary, how nice to see you!" She pulled the startled woman into a quick hug.

Julia didn't even have enough conscience to look guilty. She tucked a strand of hair behind her ear and innocently fingered the edge on a bolt of material. "Victoria. The girls look well rested, but you look positively tired this morning. Did you have a rough night last night?" A smirk flattened her lips.

Mary gasped.

"Julia, you're here too." Victoria turned towards her as though seeing her for the first time and spoke the words through a smile clenched so tight she felt sure if someone tapped her cheek her face would shatter like glass. Why she let the woman get to her she would never know. But the very thought of Rocky having any interest whatsoever in this conniving little strumpet sent a blast of fire coursing through her so assuredly that she wanted to slap the innocent smile right off of Julia Nickerson's face.

She turned back to Mary before she could actually follow through on the temptation. "Mary, I don't think you've met the girls. This is ChristyAnne and this is Damera." She pulled the girls around in front of her with a hand to each of their shoulders. "We're here to buy dress material."

"Lovely!" Mary's face brightened. "It's a pleasure to meet you, girls." She held her hand out to both of them. ChristyAnne shook her hand but Damera, thumb planted firmly in her mouth as usual, merely buried her face in Victoria's dress. "That's alright." Mary ruffled the hair on top of Damera's head. "You'll get to know me at church and then I'll have the pleasure of shaking your hand another day. Well," she held up a bolt of green cotton, "I have what I came for, so I'll talk to you another time."

Victoria smiled and only then realized that Julia had disappeared as well. With a sigh of relief she set to helping the girls pick out material in their favorite colors.

Still, she couldn't keep her mind off of Julia's words. *There's no possibility she and Rocky were ever an item!* Yet, doubt clenched a fist around her heart. She sighed as Damera quietly glanced back and forth between a bolt of pink gingham and one of blue calico. Why couldn't she just trust his word? He'd said he wouldn't leave her. That she was stuck with him, in fact. She needed to just quit worrying about it and concentrate on finding a good home for the children. And it was Julia Nickerson, of all people. Of course Rocky had never had anything going on with her.

She added two pairs of woolen stockings to the growing pile in her basket.

Julia Nickerson and Rocky! Really!

CHAPTER EIGHT

Rocky clomped down the boardwalk. A misty drizzle had settled over the valley and all of Shilo had headed indoors, it appeared. *Good.* That meant it would be quiet at the jail today. He adjusted his hat as he pondered Hannah's advice. *Fine.* So he had to court Victoria to convince her that he really did care. He could do that. Couldn't he?

Just ahead of him Julia Nickerson emerged from the mercantile.

Great. He spun on his heel and started for the alley between the store and the bank. The last thing he wanted was to talk to Julia, right now.

"Rocky!" she yoo-hooed, her boots clicking rapidly on the boardwalk as she ran to catch up to him.

Groaning inwardly, he eyed the path of his intended escape with longing. He refused to turn around, and scowled at her when she scuttled up next to him. He settled one hand on the butt of his pistol, hoping she would get the picture.

She batted her eyelashes. "Why isn't it just a coincidence, us running into each other, like this?"

"Julia." He tipped his hat. The least he could do was greet the oblivious woman politely. "Are you home for awhile then? I thought you would be off to New York for another run of the orphan trains."

"Oh, I'm home for good. One trip was more than enough. I think I've done my good deeds for the next ten years all in that one trip." She giggled and sidled much too close for propriety, even if he weren't now a married man.

He tried to step back, but she slithered one arm around his and coiled it as tightly as any snake ever could.

"Why you are looking positively glum. You poor dear. We

both know Victoria isn't the woman for you." She pressed herself even closer and stood on her tip-toes tapping the end of his nose with her fan. "Why don't you just put an end to this pretense of a marriage? You know it isn't making you happy."

Rocky dared not look down. Her face was so close to his that if he did.... Well... A shudder coursed through him. He didn't even want to think of what she might do. "Julia," again he tried to step away, but she was stuck to his arm like glue, "I'm quite happy, really." He lifted his chin and leaned away from her.

"Oh, posh! It's plain as day that you aren't happy right now." She squeezed his arm and flipped open the frippery of bamboo and lace, flashing it back and forth before her face so rapidly that a feather came loose from her hat and floated toward the ground.

Rocky begrudged it its freedom.

"You should just put her aside quietly. You know no one would blame you. Annulments happen all the time. Everyone will understand that you only married her to save those dear children."

Rocky suppressed the growl building in his chest. "Julia you are right, I'm not happy right now. But—"

A gasp directly behind him sent dread spiraling down his torso like an unplugged drain ebbing the life from him. He turned slowly, Julia still clinging to his arm.

The children stood on the boardwalk, Victoria just behind them, her face pale as fresh-laid snow. She was so white he thought sure she was going to faint then and there. And the pain in her expression stole the breath right out of his lungs. She glanced back and forth from him to Julia still wrapped around his arm. Slowly she drew her shoulders back. Her jaw jutted off to one side and her brows lowered. Then her cheeks flamed hot red and fire lit her beautiful blue eyes.

"Children come on, we've got to get to the school so you can meet your teacher." She would have bowled him over and tromped across his chest with her tiny booted heels, but Julia pulled him out of the way. Victoria pushed by followed by the children. The girls glanced up as they passed. Bewildered frowns on their faces, they looked from him to Julia and back.

Oblivious to the whole affair, Jimmy tromped by at the tail end of the line. He didn't even spare Rocky a glance. "Aw, Miss Victoria, do we hafta go to school?"

"Yes! And I don't want to hear another word about it!"

Rocky closed his eyes, his shoulders slumping. *Great.*

Julia sniffed. "There, you see? She doesn't even care enough about you to stay and fight for you. Any girl who loved a man would have stayed to fight for him, Rocky. I would have."

"Miss Nickerson." Rocky jerked away from her so forcefully that she gasped and stumbled a couple steps to catch herself. Anger surged and he trembled all over. "I'll thank you to keep your meddling nose out of our affairs. I'm married to Victoria and I plan to stay married to her. As I recall, you were the one that insisted we could only have the children if we were married. But I asked her because I wanted to. Not because you forced me to. I'd planned to do it at some point anyhow. It was just a matter of time." He took two steps before spinning on his heel and leveling her with a glare. "And I certainly wouldn't want to have the likes of you fighting for me!"

Julia's jaw dropped and she set her fan into rapid motion, her wrist flipping back and forth so fast there was nothing but a blur before her red face.

Presenting her his back once more he stormed down the boardwalk towards the sheriff's office. He needed to talk to Pa about taking a few days off.

He sure hadn't kicked off his new plan to prove his love with too grand a start.

The stage pulled to a stop with a shouted, "Whoa!" from the driver and the jangle of trace chains. A thin mist grayed the day and chilled Simon Saunders to his bones. He lumbered down the step and hurried over to the awning in front of the bakery. Stuffing his hands into his armpits, he scanned the street of Shilo, shoulders hunched.

Bank. Good. A bank always came in useful for something.

Mercantile. He'd need a warmer coat. His other one was too scruffy for the charade he would pull this time.

School house. He sniffed. School was a waste of everybody's time.

Sheriff's office. He swallowed.

"Hurry up with my bag, would you?" Blasted stage driver was moving slower than spring thaw after a long winter.

"You shore are all fired ill tempered for a man of the cloth." The stage driver spat a stream of tobacco down onto the street and glared at him.

Simon grimaced. Maybe he wouldn't be able to pull off the role of parson. Then he shook himself. He could do this. He smiled thinly. How many cons had he pulled in his time? This one would prove easy enough.

"Sorry friend." He held his hands up, palms out. "You're right, of course. It's just been a long trip out here. But that gives me no call to get irritable. Forgive an old sinner who is still learning to curb impatience?"

No telling where the goon lived. The driver might be a resident of this exact little town and if he didn't keep up the act, he'd soon be found out. Word traveled fast in the West.

"No hard feelings, Parson. None at all." The man tossed Simon's satchel to the ground and then spat a stream of brown sludge onto it. "Oh. I'm right sorry. I didn't mean to hit your bag."

Simon suppressed a growl, smiling tightly instead. "No harm done, friend." He snatched a hanky from his back pocket and wiped the mess from his bag. There was no way this had been an accident. If he didn't need this con so bad he'd pull out the pistol stashed in the top of his bag and at least give the driver a good scare. *Cussed Idiot!*

Grabbing up the bag by its handles he hurried down the boardwalk waving over his shoulder. "Thanks, now." *You can bet I'll be remembering your face.*

A jacket from the mercantile and a place to stay for a month or two and his plan could begin. His pace increased as he neared the Sheriff's office and he nearly collided with a young man coming out the door.

"Pardon me, Parson." The man stepped back and reached out a hand to steady him. "You alright?"

Simon ran a finger under the suddenly too-tight clerical collar as he eyed the silver star the young man was shoving into his breast pocket. *You're a parson, man. And you've put on fifty pounds. No one is going to recognize you.*

"Oh, yes, I'm fine." He forced himself to meet the young man's gaze. With sudden clarity he recognized the man before him. He was the one from the paper; the one in the wedding picture with Victoria.

Her new husband was a deputy. A deputy! The smile had been on his face too long. The young man eyed him quizzically. Shaking himself out of the frozen stupor Simon stretched out his hand. "Sorry, just a bit distracted. The name's Baxter. Baxter Cane."

"Rocky Jordan." The young man took his hand. "Welcome to our town, Reverend. Can I direct you to anywhere in particular? To Reverend Hollybough's house perhaps?"

"Oh, no, no, no." *The town already has a Parson.* Of course they did. *Think.* "I'm just on a little sabbatical, so to speak." He put on an appropriately somber expression. "Lost my wife of 20 years about a month back and I'm, well, I needed a little break from my congregation and routine. So I headed out west here for some time away. Time to myself."

The sobriety must have worked because Jordan's face softened. "I'm sorry to hear that, Reverend. Where are you from?"

"Boston."

"Are you just passing through, then? Or will you be staying here awhile."

Simon smoothed a hand down his chest and scanned the street as though deep in thought. "I think I'm hearing the Good Lord say I'll be staying here awhile, Son."

"Well, then let me direct you to the boarding house. I can walk you there, if you like?"

"Oh, no, no, no." The last thing he wanted was to spend more time in the presence of this deputy just yet. He would have to later of course, but for now he'd given just enough information to start things rolling in his favor. "I need to stop into the mercantile and then I can find my way to the boarding house on my own if you'll just point me in the right direction."

"The only boarding house in town is on Second Street, right behind the bank."

Simon held out his hand. "Much obliged." He gave what he hoped was a friendly smile.

"Sure." Jordan took his hand. "Welcome to Shilo."

With a sigh, Simon hurried down the walk. That could have gone better. But he'd done some pretty quick thinking on his feet. He smiled. Yes sir, this con was going to be fun.

Victoria had dinner nearly ready when Rocky arrived later that evening. He came in the kitchen door carrying a valise. She watched over the top of the sideboard that separated the kitchen from the dining table as he walked through the dining room and disappeared into the living room. He reappeared a moment later without the bag and she realized he hadn't met her gaze since he came in.

She swallowed.

Even after his betrayal this afternoon, her heart still climbed into her throat at his presence. All afternoon she'd been trying to decide what had actually been going on between he and Julia, but now, the fact that he didn't look her way confirmed what she feared. He really was unhappy here.

She shook away her ponderings and stalked to the stove stabbing the roast with the fork. The juices ran clear. Thank heavens. They could get dinner over with quickly.

Across the sideboard, she watched as Rocky approached ChristyAnne who was setting the table. He ruffled her hair and hooked his hat over the back of a chair. "Hey, how was your day today?" His voice was soft and cajoling, as though he might be sorry for the scene the young girl had witnessed today.

Victoria huffed. *He ought to be!*

ChristyAnne looked up at him and Victoria recognized the vulnerable look on the young girl's face. She felt an echo of it in her own heart.

"Fine, I suppose," ChristyAnne answered.

Victoria poured the hot water off the potatoes.

"Just fine, huh?" Rocky loosened his gun belt and hung the contraption on a hook by the front door.

"Yessir."

Victoria pressed her lips together. She hadn't been very good company this afternoon.

When she'd stopped by the school to introduce the children, Sharyah had mentioned the Rackler family. They lived just east of town and had recently lost two of their girls to a fever. They had heard about the children and had asked Sharyah to mention that they wanted to adopt the girls. That news on top of the scene between Rocky and Julia had her stomach in knots.

Probably her tension had shone through loud and clear to the children. The girls had played quietly with her old dolls all afternoon. Jimmy was outside whittling with his new pocket knife.

"Where are Damera and Jimmy?" Rocky asked.

ChristyAnne set another plate on the table. "Mera's in our room playing and Jimmy's outside." She paused then turned to face him. "I really want to thank you for keeping Mera and I together. I know things ain't, ahhh haven't, been easy for you on account of you having to get married and all, but you have no idea how hard I prayed that God would somehow keep us together." She shrugged her little shoulders as Victoria blinked back tears. "Just wanted to say thanks. Again."

Rocky glanced up then and caught Victoria looking at him. She jerked her gaze back to the potatoes and set to mashing them with a fury. *Why, oh why, did I let myself get so attracted to him? And what are we going to do now?* She spun the pot and mashed a different section. The heat of his scrutiny warmed her neck but she refused to look up.

Finally, he cleared his throat and spoke to ChristyAnne once more. "I would do it all again, if it came down to it. Why don't you go get Damera and have her wash up? I'll go find Jimmy, alright?"

"Yessir." ChristyAnne skipped down the hallway.

Rocky came into the kitchen and stopped. Victoria ignored him and channeled her frustration toward the potatoes.

He stepped toward her. "Ria, I—"

The outer kitchen door crashed open and Jimmy burst into the room.

Victoria gasped and jumped so high that Rocky put one hand on her back to steady her.

"Jimmy!" Her tone was more caustic than it needed to be. And it hardly had anything to do with the fact that Jimmy'd just about sent her heart through the ceiling.

Jimmy looked chagrinned. "Sorry. But look!" He held up a carved bear the size of an egg.

Victoria pulled in a breath of astonishment. "Jimmy! That's really good." She took the bear from him, angling it this way and that before she handed it to Rocky. She was amazed at the intricacy of it. The bear's fur was carved in small sure strokes and there was even a tiny fish dangling from its mouth.

"This is really good, Son." Rocky punched Jimmy in the arm. "That's quite a talent you've got there."

Jimmy scuffed a toe across the floor in an aw-shucks manner but the glow on his face could have lit up a ball room.

Victoria smiled at the boy's delight.

"Get washed up for dinner, alright?" Rocky handed the bear back.

Jimmy's shoulders slumped slightly and he turned away.

"Jimmy," Victoria stopped him before he could shove the bear into his pocket, "I'd love to have that carving on my windowsill to look at while I'm here in the kitchen. Would you mind letting me have it?"

"Sure." Jimmy shrugged as though it wasn't a big deal, but joy twinkled in his eyes.

The girls bustled in just then and, even though she'd repeatedly asked them to wash up outside, all three headed straight for the kitchen pump. Victoria didn't chastise them. She wasn't about to send them all out and stay in here alone with Rocky.

Rocky made small talk with the children throughout the meal, while Victoria picked at her meat and potatoes listlessly and tried to block out the image of Julia Nickerson pressing herself up against him. While it had been obvious that Rocky wasn't too pleased to have Julia clinging to him, he *had* said that he wasn't happy here with her and the children. She sighed. She didn't want him staying out of a sense of obligation and living an unhappy life. What kind of a person would she be if she expected that of him?

On top of that, when the Racklers adopted the girls she wouldn't really need Rocky to stay around anymore. She'd stopped by to talk to Hannah after hearing the news from Sharyah, and Hannah had said she could make room for Jimmy at the orphanage. So they wouldn't have to worry about Julia's threat to make sure they were taking good care of the children. Yes, once they found the children good homes, she would grant him an annulment and move on.

Victoria glanced at each child in turn. She swallowed away sadness at the thought of them leaving and knew she wasn't quite ready to give them up yet. They were just getting settled. Surely they deserved a few more days to get accustomed to the area before they were passed along to another new situation. But would that only make the inevitable parting all the harder?

Rocky unabashedly studied her. She could feel the prickle of his attentive gaze, even though she carefully kept her focus elsewhere.

She suppressed a groan and chomped down on a piece of roast. Why oh why had she let herself fall in love with him? Nothing but tragedy came from giving too much of your heart to anyone – well, anyone but children. Best she try and keep her distance from him. The less she spoke to him, the less entangled her heart would become.

Finally the torturous meal wound down. She rose and poured Rocky a final cup of coffee.

He leaned back in his chair and crossed one ankle over the opposite knee. "Got school tomorrow. So I want all of you into bed early. Head for your rooms and get into your night clothes, then you can play for a little and Ri— ah, Victoria – and I will be in to say goodnight after a bit. We've got a couple things to talk about, until then." He pinned her with a look.

Jaw clenched, she set to clearing the table, dishes clanking. The last thing she wanted to do was discuss the scene on the boardwalk today. *I do need to tell him the news about the Racklers.*

The children headed down the hall and Victoria spoke before he could broach the subject she knew was on his mind.

"I spoke to Sharyah today. She says the Racklers, the family from just east of town, would like to adopt the girls."

Rocky swallowed and the pained look that crossed his face surprised her.

He balanced his coffee cup on his knee and toyed with it, twisting it around and around. "What do you know about them?" He glanced up at her.

She shrugged. "Not much. They recently lost two of their girls to a fever. They have two other children at the school, but I think they've only lived here about a year and they mostly keep to themselves." She took Rocky's empty plate and stacked it on the pile before her. "Sharyah says their children are always well fed and groomed. And they are good, hard working folks."

"But I've never seen them at church."

That had been one of her concerns, as well. "Sharyah says they attend in Salem. Mrs. Rackler has a sister there. So they make the drive each week."

He cleared his throat and twisted the cup some more. "Well, it sounds like they will be a good family for them. I know Sharyah would never recommend them if they were questionable."

Victoria released a puff of air. "I was thinking the same thing."

"What about Jimmy?"

She blinked hard. "Hannah says that she should be able to squeeze another cot into one of the boys' rooms at the orphanage and Jimmy could come if it's just him."

He rubbed a hand across his face. "We'll have to tell them."

She nodded. "I thought we might give them one more day? Tell them tomorrow night at dinner?"

"Sounds fine. Now…," he set his cup on the table and leaned forward looking up at her, "let's talk about earlier this afternoon…."

She'd rather do just about anything than listen to his excuses for admitting his unhappiness to Julia. She thumped two plates together and scooped the silverware into one hand.

The room filled with stiff silence broken only by the clanking dishes. Rocky cleared his throat as though waiting for her to say something, but Victoria made no reply.

Rocky's chair scraped across the floor as he pushed away from the table. "Ria—"

She fled to the kitchen and set the stack of dishes into the sink. She worked the pump handle furiously. The rest of the dishes on the table could wait until Rocky headed to the parlor to read the paper. She wasn't about to go back while he was still there. Alone. And wanting to talk. She had no idea what to say to him. She huffed. Somehow, *Why did you make me care so much for you, only to break my heart*? sounded too pitiful.

She heard a noise behind her and froze for just a moment.

Rocky set the leftover potatoes and the platter of meat on the sideboard next to her. "I'll get the rest," he said, and headed back to the table.

Victoria suppressed a groan and poured the hot water from the stove into the sink, ignoring the temptation to escape out the back door. Instead, she immersed her hands in the warm soapy water. Why couldn't he be like other men and go read the paper after dinner?

Rocky set another stack of dirty plates next to her and picked up a dish towel.

Panic sent her heart to racing. Surely he didn't plan to stay in the kitchen and help with the *dishes*. "Newspaper's on the end table by the settee. It won't take me long to get these done."

"I'll dry."

She sighed and didn't meet his gaze. Merely wiped down a plate and dropped it into the rinse water, jaw set. She wished he would just get on with what he had to say as long as he insisted on staying. What was he going to tell her? Maybe Julia had been right. Had that been frustration with Julia, or guilt over getting caught, on his face when he'd first spotted her on the boardwalk this afternoon? What if he and Julia *were* an item? She cast him a glance out of the corner of her eye. Was he that foolish? To get involved with the likes of Julia Nickerson? She rolled her lips into a pressed line. She didn't think he was, but her eyes certainly hadn't deceived her. Or her ears either.

He didn't say a word the whole time they worked side by side to get the dishes done. But as she drained the water and wiped down the sink, she felt him come to a stop directly behind her. A tremor tightened her shoulders and she swallowed.

"Ria," he whispered into her hair, "you misunderstood what you saw today."

He was so close she could smell the masculine scent of soap and saddle leather that always accompanied him.

"Did I?" The words came out on a tiny squeak and frustration coursed through her. Why couldn't she at least sound self-assured around him?

She pinched her lips together and tried to step away, but he used the movement to catch her elbow and move her into the corner of the kitchen cabinets; then had the audacity to settle one arm against each cupboard.

He leaned in. "Yes, you did." There was an intensity on his face that she didn't ever remember seeing before.

She swallowed. "Everything I saw and *heard* seemed pretty clear. You don't have to lie to me just to make me feel better."

His brows lowered and a muscle along his jaw tightened as he stepped a little closer. "I'm going to ignore the fact that you just called me a liar, for a moment." A softness crept into his expression. "What did you hear exactly?" He lifted one hand to push back an escaped curl, his touch whisper-soft against her cheek.

Tremulous quivering burst to life in the pit of her stomach. She willed it away and opened her mouth to tell him exactly what it was that she had heard....

What had she heard, again?

"Um..." She took in the day-old stubble that dusted his firm jaw, the small white scar that peeked out from under the dark curl drooping over his forehead, and the way he worked one side of his lower lip with his teeth, and couldn't quite remember what it was she wanted to say.

A crinkle appeared at the corners of his deep brown eyes and his fingers caressed her cheek more firmly as he bent even closer. "Having a hard time thinking, Ria?"

She put her hands out to push him back, but her traitorous arms stopped short and her palms just rested there against his broad chest feeling the heat of him through his shirt. She closed her eyes briefly and worked the dryness out of her mouth. *Focus.* "You said you weren't happy here with me and the children."

A knock sounded at the front door.

Ignoring it, he took her face in both his hands, "That's not what you heard. You came up in the middle of a conversation."

The remembrance of Julia clinging to him sent a surge of pain through her belly. She pierced him with a glare. "I'm not deaf. Or blind."

"Ria—"

The knock sounded again, more firmly this time and a low growl of frustration escaped Rocky's throat.

He sighed. "Really, it wasn't what it sounded like." He gestured for her to wait. "I'll be right back, just... I'll be right back." He stalked off to see who was at the door.

Victoria's knees went to mush as Rocky stepped out of sight and she grabbed at the sideboard and hung on for dear life. She couldn't suppress a sigh of exasperation. That man just might be the death of her.

She only had a moment to collect herself before Rocky came back with an odd look on his face. "There is a parson at the front door? Claims he needs to talk to you?"

"Pastor Hollybough?"

He shook his head. "No. Says his name is Cane. Baxter Cane."

Victoria frowned. "I don't know a Baxter Cane."

Rocky shrugged. "I showed him to the living room. I bumped into him in town earlier today."

"Oh?"

"He told me he'd recently lost his wife and needed some time away from his church."

"What does he want with me?"

Rocky shrugged again. "Not sure. He just said it was important that he be allowed a few minutes of your time."

She swallowed. She didn't want to sit in there alone with a stranger. "Will you come with me?"

His face softened. "Sure."

"Just let me put together a tray."

Rocky waited while she gathered coffee, cream, sugar and a plate of cookies, then led the way back to the living room.

The man waiting there was of medium height and heavy build. He paced the room, hands clasped behind his back, a Bible tucked under one arm. His thin gray hair, slicked back with pomade, stuck to his head like so many pieces of yarn and the flesh at his neck drooped over his clerical collar, but there was a quietness in his expression. When he looked up and saw her he took in a sharp breath and froze.

A tremor of unease pulsed and then stilled. He looked harmless enough. She set the tray on the side table and curtsied. "Hello, I'm Victoria. Roc—, ah, my husband tells me you wanted to see me?"

The parson stared at her, his jaw slightly slack, and Rocky took a step closer to her side. She felt his hand come to rest low on her back and wondered briefly at the comfort it gave her. She stretched her hand from the Parson to the tray. "May I offer you some refreshments?"

"Uh," the man seemed to give himself a mental shake, "certainly, yes. That would be fine, thank you."

"Cream? Sugar?"

He nodded. "Both, please. And thank you."

Victoria turned to fix the coffee as Rocky said, "Please, have a seat, Parson."

The settee springs protested as the man settled his bulk.

Victoria handed him a cup and saucer with a cookie on it and pretended not to notice the trembling in his hands. "Rocky?" She tipped her head in the direction of the coffee service.

He nodded. "Sure. Just black."

Finally, Victoria eased herself into a chair and cupped her palms against the warmth of her own cup.

The parson stirred his coffee and slurped noisily, then picked up the cookie and nibbled on the corner before he tossed it back down. He stirred his coffee again, fidgeted, opened his mouth, then snapped it shut and stirred some more.

Victoria glanced over at Rocky, who cocked an eyebrow and shrugged.

Finally, Victoria took pity on him. "How may I help you, Reverend?"

"Well, ah, you see…" He glanced up. "I'm sorry. You just look so much like her. I'm not handling this very well." The coffee cup rattled against the saucer as he set it on the table next to him.

Victoria frowned. "Look like who, Reverend?"

The man glanced back and forth between her and Rocky and then sighed. "My late wife. You are, or were, our daughter." He paused. "No, not 'were'. Are. You are our daughter."

★

Chapter Nine

The room tilted and went dark around the edges. It was as if she was seeing things from the end of a long tunnel and everything in the room grew fuzzy except the man's face and fidgety hands.

"Excuse me?" Rocky reached over and took her coffee, setting it on the table between them.

"What?" Her voice sounded thin, breathy, far away.

The parson cleared his throat. "I know it must be hard to take in." He glanced at Victoria with pain-filled eyes. "You see before your mother and I came into the church, we were…, er, living in sin. And when we found out Millie was expecting you, well, we did get married, but we didn't have any money and we just didn't feel we were ready for children – didn't feel we could provide for you yet, so we gave you up for adoption."

Victoria blinked and picked up her cup, gulping a large unladylike swallow.

"Several years later when we, uh, came into the church, we realized what a mistake we had made. Well actually, even before that we knew it was a mistake. But we've searched for you since that time." He picked up the coffee cup and looked into the bottom of it. "It wasn't until just recently, when I saw your announcement in the paper about getting married, that I found you. I knew it had to be you. You look so much like my Mimi."

Rocky leaned forward. "Mimi?" he asked, skepticism lacing his tone. "A moment ago you said Millie."

Victoria frowned. Why was he speaking to the man like that?

Unruffled by Rocky's manner, the parson stared at a spot on the wall, smiling fondly as though he could see someone there. "Millicent, her name was. Most folks called her Millie. But a little tyke in our church couldn't pronounce her name right. He started calling her Miz Mimi. And it sorta stuck with me. I called her that once in awhile. My Mimi." He sighed and drained his cup then let it dangle between his knees as he turned his gaze back on Victoria. "How I wish she could be here to see you, child. You are beautiful. And, from what I read in the paper of your helping orphans, everything we hoped you would be."

Warmth enveloped Victoria and she smiled. Her father. Her real father. Sitting here in the same room with her. She could hardly take it in. She glanced at Rocky. He did not return her smile, but looked back seriously, his lips pressed into a hard line.

Her joy stuttered and she cocked her head. "What?" she asked softly.

Instead of responding to her, Rocky turned to the man. "What do you want?"

Victoria gasped. "Rocky!"

The parson stood to his feet with a sad smile. "Not a thing, young man. Not a thing but to be allowed to spend time with my daughter and get to know her a little." He turned to look at her. "As long as that is okay with her."

Victoria stood up. "Of course. I would like that." She narrowed her eyes at Rocky. How could he treat this poor old man so callously?

The parson smiled largely and patted a hand over his shirt pocket. "I'm so thankful. I only wish your mother could be here to meet you too."

Rocky made no comment, just folded his arms, his jaw jutting off to one side.

Pinching her lips together Victoria decided to ignore him for a moment. She couldn't suppress the joy, elation even, welling up inside her. After all these years, she would finally have some answers about her real family. And she didn't come from trash, as she'd been accused as a child. Her daddy was a minister. Relief swelled until it filled her chest.

"Well, then..." He turned and set his cup on the saucer and retrieved his Bible from its spot on the settee next to where he'd been sitting. "I'll be on my way. I'm staying down at the boarding house in town, and I'll be seeing you at services on Sundays." He tucked the book under his arm in a gesture that said the book was as at-home there as it was on his pulpit. He smiled at her, a full smile that allowed the joy to spill out of his eyes. "I'm looking forward to it, child."

She couldn't just let him leave without an invitation back. "Ah, can you come to dinner… say Wednesday evening? We'd love to have you." Her gesture included Rocky, even though the look on his face said he'd be less than welcoming of the man's return. Brushing aside his apparent concern, she waited for the minister's reply.

"Of course, child. I'd be more than happy to join you for dinner on Wednesday. What time should I come by?"

"How about six?"

"Six it is." His smile stretched again. "See you then, child."

Rocky stepped back into the room after seeing the parson to the door and watched Victoria straighten the parlor. He folded his arms and waited, feeling uneasy with the lightness in her step and the spark of life in her countenance that he hadn't seen for days.

Humming, she gathered the coffee cups and leftover cookies and placed them on the tray. She paused when she noticed his watchful gaze. "I can't believe you treated him like that!"

He rubbed his jaw as he debated the best way to caution her. "I don't want you to get your hopes up about this man."

"What do you mean?" The light in her expression faded slightly and he hated that he had caused that.

Reaching out, he took the tray and preceded her into the kitchen. "We just don't know anything about him. He could be who he says he is, then again, he could be someone else. All I'm asking is that you play it cautiously until we can find out a little more."

He didn't add that the man had "con" written all over him, but he couldn't disguise the implication in his tone.

She snatched up a cloth and furiously swiped the top of the side board. "He's a minister! Surely you aren't saying he's lying?"

The edge of hurt and defeat in her voice was like a knife in his chest.

"Ria." He reached out and stilled her hands, folding them snugly within his own.

She turned her face away, and tilted her chin up.

He refused to give in to the grin that wanted to escape at her little-girl-stubbornness. "All I'm asking is that you don't give your trust to this man all at once. If he is who he says he is, I'll be the first one to be happy for you, you know that. But if he isn't, I'll be the first to put a fist down his throat, too. And I don't want you getting hurt. So just be cautious, alright?" He reached out and touched the mulish point of her chin.

She glanced up at him and he held his breath, hoping she would see reason. Finally her stance softened. "You're probably right. I'll try and be careful."

He allowed the grin to come then. "Of course, I'm right, Mrs. Jordan." Any remaining spark in her eyes dimmed at the reminder of their marriage and earlier unfinished conversation. He could have kicked himself but he needed her to know his side of things.

She rolled her lips in and pressed them together, stepping back.

He tightened his hold on her hand. "So we're back to that?"

She sighed. "I just don't want you to be unhappy. I know you were practically forced into marrying me."

"Ria," he stepped toward her. "That's not—"

"Mrs. Jordan!" ChristyAnne stormed into the room. "That ol' Jimmy keeps tossing dirt clods into Mera's an' my room!"

Victoria jerked back. "Oh my!" Pressing one hand to her forehead, she glanced at him. "The children' first day of school is tomorrow, we really need to get them settled down and in bed. Could you see to Jimmy, please?"

He sighed and stomped through the living room and down the hallway as he mumbled, "I'll see to Jimmy, alright."

By the time he'd given Jimmy a thorough talking to about the inappropriateness of bringing dirt clods into the house – much less throwing them at others – and supervised the boy's sweeping job, Victoria had disappeared into her room. He stood outside her doorway for a moment debating on whether to knock and insist that she listen to his explanation of what happened between him and Julia, but then decided against it.

He gently massaged his aching shoulder as he headed towards the couch. He would talk to her first thing in the morning, Dad had given him the whole week off and he planned to put it to good use convincing his wife that he really did love her.

CHAPTER TEN

Victoria sat up with a start, the covers tumbling about her in a soft heap. She blinked at the light streaming through her window. "Wha—! Oh! Of all the days to sleep late!" She lurched out of bed and fumbled into her dress with sleep-klutzy fingers. Had the rooster crowed? If so, she hadn't heard it today.

Of course, she had lain awake long into the night thinking over everything that had happened the day before and trying not to worry about any of it, but failing miserably.

Swiping her hair up into a loose bun she stuffed pins into it as she rushed down the hallway and threw open the girl's door. "Time to get up, girls. I overslept and we are going to be late for school if we don't hurry."

She hustled back down the hall and burst into the living room. "Rocky?"

He bolted upright on the couch and rubbed a hand over his face in sleepy confusion. "Huh?"

"We oversle—oh!" She had seen him without his shirt several times as he worked, or when she helped him change his bandage, but somehow the sight of his well-muscled torso combined with the morning bristle shading his jaw and the tousled splay of his hair seemed far more intimate. At the quirk of his eyebrow she realized she was staring. With a small gasp she turned her back to the sight. Wishing the heat crawling up her neck away, she cleared her throat. "Ah… we overslept. I'm working on getting the girls up. Could you get Jimmy, please?"

The scratch of his hand rubbing across his cheek and the long inhale of a yawn filled several seconds before he replied, "Yeah, sure."

Hurrying back down the hall she was satisfied to see both girls out of bed and getting dressed. "Morning," they both mumbled.

"Morning, girls. As soon as you two are dressed, bring the brush to the kitchen and I'll help you with your hair."

A few moments later, Victoria had just poured three round flapjacks onto the griddle when Rocky sauntered in. "Jimmy's up and around. Should be out in a few minutes." He tapped his palm to the side of the coffee pot and looked perturbed to find it barely warm.

Victoria felt chagrinned and relieved at the same time. If there was no coffee then he wouldn't be tempted to stay and drink a cup before he did the chores. And that meant that they could put off that dreaded conversation about Julia for another day. "Coffee should be ready as soon as you get in from chores. Sorry."

"Guess I'll have to wait then."

"Mmm-hmm." She held her breath hoping he would go out and not bring it up.

"Wonder if there is something wrong with the rooster, or if we just didn't hear him this morning?"

"Mmmm."

"Hope I can find the right end of ol' Bess." The sound of a grin tinged his voice.

She suppressed a smile, not wanting to engage him in conversation right now. "Mmmm-hmmm."

"Well, I guess I ought to be getting to the chores."

"Okay. I'll send Jimmy out to help as soon as he makes an appearance." She held her breath.

Finally the click of the door followed by silence told her he'd gone out.

She let out her breath and checked off a mental list of everything she needed to get done before the children left for school. *Flapjacks, cooking. Coffee's on. Girls' hair, in a minute. Set the table! First check the food.* Victoria peeked at the underside of one flapjack. *Not quite ready yet. Cook faster!* She spun around to grab the plates from the cupboard and let out a squeak of surprise to find Rocky still there.

He grinned unrepentantly. "If I can't have coffee, at least I can look at the prettiest gal this side of New York. If that doesn't wake me up, I don't know what will."

For the second time that morning, Victoria felt heat crawling up her neck but she had things to do. She brushed past him, trying not to enjoy his flattery too much. Yet his words added to her confusion over the scene she'd witnessed on the boardwalk yesterday. She'd clearly heard him say he wasn't happy. And, after all, he'd known her most of her life and never shown so much as a hint of romantic interest in her. *Except for right after Mama's wedding, when he told me he wanted to court me.* She dismissed that thought and snatched up the stack of plates.

"Victoria," Rocky's fingers settled gently around her elbow.

She stiffened and clutched the plates to her chest. "Rocky let's not—"

ChristyAnne and Mera stepped into the room. "We're ready for you to do our hair, Mrs. Jordan."

Rocky growled so loudly that both girls took a step back and blinked up at him. Victoria pressed her lips together to hide a smile of relief and she winked at the girls to let them know Rocky wasn't really upset with them.

He stepped closer, the warmth of his breath brushing her ear as he whispered, "We are not done with that conversation, Ria. So don't think you can get out of it."

She did not meet his gaze as he grabbed his hat from the peg by the door and eased it onto his head. Neither did she relax until the door clicked shut behind him.

She sighed, her shoulders relaxing. *Saved by the children, yet again.* "Now girls, let's – ah!" Black smoke billowed up in aromatic clouds from around the flapjacks.

She shoved the plates into ChristyAnne's hands and snatched up the pot-holder rushing the smoking pan out the door.

Rocky, halfway across the yard to the barn, chuckled as she scraped the black blobs into the slop bucket. "Cade's pigs will thank you for that little oversight," he called.

"This is your fault, Rocky Jordan!"

He smiled and sketched a bow. "And it was my pleasure."

She quickly turned her back before he could see her grin.

Back inside, she greased the griddle and then poured three more flapjacks. When Jimmy stumbled in with his hair spiking out from his head in all directions, she told him to go help Rocky with the chores.

She brushed and plaited the girls' hair and flipped flapjacks until Rocky and Jimmy came in and finally everyone sat around the table to wolf down a hurried breakfast.

Mera tugged on her skirt expectantly and she realized the little tyke had asked her a question. "What was that, honey?" Victoria directed her attention to the little girl, pushing down her frustration with the morning's events.

"Do you fink my teachuh is gonna wike me?" Mera's attention never left Victoria's face as she reached for her milk and took a long drink.

"Of course she is! Don't you remember meeting her yesterday and how nice she was?"

She nodded, her upper lip still buried in the white froth, and sloshed milk down the front of her dress.

Victoria snatched up a towel and dabbed at it. "Well she isn't going to be any different today. She's still going to be kind to you."

"Besides," Rocky spoke up, "she's my sister, so she has extra incentive to be nice to you. If she isn't I'll go over there and tickle her until she promises to behave!" His eyes twinkled at the little girl over the top of his coffee mug.

Mera giggled and stuffed a wad of flapjack into her white-rimmed mouth, her gaze fastened on Rocky who was swiftly and obviously becoming her hero.

Victoria swallowed away the tender swell of emotion tightening her throat. She couldn't start thinking of them as a family. "Remember now children, what we talked about yesterday. Miss Sharyah is going to have each of you take a few tests. She'll ask you to read a little and do some ciphers, just to see where you are at, so she knows what grade to put you in."

ChristyAnne and Jimmy groaned.

Mera wrinkled up her nose. "Whatsa Ciphuh?"

Jimmy rolled his eyes. "It's math you dolt!"

"Jimmy!" Rocky's voice held the force of a whip. "I don't want to hear you speaking to a woman like that again. Especially not your sister!"

Victoria's brows arched. *Surely he's not starting to think of us all as a family?*

Rocky met her gaze, something like surprise in the depths of his own eyes.

"She ain't my sister," Jimmy mumbled.

Rocky cleared his throat. "Yes. Well… while you are here with us we would like you to think of yourselves as siblings. We want this to be as much a home for you as it can be. Now," he stood, "it's time to head to school. Everyone grab your lunch pail."

Victoria leapt out of her seat. "Lunch!" She couldn't believe she'd forgotten to make the lunches.

Rocky looked surprised, but quickly rallied to help as Victoria rushed for the kitchen.

"Ah… okay, tell you what?" Chairs scraped as the children stood to gather around Rocky. "You two help Ria get the table cleared and the lunches made. And Jimmy and I will go out and hitch up the buggy and we'll drive to school today. That way you won't be late."

Relief eased her slight panic as she rolled three leftover flapjacks around some cheese. It may have been a disaster of a morning but at least due to Rocky's kindness, the children wouldn't be late for their first day.

She'd never felt more relief in her life than when the children climbed into the buggy and Rocky drove them out of the yard.

She sank down onto the top step and laid her face into her hands, elbows resting on her knees. Her legs splayed in unladylike abandon and she didn't care a whit. She groaned. "I am *not* cut out to be a wife and mother!"

It was only a moment before her head popped up. "I didn't make Rocky a lunch for work!"

Cade Bennett stood and slowly removed his hat, curling the brim into his palm as he swiped his forearm across his brow. The morning air still held a nip of chill, so his damp forehead had nothing to do with heat. His horse snorted and side-stepped, tossing him an 'it's-about-time' look. Cade patted the horse on the neck. "I know, I know."

The small white schoolhouse stood silent. Sharyah had gone in several minutes earlier and if he was going to have time to talk to her before the students started arriving, he'd better get down there. He eyed the school-house door and swallowed, willing his heartbeat to ease into a calmer rhythm. Settling his hat back on his head, he glanced down at the small pile of evergreen needles he'd shredded. He gave the pile a swift kick and returned to his perusal of the school.

He sighed. "Just go talk to her, you idiot." With a determined stride, he started down the hill toward the small clap-board building.

He hadn't been able to think of anything else but Sharyah since she'd slapped him at Victoria's house after the wedding. Truth told, he still had no idea why she'd slapped him. He rubbed a hand over his jaw as he stepped past the tree swing and into the school yard, still remembering the sting of her hand. But more than that, the pain in his heart. A pain that hadn't dissipated since. What had he said to upset her? She was like a sister to him and he wouldn't be able to put this behind him until he figured out what he'd done.

His boots thumped on the stairs and when he pushed open the door at the back of the room, Sharyah was looking at him from where she'd obviously been cleaning the chalkboard behind her oak-plank desk.

"Hi." He cleared his throat. *That was a lame greeting.*

Today she had her long golden-blonde hair done up in a braid and wrapped around her head. How she kept all that mass of curls from falling all around her shoulders, he had no idea.

Sharyah had some of the prettiest hair he'd ever seen when it hung down about her shoulders – thick and curly and forever in disarray. Right now, with it pulled back, she looked prim… and stern.

Her brown eyes hard and dark as granite, she turned back to her task. "What do you want? You can't be here alone with me. You know the gossip that will start."

The edge of steel in her voice told him he hadn't been forgiven for his unknown transgression yet.

She wiped great dark swaths across the chalkboard with a damp rag, her movements swift and jerky.

She was right about the gossip. But he'd be gone before anyone arrived. "Uh…" He cleared his throat again, wishing she would look at him. Pulling the door shut behind him, he entered despite her lack of invitation. "I wanted to, uh…, talk to you about the other day. I only need a moment of your time."

Her hand paused mid-swipe, but only for a second, then she continued on almost as though she hadn't heard him. He could imagine smoke coming out of her ears and heat waves radiating off her slender, stiff shoulders.

Mystified, he eased down onto the bench at the front of the classroom and tossed his hat down beside him. "Sharyah, I have no idea what I did to make you so angry with me. But you are like the sister I never had and I can't stand the thought of you being mad at me. Please… just tell me what I did, so we can talk about this."

She froze again. Her back remained toward him, the high upper corner of the chalkboard still dusty white.

He waited, but she held her silence.

Finally her spine stiffened and she took two swift strides over to a basin of water and dipped her rag in. "If you don't know what you did, there is no point talking about it, I guess."

She angled him a glare full of venom and wrung the rag so tight, he wondered if she was fantasizing about it being his neck.

Frustration coursed through him. He stretched his arms wide and then clasped his hands behind his head. "Sharyah, I'm sorry, I don't know what I did. Just tell me so I can apologize. I've obviously offended you, somehow."

Dropping her gaze, she stalked over to a low stool and bent to drag it with her to the end of the chalkboard she still needed to clean.

Were those tears she was hiding? Swiftly he came to his feet and stepped over to help.

"I have no hard feelings, Cade." Her voice trembled, low and husky.

She is *crying*.

Her concentration on the stool, she was backing up quickly and headed in a collision course with him.

Instead of moving out of the way, he folded his arms and waited.

"I'm sorry I lo—ah!" Her words ended on a yelp as she thumped into him and spun around out of reflex.

He cupped her arms and held her steady.

She stood so close he could see the amber flecks amplified by the tears in her large dark eyes, and hear her quick intakes of breath. Chalk smeared the dusting of freckles across her small, upturned nose, but he left it be. Her normally smiling mouth pressed into a thin line and she squeezed the rag so tightly that water dripped down the front of his shirt.

He grinned and pried the rag from her clutch. "Let me get that for you before I'm wetter than a fish."

She glanced down at the dark, wet patch on his shirt and brushed at it. "Oh, I'm sorry." Her cheeks bloomed red and he paused, curious at the sight.

She's certainly no longer a little girl, is she? He swallowed and turned slowly to rub the last of the chalk from the board.

Behind him, Sharyah dashed the tears from her cheeks. Cade was the last person she wanted to see this morning. Well, that was actually a lie. But why did he have to show up here, right now? She stacked up several books and straightened her desk. *Heaven have mercy, how did I get myself into this situation?* Her hands trembled and she clutched handfuls of her skirts to hide the fact as Cade turned from wiping the last spot on the board.

"There. Done." He handed her the rag and folded his arms across his chest in the way he had when he wasn't about to let something slide.

She suppressed a groan and carried the water basin to the back door. Tossing the contents, she tucked the basin back into its cupboard, flipped the rag over the hook to dry and turned to grab the day's lesson plan from her desk.

Maybe she could bluff her way out of this. "Cade, I'm sorry I slapped you. I was having a very bad day that day. It was nothing you did, honest." *Liar.* She picked up a piece of chalk and carefully wrote "Primer One" on the board. "So I'll see you on Sunday, right? At the school's Mystery-Basket Picnic Fundraiser?"

Before she could write anymore Cade swiped the chalk from her, a grin on his face. "Okay, so this is how you are going to play this?"

She didn't dare meet his gaze. Her heart had almost pumped right out of her chest when he'd steadied her earlier. She glanced from side to side. If only some children would show up early. She'd rather face the gossip than one more minute alone with Cade. Maybe she could come up with an excuse to go outside. But he stood between her and the door. She contemplated the back door, but the steps weren't fixed yet and she refused to jump three feet to the ground just to avoid talking to Mr. Stubborn.

A glimmer shone in Cade's eyes, telling her he knew exactly the predicament she was in.

He doesn't know the half of it!

Cade dropped the chalk into the dish on her desk then cupped his chin in contemplation. "I'm having a hard time believing that the cool, calm, level headed Sharyah Jordan just lost her temper and slapped me for no good reason. But," he shrugged and stuck out his lower lip, "if you want to do this the hard way, we can."

Sharyah shifted from one foot to the other. She should just tell him, but the humiliation was more than she could handle. *He's going to figure it out anyway. It's only a matter of time.* She held her silence and stared at the top button on his shirt miserably.

Cade held aloft one finger. "So, I guess I start at the beginning. This might take awhile." He reached for the lesson plan she still clutched tightly in one hand.

With a sigh of resignation, Sharyah relinquished the papers and Cade thumped them down on her desk with a satisfied look.

"Now," he turned back to her. "After the wedding Hannah asked us to go and help pack Mrs. Snyder's things over to the Doc's place." He arched a brow, as though asking if that was a good place to start.

Sharyah nodded, her mind scrambling for a way out, even as she resigned herself to the inevitable. She smoothed her hands down her skirt.

Cade arched a brow. "Oh, see? We're getting somewhere now, because you only do that smoothing thing when you are nervous or out of sorts."

Sharyah's hands stilled and she tipped her chin up as she deliberately clasped her hands behind her back. "Can you please just accept my apology and go home?"

His grin sprang back into place and he tossed her a bold wink. "Then," he held up a second finger. "We were in the parlor and you said what a beautiful wedding it was, what with Victoria standing up with her mother and all. And you asked me what kind of wedding I wanted to have when the day came to be my turn. And…." He stilled and his hand went back to cup his chin.

Sharyah's heart forgot to beat. She could see by the look on his face that he'd figured it out.

As though testing the words, he went on slowly. "I said there was no woman in the world worth the trouble of getting hitched to and then you slapped me."

She closed her eyes, never before had she wished that a hole would open up in the ground and swallow her, but today she did. A tiny hole, just big enough for her and no one else. Then she could go and wallow in her humiliation all alone.

The silence lengthened and stretched so tight she finally

peeked to see if Cade had stolen away on cat feet. Her shoulders drooped. No such luck. He stood before her, a totally blank look on his face.

Her stomach surged on a bit of elation. *He still doesn't know. Oh, thank you God!* "Are we done now? Seems to me you remember things pretty accurately." She reached for her lesson plan.

But he brushed her hands back. "No, oh no, we are not done. I'm no closer to knowing why I got slapped than when I walked in here and I'm not leaving until I know. A guy's got to know what to avoid saying or doing so he doesn't go around getting slapped all the time." He tipped his head and settled his hands on narrow hips.

"Cade!" She sighed and dropped her arms to her sides in exasperation. He never took anything seriously. "You are such a dolt!" She couldn't believe that had just popped out of her mouth, and one hand flew to cover her lips as though to keep any other wayward words from jumping out of their own accord.

He laughed. "Good! See? Now we are getting somewhere. Just tell me how I offended you enough to make you want to slap me!" He lifted his palms to shoulder height. "Did you think I really meant it as an insult against all women? Surely you know that I was just kidding, right? There's obviously some woman, out there somewhere," he gestured to include the world outside the school-house windows, "who will be worth the trouble, one day. But I certainly haven't met her yet. And that's all I was saying. Is that why you slapped me?"

Sharyah clenched her eyelids tight and willed herself not to slap him again. She had loved Cascade Bennett from the time she knew what the opposite sex was. And he'd always thought of her as a little sister. But after the wedding she'd imagined that he'd been flirting with her, that he was actually enjoying her company as a woman, not just as a little sister. And then he'd said no woman in the world was worth the trouble of getting hitched to. Just like he was saying right now. It had been like a knife shoved into her chest and she'd reacted to the pain on her first instinct. Oh how she wished she'd held her itching palm in check. Because now this stubborn man would hound her all the way to heaven's gate, wanting to know the reason, and he was too… man-like to figure it out himself. And not a thing on God's green earth could entice her to admit to him that she loved him, had loved him for as long as she could remember.

So… She opened her eyes and dropped her hand to her side. "Yes, Cade. You are right. You can't just go around insulting women. I had to stand up for all women everywhere and that's why I slapped you. Please forgive me, like I said, I was having a really bad day."

His eyes narrowed and he folded his arms. "I don't believe you." He stepped toward her a dawning look of realization on his face. "Wait a minute, you don't, you weren't… Sharyah?" He reached out to take her hand a look of pity on his face.

Panic surged. She backed away from him so fast that she tripped on her hem. She would have sprawled in a heap if not for his lightening fast grab of her waist. She settled her hands against the corded muscles in his forearms, frustrated with the heat in her cheeks.

"Shar," he touched her chin, tipping her face up and studying her intently. "When did you morph from a little girl into such a beautiful woman?" His voice barely carried to her.

"Ah." The word came out on a tiny squeak. "I really need you to get going. The students are going to be here any min—"

"What is going on here?" The voice cut through the morning air with the force of a whip.

Sharyah felt her humiliation rise as she glanced down the aisle to see her brother and the three orphans he and Victoria had taken in staring at them. The girls grinned. Rocky, his arms folded, glared passionately. The little boy took in Rocky's stance and mimicked him without a moment's hesitation.

She pressed away from Cade and mercifully he didn't stop her. How had they missed the sound of the door opening? "Rocky, good morning. Nothing is going on. Cade was just leaving." She shot Cade a meaningful look she hoped he would recognize.

Smoothing her hands over her skirt, she hurried down the aisle. "ChristyAnne, Damera, Jimmy, welcome to your first day of school. I've prepared a desk for each of you. As soon as school gets started today I'll have you each take a few tests so I'll know better how to prepare your lessons. But for now, you can hang your coats in the entryway and then I'll show you to your seats."

Mercifully, other children started filtering into the room as the three turned to do as she had said. The men glared at one another as though they hadn't been life-long best friends, but rather enemies. "Rocky, please." She lowered her voice and stepped closer to him. "Nothing was going on. Just drop it and leave."

Rocky tore his gaze from Cade and met her gaze. "It's a good thing it was me who walked in and not one of the other parents."

"Yes."

"You okay?"

"Yes." She forced a smile.

He didn't look convinced, but he slid his hat back on his head. "Alright, I'll take your word for it." Rocky turned and left, but not before he cast one more hard look in Cade's direction.

Sharyah let out a breath on a bit of relief. One down. Now just one more stubborn man to get out of her classroom. As the students started settling into their desks, she turned a pleading look on Cade. Amusement danced in his expression and she felt her anger spark at that. How could he find this funny. She had been humiliated in front of several of her new students, not to mention her brother. Her eyes narrowed. But thankfully she was spared from giving him the sharp side of her tongue, because he held up his hands in an "I surrender" gesture and reached for his hat on the front bench.

Settling it on his head, he pulled the brim low and tilted his head to meet her gaze. "Seeing that we didn't get to finish our conversation, Miss Jordan, when can I expect that we might finish it?"

Aware that her students were studying her, she smiled smoothly. "I'm sure I'll be seeing you at church on Sunday, Mr. Bennett. Perhaps we can finish our conversation then."

Giving his hat another tug, Cade smiled. "I'll be looking forward to it, Miss Jordan. You can certainly count on my donation to the school's fundraiser."

The titter of laughter that followed Cade out the door did nothing to ease her fears over the gossip this morning's events would elicit in town. She sighed. That was the last thing she needed. But what was done, was done.

She clapped her hands. "Children, please open your primers to today's lesson. Jimmy, ChristyAnne and Damera, come to my desk please." *God, just get me through this day.*

CHAPTER ELEVEN

Victoria had just finished up the morning dishes and started on a batch of cookies when she heard Rocky drive the team into the yard. She frowned. She'd thought he would go to the livery and leave the team there so he wouldn't be late for work. She'd planned to drop the forgotten lunch off with his father a little later, when she knew Rocky would be riding his rounds of the town. Well, maybe he'd forgotten something. She huffed in frustration. She'd really been hoping not to see him again until this evening when the children would be home.

She bumped the coffee pot further from the center of the stove so it would be cool when he came in. Maybe cold coffee would hustle him out the door to work sooner.

A few minutes later he pushed through the kitchen door and hung his brown Stetson on the peg.

She tried to act calm. "Hi. Forget something? I made you a lunch. It's there by the door." She gestured in the general direction but stared down at her cookie recipe, hoping he would just get what he came for and then go.

"MmHmm." He sidled up beside her and leaned his elbows back onto the counter, peering up into her face.

She dumped a measure of flour into the cookie dough and, too late, realized she'd put in double what she needed. *Drat!* Why could she never seem to concentrate when he was around? She reached past him for another egg and more sugar. "You better get it and get going. You're going to be late for work." She cracked the egg against the side of the bowl.

He smiled. "I don't have to go in to work today."

Her hands stilled. "You don't?" She hoped he hadn't noticed the squeak in her voice.

"Nope." He took the egg shells from her, dropping them into the compost bucket by the back door.

She frowned. "But you just—I thought—"

Strolling to the stove, he pushed the coffee pot into the center, then grinned at her over his shoulder. "I forgot to tell you I didn't have to go to work today." He winked. "Also forgot to tell you not to worry, that we'd be able to finish our conversation from last night without interruption as soon as I got home."

Her face heated and she stared down into the batter. *Now what?*

"Of course," he ambled over and placed his palms on the counter next to her, "if I had done that, I suspect you'd have been long gone to the orphanage or into town by now." He grinned and bent close enough that his shoulder touched hers. "So maybe I didn't forget. Maybe I just neglected to tell you."

She couldn't avoid the magnetic pull of a smile. But she didn't dare meet his gaze and she scooted away from his touch.

He followed and leaned close again. His face was only inches from hers and if she looked up there was no telling what might happen. She poked at the dough with the end of her spoon. There was something wrong with it, but for the life of her she couldn't figure out what she'd done.

"Ria," he whispered, "look at me."

She closed her eyes and gave a little shake of her head, willing away the desire to collapse into his arms and allow all her protective walls to crumble.

He bent nearer, his breath brushing warmth against her cheek. "I'd marry you all over again, even if there were no orphans involved."

So he says now.

At his chuckle, her eyes flew open. What could he find humorous at this moment? Despite herself, she met his gaze.

One finger tapped the end of her nose. "Don't get that stubborn lift to your chin, Mrs. Jordan."

A mere fraction of an inch separated his lips from hers. She swallowed and stepped back. "Rocky—"

He lifted a hand to silence her and his thumb traced a warm path from one corner of her mouth to the other. "I know what you think you heard. But I'm telling you, it wasn't what it sounded like. Now I have one question before we start this again. Have I ever lied to you?"

She frowned and shook her head. He hadn't removed his hand yet, she could do no more than that.

"That's right. So what makes you think I'm lying to you now? What I said to Julia had nothing to do with you and me. She told me I looked unhappy and I was about to tell her I was unhappy with the way she had accosted me on the street! Not that I was unhappy with the fact that I'd married you." He dropped his hand to his hip, but didn't step back.

She felt her knees go weak. "Really?"

"Really."

"So you're not in love with Julia?" She knew he wasn't, but she wanted to hear him say it.

There was a short pause and then he gave a long bark of laughter. "No! Not even a little bit."

Her heart lurched. "Oh. Good."

His laughter settled into a warm, intimate smile as he trailed his fingers across her cheek bone and tucked a stray curl behind her ear, his gaze roving over her face. "You, on the other hand, Mrs. Jordan... You, I am in love with." He let his hand settle against her shoulder his thumb still stroking her jaw.

"Oh." The word was breathy and barely discernible. "But you were so frustrated the other day when you found out...." She stared at his shoulder no longer able to look him in the face.

Rocky sighed. "I'm sorry about that. I was irritated that you felt I'd think less of you just because you were adopted."

Her gaze flew to his. "And you don't?"

"No."

She swallowed. "What if... what if that man isn't really my father and my ancestors were bad people? Or what if he is my father but he turns out to be a con man?"

"That doesn't matter."

She studied his shoulder again. "It matters to me."

"Ria," he tipped her chin up with his thumb, "you are a good person because of your choices and because of who you are in Christ, not because of the blood that flows in your veins."

"I know." She pressed her lips into a pinched line. How did she tell him that she questioned God's love, most days and she wasn't at all sure she was the good person he thought her to be. She'd always struggled with believing God could really love her. Maybe it was because of her lineage. She glanced up and met his gaze, trying to find the words to tell him.

His fingers skimmed along the curve of her chin and traced her mouth, ever so softly. And he must have mistaken the look on her face because he leaned in with clear intentions. She jerked and turned away.

"Ria, why are you so afraid of letting me get close?"

"I just…" She shrugged.

"You can't avoid all of life's pain, you know. Life is full of all kinds of ups and downs, love, loss, pain, happiness. I just hope you don't throw away your allotted moments of blessing by constantly expecting the next tragedy."

Was that what she was doing? "It's just…" She pushed the spoon into the dough. How did she make him understand something she had a hard time understanding herself?

He reached deep into his pocket and withdrew something. Then held it up between his thumb and finger for her to see.

It was a ring.

Her mouth dropped open as she pressed one hand against her heart and studied the small gold band.

"I'm not going anywhere, Ria. And I meant my vows." He reached hesitantly for her left hand and when she didn't resist he slid the ring onto her finger and then enveloped her hand between both of his. "So don't think you and I last only as long as we have those children. You and I are forever, and I, for one, hope that we can be happy together during the good times, and a strength for each other in the bad ones, because I'm sure we'll have our share of those, too." He dropped a quick kiss onto her fingers and then let her go, reaching past her to snitch a pinch of cookie dough. "I'm going to do some checking on the Racklers." He went out then, shutting the door behind him.

She leaned back, stretched her arm out, and stared at the shiny gold band on her trembling hand.

Rocky raked up the last of the straw and shoveled it into the wheel barrow. Pushing his hat back on his head, he studied Jimmy through the open barn doors. He'd sent the boy outside to feed the chickens. The lad had taken the bucket of feed and dumped it all in one big pile and was now attempting to lasso a corral pole. He chuckled at the way the boy's jaw jutted to one side each time he canted forward and tossed the saggy loop. But he had to admire his persistence. Jimmy hadn't snagged the pole yet, but he hadn't given up, either.

The chickens scrabbled and flapped. They would set to fighting in earnest if he didn't get out there and amend the situation. Laying the shovel against the barrow, he pulled off his gloves and stuffed them in his back pocket.

"Jimmy, come here please."

Jimmy glanced over his shoulder. "Yes, Sir. Coming."

Someone had taught the boy some manners. Rocky wondered what his story was.

When Jimmy stepped up to his side, he gestured to the chickens all battling to get to the one small pile of feed at the center of the milling round of feathers. "When you put down feed for chickens you need to scatter it so they all get a chance. Otherwise the stronger ones fight off the weaker ones and then we get injured chickens and a flock that isn't healthy."

"Oh." Jimmy studied the birds, a light of understanding leaping into his intelligent eyes.

Rocky clapped him on the shoulder. "Wade on in there carefully and scatter the seed like it needs to be."

"But I might get pecked!"

Rocky suppressed a grin, rubbing one hand over his jaw.

"Doesn't hurt much. And it'll help you remember to do it right next time."

The boy sighed. "Yes, Sir."

As he slowly made his way through the churning flock, he looked like he was heading to his doom. The chicken's cocked their heads and cackled, flapping their wings and dashing out of his path, only to dart back in front of him on a beeline toward the feed. When Jimmy reached the pile of cracked corn at the center he studied it for a moment then looked over as if to ask if Rocky really meant he had to reach his hands down in there and risk the pecking.

Rocky nodded and folded his arms. A grin threatened as the boy clenched his eyes shut and shoved his hands down into the flailing, pecking pack.

Jimmy came up with a double handful of feed though, and he tossed the corn as far as he could. His face lit up with wonder as several chickens squawked and flapped after it. The boy looked over, pleading in his expression.

Rocky pushed aside the inclination to step to his rescue. He pointed at the corn again and gestured that Jimmy should repeat the action.

Jimmy sighed.

After two more times, each followed by the pleading expression, Rocky decided that was enough and motioned the lad back toward him. He socked a punch to his shoulder. "You did good, Son."

The glow that lit Jimmy's face over the simple compliment made Rocky wonder if he'd been encouraged much in his life.

"I'll do it right next time."

"Glad to hear it. Now," he sauntered over to the lariat the boy had left lying in the dirt by the corral, "would you like me to help you learn to rope?"

"Would you?!"

"First thing you need to learn is that you have to take care of your rope. You never leave it lying around in the dirt. You do that and it gets all kinds of grime in it that wears at the fibers and ruins a good rope."

"Oh. Okay, I'll remember." Jimmy nodded in all sincerity, a look of pure adulation on his face.

Rocky swallowed away the lump forming in his throat. "Step over here and I'll show you how to tie the knot so your rope will slip through nice and smooth."

Jimmy studied his fingers as he formed the knot and proved to be an adept learner.

"Good." Rocky shook out a loop and gave it a few easy swings around his head. "The next thing to learn is to keep your loop nice and smooth and steady. Just like this." He held the rope out for the boy to see. "You hold it here. Like this." He let the lad study how his hand lay on the rope, holding both the loop and the feed line in one hand.

Fifteen minutes later when Jimmy had learned how to keep a fairly steady loop and had even managed one fluke snag of the corral pole, Rocky stepped back. He needed to finish up the chores so they could go in to dinner. "You just keep practicing. You'll be a regular cowboy before you know it."

Jimmy's face brightened. "Thanks!"

Rocky bumped the boy's shoulder again. "You're a quick learner."

His enthusiasm flickered. "That's not what my pa used to say."

Rocky felt the words like a mule-kick to the chest. He shoved his hands into his back pockets. "He still alive? Your pa?"

One shoulder hitched. "Don't know. Most likely."

"How did you come to be riding the orphan train?"

The boy pulled the rope across his palm and a tremor laced his voice when he spoke. "Pa…, he said he couldn't take care o' me no more." He gulped. "That I was too much trouble and I cost too much. So he took me down to the orphanage one night and left me there. I thought about striking out on my own, but," he scuffed his toe, "I didn't know where to go, so I just stayed and slept in the doorway. The next morning the orphanage people told me they didn't have any room, but a kid who was supposed to ride the train that day, had died in the night." His throat worked. "So they let me come in his place."

Rocky clenched his fist on a wave of agony for the boy. "How long ago was that?"

Jimmy shrugged. "Not sure exactly. The days all sorta ran together like. However long it takes for the train to get from Chicago to here."

Less than two weeks. The boy had been abandoned by his father less than two weeks ago. Then had been subjected to scrutiny, and subsequently passed over, at every stop between there and here. That explained a whole lot about his prickly behavior.

He cupped a hand to the back of the boy's neck and gave him a jostle. "Well, I for one am glad that the Good Lord worked it out so that you and I could meet."

Moisture shone in the lad's eyes. He blinked rapidly and rubbed them. "I think I got some dust in my eyes."

Rocky allowed him the small deception and started to turn back toward the barn.

"Sir?"

He paused.

Jimmy cleared his throat and dragged a toe through the dirt. "I never met anyone as nice as you and Mrs. Jordan."

Rocky smiled and cuffed the boy's head gently. "Well, I won't be so nice the next time you feed the chickens the way you did today."

Jimmy chuckled. "Don't worry. I don't ever want to have to reach down into a pile o' pecking chickens again!"

A short bark of laughter escaped. He held his hand out for the lariat. "Go on and get washed up for dinner now. Let Victoria know I'm almost done and will be in momentarily. I'll hang this back in the tack room for you"

As the boy bounded off toward the pump, Rocky angled a glance toward the heavens. *Lord, for however long I have that boy in my care, help me to show him how special he is to You.* The next thought, the one about what life would be like around here after the children found other homes, had him swallowing away his dread.

The Racklers, by all appearances, were indeed the perfect place for the girls to go. They had a well-run ranch with plenty of room in the house for the girls and plenty of money to provide for them. They'd been more than happy to answer all his questions and by the end of his time with them he knew that the girls would be well taken care of.

That didn't mean he would miss them and Jimmy any less. He pushed the thought aside. He would deal with that moment when it came.

★

Chapter Twelve

Dreading the news they would need to tell the children tonight, Victoria settled the platter of crisp fried chicken into the middle of the table just as Jimmy burst through the back door.

"Mr. Jordan says to tell you he'll be along in just a few minutes. Did you see me roping?" His eyes sparkled with delight.

Using a towel, she opened the oven door and pulled out the bowl of mashed potatoes she'd put there to warm. "I'm sorry. I missed it. What were you roping?" She motioned with the bowl at the door he'd left wide open. "Get the door, please."

He pushed it shut with the toe of one boot. "Just the corral pole, but Mr. Jordan showed me how to swing a loop and I'm getting better. I even caught it once."

She smiled at him as she placed the potatoes on the table. "Well, if anyone can teach you to rope, it's Rocky. He spent lots of summers working out on the Bennett's ranch just outside of town. The girls and I will have to come out and watch you try again after dinner."

"Aw, it's no big deal." He shoved his hands in his pockets, but she could see a spark of hope light his countenance.

"I'd love to watch. But dinner first. Call the girls, would you? Then wash up."

"I already washed up, but I'll get the girls." He bounded through the living room and down the hall calling their names and all three bounced back into the kitchen just as Rocky came through the back door.

After they had all washed and everyone was seated at the table and the grace had been said, Victoria handed the platter of meat to Rocky. She noted that his face seemed tight as he studied the children. After a long moment he addressed them. "So how was your first day of school?"

"Great!" ChristyAnne's eyes sparkled.

"Terrible." Jimmy's shoulders slumped.

Damera remained silent with an impassive shrug.

Rocky caught Victoria's attention across the table and arched one brow. After a brief moment he looked at ChristyAnne. "So tell us about it."

"Well, when we first got there she tested us and then she gave me a shiny slate for Mera and I to share, and Jimmy got one all to himself. We are supposed to do our sums on it at night and bring it back for her to see in the morning. And at recess Mera and I met Elsa and Daria Reed. Their dad is the banker in town and they had on the prettiest dresses you ever saw. And we played jump rope and pushed each other on the swing. And at lunch they shared a piece of penny candy with each of us!"

"I didn't get no penny candy," Jimmy grumbled. "And I got put up a grade higher than I'm supposed to be. The sums are going to be impossible!"

ChristyAnne sniffed. "You didn't get any candy because you kept pulling Elsa's pig-tails. What girl would want to give a boy candy when he does mean stuff like that?"

Rocky grinned and stuffed a huge bite of roll into his mouth. He met her gaze again and winked slyly. Tucking the food into his cheek he said, "I remember pulling on a certain pretty red-head's braids a time or two, myself."

Victoria concentrated on her plate and pushed away the memories of the pleasure that had given her.

"Well, I think it is dumb for boys to pull girls' hair! And so does Elsa!"

"Aww," Jimmy grinned, "I think she kinda likes it!"

Victoria didn't dare meet Rocky's gaze. "Just make sure you are acting like a gentleman and not a hooligan."

ChristyAnne arched her brows and gave her a pointed look. "I think it is going to take some doing to get him to act like a gentleman!"

Rocky cleared his throat and ChristyAnne dropped her head guiltily and mumbled an apology into her mashed potatoes.

Jimmy sighed and angled a look toward Rocky to see if he had to make a response. At the stern quirk of Rocky's brow his shoulders slumped. "It's okay."

Silence reigned for a time, but after a moment Damera plunked her milk back on the table and announced, "An' dere is a boy who wikes ChrissyAnne." She nodded her little head emphatically, curls bobbing.

"What boy?"

Victoria nearly choked on her potatoes at the look of fatherly concern that immediately etched Rocky's face. She glanced around the table, then closed her eyes in dread. What would life be like when they were all gone? Could she and Rocky actually let them go? Couldn't they be the family these children needed? She studied them again.

Jimmy laughing at the pretty blush on ChristyAnne's cheeks. Damera with her perpetual milk mustache and dancing brown eyes laughing along. Rocky looking back and forth between them all and waiting for an answer to his question.

She studied the ring on her finger. If Rocky really meant to stay with her... well... she would talk to him about their options after dinner. She focused her attention on the conversation once more.

"...vorson!" Jimmy fanned his cheeks with one hand and pretended an attack of the vapors. "Charley Halvorson!" He crooned the word and made smooching noises across the table.

Rocky's shoulders relaxed. And Victoria couldn't deny that she felt a little of the same ease. The Halvorson's were good, God fearing people.

"Charley Halvorson!"

Rocky gave one snap of his fingers. "That'll be enough of that, Jimmy."

When Jimmy lapsed into silence ChristyAnne made a little dismissive noise but there was still a pink tinge to her cheeks. "That boy is awful! He put an ugly, green, splotchy frog on my seat after lunch! And Miss Jordan had to—" She shuddered. "She had to pick it up and take it outside."

"It was a cute fwog," Damera countered around a bite of chicken.

Rocky grinned at Victoria across the table and she remembered the time he'd put a toad in her lunch pail right on top of her apple. She hadn't been able to eat an apple for a whole month after that and she'd been wary of pulling the towel off her pail for the rest of that year.

"Frogs are not cute!" ChristyAnne scooped two peas onto her spoon and quickly swallowed them down with a chaser of milk.

"It was just a little ol' thing. And it took us all lunch time to find one. Then you had to go and scream at the top of your lungs and have Miss Jordan let it go outside." Jimmy shook his head in disgust as he shoveled in a mouthful of potatoes. "All your screeching and caterwauling probably scared the stuffing right out of the little guy."

Rocky coughed and snatched up his coffee, hiding his mouth with a long sip, but his eyes twinkled at her over the rim of the blue tin cup.

"Let's hope I scared it into hopping far away from the school so that Charley Halvorson can't find it again tomorrow." ChristyAnne rubbed her hands up and down her arms and made a face that could have curdled fresh-skimmed cream.

Victoria turned her escaped bit of laughter into a sneeze and hastened to the kitchen where she busied herself preparing a plate of cookies for dessert. They hadn't turned out too bad, despite the fact she'd never figured out what went wrong with them earlier.

When she came back in Rocky's face had turned serious. His tin cup clinked against the table. "Listen children, Victoria and I have some news that pertains to each of you."

Victoria eased back into her chair and set the cookies down in the middle of the table.

"Cookies!" Jimmy scooped up three and a whole one

disappeared into his mouth. Then he tossed Rocky a guilty look. "Sorry. I'm listenin."

"Ah…"

Victoria offered the plate to the girls as Rocky twisted his cup in a circle on the table.

"Well…" he looked at her for a moment then turned his focus on the girls, "there is a very nice family just near here that would like to adopt you both together."

"Oh." ChristyAnne's cookie stopped halfway to her mouth.

Damera glanced uncertainly between her sister and Rocky with such a look of confusion that Victoria pressed her lips together and studied the blue calico of her skirt, willing the tears to remain locked away.

"So, who are they?" ChristyAnne's voice sounded a little breathy and far too grown up.

"Well," Rocky cleared his throat, "their name is Rackler and they have a fine ranch just east of here. They have… they have two other children, so you'll have a brother and a sister right off, and there will be horses to ride, and you each will have your own room…."

The despair on Rocky's face begged for intervention. Victoria leaned past Damera and covered ChristyAnne's hand. "We know this is going to be hard, but after a few days you'll know them just as well as you know us, and you'll be just as happy with them as you are here."

"Yes'm." ChristyAnne mumbled the word into her plate.

Jimmy fidgeted in his chair and Rocky met her gaze miserably. She made a snap decision. "Jimmy, no place has been found for you yet, so you'll be with us yet awhile."

Rocky blinked, but then nodded in agreement and his shoulders relaxed slightly. "I invited the Racklers to dinner when I was out at their place today. How does Friday evening sound to everyone?" He arched a brow in her direction and she nodded that it was fine.

ChristyAnne looked up. "You mean we don't have to go right away?"

"No." Rocky's face softened and he shook his head. "We wanted to give you all a chance to get used to the idea. The Rackler's children also need some time to adjust to having new siblings. We know you've already met the children, but we'd like you to meet Mr. and Mrs. Rackler on Friday and then we'll see from there what day would be best to... make the transition."

ChristyAnne threw back her shoulders and lifted her chin perceptibly. In just a few moments she'd turned from a little girl into the fierce protector they'd caught a glimpse of in the train station that first day. "Whatever you say, sir. And I'll forever be grateful to you both for helping to keep Damera and me together. We'll be alright." She reached out and took her sister's hand in her own trembling one and gave it a little shake. "We'll be just fine. Friday for dinner. Yes, that sounds fine, doesn't it, Mera?"

Damera nibbled on her cookie making no comment.

Jimmy shuffled his feet. The silence stretched so tight she thought she might hear it snap.

Finally Rocky said, "So Damera. You haven't said too much. How did you like school today?"

She set her cookie down carefully and dusted her hands. "I wike Dawia an' Miss Jowdan was nice too..."

"But...?" Rocky questioned.

Jimmy snagged two more cookies.

Victoria frowned at him but a sniffle from Damera arrested her attention.

"Oh, honey." She slid a hand over the little girl's head. "It's going to be okay."

Scooting her chair back, Damera darted out of the room, tears streaming down her cheeks.

Victoria blinked at Rocky.

He rubbed a hand across his jaw and looked down at his plate.

ChristyAnne pressed her lips into a grim line. "Our mama used to teach us school. And Miss Jordan looks a lot like Mama did. That was a little hard, but...." She rubbed her hands together and Victoria felt a swell of emotion crash over her.

"Oh, honey." She reached out and squeezed ChristyAnne's hands. "I'm so sorry."

The little girl sighed. "Best I go talk to her."

She'd taken on quite a burden for a child so young. Life just wasn't fair. Victoria met Rocky's gaze briefly before she looked back and said, "Let me go talk to her this time, okay? You stay here with Rocky and Jimmy and have a cookie while I go see if there's anything I can do for her." At ChristyAnne's attempted protest she added, "I'll call you if I need anything. I promise."

Damera was curled up on her side in the middle of the bed, her thumb in its usual position.

Victoria eased down by her side and fluffed a pillow as she rested back against the headboard. "Come here, Sweet Pea." She patted her lap.

Damera rolled toward her and crawled up into her lap, resting her cheek against Victoria's chest.

Wrapping comforting arms about her, Victoria simply held her, rocking gently. *Father give her comfort. This little one has already experienced so much tragedy. Through me, wrap Your arms around her.*

After several long moments Rocky peeked in the door and then came over to stand by the bed. He bent down to Damera's eye level. "You alright?"

Damera tipped back her head and looked back and forth between them. "Can't I be yo' wittle guhl?"

As though he'd been kicked in the chest, Rocky straightened and swallowed, blinking rapidly a few times.

Victoria closed her eyes. *Oh sweet Jesus… How do we respond to that?* She would promise the little girl the moon in a heartbeat if it wasn't for … so many things.

Rocky rubbed the back of his neck and glanced from Damera to Victoria, holding her gaze. His dark eyes softened, full of all the same pain she was feeling. The same longing to make promises that neither of them knew whether they could keep, or not. And she felt hope springing to life in her heart. Maybe…

Finally Rocky knelt down so that his face was directly at

Damera's level. He cupped her head. "Honey, Ria and I would love to have you as our little girl. But there are lots of things for us to consider. And right now, we feel this family, The Racklers, will be a very good place for you and ChristyAnne. Do you understand?"

Damera's lip pooched out. "You don't want me?"

Victoria heard the rush of air that left Rocky's lungs as he tipped his head back and blinked at the ceiling. "Darling nothing could be further from the truth. I would love to have you for my little girl. But so would the Racklers. I think you're really going to like them."

"But I want to stay wif you!"

He swallowed. "I know, but I'm just not sure I would be the best pa for you. And I need you to trust me that I'm trying to do what's best for you. Okay?"

Damera crawled from Victoria's lap and wrapped her little arms around Rocky's neck. "But I fink you would be the best pa, and since I'm the one who needs a pa, don't that count fo' somethin'?"

Rocky looked at her over the little girl's shoulder. She wasn't sure if the moisture she saw was because her own eyes were damp, or if Rocky was fighting tears as well.

"Honey," he patted the little tyke's back, "I'm honored that you want me for your pa."

The little girl pushed away and pressed both palms to his cheeks, looking intently into his face. "That's good, wight? Honowed?"

"Yes, honored is good, but listen now," there was a catch in his voice. "The Racklers are a fine family. After a few days with them you'll feel about them all the same things you feel about Ria and I. Only better because they will be your forever ma and pa." He gave the little girl an assuring smile and tweaked her nose, but his gaze was serious as he tossed Victoria a glance over Damera's shoulder.

Looking down, Victoria smoothed a wrinkle from her dress.

"Tell you what?" Rocky pushed the little girl back. "How

about if we let this news settle and we all have a chess tournament tonight?"

Damera's expression lit up for just a moment, then dimmed. "But I don't know how to pway chess. I don't want to pway chess."

Victoria was glad for a change in topic and gave her a squeeze. "Come on. You can be on my team. I'll show you how it's done and we'll whip everybody!"

She looked skeptical, but finally answered, "Okay."

Rocky laughed. "Well." He scooped the little girl up into his arms. "I wouldn't count on coming out the winner, young lady." He flipped her upside down and tickled her belly. "Because I play a pretty mean game of chess!"

Damera squealed, clutching at Rocky's hands.

ChristyAnne rushed into the room, a look of worry on her face, but relaxed and smiled when she saw her little sister hanging upside down from Rocky's arms in a fit of silent laughter.

"Alright." Rocky put the little girl down and shooed her toward the door. "Go have Jimmy show you how to set up the board. A challenge has been issued and the great chess tournament of 1887 is about to begin!"

Both girls scurried from the room calling the news to Jimmy.

As soon as they were out of sight, Rocky bent forward and rotated his injured shoulder stiffly.

Victoria's breath caught. "Are you okay?" She scooted to the edge of the bed and studied him.

He grinned and waved away her concern. "Yeah. It's been doing so good, I sometimes forget the old shoulder isn't what it used to be. I'll be fine."

Remembering his words from earlier, she determined she wasn't going to let her worries ruin what could turn out to be a fun evening. So she pushed the thoughts aside. "Fine, then. Let's get to playing. The sooner we do, the sooner I'll be crowned the winner." With a cheeky grin, she hurried from the room.

Forty-five minutes later, the opponents had come down to Rocky against Victoria and Damera.

ChristyAnne and Jimmy sat at the table half-heartedly

working on sums, their attention mostly focused on Rocky's king who was in dangerous peril.

Victoria whispered into Damera's ear and she reached one tiny hand to move a horse.

"Wait!" Rocky cautioned. "Are you *sure* that's the one you want to move?"

Damera giggled and looked up at Victoria for confirmation. She nodded her encouragement and gave the little girl a squeeze. "We have him on the run now! He's just scared and trying to get us to mess up!"

Rocky grinned unrepentantly and dropped one lid in a quick wink.

"Well, it's not gonna wohk!" Damera plunked the horse down on its new square with decided finality. "Check!"

"Ohhhh!" Rocky winced and clutched his chest.

Victoria chuckled. "Maybe he should be a thespian instead of a deputy, what do you children think?"

All three snickered.

"Hey!" Rocky snapped his fingers at the two sitting at the table. "Get those sums done!" The twinkle in his eye belied the overdramatized authority in his voice.

They only ducked their heads and laughed into their hands.

Rocky sighed and studied the board, pretending great sadness over the demise of his king. Finally he moved the king one space, making a great fanfare of checking to make sure he'd be safe there.

Victoria suppressed a grin, knowing he could see their queen's next move would put him in checkmate.

The children all held their breath, each one also seeing the jeopardy he was in.

"There I should be safe right there."

When he let go of the king, the two older children tittered and Damera clapped her hands in glee.

"What?" Rocky asked innocently but Victoria knew him well enough to detect the twinkle in his eye.

With a satisfied thud, Mera moved the queen. "Checkmate!"

"No!" he exclaimed. "You can't— wait— you—" Reaching out he snagged Damera from Victoria's lap tickling her mercilessly. "You are the new Chess champion!"

ChristyAnne and Jimmy piled on top of Rocky and joined in the fun. Their peals of laughter brought a sudden onslaught of tears, and Victoria swallowed away a lump of sheer happiness stitched with longing.

Rocky glanced up from the middle of the pile of squirming children. As he caught sight of her tears momentary concern flickered in his gaze, but then his features softened into understanding.

"Alright!" He sat up, sprawling Jimmy into a heap on the floor. "Time for bed. We have school in the morning."

Half an hour later as Victoria emerged from tucking in the girls, Rocky was just heading down the hall from Jimmy's room. He paused, rested his hands on his hips and angled her a look. "You going to be alright?"

She sighed. "Yes. When do…Did the Racklers say when they want to come get them?"

He swallowed and looked down at the floor. "I told them I felt the children needed at least a few days to adjust to the idea. That's why I didn't have them come to dinner earlier in the week. Let's just give it until Friday and we can talk with the girls and with the Racklers after that and see where we go from there."

Smoothing at an invisible wrinkle in her skirt, she tried to keep her voice even. "Alright."

Victoria had never felt so terrible about a decision before. The Racklers were good people. It wasn't like they were giving the girls to an awful family. It was the fact that they were considering giving them to another family at all. Yet this had been the plan from the beginning.

Rocky pinned her with a look. "I knew this was going to be hard for you. I just never dreamed how hard it would be for me. Someday, I'd love to have a family…children." He swallowed. "Every time I've ever considered having a family… you were part of the picture."

Victoria felt her heart give a double-thump in her chest. Would he consider...? She glanced up and pressed her lips together as she studied his face. Finally, she could withhold the question no longer. "Would you consider keeping them?"

Folding his arms, he narrowed his eyes. "I know how you feel about me being a lawman. And I figured that you definitely wouldn't want to have children to complicate matters, just in case something ever happened to me."

Victoria's world tipped and she was ever so thankful for the wall behind her as she leaned back against it. He was right, that's how she should feel, but somehow...something, had changed.

He rubbed the back of his neck. "But I can see that you are just as head-over-heels for these children as I am." He stepped toward her until he was so close she could feel the heat of his breath warming her face. "With you, Ria...family seems... right." He caressed her chin with a short stroke from one finger as he studied her lips. Then he gave a little jerk and stepped back, his gaze snapping to hers. "But hard as it is to admit, Julia had one thing right. We can't give children the kind of home they need unless our relationship is where it ought to be as a husband and wife." He released a short puff of air and stepped back. "I'd love to have children in our home one day. But unless you can come to terms with our relationship and my job, I don't think we'd provide the best home for them. And—" He scrubbed one hand over his face. "I'm not just talking about, ah, intimacies." His eyes flicked towards her bedroom door.

Her face flamed and she looked down, studying the tips of her shoes.

"There's more to a marriage than that. I'm talking about you wanting to be with me for more reason than just to keep these children. About trust, openness, and communication. Intimacy is just a symbol that those other things are already taking place in a relationship. Kind of like the ultimate trust, openness and communication." He shrugged. "At least that's how I've always imagined it would be. And those things may take us awhile.

Until then… hard as it may be, I know it's not in the children's best interest to be here with us."

With that, he left her standing there and it wasn't until he'd disappeared around the corner that she realized she was holding her breath and let it go in a rush.

Simon Saunders stepped in out of the moonless night, cast a quick glance around the room and pulled his hat low over his forehead, then settled himself at the bar and lifted his finger. Conrath's Saloon looked and sounded like every other one he'd been in over the past twenty years. Dim. Smokey. And loud.

Good. If he kept his visit short, no one would even notice he'd been here.

"What'll it be?" The bartender yelled over the plinking of the piano in the corner.

"Whiskey!" As he waited, Simon's attention honed in on the sashay of a barmaid carrying a tray of drinks. She stopped at a poker table and set a round of frothy mugs to the right of each player. The cut of her dress announced to each man what he should plan on doing with his winnings.

Simon smirked. Too bad she wasn't serving him.

The barkeep set his drink before him and dried his hands on his stained apron, waiting expectantly.

Simon fumbled in his vest pocket and pulled out a five dollar gold coin, laying it down with a *snap*.

The bartender gave the coin a brief glance, then paused as his eyebrows rose.

Good. He had the man's attention.

"I'll get your change." The man reached for the coin.

Simon beat him to it, pressing his finger into the middle of the Half Eagle and pinning it to the bar. "I don't need any change if the information is right."

The man set his beefy hands on the counter and leaned into them. "Yeah?"

"You know a family in town by the name of Snyder?"

"I know 'em. They don't come in here, though." He swiped his mouth across one arm, scanning the other patrons at the bar as though worried they might be eavesdropping.

Simon lowered his voice, but the raucous music and rumble of other conversations should block theirs from anyone else's ears. "They have money?"

The bar tender pushed out his bottom lip, glancing across the room in thought. Finally he shook his head. "Not so's you'd notice. The old man, he died several years back. But he was a lawman plain and simple. Never flashed any money around." He shrugged. "The wife and daughter, they stayed on after he passed. Same house. Never known them to be extravagant spenders, either. Nope. My guess would be they don't have much."

Simon felt a curl of satisfaction as he lifted his finger from the coin. He tossed back his drink and started to stand, but at a sharp look from the bar tender, he paused. "What?"

"Mister. I don't know what your plans are, but the Jordans are the law here abouts. Word about town is the daughter just married one o' them. I'd watch my step, if I were you."

Simon pulled out his best aw-shucks grin. "Why, Rocky Jordan himself invited me to dinner tomorrow night. He wouldn't o' done that if he thought I was a danger, now would he?"

The man never lost his look of skepticism. "Just watch yourself." He picked up the coin and pocketed it.

Simon tipped his hat in acknowledgment and stepped back out into the night. He might not be too late after all. A grin split his face. "Mags, darlin'," he whispered. "You'll get yours yet."

★

Chapter Thirteen

The next morning after the children had left for school Rocky sauntered into the kitchen. "Do you have time to go on a short walk with me this morning? I have something I want to show you."

Victoria surveyed the pie dough she'd just started mixing. "Can you give me a couple hours?"

He snagged his hat from its hook and pushed it back onto his head. "Sure. I've got a couple things I need to see to out in the barn. I'll come back then."

Where could he be taking her? Various scenarios and possibilities ran through her mind as she finished the dough and chopped the apples, mixing in sugar and cinnamon, but for the life of her she couldn't come up with a reason he'd need to show her something.

The rattle of the buggy stopped outside the door just as Victoria was sliding the last sheet of small apple tarts from the oven.

Jimmy had practically devoured the entire batch of cookies she'd made the day before. His delight had been so palpable she hadn't had the heart to tell him he couldn't have any more. And she'd packed the last of the batch into the children's lunches this morning.

The door opened and Rocky hung up his Stetson. "Mmmmm, smells good," he proclaimed as he filched two tarts from the cooling rack. One of them disappeared in a single bite and Victoria gawked at him. "I hope to goodness Jimmy never sees you do that!"

Swallowing it down, he grinned. "I'll tell you the same thing I always tell Ma. Make them bigger if you want me to take bites."

He held aloft the second tart and shoved the whole thing into his mouth with an unrepentant twitch of his lips.

With a dismissive wave of her hand, she nodded to the buggy. "I thought you said you wanted to go for a walk?"

He spoke around the mouthful. "We'll walk. We just have a bit of a drive first."

Her curiosity got the best of her. "Where are we going?"

He sloshed some coffee into the bottom of a cup, swirled it around and then drank as he tossed a wink in her direction, but didn't reply.

"Ah, so you're not telling me?" She placed the empty baking tray into the sink and pumped water onto it.

"Nope, not yet."

"Well, a girl likes to know where her man is taking her, you know."

He stilled and she realized too late what she'd said.

"Your man, huh?" He sidled up next to her and bumped her with his shoulder. "I like the sound of that, Mrs. Jordan."

Blast her pale skin that seemed to forever be heating under his watchful scrutiny. She scrubbed the cookie sheet with a venom and refused to meet his gaze.

He chuckled softly and trailed a knuckle down her neck just behind her ear. His voice lowered to a whisper that brushed warmth against her skin. "You are a very beautiful woman, Ria." He pressed a gentle kiss to her hair and then stepped away. "I'll meet you at the buggy."

She managed an "Okay" before he disappeared out the door. Giving herself a few moments to gather her composure, she finished cleaning the kitchen before she finally descended the stairs and allowed him to help her up onto the buggy seat.

When he had settled beside her and snapped the reins starting the buggy down the road, she angled him a glance. "So where are we going?"

He chuckled. "I see that patience is not one of your strong suits."

"You're really not going to tell me?"

He angled toward her, his gaze roving over her face for a long moment before he replied, "I'm enjoying this just a little too much to put an end to the fun, now."

She released a puff of breath and settled her hands into her lap, fiddling with her fingers. "Are we going to the school?"

He tipped back his head on a laugh. "No."

"To your parents?"

"Nope." His grin was full of diabolical mischief. "I think I'll prolong your torture for a bit."

She sighed. "Oh fine!"

"Sit back and enjoy the beautiful day, Mrs. Jordan. I might even take the long way just to extend your misery."

She gave him a syrupy smile. "You're such a gentleman!"

He laughed again. "Why thank you, ma'am."

Rocky took the main road through town. The sun cocooned the day in warmth and Mr. Halvorson sat on the bench in front of the mercantile smoking his pipe and jawing with Mr. Reed from the bank. The Halvorson's coon hound lolled on the boardwalk, belly-up in a patch of sunlight. As they passed the school on the edge of town, the children were out for their mid-morning recess and Victoria caught a glimpse of ChristyAnne and Mera playing jump-rope with the Reed girls in the school's side yard. Jimmy and Charley Halvorson each stood on one end of the teeter-totter trying to see who would be the first to dislodge his opponent. She spotted the two children she presumed to be the Racklers' crouched in a group playing marbles in the dirt. She swallowed and turned her focus back to the road stretching out before them.

Rocky seemed to sense her mood. "What do you think of Cade and Sharyah?" he asked, as he smacked the reins down to encourage the horse up the small grade by the school.

"They would be good for each other."

"He was at the school the other morning when I dropped the children off."

"Really?"

"Didn't exactly look like brotherly affection between them when I walked in the door." The muscle in his jaw pulsed.

"They were there alone together when you arrived that morning?"

He nodded.

"Well," she shrugged, "you know how Cade is. He never worries about what the gossips will say. But I know he and Sharyah would never do anything improper."

"He was practically kissing her when I walked in!"

"Really?" She clapped her hands in excitement. "Well! It's about time!"

Rocky slanted her a glare. "That's my little sister you're talking about."

Victoria laughed. "A little sister who can more than hold her own against the likes of Cascade Bennett. Besides, she's been in love with him for years and you know it."

He thought about that for a moment. "Well, that's probably true."

"You know it's true."

"Kind of like I've been in love with you for years."

She snorted dismissively.

"No. It's true. You asked me the other day why I'd never called on you. Well, because I didn't think my heart could handle it if you rejected me. Besides, I knew how you felt about lawmen. That's why you broke it off with Sky."

That wasn't the reason. *But he doesn't need to know that.* Then she remembered his comments from the night before. A good marriage started with trust and communication, he'd said. She pressed her lips together. Trust made one vulnerable. Yet... she glanced at him sideways, studying the firm set of his jaw dusted with stubble, the curls of dark hair showing just beneath the brim of his hat, the way the muscles in his forearms rippled as he held the reins. What person in the world would she rather be vulnerable to than the man beside her?

"Um, actually..." she cleared her throat and studied a white spot on one horse's haunch, "I do worry about you being a lawman. But I broke it off with Sky because courting him didn't seem to make you jealous."

"Whoa!" Rocky pulled back on the reins and the horses came to a stop, bobbing and shaking their heads at the unexpected treatment.

Oh, mercy, she'd done it now.

Rocky turned to face her on the seat and warmth crawled over her cheeks. "Those are some very enlightening words."

She swallowed. Well, she'd started this so she might as well finish it. "I kept reminding myself that you were a lawman. But..." she turned and met his gaze, "nothing seemed to work."

"Well, you are just full of surprises."

"So, where are we going?" She slipped it in innocently hoping to catch him off guard, maybe change the subject.

He only grinned and winked as he slapped the reins down and the buggy started forward again. "You really need to work on that patience thing. Nice try, though."

But a few minutes later when he took the Bennett cut-off she knew exactly where they were going. "We're going to the Bennett's, aren't we? Why are we going out there?"

He chuckled. "You know what they say about curiosity, don't you?"

"Well, I'm not a cat so I'm not in any danger."

"Mmmm, a kitten maybe. Cute as one, anyhow. But I've never seen a red kitten." Holding the reins in one hand he settled his arm along the back of the bench and fingered the tendrils of hair by her ear.

She glanced into her lap, trying to ignore the shiver that raced down her spine and then zipped back up to settle in her stomach.

"So you're adopted. Tell me about it."

She stiffened. Then sighed. She'd started down this road of vulnerability, so she might as well finish the journey. She gave a little shrug. "There's not much to tell. My mother took me to the foundling hospital in New York when I was just two days old and dropped me off. I've never seen her or my father again... until the other day. I was sent away on one of the orphan trains just two days after I arrived at the hospital, and Mama and Papa adopted me at a stop in Nebraska. From there we moved here."

She swallowed before she spilled the whole sorry story about how the children at school had taunted her because of her status.

Rocky wrapped the curl around his finger. "So that partly explains your tender heart for other children that ride the orphan trains." He paused for a moment, then continued, "Must be some reason you haven't told anyone you were adopted for all these years...."

Pushing down the lump that rose in her throat she looked out across the field. *Just tell him the whole ugly truth.* "Lots of people look down on adopted children. I needed some time to heal when we first arrived here, and then it just never seemed the right time to bring it up."

"Time to heal from what?" There was a hard edge in his voice when he spoke.

She glanced at him, but she could tell that the hardness was directed at the people who had hurt her. "People's meanness, mostly." She picked at a thread in her skirt. "One girl always claimed that my birth parents must not have loved me, to drop me off and abandon me. Then all the children would chime in with how ugly I must have been, that they took one look at me and ran me to the nearest foundling hospital." She sighed. "Every day for the first year of school, I put up with the jeering. Icky Vicky, they called me." She grimaced. "Then I started fighting back."

Rocky dropped his hand to hers and squeezed. "That's my girl."

She shook her head. "It did me no good. It only spurred them on. My parents tried to talk to the school master, but he must have felt the same way as the children because he would only smirk when he heard their comments to me and then turn his back and walk away. After awhile the children didn't even try to conceal their ridicule anymore. They would goad me until I finally blew up and attacked one of them. It was their entertainment. Most of the children were older than me and knew I wouldn't be able to really hurt them. The day I came home and asked my mother the meaning of 'vile whore', was the day my father finally paid the school master another visit. We left town the next day, but I remember as we drove by the school house, Mr. Habersham stepped out onto the porch to ring the bell and his face was all swollen and black and blue."

"Good for your dad!" He paused for a moment then tightened his grip on her hand. "Thanks for telling me about it."

Victoria nodded. "At least now I know why I was given up for adoption."

He cleared his throat. "If the story Baxter Cane told was true."

She sighed and nodded, wondering if the man really was who he claimed to be, even as she realized they had come to a stop by the side of the road and the Bennett's ranch lay just ahead. "Oh, you didn't have to stop for me."

He laced his fingers through hers and leaned toward her. "I would do anything for you."

The magnetic pull of his gaze captured and held hers and she took solace in the wonder that he cared for her even after all he knew about her. After the heaviness of her story she felt the need to lighten the mood. "Anything?"

He nodded. "Anything."

"How about telling me why we are going to the Bennett's?"

He threw back his head on a laugh then winked at her. "Anything but that, Kitten Red. Anything but that."

With a deft flip of his wrist he set the buggy in motion again and within moments they were pulling to a stop in the yard of the Bennett's ranch. Rocky came around to her side and reached up to help her down, his hands cupping firmly around her waist.

As her feet settled on the ground, she whispered, "See, I knew we were coming to the Bennett's ranch." She gave him a teasing poke.

He tapped the end of her nose. "Not only a cute kitten, but a smart one as well. Come on Miss Curiosity, and I'll show you why I brought you out here, because after what I said last night about communication and trust, I realized I haven't been completely open with you, either. There's something about me that I haven't shared with you."

Really? Her mouth gaped open but before she could form a reply, Brenda Bennett stepped out onto the back porch of the ranch house drying her hands. "Rocky and Victoria! How nice to see you two out here. Congratulations, by the way. I was so pleased when Smith came from church and told me your exciting news. I was home with a terrible headache that morning, and I was so sorry to have missed giving you my best wishes."

Rocky's boots thudded on the boards as he bounded up the steps and pulled the woman into a hug. "Thank you, Mrs. Bennett. We know you would have been the first to wish us well if you had been there."

"Of course I would have. I just can't wait to meet those three children. I'm sure they are all just as cute as kittens."

Rocky grinned, met Victoria's gaze and dropped one eyelid. "Yes, ma'am, they sure are."

"Well, come in, come in." She gestured Rocky past and pulled Victoria into a quick hug. Before following them into her cheery red and white kitchen, she gave the dinner bell dangling at one end of the porch three quick whacks that rang out across the yard with a loud clang. Coming through the door she pushed the coffee pot into the center of the stove. "I just pulled a cherry pie from the oven. Sit. Sit." She flapped her hands toward the kitchen table and then set about slicing enormous pieces of pie.

Rocky held out a chair for Victoria and then took the one next to her as Mrs. Bennett placed the tangy scented confection before them along with a pitcher of heavy cream. She was back in a moment with steaming cups of coffee and the sugar bowl.

Mrs. Bennett leaned heavily on the table as she eased herself down into her chair and Victoria felt a prick of worry. "Are you okay, Mrs. Bennett?"

The woman waved her hand. "Now that you are married you best call me Brenda, dear. And yes, I'm just fine." She lifted the cream pitcher and started to pour some into her cup just as the back door flew open and Cade burst in.

"Ma!" He stopped in his tracks, his gaze fixed with relief on his mother sitting at the table. "You're alright."

"Of course I am dear. But look what you've made me do." She gestured to the table where she'd sloshed cream.

"I'll get it."

Cade plucked a rag from the kitchen sink. He met Rocky's gaze for a moment and Victoria could see that they both had yesterday morning's incident at the school on their minds. It gave her great pleasure to see Cade's face color before he finally looked away, wiped up the cream and tossed the rag back into the sink.

"Mmmm, pie. Do I get a slice, Ma? Or is that only for special guests."

"It's only for the guests," both Brenda and Rocky replied together.

Victoria chuckled and added a slosh of cream to her own coffee and a drizzle to the top of her pie. The first mouthful eased across her tongue, sugary sweet tartness smoothed out with the flavor of the cream. Like the taste of heaven on a fork. She closed her eyes and savored the melding. "This is delicious, Mrs. Ben— Brenda. I'd love to get the recipe from you."

"That was my grandmother's recipe. Of course dear, I'll get it for you." She started to rise, but Cade motioned her back to her seat. "I'll get it, Ma. You just sit."

Victoria noticed a slight frown on Rocky's face when she complied without so much as a protest. "Thank you, dear. It's in the tin on the counter by the stove. Just bring the whole tin, I'll find it."

Cade set the recipe box before her and plunked himself into a chair pulling his slice of pie closer. His gaze focused on Rocky. "So, you here about the horse?"

Victoria's eye brows peaked as she slipped another delicious morsel from her fork.

Rocky's eyes found hers and crinkled at the corners. "Yep. Sure am." He gave her a bold wink and then turned back to Cade. "And kittens. Got any kittens?"

Victoria almost choked on a cherry. Hurriedly, she downed a sip of coffee.

He patted her on the back and bumped her with his shoulder. "You still breathing?"

She narrowed her eyes and gave him a 'we'll discuss this later' look to which he replied with an unrepentant grin just before shoving a huge bite of pie into his mouth.

Cade glanced back and forth between them with a speculative gleam in his eyes.

"Here it is." Brenda produced a recipe card. "Get me a paper and pencil from the desk in the study, would you dear?"

Rocky shuffled his feet and looked from Brenda to Cade with a small V of worry between his brows.

Cade gave a nearly indiscernible shake of his head to quiet any questions from Rocky as he stood and replied, "Sure, Ma. Be right back."

As soon as Rocky finished his slice of pie, Victoria subtly pushed her half eaten piece toward him. Mrs. Bennett's attention was still on her recipe box, and while the pie tasted wonderful she simply couldn't eat that much. Yet she didn't want to hurt the woman's feelings.

Rocky switched their plates quickly and set to eating again. With a grin he reached over and snagged the coffee cup out of her hand. His was empty.

"You two are acting just like old married folks," Mrs. Bennett said, peering up at them through her eyebrows.

Victoria grimaced inwardly. "The pie was delicious, Mrs. Bennett, really. I just—"

Rocky reached out and squeezed her hand, stilling her apology. "She just noticed me eyeing her pie and saw it as a way out of having to fix me lunch in an hour."

Cade appeared with paper and pencil and set them on the table by his mother.

"Thank you, dear. Now," she gave him a piercing look, "I'll be just fine, so you go on and show Rocky that filly you've been bragging all over about and quit your worrying."

Cade dropped an affectionate hand on her shoulder. "Yes'm. And thank you for the pie." He lifted the last portion of his slice from the plate in a jaunty salute. "I hope you aren't sending the rest of this home with Rocky. You still make the best cherry pie of any woman I know."

Mrs. Bennett huffed and slapped him on the arm. "You say that to all the women and of course the rest will go home with them. I can make you another one tomorrow."

Cade dramatized the look of hurt on his face and his mother chuckled.

"Go on with you now. And don't you think that we mother's don't talk. Especially about you two charmers." She glanced back and forth between the two men.

Rocky smiled as he rose to follow Cade out the door. "Thanks so much for the pie, ma'am. Your pie comes in second only to Ma's in my book and if you don't mind, you can tell her I said so the next time you get together to talk about Cade and me." He reached to help Victoria with her chair.

Mrs. Bennett gave a soft chuckle, even as a far away thoughtfulness leapt into her gaze. But after only a moment she seemed to shake it off and chuckled again. "Get on with you now." She shooed him out the door. As Victoria walked past her, she added, "You're going to have to keep an eye on that one."

Victoria smiled. "Yes, ma'am. I believe you are right. Maybe even two."

Rocky placed a hand to his chest looking hurt but he jabbed her in the ribs as they headed out the door and then took her hand to help her down the steps.

Victoria tried to ignore the way her stomach pitched into a pleasant roll as the warmth of his fingers wrapped around her own.

Just ahead of them Cade shoved the last section of his pie into his mouth and gestured for them to follow him.

Victoria slowed her steps purposely and leaned toward Rocky. "We are *not* taking home a kitten!"

"Awww, come on!" he whispered. "Just think of the joy on Mera's face when we bring a cute little guy home. Then maybe, if all works out with the Racklers, she can take it with her when she goes. Might help with the transition."

Victoria gave him her best 'I'm not convinced' face. "I'm going to be the one who has to take care of it at home. Feed it. Make sure it isn't jumping up on the table and side-boards!"

He pulled back and looked at her. "He's going to live outside in the barn! Catch mice and maybe get a squirt or two of milk in the mornings."

"We can't bring a poor little kitty home and make it live outside! What about in the winter? It would get cold!"

He grinned. "Oh good. I was hoping you'd feel that way. We'll just bring the horses in during the winter too."

"Rocky!" She smacked his arm.

He rubbed his shoulder. "Ow!"

"You are impossible. There is a big deal of difference between a horse and a poor little kitty."

"Are you two coming? Or are you going to stand there looking moony-eyed at each other all day long?" Cade called from across the yard.

With surprise Victoria noted that they had come to a halt as they talked.

Rocky slipped his arm behind her so that their joined hands rested at the small of her back and tipped his head towards her. "I'd rather stand here looking moony-eyed all day long. What do you think?"

Victoria chuckled. If she were honest she'd admit that's what she'd rather do, too. Instead she said, "I want to see this oh-so-secret horse that you wouldn't tell me about."

He placed a hand over his heart. "I'm crushed." He glanced across the way toward Cade and called, "The woman would rather look at the horse than make time with me. So I guess we go on to the horse."

"Smart woman!"

Victoria giggled and trailed after Rocky, even as she realized that the walls she'd carefully erected around her heart to keep it safe from the very man holding her hand were crumbling brick by brick and she didn't want to reconstruct them. Not even a little bit.

CHAPTER FOURTEEN

"Oh she's beautiful!" Victoria gasped as she propped her arms across the top rail of the corral.

"Yes she is," Came Cade's reply. "That there is one of the horses that Jason found on his and Nicki's spread. They were running wild on a back section of their property and as far as we can tell many of them had never encountered humans before a few of us went in to round them up. Rocky's had his sights on this girl since he first laid eyes on her down in that little valley. She was as wild as can be, but she's come a long way in a short time and once I finish her training she will be one fine brood mare."

Rocky leaned against the rails next to Victoria and watched her face. He was pleased by her awe as she watched the mare across the paddock. "She's a line-backed dun." He rested his chin on his arms and simply let Victoria take in the animal for a little while. The mare was putting on a show. She trotted from one end of the corral to the other, her head held high, her neck arched and her tail raised. The soft tawny color of her hide contrasted with the crisp black of her mane and tail and the long black line down her back. At the center of the corral the horse came to a stop, her flank to them but her head tilted in a way that showed all her focus was on the three of them. The skin along her side rippled and her tail flicked over to dispatch a pesky fly, then she turned her head and looked directly at them.

"Hey there." Victoria climbed a rung higher on the fence as she cooed, holding out one hand palm up. "Come on then, you know you are ever so curious as to what we are all about. Yes you are. Come on over here and let me give you a good scratch behind your ears."

The horse's ears perked forward at the cajoling tone of Victoria's voice.

"Yeah. That's right. Come on then. Come on."

With a snort, the mare bobbed her head, her black nostrils flaring as she tested the air. Apparently satisfied that there was no danger lurking near the three of them, she took two cautious steps forward and stretched her neck out as far as it would go to sniff at Victoria's hand.

"That's right," Victoria continued in her sing-song voice. "Come on. I'm not going to hurt you." She quieted then, but kept her palm out.

Rocky admired her calm assurance around the animal. Maybe talking her into buying wouldn't be as big a deal as he had feared. He wanted to start his own herd and this mare showed the exact strengths he'd been keeping his eye out for. The sooner he could get a good herd started, the sooner he could step down from his deputy job, and he knew that would bring Victoria some relief.

His hesitation rose from the fact that he'd never told anyone he didn't really want to be a lawman for the rest of his life. Dad kind of assumed he and Sky would take his place one day, but that had never been Rocky's dream. Nor Sky's either, if he didn't miss his guess. Cade was offering him a fair price and with the aid of Sky's stallion this mare ought to throw a right nice foal.

The horse took two more steps and Victoria gently laid her hand against the side of her nose. The mare snorted and bobbed her head again, but stayed steady.

"That's right beauty. Yeah. You don't have anything to be afraid of from me. Rocky she's beautiful," she continued, addressing him in her soft sing song voice.

He didn't reply, not wanting to scare the filly away. This was the first time he'd seen the horse willingly approach someone. It was a tribute to Cade's gentle training and the mare's calm disposition that she was doing so this soon.

Behind them, Smith Bennett poked his head out of the barn and called for Cade. Cade stepped away quietly, but with a sudden prick of her ears and a flip of her tail the horse jolted back and trotted away across the corral.

Victoria stepped to the ground and Rocky tilted his head on his arms to look at her. "I brought you out here because she's for sale and I'd like to buy her."

"You don't have to ask me." She splayed her hands. "Do what you want to do."

"What I want to do is talk to you about it. I don't want to start out our life together making decisions on my own. I want your input. And… I don't want to be a lawman for the rest of my life."

She blinked. "You don't?"

He shook his head. "I knew you would never be comfortable day in and day out with me wearing a badge. That's why, the moment I saw her," he nodded toward the horse, "I knew I wanted her to get my herd started."

"But… you were at Jason's place in the spring… wait… you?"

He winked at her. "I told you… I've been in love with you for a long time. And I figured my chances of getting you to let me come calling would be a lot better if I could come as a rancher instead of a lawman."

"So…?" Her hands fluttered up near her throat and he hoped that was a good sign. "You would give up your work for me?"

He nodded. "For you. For me. It's what I've wanted for a long time. I just need to find a good piece of property where we can get started. And I'd like it to be close to home, so you don't have to move too far from your mother."

"Oh." She glanced back across the paddock at the mare. "How much is she?"

"He's asking seventy-five dollars for her."

Her brows arched at that figure, as he'd known they would. "Do you have that much?"

He nodded. "Yes. *We* have that much. I've been doing a little saving for this very reason."

"Well then…," Victoria's lips tilted up into a soft smile as she watched the animal across the pen, "my input is she has to stay out in the barn, even in the winter."

He chuckled. "Deal."

Cade came out of the barn. "So, do I have a sale?"

Rocky stood and stretched his arms above his head. He hadn't realized how tense he'd gotten today waiting for Victoria's thoughts on this. "Yes, you do. I'll have the money for you just as soon as she's fully broken." He held his hand out in his friend's direction.

Cade smiled as he accepted the hand. "Sounds good to me."

Rocky changed the subject. "What's wrong with your ma?"

Cade sighed and focused on the side of the clap-board house across the yard. "She hasn't been herself lately. She's been getting severe headaches that are so bad she can't even stand up. She pretends everything is fine, but...." He shrugged. "I'm worried about her."

"What does Doc say?"

"Well, he stopped by to see her before he left on his trip. He was honest enough to say he didn't know what might bring on such sudden headaches but he would do some more research and get back to us."

Rocky clapped him on the back. "Sorry. We'll be sure to add her to our prayers."

Victoria nodded. "I was so worried about Mama a while back, but Doc fixed her up just fine. I'm sure he'll come up with something to help your ma, too."

"Thanks." Cade nodded. "We appreciate the prayers and I know Doc will do everything he can." He turned back toward the barn. "Come on, I've got those kittens to show you."

Rocky waited for Victoria to precede him. "You don't happen to have a red one, do you? Red kittens happen to be some of my favorites."

"Red?" A puzzled frown creased Cade's forehead and he glanced back at them over his shoulder.

Rocky enjoyed the blush that washed up the back of Victoria's neck.

"Mmmm. Red ones. They're just so... cute. Especially when they have a dusting of freckles and curly hair."

Cade came to a halt and spun around. "Wha—Oh!" A light dawned in his expression as he darted a glance from Victoria's red face to Rocky.

Rocky grinned.

"You've made a sniveling romantic out of my best friend, Victoria."

Rocky laughed out loud. "Your day is coming Cascade Bennett. Your day's coming."

On the way home from the Bennett's with the tiny little calico kitten wrapped in a cloth and resting on Victoria's lap and the leftover pie tucked into the luggage boot, Rocky pulled to a stop just before the cutoff to the church and Pastor Hollybough's house. He glanced over at Victoria. "I'd like to invite the Hollyboughs to dinner tonight, too, if that's alright with you. I figure if anyone can determine if someone is a minister it would be another minister."

Victoria rubbed the soft ear of the purring kitten. "Why don't you believe he is who he says he is?"

He sighed and rubbed a hand across his jaw, looking off across the field. "I don't know exactly. Just…, when you've been a lawman for a bit you get to recognize the look of a con and this somehow feels like one to me."

"I see." She pressed her lips together. "So do you think he really is my father and a con man? Or is he even lying about being my father?"

He shrugged. "I don't know."

"Why would he want to con me? I have nothing. What could he possibly have to gain?"

"I don't know."

"Maybe he was just nervous and didn't know how to tell me."

"Maybe."

She stroked behind the kitten's ears, eliciting a loud purr. "He probably is my father and a con man. That would make sense with my life."

"Hey." He reached out and touched her hand. "Where you

come from doesn't have to determine who you are. You will still be a beautiful, loving, caring person no matter what your lineage is. In Christ we can put all that behind us, remember?"

She blinked back tears. "I know."

"It's going to be fine, Ria. I'm going to walk with you through this, each step of the way."

"I know. I'm just scared."

"Scared of what?"

She pulled in a shuddering breath. If she told him there would be no going back. But who was she kidding? She didn't want to go back anymore. "I feel like every person that I've cared for, God has taken away. First my dad. Now Mama is married to Doc." She met his gaze briefly, but couldn't hold it. "I care for you. And I don't want to lose you."

"Hey." He scooted closer to her on the bench and cupped the back of her neck with gentle fingers, tipping his head down to peer into her face. "You're not going to lose me. I'm not going anywhere."

"I know you wouldn't purposely leave me. I… I just don't ever want to feel the pain I felt after Daddy died, again."

Rocky swallowed. "And will keeping me at arm's length make you feel any better if something does happen to me? You know that even when I do take up ranching, there will be dangers."

She folded her arms, careful not to jostle the kitten, and stared out across the field beside them.

"You're only robbing yourself of the happiness the Lord wants for you."

Was she?

"You know why worry is a sin? It's a lack of trust in God."

She didn't want to hear that. She clenched her jaw and tilted up her chin. "What has God ever done specifically for me?" She pressed her lips into a line and studied a tree across the way.

Rocky bent even closer. "The other day when you didn't believe that I was telling the truth about Julia, you basically called me a liar. You're doing the same thing with God right now. He sent His Son to die – specifically for you. His Word says he cares and wants only the best for you, but you don't believe him. You've been so busy trying to keep yourself from getting hurt that you aren't letting God do the very thing that he longs to do."

She scratched the kitten under its chin. The Bible did say that. She felt some of her stubbornness drain away and her shoulders eased, but she still didn't meet Rocky's gaze.

He sighed and fiddled with the reins. "In the twenty-third Psalm, a Psalm that is talking about the valley of death, it still talks about the comfort God offers us in the midst of hard times. Keeping me at arm's length doesn't keep me safe. It's a selfish act on your part. You either believe God is who He says He is, or you don't. Which is it? You think about it and you'll see that if you look at things the right way, you'll be able to see what God has done *for* you. Not what He's done *to* you."

She looked up at him and guilt washed over her. She was being so ungrateful. Like a little child who hadn't gotten a penny-candy at the mercantile. She released a puff of pent-up breath and laid her palm over the bullet wound in his shoulder. "You're right. He brought you home to me."

His face softened and he nodded. "You remember the verses in the end of that Psalm where it says, 'You prepare a table before me in the presence of my enemies'?"

She nodded, her lips pressed together.

"I feel like God has done that for me so many times. Even in the midst of danger, God gives us good things. I can't promise I'll outlive you. But I can promise that our days together will be the best days of our lives. And I can promise that God loves you and only wants the best for you. He leads us each down a path that He knows will brings us closer to Him. And if God asks you to go through losing another person you love, I know He will give you the strength to make it through that time."

She blinked back the tears threatening to overflow. "I just don't know if I would be able to make it, if something happened to you."

"Sure you would." He chucked her under her chin. "You've made it all these years without me."

She huffed a laugh, even as she brushed back more tears.

With a deft flip, he looped the reins around the brake handle. Both hands now free, he turned back towards her and cupped her face. His thumbs swiped the wet tracks from her cheeks, and when his head dipped toward hers, she could no more pull away than she could breathe. Her arms rose and wrapped around his neck. The kicking of her heart vibrated the walls of her chest. And then his lips were on hers. Softly, slowly, smoothly, his mouth caressed hers, the stubble on his jaw prickling.

Her fingers curled into the hair at the back of his head, knocking his hat askew. She parted her lips, hungering for more.

He mumbled something low and warm as he scooted closer and increased the fervency of the kiss.

Then with a dash of cold clarity she realized just how much of herself she was giving away and she jerked back with a gasp. The kitten mewled at the sudden jolt as she pressed the back of one trembling hand to her mouth.

A question flashed across Rocky's face and then understanding lit his eyes. His shoulders sagged slightly as he looked out across the field beyond her. For a long moment they sat as though frozen in time, and then he sighed and met her gaze. "We're going to get through this, Ria. One day we're going to look back and be amazed at how far God has brought us."

She swallowed and shook her head. "I don't know if I can, Rocky. I've been hiding for so many years, I don't know how to…." She let the thought trail off with a shrug.

The knuckles of his hand trailed down her cheek. "You made a good start today, Ria. Don't pull away from me now."

She didn't respond. Didn't want to respond. Didn't want him to know how hopeless she felt to pull away from him. She'd given away too much of herself, and the fear of what that might cost her, nearly took her breath away. Looking down she resettled the kitten in her lap and scratched it softly under its chin.

He studied the fields for a moment longer, then finally gave a little nod of seeming resignation before he scooted back to his side of the bench. "Back to tonight. I only want to be careful about Parson Cane because I care so much for you."

She didn't trust herself to answer.

"So? The Hollyboughs?"

"Yes. Let's invite them." The words came out on a warbled whisper.

"Alright then." With a click of his tongue and snap of the reins, Rocky set the buggy rolling down the lane toward the parsonage.

Victoria rubbed her forehead pushing at an incoming headache.

★

CHAPTER FIFTEEN

S imon Saunders adjusted his coat and collar one more time, giving himself an assessing gaze in the mirror. He practiced a smooth fatherly smile. Yes it worked. "Maggie, dear." He ran a hand across his cheeks making sure they were clean shaven and smooth. "You are going to lose, in the long run. I've found our girl and I'm just about to recover all that you stole from me." Setting his bowler at a jaunty angle on his head, he nodded approval at his reflection. "Yes sir, Mags. Just a few more days and all your attempts will have been in vain."

He stepped out into the hallway of the boarding house and almost had his door shut when he remembered the Bible sitting on the chair where he'd tossed it when he got in last night.

"Get yourself together, Saunders," he muttered.

The trek through town took him through the back alley behind the sheriff's office. He didn't realize he was rushing until he almost walked into the arc of water that the lady from the mercantile tossed out her back door.

"Oh, I'm so sorry!" she gasped.

Simon gritted his teeth but then snatched his hat from his head. "Don't you worry about a thing, Ma'am. I shouldn't be in such an all-fired hurry. I'm just running a little late for a dinner engagement."

"Well, I'm so glad I didn't douse you with my wash water!" she giggled.

He forced a smile to spread. "I'd have to say I am too, Ma'am." Adjusting his hat he tipped the brim in her direction and continued down the alley at a slower pace. Annoying woman!

The walk out to Victoria's place was longer than he remembered and the blasted Bible felt like it weighed more than a half grown hog by the time he crested the low ridge above her home. He was panting for breath when he reached her porch and gave himself a moment to catch his wind.

Scanning the yard, he frowned at the buggy tied up to the corral. She must have visitors. He hoped they weren't staying for dinner. He had planned to get right down to the questions he had about the locket and key tonight, and he had just the story for the cover, too. He straightened his coat one last time before climbing the front steps and knocking on the door.

Her deputy husband answered the door. The man's lips smiled, but Simon could see the hesitation in his expression.

He was going to have to be smooth as butter to pull this off.

"Come in, Reverend." The younger man stepped back and gestured him inside. "I'd like for you to meet our own pastor."

Another Pastor? Confound it all!

A man about his own age stood from the settee and stretched out his age-spotted hand.

"Parson Cane, this is Pastor Hollybough." The husband motioned to the other man. "Pastor, Parson Baxter Cane."

Simon's collar seemed to tighten as he shook the man's hand and took in his casual clothing. He wore faded denims and a flannel shirt, rolled up to his elbows. Didn't parsons always wear their clerical attire? He nodded a greeting.

"It's a real pleasure to meet you." Pastor Hollybough's eyes lit up as they landed on the Bible tucked under his arm. "Ah, you've brought the Good Book with you. Excellent! I've had a question burning in my mind for several weeks about a passage in Romans, and I'm so looking forward to discussing it with another man of the cloth."

Simon hoped his eyes hadn't bulged as much as he felt like they had. *There's a book about Romans in the Bible?* Quickly he composed his features. "Certainly. Certainly. It would be my pleasure. I'm sure we'll have plenty of time for theological discussions after dinner." He congratulated himself on that bit of a save. Somehow, between now and then he would have to come up with an excuse to get out of here as soon as the meal concluded. Maybe tonight wasn't going to be the best night to get the information he needed from the woman. *Blast!*

"Oh I'm sure we have a few minutes here before dinner is ready," Rocky supplied with a too-friendly smile. "Come on in and have a seat, Parson. If you'll excuse me, I'll just go let Victoria know you've arrived."

Baxter watched the young man walk away, feeling like a convict with a noose around his neck watching his executioner pull on a black hood. *Think man!* "Ah, you know? If you don't mind, before we launch into this discussion on the Romans I need to find the water-closet. The walk out here from town... you know."

"Ah, yes. I understand. I believe their privy is out back." Pastor Hollybough gestured through the door and around the corner of the house.

"Thank you." Simon turned and started out.

"Uh? Don't you want to leave your Bible here?"

He paused and glanced down at the book still tucked under his arm. He smiled sheepishly, pulled it out and set it on the table by the side of the settee. "Of course. I've just gotten into such a habit of carrying it with me everywhere since my Millie's passing that I almost forgot it was there." He ran a hand over the cover in what he hoped was an affectionate gesture, then looked up at the Reverend. "I'll be back in a moment." And with that, he made his escape to the outhouse.

He stayed for as long as he dared without embarrassing himself and slowly worked his way back to the house counting on all the mercies of heaven to save him from having to discuss gladiators and Caesars with that man of the cloth. As he washed his hands in the basin by the door, he'd never been more relieved in his life to hear the call that dinner was ready.

CHAPTER SIXTEEN

Victoria watched the man who claimed to be her father carefully throughout dinner. She had set him at the end of the table with ChristyAnne and Jimmy on either side of him. It was curious that he'd come to dinner in his suit. She wondered if he always wore a suit and where he got the money to do so, if he did. Pastor Hollybough only had one suit and he rationed the wearing of it to Sundays and very special occasions.

Jimmy eyed the man as he passed him the potatoes. "Why do you carry your Bible with you everywhere you go, Parson?"

The man plunked a huge portion of potatoes on his plate and then set the bowl back on the table in front of him without passing it to ChristyAnne. Victoria suppressed a grin at the roll of ChristyAnne's eyes as she reached for the bowl and took a serving before carefully holding it for Mera.

"Uh, well son, one never knows when the Good Lord is going to give you a revelation. It's important to have the good book along just in case," the parson said.

"Oh." Jimmy seemed willing to accept that explanation but pastor Hollybough spoke up.

"One also never knows when they might have need of the Good Book to minister to hurting souls, young man."

"Really? Like what kind of hurting souls?"

Pastor Hollybough shrugged, "Maybe someone who has a loved one that's sick. Or a man who's working really hard but can't seem to make ends meet. Lots of people questioning God every day. And all the answers they need are right there in that book, Son."

"Oh." Jimmy studied his plate with a thoughtful look on his face.

Victoria tried to ignore the fact that the Parson once again took a large helping of meat and then set the platter on the table, totally ignoring ChristyAnne's waiting hands. But one glance at Rocky and the way he hacked at the steak on his plate like he needed to kill it before putting it in his mouth, and she knew that she wasn't the only one who had noticed the man's selfishness. Even Mrs. Hollybough's lips pinched into a disapproving frown.

Her hopes that Rocky might be wrong about the man ebbed further and further away and she felt despair welling up inside her. She really did come from vile blood. The man was posing as a minister, for goodness sake!

A fork crashed loudly against a plate and the next thing she knew Rocky took her by the arm and practically lifted her out of her seat.

"I need your help for a minute." He looked around the table. "If you all will excuse us, we'll be right back. Children, best behavior, please." And with that, he pulled her through the kitchen and out the back door.

Pressing her back to the wall of the house he tilted his head down and looked into her face. "Ria, are you alright? You got so pale I thought you were going to pass out." He patted her cheek.

She let the tears she'd been holding at bay fall. "I really do come from an awful family. He has to be my father. How else would he have known I was adopted?"

"Ah, Kitten." He cupped her head against his chest and enveloped her with strong arms. "Remember what we talked about this afternoon. First, we don't know for sure that he's your real father. He could have found out about the adoption some other way. Second, even if he is, that doesn't make you a terrible person. Your past is hidden in Christ and your life is what you make of it in Him, nothing more, nothing less."

"I—I—know." She sobbed into his shirt, gripping handfuls of it in her fists.

He dropped a kiss against the top of her head. "Come on, now. You can do this. You remember that time Cade, Jason, Sky and I got into a fight over you and you waded into the middle of us and set us all in our place?"

The reminder of that day made her laugh even through her tears and she nodded.

"If you could handle the four of us back then, you can handle this one old codger now. We have to go back inside and finish out this meal." He cupped her chin and tilted it up so he could look her full in the face. "You think you can do that?"

The concern in his deep brown eyes almost set her off again, but she hauled her composure up from the depths of herself, sniffed and swiped at her tears with the flats of her fingers, then nodded.

"Why don't you go over to the pump and splash a little water on your face? That always makes Sharyah feel better after she's had a cry. I'll make your excuses until you come back in. Take as much time as you need."

He started to walk away but she stopped him with a touch on his arm. She held his gaze for a long moment before she finally said, "I couldn't do this without you. I'm so thankful you're here."

His face softened and he pressed his palm to her cheek. "Yes, you could. You have so much more strength than you know, Ria, because no matter where you go, God is on your side. But this time you don't have to face it alone, and I'm thankful to be here to help you walk through this." He reached out and tucked a curl behind her ear. "More than you know." Stepping away he motioned her toward the pump. "I'll see you back inside."

When she arrived back in the house a few minutes later everyone had already finished eating so she set about serving the apple pie she'd made earlier.

Just as he was finishing his last bite, Mr. Cane (she refused to call him Parson for another moment) started to choke. His face turned a mottled red and his fleshy cheeks vibrated with fervor as he tried to pull in a breath. Victoria, her coffee pot frozen in mid-pour, watched the changing hues of his face in horror.

"Oh my!" Pastor Hollybough exclaimed.

Rocky leaped from his chair and gave the man such a whack on the back that Victoria startled and sloshed coffee onto Mrs. Hollybough's plate. Catching herself, she planted the coffee pot firmly on the table and looked back at the man whose bulging eyes appeared as though they might pop from his head at any moment.

Jimmy and ChristyAnne tittered as Rocky whacked him again and the man coughed convulsively and then finally took a huge gasp of breath, his jowls jiggling like the wattle on a turkey.

He stood and swiped a trembling hand across his face. "Ah… If you good folks will excuse me, I think after that bit of embarrassment I will hustle on back to the boarding house and get myself some rest." He pulled his bowler from the peg by the door and twisted it around by the brim, looking at Victoria. "You're as fine a cook as your mother ever was, young lady. She'd be right impressed if she could be here to meet you."

Victoria didn't trust her voice so she merely nodded her thanks.

"I'll see you out," Rocky said and held a hand toward the door for the man to precede him.

Simon started out, recalled that the blasted Bible still rested where he'd left it on the table at the end of the couch and turned back for it. He almost rammed into the husband, but the man was agile on his feet, and he leaped back out of the way.

Confounded idiot.

He'd had everything under control with his little choking display. When he started his act, to get out of having to discuss the Romans with the minister, the small piece of crust had been all set just near the back of his throat so that when he coughed, it would pop out onto his plate. Then the husband had darted over and given him such a surprisingly painful whack that he'd gasped and the crust had lodged in his throat for real. For a few eternal seconds, he'd thought for sure that his resting place this evening would be boot hill and not the boarding house.

Snagging the Bible and tucking it under his arm he waved farewell to Victoria, the minister and his wife, and the children once more. For some reason they were all staring at him, jaws slightly slack. He had a feeling that this evening's con hadn't gone so well.

As Rocky followed him out the door he realized the young whelp had probably saved his life with that second whack, but – he rolled his shoulders – he was going to be feeling the effects of it for a couple days.

He turned at the end of the walk and stretched his hand out to the husband. "Son, thank you for having me tonight. I rightly appreciate you allowing me the chance to get to know my daughter."

The younger man folded his arms and ignored his proffered hand. "I want you to stay away from my wife." The look on his face was one of feral intensity.

So the con had been even worse than he'd thought. It had been a little strange when they both got up and left the room so quickly. He should have known that the role of minister was one he, of all people, would be hard put to pull off. Still, he had to try and smooth things over. "I—I don't understand?"

"You understand perfectly well. I don't know what your real name is but if you're a minister then I'm no lawman. I have no idea what you want with my wife, or if you are even her real father but I want you to keep away from her. She's got enough to deal with right now without having to wonder and worry about you, too."

Simon's heart rate quickened. If this pup started doing a little research on him there was no telling what he might find. And he had no intention of going back to prison. Still, there was nothing he could do right at this moment, so he stubbornly clung to his role. "Young man, I honestly have no idea what you mean by these seeming accusations. But I've done nothing wrong. Your wife is my daughter and while I'm not proud of some of the mistakes I've made in the past, they are just that, in the past. I'm trying to put things right, and I hope you will not stand in my way. For now, I will say good night and I wish you all the best until we meet again. I hope that you will not rob your wife of the happiness of getting to know me."

"How do I even know you're her real father?"

Simon's eyes narrowed. "You just ask her if her mother left a locket in her possession. Silver and shaped like a heart. Engraved on the back are the initials M. S. for Millie Suzanne." *Or Maggie Saunders as the case may be.* "There was also a small rag doll, Millie sewed with her own hands."

With that he presented his back to the young devil and hoped the erratic thumping of his old ticker couldn't be heard. He needed a drink. He was getting too old for this. *That's why you need to make this one pay. This will be the job that sets you up for the rest of your life and you know it. Just stay calm!*

He glanced back. The man still stood at the gate like a formidable guardian, his gaze practically boring holes through the dusk between them.

Simon sighed. Sure he needed this. But it wasn't going to be easy.

He needed to rethink his strategy.

Victoria went through the next day in a semi daze. Rocky had come in and asked her about a locket with the initials M. S. engraved on it. She'd pulled hers out and showed it to him. Mama had said the locket and the doll were the two things that came with her when they adopted her. They'd been left with her at the foundling hospital.

With each new bit of evidence she grew more and more confident. That awful man really was her father. How else would he know about her locket? But why would he be in town posing as a minister, when it was quite obvious from his behavior that he was anything but?

She sighed and pushed thoughts of the man from her mind.

It was Friday morning and later tonight the Racklers would come for dinner. But first, Mama and Doc were to arrive this morning in Salem on the ten o'clock train.

Victoria had hustled the children out the door and now finished up the dishes with trembling hands. What was she going to tell her mother about her and Rocky? And about Baxter Cane? How would Mama handle that news?

Rocky would drive her to the train depot and she had rehearsed various scenarios over and over on how to explain both situations to Mama, but none of them seemed adequate.

She heard the buggy pull up at the back door and Rocky poked his head in. "Ready?"

"Almost. I'm just finishing up these dishes."

He tossed his hat down on the side-board and stepped over behind her. Placing his hands on the counter on either side of her, he looked down from one side.

She kept washing the pan she was working on, willing her heart rate back to normal and refusing to meet his gaze.

"Nervous?"

She chuckled. "Yes."

"Me too," he grinned.

"You don't have anything to be nervous about. Mama is going to be thrilled to have you as her son-in-law. I'm the one who's going to be in trouble because she wasn't at the ceremony."

His voice lowered. "She'll come around to forgiving you when you produce her first grandbaby."

She felt the heat climb her neck and pumped water to rinse the pan.

All week long Rocky had been most attentive. Bringing her flowers one day, a stick of candy from the general store the next. He'd popped into the house at the most inconvenient times – or convenient, for breaking her walls down even further – to compliment her or tease her or both.

Now, he pressed a kiss to her jaw just below her ear. "You're so beautiful when you blush, Mrs. Jordan." The whisper wafted warmth across her cheek.

She felt sure her face could rival the tint of a red summer poppy and her heart hammered in her ears as she set the pan into the drain board. With nothing else to wash, she rested her hands on the rim of counter between her and the sink.

He nuzzled the hair by her ear.

She resisted the urge to turn in his arms and give in to the desire weakening her knees. She needed to change the subject. "How am I going to tell Mama about Parson Cane?"

He settled his hands on her shoulders. "Your Ma is a very understanding woman, Ria. She only wants happiness for you. If Cane really is who he says he is, I'm sure your mother will be thrilled that he finally found you."

"I know, but— What if—"

Gently he turned her to face him. "No what ifs, remember? You can't worry about what others are, or what they think of you."

She gave a tiny nod. "Alright. I'm done. We can go now." Despite her desire to project self-confidence, her voice came out in a tremulous whisper.

"Everything's going to be fine, but," he grinned and bent closer, "I need a kiss. It might be the last one I get before your mother kicks me out of the family."

She laughed and splayed her palms against his chest. Pressing him away firmly, she gave him as stern a look as she could muster. "We need to go. Now. Or we are going to be late for the train. Then we'll really have some explaining to do."

He grinned unrepentantly and reached past her to lazily snag his hat. "Might be worth it, though." One lid dropped.

She cleared her throat and looked away. What scared her silly was the fact that she felt exactly same way.

★

Chapter Seventeen

The train chuffed to a halt with a huge puff of steam and clatter of wheels.

Rocky placed one hand to the small of her back. "Do you want me to tell them? Or should you?"

Victoria *zinged* the locket on her necklace back and forth, back and forth. She wanted to take the easy way out and make him tell them, but it was her mother, after all. He'd already had to tell his own parents about their marriage. And Mama really should hear about Parson Cane from her. "I'll tell them."

The door to the passenger car opened and the conductor stepped out onto the top step.

Zing. Zing. Zing.

Rocky reached out and stilled her hand. "You're going to break your chain, if you don't quit. She's your mother. She's going to understand. She loves you."

He was right, of course. She tucked her hands behind her and clasped them tight. Still – she rolled her lips in and pinched them together – she'd rather be almost anywhere else than here at this moment.

Mama and Doc were the first two passengers off the train.

Of course.

Mama turned and saw them, her face lighting up like a summer bonfire. "Honey!" she waved her lace kerchief. "Hi!"

Victoria raised her hand in greeting as Mama rushed toward them and Doc trundled after, carrying both of their valises.

Mama pulled her into a firm embrace. "Oh, we had such a lovely time. Hi, Rocky." She squeezed his arm.

Rocky resettled his hat on his head. "Ma'am."

Mama turned back to Victoria, her eyes sparkling with glee. "Doc reserved us rooms at the Palace Hotel on Market Street! The view of the city from our window was just spectacular! And the food!" She flapped her hanky in an expression of delight. "Oh, it was just amazing! Wasn't it, dear?" She paused long enough for Doc to nod his head in sage agreement and greet the two of them. "So tell me all about what happened while we were away."

That was an opening if ever Victoria could ask for one. "Well—"

"How's Hannah? And the children at the orphanage?"

"Ah." She quickly changed tactics. "They're fine. But I wanted—"

"You didn't try and run to the depot the day of our wedding did you? I thought of that after Doc and I were already settled in for the night. I hoped you didn't exhaust yourself by trying to do that on such a busy day."

"Actually—"

"Dale, honey, we better hurry. I think our trunks will be set off inside." Lifting her skirts, Mama bustled toward the depot.

Victoria angled a glance in Rocky's direction with an exasperated sigh.

He grinned at her and nodded his encouragement with a quick wink. Placing a hand to the middle of her back he pressed her after the departing couple. "This is better than a traveling circus," he whispered in her ear.

She giggled and gave him an elbow to the ribs. "Hush or I'll make you tell them."

"My lips are sealed."

Mama chattered and interrupted all the way back into town and by the time Rocky pulled the buggy to a stop in front of Doc's little bungalow, Victoria still hadn't found an opportunity to share their news.

"Oh, my! I've chattered on all the way home. Rocky, thank you for escorting Victoria to pick us up."

Rocky tugged at the brim of his hat. "My pleasure, Mrs. Martin."

Doc clambered down and reached up to help Mama from the seat as Rocky helped Victoria from his side.

Victoria headed around to the back of the buggy by the luggage hold.

"Ah? Mama? I—"

"How's your shoulder?" Doc looked at Rocky.

Victoria huffed.

Rocky's lips twitched even as he nodded. "It's good. I'll drop by later this evening and let you have a look at it."

Doc pulled the two valises from the hold, while Rocky lifted the big steamer trunk from the back and set it on the ground.

Mama wrapped Victoria in a tight hug. "Thank you so much for picking us up, honey. We so appreciate it."

Victoria heaved a huge sigh as she stepped back.

"What is it, dear?"

Rocky chuckled and Victoria scalded him with a glare.

He made a key turning gesture in front of his pinched lips.

She turned back to face Mama's questioning look. "I've been trying to tell you something ever since you got off the train, Mama. So if you could just please…." She patted her palms toward the ground a couple times. "After your wedding, Rocky drove me to the train depot in Salem. There were 3 orphans left who had no homes to go to and Hannah had no more room at the orphanage. Julia Nickerson of all people was the Society worker in charge and she was going to give one of the girls to Mr. V from the dairy and send her little sister back to New York. And I couldn't let that happen. But she wouldn't give them to me because I was single."

A dawning look of realization swept over Mama's face and she took a step back, her jaw dropping as she glanced from Victoria to Rocky and back.

Victoria nodded. "Rocky and I got married last Saturday." She heaved a sigh of relief to have at least half the news out in the open.

"You…? Oh my! Well…" Mama's gaze still darted back and forth from her to Rocky, her mouth opening and shutting like a fish out of water as she massaged her throat.

Rocky rubbed the back of his neck and kicked at a pebble on the ground.

Victoria held her breath as she folded her hands together and rolled her lips into a tight line.

And the silence stretched.

Doc stepped up beside Mama and wrapped an arm around her shoulders. "I believe the words she's searching for are, 'Congratulations children, we're so happy for you.'" He grinned and stretched his hand out to squeeze Victoria's fingers.

Mama recovered. "My! Oh yes! I'm so happy I just don't know what to say!" Tears filled her eyes and spilled over to trail down her cheeks and she lurched forward and jerked Victoria into her plump, firm hug. "Oh honey, I couldn't be more happy. Surprised. But totally ecstatic! Really."

Victoria and Rocky both released huge puffs of air at the same time and she couldn't deny her relief as she joined the others for a laugh.

"Wait a minute!" Mama set Victoria out at arm's length. "You mean we have three grandchildren!?"

"Well... No." She met Rocky's gaze. "The Racklers from east of town are most likely going to take the girls at some point soon. They are coming to dinner tonight so everyone can meet for the first time. We aren't sure what will happen with Jimmy yet."

"Why don't you two keep them?" Mama asked. "I think you'd make fine parents!"

Silence held the little group in its clutches for a moment until Victoria finally stuttered, "Uh, we don't... Rocky doesn't... We were just glad to be able to keep the girls together."

Mama opened her mouth to say something more, but Doc cleared his throat and wrapped one arm around her. Mama met his gaze for only a moment, then snapped her mouth shut.

Doc reached for Rocky's hand. "Thanks so much for picking us up. Much obliged."

"There's one more thing," Victoria inserted quickly.

Mama and Doc stilled.

"Something else happened this week, Mama. A man..., a man claiming to be a minister came to the house the other day and he...." Victoria glanced up at Rocky, needing to draw strength from him, somehow. Rocky nodded his encouragement and rested one hand at the back of her neck.

"He what, dear?" Mama asked.

Turning to study Mama's face, Victoria clasped her hands together. Would Mama be hurt by the fact that she had wanted to get to know Baxter Cane? And how would she feel when they told her the man was probably a con artist?

"He said he was my father, Mama. My birth father."

"Oh, honey!" True joy laced Mama's tone as she pulled her into a quick heartfelt embrace and then set her at arm's length. "How wonderful for you! Does he have a wife? What—?" Mama jolted to silence and tipped her head to one side in the way she had when pondering carefully. "You don't seem happy dear. Why not?"

Victoria's stomach tightened up. "No, he doesn't have a wife. She passed away awhile back, but he saw the announcement about Rocky and I in the paper and said he knew it had to be me because he says I look so much like her."

"Well, she must have been a very beautiful woman then." The unanswered question still lingered on Mama's face.

Victoria pressed on. "The thing is.... We had the man, Baxter Cane he says his name is, over for dinner the other night. And by the time he left…, Rocky and I were convinced he wasn't a minister at all."

One of Mama's hands fluttered to her cameo pendant and she paled as she glanced back and forth from Victoria to Rocky, eyebrows raised.

Rocky cleared his throat. "I'm not sure who the man is, he might be Victoria's real father, but if he's a minister I'll eat my hat."

"Oh dear!" Mama gripped one of Victoria's hands.

"Now Clarice," Doc chastised softly. "Don't get yourself all in a dither."

"Everything will be fine, Mama."

Rocky nodded. "I've asked the man to keep his distance, for now, until I can do some more checking on him. But we wanted you two to know, right away." Rocky fixed Mama with a look. "Were you told anything about Victoria's past when you adopted her? Any information at all might help us determine who this man is."

Mama shook her head. "No. We were told nothing about her past. Only that she was just two days old when she was left at the Foundling Hospital in New York. The locket she wears, and the doll on the table by her bed, came with her. And that was all. We didn't ask any questions. We were just so happy to have her."

"Alright. Not a problem. I'm going to do some looking into the man's past and see what I can find. For now, we'll just play things safe."

"Oh honey!" Mama pulled Victoria into another embrace. "I'm so glad Rocky is there with you at the house! And you bring those children by real soon. I've got grandkids and I want to meet them!"

Victoria chuckled and allowed Rocky to help her up into the carriage.

As they drove away, Rocky leaned over and jostled her with his arm. "We lived to tell about it."

She didn't fall in with his joviality. "Mama thinks we should keep the children."

Elbows resting on his knees, Rocky stared out over the backs of the horses. "Yeah."

She glanced at him. "Do you think… I mean… what if I…" Her face heated and she focused on the passing fields. Would she be willing to risk everything and love this man, if it meant being able to keep the children?

Rocky was silent for a few moments before he finally said, "I think I stand by what I said the other day. It's gonna take us a bit to get settled into married life. I think you—we—still need some time to… adjust to this. For now, I think we should move ahead as planned. The Racklers are a good family. The girls will be well taken care of there."

She wanted to protest that they could do it all, but at that moment they drove past the boarding house and she glanced up and saw Baxter Cane watching them from his second story window. He lifted a hand in greeting and she returned the gesture, but a shiver of apprehension ran up her spine.

She frowned. Rocky was probably right. She was the least likely candidate around for a good mother.

The Racklers' wagon rumbled into the yard promptly at six that evening. The flock of chickens cackled and scattered, disgruntled by the fact that their evening feeding had been disturbed.

Victoria quickly set the cinnamon apple pie she'd just pulled from the oven on the cooling rack as she heard Rocky call a greeting to the family from near the barn. "Girls!" she called as quietly as she could but so they would still hear her. "Come quickly, please!" She wanted to look them over one last time so they were sure to make a good first impression.

Jimmy rounded the corner whistling an innocent tuneless ditty. "Jimmy! Run out and coop the chickens please. Did the girls hear me?"

"Yes'm. They needed to use the necessary. They said to let you know they'd be in directly."

"Oh…" Had there been an odd light in his expression as he said that? But she didn't have time to question him because he'd already dashed out the door, leaving it gaping open, like usual. "…alright." With a sigh she picked up a towel and wiped her hands as she stepped out onto the back porch and smiled at the Racklers who were approaching with Rocky leading the way.

Mr. Rackler was tall – a good head above Rocky's height – and broad of shoulders. But his stature seemed diminished because sadness draped him like a cloak, and his shoulders sagged as he shuffled across the yard. His focus never left the hat that he spun around and around in his trembling hands.

Mrs. Rackler, hands folded in front of her, walked along beside him, her own countenance, haggard and weary, blanched gray by the stark black of her dress.

Neither of the children looked much happier. In fact were she to guess, she'd venture that sheer resentment glittered in their sad eyes.

She couldn't blame them really. After all, their parents planned to bring two new children into the home. She supposed they would see it as an attempt to replace their lost sisters.

Although Victoria immediately noted their brand new buckboard and the store-bought clothing that showed no signs of patching, she couldn't help but wonder if this family was indeed right for the girls. So much grief emanated from the four people before her she wanted to weep on their behalf.

Was this really the family God wanted the girls to join?

Switching the towel to her left hand she held her right out to Mrs. Rackler in greeting. "Hello." She smiled. "We're so glad you could join us for dinner this evening."

"Thank you." The woman returned her shake with a smile that didn't quite reach her eyes. "I'm Mary. This is my husband Tom and our young ones, Paul and Suzette."

"Ma'am." Tom dipped his chin.

The two children merely studied their shuffling feet.

Victoria wished she could pull them into a comforting embrace. Instead, she filled the awkward silence that followed with, "Nice to meet you all." She gestured to the open door behind her. "Please come in everyone. Dinner is ready."

Mary glanced behind her expectantly. "Are our girls here?"

Victoria felt her stomach roll at the word 'our' and darted Rocky a glance.

Hands resting on his hips, he pressed his lips together, and kicked at the ground with one toe.

She swallowed. This wasn't going to be easy. Realizing Mary still waited for an answer she hurried to say, "Uh, the girls are out back for just a moment but I know they are excited to meet you." Pressing away her hesitation, she hoped God would forgive her for that little stretch of the truth. The fact was, the girls had been irritable and cranky all day long.

Everyone had been seated and the food placed on the table

before Victoria realized ChristyAnne and Damera still hadn't made an appearance.

"Uh," she smoothed one hand down over her apron, "if you'll excuse me for just a moment, I'll go and see what's keeping the girls."

Rocky nodded then turned his focus on Tom. "So, how are the springs holding out on your ranch this year?"

"Well, I was a little worried after that last dry spell, but…"

Their conversation faded as she stepped out the door and made her way around back to the necessary. "Girls?" she called.

She heard some shuffling noises from inside the outhouse, then silence. "The Racklers are here. Dinner is on the table and everyone is waiting on you."

She heard the cork-pop of Damera's thumb coming out of her mouth. "Tell 'em to huwwy up an' eat 'cause it stinks in hewe!"

"Mera! Shhh!" ChristyAnne hissed.

Victoria felt the first premonition of dreaded realization. *And Jimmy knew what they planned*! She reached for the door. "Girls you need to come out right now. The Racklers are very nice people and they've come a long way to meet you!" The door wouldn't budge.

"We aren't coming."

"ChristyAnne, unlatch the bolt and open this door."

"No," both girls chorused in unison.

Tossing her hands in frustration, Victoria looked around as she thought through the situation. She could pry open the door and force them to come inside, but that would take some time and she wouldn't put it past ChristyAnne to say something outlandishly shocking to the grieving family inside. Besides that, everyone sat waiting for her to come back in and she didn't want to keep them. She huffed. There was nothing for it but to go get Rocky and see if he could talk them into coming out.

Back at the house, when she stepped through the door, everyone looked up expectantly.

"Uh…" Her focus honed in on Jimmy and he stared guiltily down at his plate. "The girls…," she transferred her gaze to Rocky, "are a little nervous…." She gave a quick shrug. "They've locked themselves in the outhouse. I asked them to come out, but they wouldn't."

Rocky started to stand, but Mary Rackler threw her hands up to her face and let out a loud sob, and he sank slowly back into his chair.

"They don't want to meet us, Tom! How could our girls not want to be with us?!" Mary's shoulder's shook.

Rocky looked at Victoria as though asking her what to do now.

But Tom lurched to his feet, before she could decide how to respond, and hurried over to ease his wife's chair out. "Now Mary. I told you this was all too soon. Come on darlin'." He lifted her to her feet and pulled her to his side with one arm. Casting Rocky and Victoria an apologetic look he gestured for Paul and Suzette to stand. "Listen, I'm real sorry. Can we put off meeting the girls for a couple weeks?"

A surge of relief washed over Victoria even as she heard Rocky say, "Certainly. Not a problem."

"It's just been a hard couple of weeks, if you catch my meaning," Tom continued.

"We understand," Rocky assured. "Why don't you just get a hold of me when you think you'll be ready to meet them?"

"I'll do that."

Victoria lifted the man's hat off the peg by the door and handed it to him.

"Thank you, ma'am." He motioned with it for Paul to head out the door. "Get the team, son."

"Yes, sir." Paul shuffled by, casting his mother a worried glance.

Victoria felt the heaviness of their grief wash over her. She folded her arms and blinked back tears as she watched them shuffle across the yard and climb slowly into their buckboard.

Suddenly she realized they hadn't even gotten to eat any dinner. "Oh! Rocky ask them to wait for just a minute and I'll send some dinner home with them." Quickly, she snatched up a basket and a towel as Rocky headed out the door. "Jimmy get me three of the empty canning jars from the pantry." She filled the middle of the towel with the crisp golden fried chicken and tied the corners together, then filled two of the jars Jimmy brought out with mashed potatoes and gravy and the third with green beans. She tucked all of them into the basket and carefully eased the pie in next to them."

"Not the pie!" Jimmy protested.

She gave him a hard look. "Yes, the pie. You knew exactly what the girls were planning and you never said a word to me. And just look at the hurt this caused Mrs. Rackler. Now quickly," she pressed the handle into his hands, "take this out to them."

Jimmy grumbled but complied and Victoria leaned back against the sideboard, her legs suddenly too weary to solely support her weight. What a mess! Hard as it had been to think of the girls going to another family, she never would have wanted to hurt Mrs. Rackler like that. Obviously the girls hadn't realized how hurtful their actions would be to the still-grieving woman.

She sighed. How should she and Rocky handle this? The girls only wanted to stay on here with them. Could they blame them for not wanting to move on again after they'd found a measure of happiness here with her and Rocky? Still, they couldn't just let the situation pass as if nothing had happened. The girls had been downright disobedient and Jimmy had been deceptive.

What had they all been thinking?

A few moments later she jolted upright as Rocky banged through the back door followed by three very meek children.

Stopping by the table, Rocky gestured for each of them to sit but he himself remained standing, hands resting on his hips and fury radiating from his face. "ChristyAnne? Would you care to explain your thinking today?"

In the face of Rocky's anger ChristyAnne looked befuddled, and large tears pooled in her big dark eyes.

Victoria's heart melted at the sight and her lips pressed together as she rested one hand against her chest.

"We only wanted to stay here with the two of you."

"Yeah. We love it hewe!"

Rocky's feet shuffled at that proclamation and Victoria peered over at him to see what his next course of action would be.

"Well," he cleared his throat, "what you did was wrong. A lady's feelings were very hurt, not to mention the fact that you directly disobeyed Victoria when she told you to come out. So," he sighed and looked over at Victoria, pain radiating from his eyes, even as he continued to speak to the girls, "you won't – uh, you won't get any dinner tonight. Both of you go to your room."

Victoria could tell that was probably the hardest thing he'd ever had to say to anyone.

"But Damera can't sleep when she's hungry! You can't do that to her!" ChristyAnne stamped one foot.

A muscle pulsed in Rocky's jaw. He speared ChristyAnne with a look and he lowered his voice. "Young lady, do not make me repeat myself."

Victoria wondered if the children had heard the tremor that laced his tone.

Jaw jutted off to one side, ChristyAnne tilted her chin up with all the air of royalty and stood slowly, regally, to her feet. She paused there, assessing Rocky for a moment, the glitter of decision in her dark eyes.

Victoria held her breath. *Please don't challenge him, child.*

Jimmy's feet shuffled and Damera glanced back and forth from ChristyAnne to Rocky for a moment before she pulled her thumb from her mouth, slid off her chair, and walked toward their room.

The air of challenge in ChristyAnne's expression dissipated and her shoulders slumped. She turned and quietly followed her sister from the room.

Releasing a puff of breath Victoria sank down into her chair.

Jimmy let out a low whistle and reached for a dinner roll. "WhooEee! That was some stunt they pulled, huh?" A twinkle danced in his eyes.

"Jimmy?"

The roll stopped half way to his mouth and he glanced up to meet Rocky's scrutiny. "Yeah?"

"Am I correct in my understanding that you knew what the girls were up to, yet you didn't say anything to Victoria or me before the Racklers got here."

Jimmy glanced back and forth from the roll to Rocky. Finally, he tossed the roll back with a disgusted snort. "Yes, sir. In fact," defeat cloaked his stance as he studied the table sheepishly, "it was all my idea."

Rocky cleared his throat. "Well then. You can head for your room, too."

As Jimmy shuffled from the room Rocky sank into his own chair at the opposite end of the table. Leaning forward he planted his elbows on his knees and dropped his face into his hands. After a long moment, he turned his head to look over at her. "You think that was the best way to handle it?"

She shrugged. "I might have let them eat dinner, and given them extra chores to do instead, but I don't think you were too hard on them."

A grimace flickered across his features. "Well, let's just hope they learn their lesson the first time, because I don't ever want to have to do that again."

She couldn't prevent a grin. "Daddy used to take me on a picnic fishing trip the next day after he had to discipline me."

"You?" Rocky thought for a moment. "Whatever could you have done to need discipline?" The sparkle in his eyes belied the seriousness of his tone.

A chuckle escaped her lips. "Once upon a time there was this very annoying boy who put a toad in my lunch pail."

He smiled softly now.

She arched one brow. "The next day at school, I broke his slate over my knee, after he dipped my braid into his ink-well."

His head tipped back in a full blown laugh. "I'd forgotten about that!" He leaned forward, studying her face intently. "If it's any consolation, I don't think I was comfortable sitting down for a full two days after the Infamous Ink-Well Incident of…, what year was that…? 1880?"

"Yes. I was ten and you were twelve, that year."

"I didn't mind the paddling. Or even the soreness afterwards. What I hated was that Miss Childers wouldn't let me sit behind you for the rest of the year." His gaze roved over her hair before it captured hers again and he added, "I always was more interested in your beautiful red curls than I was in arithmetic."

She felt her face heat and turned to look at the floor.

After a long moment he turned to examine the meal on the table. "A picnic, huh?" He reached for a roll. "Well if we're going on a picnic tomorrow, you best save that chicken." He sighed and snagged two more of the golden orbs. "I have a harness to finish repairing."

As she watched him walk out through the kitchen she wondered just why it was that she couldn't seem to let that wonderful man past her emotional barriers.

Rubbing one hand over her full tummy, ChristyAnne watched Mrs. Jordan tuck the last of the leftovers into the picnic basket. Mrs. Jordan's Mama and her husband had come along too, and ChristyAnne had known she would like them from the moment they drove up in their buggy and handed each of them a long stick of hard candy from the general store. Part of hers still rested in the pocket of her dress for later, but Jimmy had gobbled his down in the first five minutes.

Across the way Mera squealed in delight as she swung through the air on the knotted rope that Mr. Jordan had climbed up and tied to an old maple tree's branch. Each time she swung back toward Mr. Jordan, he reached out and tickled her. Mera was squirming and giggling like ChristyAnne hadn't seen her do in a long time.

ChristyAnne leaned back on her arms and refused to allow a smile, not quite ready to let go of her frustration with their punishment the night before. Although, she *had* been surprised at how quickly Mera fell asleep. Probably the fact that she'd been eating well for a couple weeks before the missed meal had helped. Reluctantly, ChristyAnne admitted that it hadn't hurt them too much to miss dinner last night. She especially felt better now that her tummy was full from the huge breakfast Mrs. Jordan had made and then the yummy left over chicken and fried potato patty lunch they'd all just shared. The peach pie Nana Martin had brought wasn't bad either.

She sighed and watched Mr. Jordan grab the tail of the rope and pull Mera back and up before he let her go again.

A wood chip landed in her lap and she turned to frown at Jimmy.

He grinned. "Smile. Your face is scaring the wildlife for miles around."

Nana and Doc chuckled.

She glared at him, sitting there on the rock whistling tunelessly and carving another dumb animal that Mrs. Jordan would probably fawn over and put in her windowsill.

"If anything is scaring them, Jimmy, it's the stupid song you've been whistling all morning!"

"ChristyAnne!" Mrs. Jordan stood to her feet and lifted the picnic basket to her hip. "Fold up the blanket and come with me please."

Great! Now he'd gotten her in trouble again. She stood, shook off the blanket, folded it with swift sharp movements and then followed Victoria to the wagon several feet away. The horses bobbed their heads and swung around to look at her as she dropped the quilt into the back right corner of the bed. One flicked its tail at a fly, then they both turned back to munching grass.

From the corner of her eye she saw Mrs. Jordan fold her arms. *Here it comes! She's gonna stand up for Jimmy again and tell me how mean I'm being to him!*

"ChristyAnne, I want you to know that it was never Rocky's or my intention to force you to go live with the Racklers. We invited them to dinner specifically so you could meet each other and see if everyone, including you, thought it could be worked out. I'm sorry it was so upsetting to you, and that you felt your only option was to hide away in the outhouse. I hope next time you take issue with something we ask you to do, you will have the courage to come and talk to us about it."

ChristyAnne folded her arms and huffed. "Why should I come talk to you? You don't even want us! I don't see you kicking Jimmy out to go live with someone else!"

"Oh, honey. Rocky and I not keeping you has nothing to do with you and Mera. Nothing at all. Honestly, Rocky and I just don't feel that our…, that we…, we just don't get along well enough to have children in our home. And the only reason Jimmy was staying on for a bit is that we haven't found a family for him yet." Victoria stepped forward and tried to wrap her in a hug.

ChristyAnne took a quick step back. "You two get along better than my mama and papa, and they had children."

Mrs. Jordan's face washed pale. She swallowed and glanced over toward the make-shift swing. "That may be, but grown-up issues are often a lot more complicated than they appear." Mrs. Jordan met her gaze again. "We really are trying to do what we feel is best for you and Mera."

The tears that sprang to Mrs. Jordan's eyes made ChristyAnne feel a little sick inside and she rushed forward and wrapped her arms around her.

Mrs. Jordan pulled her close and soothed one hand over her hair. "I know this is hard. We just have to trust that God will lead us all through this, okay?"

ChristyAnne nodded, her cheek still pressed against Mrs. Jordan's shoulder.

I suppose it wasn't very nice of us to pull that hiding trick on the Racklers. She hadn't known it would hurt the woman's feelings so badly, but she maybe should have thought about it a little before going along with stupid Jimmy and his plan.

Still, even though she felt bad for hurting the woman's feelings, that didn't mean she wanted to go and live with that family. She and Mera were happy right here with the Jordans and she planned to do everything in her power to keep them there.

She angled a look up at Mrs. Jordan. An apology probably

wouldn't hurt. She cleared her throat. "I'm sorry for the… way we acted last night."

Mrs. Jordan gave her another squeeze. "I know you are, darling. Let's just move on and let the past rest in the past, shall we?"

ChristyAnne nodded, suddenly feeling like she could fly. "Can I go swing with Mera for a bit?"

A smile lit Mrs. Jordan's blue eyes. "You most certainly can. Then when you are done, how about you help me plan how to decorate our basket for the doings tomorrow?"

Through the sheen of tears still blurring her vision, Victoria watched her dash over to where Rocky and Mera giggled together. *Lord*, she turned her face to study the sky through the fluttering leaves overhead, *I really want to keep these children.* She glanced at Jimmy. *All of them.*

Remembering Rocky's word from a few days ago, she looked over at him. Could she really let go of all her carefully constructed walls and let him fully into her life? Give him trust, openness, love…., *intimacy*? Her breath eased out through pursed lips. And all that without taking it back again?

He would want to know if she was offering simply to keep the children. Would she be?

She watched him help Mera off the rope and bend down so she could climb up onto his back as ChristyAnne grabbed the swing and clambered up until her feet could rest on the highest knot.

"You ready?" he called.

ChristyAnne nodded, her eyes sparkling like sun-kissed snow.

As Rocky took several large steps back, pulling the rope with him, Mera, her chubby little arms wrapped around Rocky's neck giggled and jounced. "It's fun, Sissy! Close yo eyes and tip yo head back. It feels wike yo fwying!"

Rocky grinned as ChristyAnne arched through the air with a happy screech.

★ ★ ★

Sunday morning dawned bright and clear and Victoria popped out of bed with a light heart. She glanced outside and grinned at the clear blue sky. Today was the day of the mystery-basket picnic auction fundraiser for the school. Sharyah had put a lot of effort into organizing it.

Each woman was to create a full meal. Then they were each to decorate a basket to hold the food and keep its appearance secret from their husbands.

At the auction, the men would bid to win the basket they thought was their wife's. And after all the meals had been auctioned, the man who won a particular basket would eat lunch with the woman who had prepared it. The married women's offerings would be auctioned first, followed by the single women's.

Victoria hurried the children through their preparations and then hustled everyone outdoors while she added the final touches. For her decoration she had decided to wrap the whole basket up in a lap quilt she had made the year before. The quilt was a light blue patchwork and thin enough that she could knot the corners to the braided Willow handle. Then through the center of the knots she pushed the stems of several roses and hydrangeas to create a bouquet of yellow and blue that cascaded down the front. Stepping back, she eyed her handy work and was quite pleased with the effect. She added one more rose for balance and then poked her head out the door.

Rocky sat on the seat of the wagon chatting easily with the children. Damera was beside him on the seat and ChristyAnne and Jimmy were in the bed at the back.

"Okay, ChristyAnne. You're on!" Victoria gave her a nod.

With a gleeful clap of her hands ChristyAnne hopped over behind Rocky and nearly knocked his hat off in her exuberance to cover his eyes.

"Jimmy, come and get this, would you please?" Victoria set out a separate quilt to drape over the basket to keep Rocky from seeing what it looked like.

The girl's ooohhhed and aaahhhed in appreciation as Victoria carefully carried it out ahead of Jimmy.

"I'll take you by the mercantile on your way home from school tomorrow and buy you some candy if you let me get just a peek, ChristyAnne," Rocky tried.

The girl giggled and tossed her dark curls. "That would be cheating."

"Two pieces?"

"Nope," she laughed.

Jimmy grinned mischievously. "I'll tell you what it *looks* like for two pieces of candy."

"Not a word, young man!" Victoria nailed him with a tough-as-hide-leather look.

Rocky threw back his head on a laugh. "What about you, Mera? You gonna help me out any?"

Grinning around the thumb firmly planted in her mouth, Damera shook her head. Her expression sparkled with merriment as the basket disappeared under the drape of the old quilt.

At her silence, Rocky reached out to the space where he'd last seen her. "I'll take that as a no, young miss." His hand connected with her dress and he pulled her into his lap and set to tickling her. "Why won't you help me? I'm going to starve! Or worse yet have to eat something Mrs. Halvorson makes!"

"Rocky!" Victoria gasped.

Mrs. Halvorson could take the blue ribbon at the county fair for "notoriously bad cook," but he didn't need to be letting the children in on that secret!

He chuckled sheepishly.

ChristyAnne removed her hands and resumed her seat in the wagon bed next to Jimmy. "She sent cookies to the school for all the children on Friday."

Jimmy shuddered and it was all Victoria could do to keep from giggling at the wretched face he pulled. "Not even the ducks would eat them!"

Rocky cleared his throat and gave her an apologetic look as he jumped down to lift her up to the seat. "Yes. Well. I probably shouldn't have said anything. God gifts us all in various ways. Mrs. Halvorson's gift just isn't cooking, that's all."

Mera pulled her thumb out of her mouth just long enough to pronounce, "You got dat wight!" and then popped it right back in.

Victoria covered her laughter with a pretended sneeze as she pulled the little girl onto her lap. And Rocky hurried to the back of the wagon and busied himself checking out something with the wheel. But she could see his shoulders shaking in silent mirth over the top of the wagon box, and when he finally climbed up beside her he was wiping moisture from his face.

"Get up, now!" He flipped the reins and didn't meet her gaze. The persistent twitch of his lip gave evidence to his continuing battle.

Several families that didn't normally come to church were pulling into the lot as they arrived and Victoria felt a little thrill at that. She hoped a lot of money would be raised today for the school.

She stopped Rocky by the side of the wagon as the children scurried on inside ahead of them. "I have a little something for you."

His eyebrows lifted speculatively and he cocked his head.

She pulled a baby yellow rose bud from her pocket and stepped closer to him. With trembling fingers she pinned the bud to his lapel and moved back.

Chin tipped down, the brim of his hat hiding his face, he studied the flower for several long moments, then cleared his throat as he lifted his gaze to hers. "Listen. I appreciate the gesture and all, but…" He darted a look toward the church, then pushed his hat back on his head. "I can't walk in there with a flower on my jacket. I'll never be able to walk into Samuelson's Feed again without being the laughing stock of the whole place."

"Oh." She hoped he couldn't hear the disappointment in her tone.

While they obviously couldn't tell their men what their baskets looked like, for that just wouldn't be proper, the women had all planned to pin a flower matching their baskets to the lapel of their husbands and hope he would get the hint when the time for bidding came.

But, of course the men wouldn't want to wear flowers. What had they been thinking?

"Of course. You don't have to wear it. Here…" She stepped forward and worked it free.

She started to put it back in her pocket, but as she pulled away Rocky's fingers closed around her wrist.

"I have a better idea for it." He took the rose from her and held her gaze, his thumb caressing the rushing pulse point in her wrist.

She held her breath.

After what seemed an eternity he glanced up and carefully tucked the flower into her upswept curls. He smiled softly. "Thanks for understanding, and…" He bent closer and tapped her on the end of her nose, a smirk thinning his lips. "I'll look forward to a slice of your delicious apple pie at lunch."

She sighed. Maybe he had gotten the message.

They made their way inside and squeezed onto an available pew toward the back. Rocky took one girl on each leg, and she scooted in close to Jimmy so they wouldn't crowd the family down the row from them. No one stood for the singing. They were all packed in like pickled-pig's-feet with hardly a spare space between them.

After the singing, Pastor Hollybough stepped to his place behind the podium. A bright red poppy stood out in stark contrast to his black lapel. A titter of laughter traversed the room and Victoria began to glance around.

Doc and Mama were just one row ahead and off to one side and Mama had a pink geranium tucked behind her ear. Doc was fingering his lapel and staring at the pastor's floral décor with something close to horror on his face.

Sky Jordan sat next to Brooke in the same row as theirs but across the aisle. He sported a pink rose, pinned carefully to his jacket. Sky leaned forward and caught Rocky's eye. He pushed the rose forward with a quirk of one eyebrow, as if to ask where his was.

Rocky only grinned and gave his older brother a dismissive hitch of his shoulder.

Mr. Halvorson, sitting up front and to the left, was the only other man she could see wearing a flower and he had a red rose stuffed into the top button hole of his black coat.

The congregation never really did settle down and Pastor Hollybough kept his sermon short.

As she exited and fell into place beside Brooke, Victoria took a deep breath, happy to be free of the stuffy interior of the church.

Just past the church, a long slope stretched down to Green Gulch Creek and the auctioneer's table had been set up in a small flat spot about midway down the hill.

The children ran on ahead to play by the creek with their new friends from school. "Stay out of the water, please!" Victoria called after them.

Brooke chuckled. "I'll have to be hollering that before we know it."

Victoria glanced ahead to see Sierra leaning against her Daddy's shoulder and slobbering happily on her tiny fist. She smiled. "She's such a doll."

"Thank you," Brooke returned her smile. "We feel pretty blessed."

Victoria glanced over to Rocky, the errant wonder of whether they would ever have children of their own washing over her. Her eyes widened at the sudden course-change in her thoughts and she felt her face pale.

Brooke caught the direction of her glance and took in her face. Bending down she pulled a long stem of grass as they sauntered toward the auction area and Victoria eased out a breath of relief when she let the situation pass without comment.

"I wanted to tell you that I'm sorry I haven't been out to visit you. I've been meaning to get to it. But Sierra was sick for the first couple days of the week and I didn't want to take her out. And then I seemed to come down with something. I just felt wiped out and I didn't want to come and make you all sick. I've been thinking of you, though. And I'm so glad we'll be sisters." A faraway look pooled in her eyes but she seemed to shake it off.

"I'm glad too. I guess I could have come to visit you as well, but things have been a little hectic at our place."

"Oh please," Brooke brushed the thought away with a flick of her wrist, "you have the three children and a new husband. You have no time to be running around town visiting anyone for the time being."

"I'm glad you understand."

"I absolutely understand, but one of these days we'll have to get together, just us girls. You, me and maybe Sharyah. I think that would be fun."

Victoria smiled. "I'd love that."

Rocky stepped up beside her and she gave him a sly look then turned back to Brooke. So..." she angled her head toward Sky who still walked a few paces ahead of them, "how'd you get Sky to wear that flower on his lapel?"

Brooke's face turned red and she pressed her palms together with a little nervous laugh. She cleared her throat and glanced ahead. "Speaking of Sky, I'd better catch up to him and get Sierra so he can concentrate on his bidding."

For a moment Victoria drew a blank as to why she hadn't answered the question. Then as realization hit, warmth washed her face in a crimson cascade.

Rocky cupped a hand around her waist and leaned in. His voice was low and warm against her ear. "Wish I'd thought of that."

CHAPTER EIGHTEEN

Victoria smacked Rocky and shared a laugh with Brooke who turned to catch her eye as she took the baby from Sky.

"Think we can renegotiate?"

She gave him a little push. "Go bid on the baskets. And," she lowered her voice, "make sure to win the one with red roses on it."

Victoria watched Rocky saunter over to join the men, his hands shoved into his back pockets, as she sat down next to Brooke on the grass.

Brooke smiled at her. "Sorry."

Victoria smiled shyly and concentrated on a blade of grass by her side without comment.

Glancing around, Brooke said, "Looks like a good turnout. I hope the school is able to get all the new text books and desks they need for next year."

She released a breath, thankful for the change in subject. "Yes. I was glad to see so many other families in church this morning."

Mr. Reed, who was to serve as the auctioneer, stepped up to the wooden podium and banged his gavel three times. "Ladies and gentlemen, as chairman of the school board I'd like to thank you all for coming out today. It is an honor to have so many of the fine folks from Shiloh turn out in support of our school. I'd like to say a blessing over the food and then we'll have a short word from Miss Jordan… Miss Jordan, where are you?"

"Here."

The crowd parted and Sharyah walked forward to stand by Mr. Reed.

Victoria's gaze flitted to Cade. He rubbed one hand over his cheek and down his neck, his attention fixed on Sharyah. She did look very nice today. Her dress was a shimmery shade of pale purple that complimented her skin tone and made her dark eyes seem even larger than usual. She'd twisted her golden-blonde hair up into a loose bun, but curls fell in a beguiling frame about her face. Cade's feet shifted and Victoria felt a stab of joy at his discomfort. Perhaps the man had finally developed a brain.

Mr. Reed said "Amen," and she realized she'd missed his entire prayer. She cast a guilty look around and caught Rocky studying her. He raised one finger and shook it back and forth, chastising her for her inattentiveness.

She arched her eyebrows and repeated the gesture back to him.

He merely grinned and folded his arms, fixing his attention back on his little sister at the front.

Sharyah's voice was soft but it still carried well across the crowd. "I want to thank everyone for turning out today. Men," she swept a gesture that included the section where most of the men stood, "I wish you luck with determining which basket your wife packed." A ripple of laughter filtered across the field, for everyone knew about the secret code by now. "Women," Sharyah turned her attention toward the section where the women sat. "I also want to thank you for your contribution to this cause. Without your willingness to cook for the occasion, there would be nothing to auction."

"We could pay for the privilege of a dance with you!" Jay Olson called from the back of the crowd.

Several men in the crowd stiffened and Rocky and Sky folded their arms and drilled the man with hard looks. But Cade actually jolted and Victoria watched his hands fist and unfist by his sides.

Sharyah fixed a good-humored smile on her face. "And that only adds emphasis to my thanks, ladies. Because, Jay Olson, my feet are still recovering from dancing with you in the sixth grade!"

Everyone roared with laughter, even Jay, who did a little jig and pretended to stomp on the foot of the man next to him.

Sharyah stepped back from the podium and turned the event

over to Mr. Reed once more. A few moments later she sank onto the grass by Victoria's side.

Victoria did a double take. Sharyah, her face so pale that her lips were gray, looked like she was about to be sick. "Are you okay?"

Mr. Reed set the first basket up on the podium and started the bidding at two bits.

Sharyah bent forward and planted her face into her hands. "Oh, I'm so nervous! I hate this!" she groaned.

Victoria patted her back. "You did great. You handled Jay with humor and your own touch of sass. It was fine."

"Not about that! It never bothers me to get up in front of people. It's about the basket!"

"What about it?"

"I wasn't going to make one. But then all the children told me it wouldn't be right if I didn't make one and they talked me into it. I know this is all for a good cause, but I just hate this! It wouldn't be so bad if I were married and my husband was fighting for my basket. But every time all the single men gather round and bid each other up like I'm some sort of prize possession and it is just … oh, and that sounds so vain! I give up."

Victoria chuckled at her discomfiture even as she remembered that last year Rocky had bid for the privilege of joining her for lunch, and won. They'd shared a quiet meal and she had been relieved and sad when he'd left without asking if he could see her again.

"It could be worse. You could be ugly as a pig's snout and have no one bidding on yours at all."

Sharyah giggled through her fingers. "Yes, I guess you are right."

They both turned their attention back to the auction. Sheriff Jordan – Victoria swallowed – her father-in-law, had already bid on and won his wife's basket, as had Mr. Samuelson.

As the families won their baskets they all sat back down on the grass and waited for the auction to conclude before digging into their food. It soon became apparent that poor Mr. Halvorson was bidding to win everyone's lunch but his own. The husband's groused, counted their money and raised him another time. Finally he would give up.

Mr. Reed set another contribution atop the podium. This one with red roses decorating it.

Mr. Halvorson pinched his lips together and heaved a sigh.

"Who will give me two-bits for this beautiful basket?" Mr. Reed called.

From the corner of her eye Victoria noticed Mrs. Halvorson shift as silence stretched taut over the men. Victoria's heart went out to the woman. She glanced back at the crowd of bidders and saw Rocky give Sky a nudge as he called out, "Two bits!"

"I'll give you three!" Sky hollered.

A ripple of awareness filtered across the hillside and when Mr. Halvorson's call of a dollar was raised by another man, it turned into full-out laughter. Mr. Halvorson finally won his wife's basket for three dollars and seventy-five cents, the highest price any had fetched yet.

Victoria's basket with the yellow roses was lifted to the podium next. A prickle of apprehension danced along her spine. Had Rocky really gotten her message, earlier?

"This looks like a mighty fine basket, gentlemen. Who will start the bidding?"

Jay Olson raised his hand. "Three bits!"

Mr. Reed chuckled nervously. "These are still the married women's baskets, Jay. You are playing with fire there."

Rocky pinned Jay with a glare. "Yes, Jay, you are." He returned his attention to the podium. "Four dollars!"

Four dollars? Victoria's stomach rolled. That was an outrageous price for him to pay.

Beside him, Sky grinned. "Make that four and a quarter."

Rocky jutted his jaw to one side, a glimmer of humor dancing in his expression. "You already won your wife's basket."

Sky clapped him on the shoulder. "True. But it's for a really good cause, little brother. And for a really good cause, I'm willing to eat two lunches."

Laughter erupted across the hillside and Victoria met Rachel Jordan's amused gaze from down the way.

Rocky joined in the good humor with a chuckle. "Four and two bits." He arched his eyebrows at Sky who raised the price to four and three quarters without a moment's hesitation.

Holding out his finger to the auctioneer, Rocky strode their way.

Victoria watched, curious as he bent down and whispered something in Brooke's far ear.

Brooke leapt to her feet and covered her face as she rushed back toward the church.

Victoria gasped in unison with several in the crowd. What could he have said to make her react so?

Sky frowned and glanced from where his wife had just disappeared behind a laurel bush, to Rocky, and back again. Then without another word, rushed off after her, baby Sierra still clutched in his arms.

A murmur of concern rose to a grumble until Rocky raised his hands to quiet everyone. "Don't worry folks. I'm a good brother-in-law and Brooke just likes me, is all." He grinned and turned back to Mr. Reed. "Now, where were we? I believe the bid is to me at five dollars."

Victoria chuckled in amazement as realization dawned.

Mr. Reed did the same. "Five dollars it is. Going once… going twice… SOLD to Mr. Rocky Jordan!"

"Thank you!"

Those gathered burst into applause and Rocky gave a wave of acknowledgment. He had just lifted his prize down from the podium when Sky reappeared with Brooke by his side, both of them laughing. When Rocky approached them, and said something quietly, Sky swung a friendly punch, but Rocky ducked under it.

He glanced over and dropped one lid in a sheepish wink as he made his way toward her.

She shook her head good naturedly and, when he sank down onto the grass behind her, she turned and asked, "What did you say to her?"

He jutted out his lower lip. "I simply asked her to come to the rescue of a man who only had five dollars and some change in his pocket."

She laughed. "Five dollars really is an outrageous price to pay."

He leaned toward her. "The company will be worth every last penny."

She cocked one eyebrow. "You just didn't want to give up your slice of apple pie."

He threw back his head with a guffaw. "That too."

Still smiling, she turned her attention back to the auction. Soon all the married women's baskets had been auctioned off and it was time for the baskets from the single ladies.

All the married men went and sat with their families and waited for the fun to begin. Several of the family men had first met their wives by winning her offering in years gone by. So this part of the auction always elicited great interest from the community.

Victoria felt Sharyah stiffen by her side and reached over to give her arm a little squeeze of encouragement. Four baskets remained on the auctioneer's table. Sharyah's, Julia's, and two others that belonged to the oldest Samuelson girls.

Rocky angled forward from his seat behind them. "Which one is yours, Shar?"

She sighed. "The blue one."

"Looks nice." Rocky's voice was too casual and Victoria turned to look at him. With an arch of his brows and an innocent look, he tried to shrug off her scrutiny. But when she narrowed her eyes, he broke into a grin and laid a finger across his lips.

Mr. Reed started the bidding on a basket decorated with a bright pink spray of wild peas.

Cade angled his head and looked just past her. Rocky shifted behind her. There seemed to be no more communication between the two men but Cade held his silence through the bidding on the first three baskets until Mr. Reed placed Sharyah's blue one up on the podium.

Cade opened the bidding with, "Ten dollars."

Beside her, Sharyah gasped and mumbled something unintelligible under her breath.

And Victoria grinned.

Mr. Reed raised his gavel and looked at the few single men left who hadn't yet won a lunch.

To a man, all shoulders slumped and heads shook. None of them could afford that much.

"Ten dollars going once, going twice…, SOLD to Mr. Bennett for the princely sum of ten dollars!" Bang! His gavel crashed down and the field erupted into applause as people milled about to get with their families, collect their baskets, and spread blankets across the hillside.

Rocky spread their blanket under the shade of a huge oak with Jimmy's help. And Victoria set to work pulling the contents of the basket from its depths. Fried chicken, potato salad, creamed corn, pickles, cookies, and quart jars of fresh milk. When she came to the apple pie, she stilled, and remembering his earlier quip about enjoying her pie, decided to leave it in the basket. She eased back, shutting the lid as though she'd pulled everything out.

Rocky, busy looking at a scrape on Damera's knee, didn't seem to notice.

Hannah spread her large blanket for the orphans out next to them. She never brought a meal to auction at the box lunch, but instead made enough to feed the orphans. Her contribution to the fundraiser was to give each of the orphans a penny so they could participate in the three-legged races that would take place after lunch. Each person paid a penny to enter the race. Whichever team won got to keep half the pot and the other half went into the school's coffers.

Victoria savored her final bite of crispy chicken, as a soft breeze blew across the hillside, rustling the long grasses in a soothing melody of sibilant praise.

The children gobbled down the last of their food and asked if they could be dismissed to play by the creek again. Rocky nodded and told them to come back when the races started and he would give them each pennies so they could join in the fun. A few moments later he rose from his place across the blanket, sauntered over to Hannah and dropped a handful of change into her palm.

Victoria smiled. It looked like the orphans would get to participate in more than one race each. Her heart warmed at the thoughtful gesture and then stuttered to a standstill as Julia stepped up to Rocky's side. "Victoria," Julia gave her a chilly little nod, then purred, "Rocky," and wrapped her arms around his bicep.

Rocky stiffened noticeably and Victoria felt a measure of satisfaction at the near revulsion that etched his face as he extracted his arm from her clutches.

He took a step away and settled his hands on his hips. "What can we do for you Julia?"

Julia looked a little lost with nothing to hold onto. She flipped open her fan and fluttered it in front of her face, her chin tipping up. "I thought it only fair to let you know that since I will no longer be working for the Children's Aid Society, your case has been turned over to another worker. He will be dropping by for an inspection of your place and to check on the children at some point."

"Thank you for letting us know. You have a good afternoon now." And with that Rocky dropped down right beside Victoria and propped one arm behind her back. "How about that pie?"

Victoria glanced from Julia to him and back. "Thank you for letting us know, Julia. We'll be looking for him." She offered a little smile and couldn't help but feel a touch sorry for the woman as she sashayed away, perfectly-coiffed head held high, but defeat draping her shoulders. Victoria turned to Rocky. "Maybe you shouldn't be so blunt with her."

Rocky barked a laugh. "Trust me, blunt is the only language Julia understands. And I don't want her getting any ideas into that head of hers, especially not when I have the only woman I've ever wanted sitting right here by my side. Now," leaning in to speak low near her ear, he asked, "are you going to bring that apple pie out? Or am I going to have to fight you for it?"

She giggled like a little girl and glanced down at her skirt. *The only woman he ever wanted...* Would her heart ever beat normally again?

She pretended demureness and added a touch of southern drawl to her words as she pressed one hand to the base of her throat. "Such shocking words, Mr. Jordan! A man fighting a woman for a mere slice of pie!"

He shifted toward her and his free hand landed dangerously close to the ticklish spot just above her knee. "What's shocking is that a woman would refuse to share a slice of the best apple pie in the country with her husband." One finger reached out to tap her knee. "Are you ticklish, by chance?" A devilish gleam leapt into his eyes.

"Rocky Jordan!" Her voice was a fierce whisper as she glanced around to make sure no one watched them. "We are in public. Don't you dare do such a thing!"

"Hmmm..." His lips flattened into a calculating smile and his eyes narrowed. "You have been opening up and talking to me more. Even admitted a few things that make me realize you are trying to make our relationship work. So, by rights, I should be nice to you. But...," he studied her, his face perfectly serious, "you did try to get me to bid on Mrs. Halvorson's basket so perhaps a little bit of payback is in order." His hand moved just enough so that his fingers and thumb now rested on either side of her leg. "Or..." he flicked a glance toward Sky and Brooke, deep in an intimate conversation over on their blanket, then brought his attention back to her and winked, "we could reinitiate our conversation from just before the bidding started? Something about how Brooke got Sky to wear that rose this morning...?"

Victoria lurched forward. "I'll get the pie."

His lips twitched. "I thought you might."

★
Chapter Nineteen

Simon Saunders rubbed the back of his neck and pondered his quandary. The husband had told him to stay away from the girl. But he needed to get his hands on that locket at her neck. On the other hand, with both of them occupied at the picnic, now would be a good time to retrieve the doll from her house, presuming she even still had the thing. Or would the mother have it? Maybe her mother had thrown the doll away years ago.

He grimaced. He'd deal with that if it came to it.

But there was only one way to find out. He leaned out from behind the church and peered down the hill again. The husband whispered something in the girl's ear that made her give his shoulder a push. The three brats tromped along the edge of the creek with a passel of other young'uns and looked like they planned to be there for a while.

He grinned. They were in no hurry to get home. He'd just meander out to their place and snoop around a bit.

Sharyah watched Cade polish off the last bite of his second slice of pie and grinned. "Would you like another?"

He rubbed a hand over his stomach. "I couldn't eat another morsel. This was one of the best meals I've eaten in a long time. Thanks."

"I want to thank you for your generous donation to the school's fundraiser. That was very kind of you."

"It was the least I could do. I know you'll put the funds to good use for the children."

She nodded and tucked the pie tin back into the basket. Cade wasn't acting like himself. Normally he joked constantly, but today he'd been rather quiet and thoughtful. She wanted to ask him if everything was alright. But maybe it was her stupid revealing slap that had him acting so serious and if that was the case she didn't want to have that discussion here on this hillside in front of half the town.

Still, he'd been her friend for almost her entire life.... "Is everything alright, Cade?"

He propped his arms behind him and leaned back. "Sorry. I haven't been very good company, have I?"

Sharyah covered the dish of leftover salad and put it in the picnic basket. She cocked her head to one side and met his gaze. "You just haven't been yourself."

Reaching out, he plucked a stem of grass, tucking it into the corner of his mouth. "Had a lot on my mind the last few days, I guess." He worked the blade with his tongue, his dark blue gaze drilling into hers with magnetic intensity.

Her heart pounded in her ears like the thundering feet of the children rushing out to recess each day. "I see."

The stem bobbed its way to the other side of his mouth and still he didn't break eye contact. "Ma hasn't been feeling well. She's getting headaches that bring her to her knees and put her in bed for days. Doc doesn't know what's wrong. Dad stayed home with her today."

"Oh, I'm so sorry. I knew she hadn't been feeling well. But I can see why you would be worried about her."

He tossed the first stem aside and plucked another. Rolling it between his fingers he studied it for a long moment, then looked up and met her gaze. "Thanks," he smiled, "I'm sure she'll be fine in a couple weeks. Doc prescribed lots of rest and we've been praying, of course."

Sharyah tried an encouraging smile. "I'm sure you're right."

"Anyhow," he rose to squat on the balls of his booted feet, "I need to be going, but I wanted to finish up our conversation from the other day...."

She felt a blaze ignite her cheeks. She turned away and

pretended interest in an oak across the field. "Cade, I don't want you to misunderstand…."

Actually, she did. She really did. If only he would totally misunderstand and spare her the humiliation of him knowing the depth of her feelings for him.

The intensity of his scrutiny prickled her neck and her focus flicked back to him.

Soft emotion darkened his eyes to midnight blue. "Did I misunderstand?" He broke the stalk into tiny pieces and dropped them near his feet, his attention never leaving her face.

She bit her tongue and looked away. She would not lie to him, no matter how badly the deception wanted to crawl from her throat.

There was the snap of another stem breaking and he leaned over, laying the fuchsia-bloom-studded frond of a wild pea by her knee. "Sharyah, I want to be honest with you. You caught me off guard, and at a really bad time." He focused on the growing pile of grass bits by his feet. "With Ma…." He looked up then. "I don't want to hurt you. You're like the kid sister I never had."

Her heart flinched. She started to smooth at an invisible wrinkle in her skirt, but at his pointed look of sympathy and understanding she clenched her hand into a fist instead.

"I care for you. But not in the way a man should for… there to be more."

Her short fingernails bit into her palm.

"I never noticed until just the other day what a beautiful woman you've grown into, and some man is going to be very lucky when you fall in love with him one day, but I would be less than kind if I let you hope that you and I…."

Well that left nothing to the interpretation, now did it?

Picking up the pink blooms with a trembling hand, she held them to her nose. There was no scent, just like there was no chance for her to have a relationship with Cade.

She didn't know how to reply and she couldn't bring herself to look into his face. A few moments later his footsteps receded across the hill.

She sighed but carefully maintained her composure.

The collapse could come later. At home. In the privacy of her bedroom.

Simon wheezed as he crested the last low hill before Victoria's place. Blast but this extra weight he was carrying as part of his disguise hindered him, at times. The path down from the road to their place led first past the barn. He glanced down the road behind him to make sure no one had followed him, then descended the trail and rested a shoulder into the back corner of the barn, peering around into their yard.

When he'd been here the other day he hadn't noticed any dogs and his current perusal confirmed that the place seemed to be unguarded and waiting for his entry.

He slipped around the side of the barn and soft-footed his way to the back of the house. Better to work from there, that way no one could happen by on the road and notice him.

There were two windows along the back of the little place. He tried the first. Locked. The second held fast also.

Well that left him no choice but to do this the hard way. He didn't want his presence in the place to later be detected when they arrived home. He hurried back to the barn and pushed his way inside. The work room sported tack on one wall and a table of tools along another. He searched it for what he needed and found a long pry bar that should do the trick. Hefting it, he made his way back to the other side of the house and set to work on one of the windows. It wasn't long before he heard the snap of the inner lock as he pried the window up, but he was still sweating like a roasted boar.

He swiped one arm across his brow and tossed the crow bar to one side. He would return it to the barn on his way out. Now he just needed something to stand on so he could lift himself through the opening.

A large rock rested not too far away, shavings of wood littering the ground around it. With a grunt he rolled the stone till it rested under the window. Within moments he had clambered inside.

The room he stood in looked like one shared by the two young girls. A large double poster bed rested against one wall and a dresser held two small brushes. He opened the door cautiously and poked his head out. Silence was his only greeting. The room farthest down the hall, held only one rumpled bed and had to be the boy's. That left only one other, the one in the middle, for the newlyweds to share.

He pushed open the door and let out a low whistle. "Right fancy!" Even had a carpet on the floor and a mirror over the dressing table. He gave himself a long perusal followed by a satisfied nod. No one would recognize him as Simon Saunders. He hardly recognized himself.

Now to find what he needed. Maybe the girl had left her necklace home today. He pawed through the few pieces of jewelry on the tray in front of the mirror. Not there. He sighed. Somehow he needed to get his hands on that necklace.

He turned to survey the room and stilled, unable to believe his easy fortune. A doll sat on the bedside table, one rag leg hanging over the edge while the other poked out at a jaunty angle. The fabric had faded, but it was definitely *the* doll. The legs were sewn from the fabric of one of his old shirts and the dress…. Mags had been wearing that material the day he'd met her. He'd known right then that she had plenty of money. No one wore crimson velvet unless they did. The doll's black button eyes stared, haunting him with memories of years gone by….

…The familiar comforting burn scalded his throat as he guzzled straight from the decanter, the stopper a hard ball at the center of one fist. He glared out the window – across the rolling green lawn in need of a trim, past the white fence and lost his focus somewhere in the wind-jostled field of weeds and tobacco.

The crop had been so promising this year. The rains had been good. The bugs reclusive.

But when the right honorable Senator McKenna had passed on, the slaves had all left the plantation. They'd abandoned him!

Curse the compassionate man and the stupidity of emancipation.

How was he to know that McKenna had freed every slave on the place after the war but they'd all stayed out of loyalty to him and of their own free will?

The man had paid the wretches!

After the death of the senator, the unreliable lot had up and abandoned him in the middle of the night. All but the two fools who'd stayed out of loyalty to Maggie. The sheriff, slave loving coward that he was, refused to go after them.

So he was left with unkempt fields, and now—this.

He glanced around the barren room, once more, the surge of a barely controlled temper quivering through him. Gone were the golden candelabras that had rested on the mantel, the silver tea service from the hutch, the gilt framed paintings that had hung above the settee. Across the room the safe still gaped open, as he'd left it moments ago, the interior taunting in its emptiness.

Maggie's valise lay packed and waiting by the front door.

She'd been planning on leaving him. After she stripped him of everything. Good thing he'd come home from his trip a few days early. Where would she be?

The liquor burned his throat again, and he closed his eyes as he began to slip into familiar numbness.

Had she birthed the whelp? She wasn't due for a couple weeks.

The door behind him opened and the very lady of his thoughts walked in, pulling driving gloves from her fingers.

She froze and gawked at him, her face paling.

Good. Her fear of him pulsed palpably – wrapped around her like a cloak. He raked her from head to toe. Then paused on the flat of her belly. "So I see you've birthed the child. Bring it. I want to see it." He guzzled another mouthful.

The darkie doe entered behind her. She darted him a terrified glance, swung her white shawl off of her shoulders and draped it on the hook by the door, then scuttled away into the kitchen.

Maggie pressed her palms together. "The babe died during the birthing."

He sneered. She actually thought he would believe her? He could see the lie in her shifting eyes.

A few swift strides and he had her by the throat. "I know that's a lie. What have you done with the child?"

Eyes wide with panic, she clutched at his hand. "Please, Simon. God's own truth it is! After ye— after what ye did, the babe came early."

The rage swelled from deep inside him. It curled, and wafted and churned until he could feel the heat of it stroking his neck and flowing up into his face. The strength of it clenching his fingers tight around her throat.

Maggie's legs gave out from under her and she clawed at his hand, her eyes wild and bulging, her mouth yawning in an unfulfilled gasp for air.

Pain crashed across his skull. He grunted and released his grip, stumbling sideways as shards of glass tinkled around his feet. The room tilted and he put one foot out to catch his balance, but he must have misjudged because his body slammed down hard and he could feel the cold of the wood floor against his cheek. He blinked deliberately, pushing blinding blackness back by sheer force of will.

Maggie lay just out of arms reach, chest heaving as she pulled in great draughts of air.

He shook his head. The blackness swept in and blurred the edges of his vision.

The door jerked open and banged against the wall. "Zeb! Zeb, come quick! He tryin' ta kill her!"

Simon rubbed the back of his head and staggered to his feet. He cursed the darkie soundly and surged toward her, his fingers fumbling for the red kerchief tied about her head.

Gasping like a fox on the run from baying hounds, she spun to face him and pressed herself flat against the wall as her man barreled through the front door.

Simon's fingers fell short of their intended grasp as the buck plowed into him and he tumbled backward, sprawling onto the floor once more.

Maggie crawled away toward the corner, her lungs still sucking madly for breath.

The black buck loomed huge, his clenched fists the size of sledge-hammer heads.

Think Simon. Get control. From his prone position, he stretched out his palms and tapped them toward the ground in a calming gesture. "Everyone just quiet down. I only want to know where the child is. Bring me the child and all will be fine."

The darkie kept his watchful stance. "I'm sorry massah. We cain't be bringin' you the child. It's done buried in the cemetery. You come with me now and I'll show you the parcel. You leave Miss Maggie be."

Simon studied the female, assessing her reaction to the words. Her gaze darted to the floor, but then her chin tipped up and she nodded her agreement. "Thet's the Good Lawd's truth, Suh."

Simon slid his derringer into his palm and shot the man through the leg.

Both women screamed as the darkie toppled with a cry of pain. His head lolled to one side and he passed out. The doe fell to her knees beside him. "Zeb! Zeb! Oh Lawd, Zeb Honey!" She pulled the kerchief from her head and cinched it around the red, gushing wound.

Simon calmly reloaded. He would get the information. He was good at getting information.

After several long moments she lifted her head. Hatred, such hatred as he had never seen, radiated from every trembling inch of her.

"Ah good. I see you've realized how powerless you are." He stiff-armed the gun toward the buck again. "Tell me where the child is, or today you will watch your husband die, slowly, one bullet hole after another." He spoke slowly so she would be sure to understand.

Her eyes widened, stark with fear, but fixed on something over his shoulder.

Instinctively, he ducked and spun around arms swinging in a sweeping gesture.

His elbow caught Maggie in the ribs. A sharp snap reverberated through the room. With a cry she stumbled back clutching her ribcage. The crystal vase she'd been holding over her head fell from her fingers – shattered with a piercing clash. Her foot caught in the hem of her dress. She flailed helplessly as she toppled backward. A loud, hollow *thunk* resounded as her temple smacked into the wooden arm of the settee. Her body fell limp and slumped to the floor.

He gaped at her.

"Oh, Lawd have mercy!"

"Shut up!" he snapped at the hysterical darkie, emphasizing his command with the level of the gun.

"Mags, darling." He squatted by her, feeling for a pulse in her neck. Nothing. He sighed. If she would have just been the good, compliant wife he'd thought she would be. Why did she have to be so fractious?

The red marks left by his fingers stood in stark contrast to the pale skin of her lifeless throat.

As though he could erase what he'd done, he stroked a finger across them. "Ah, Mags. We could have had such a good life together."

He paused. The locket she always wore, the one that had been her grandmother's, was not around her neck. He'd never seen her without it. What had happened to it?

A movement from the corner of his eye drew his attention. The slave trying to pull her man out the door.

Forcing his focus to where it needed to be, he demanded, "Stop." Standing to his feet, he steadied his aim. Even with her kerchief tied about the darkie's leg, a large pool of blood oozed across the floor. The man was not long for this world. Best he work quickly then.

He tilted the barrel of the gun up toward the ceiling and lowered his voice. "Tell me what Mags has been up to while I've been gone and I will help you get him to the doctor."

The doe shook her head. "I don't know nothin', Suh. Honest, I don't."

"Your buck is dying right in front of you, girl. Speak up, now."

Her gaze darted to the darkie and the expanding pool of blood around him. "I can't tell you somethin' I don't know, Suh."

He frowned. "Mags always told you everything!"

"Please Suh, this time she didn't confide in me. Said the less I knew the better." Her voice was too calm.

He jacked a second shell into the buck's other leg.

The woman screamed and sprawled out over the man in a lame attempt to protect him. "Please, please, Massah Simon, Suh. I knows nothin'! Miss Maggie, she have the baby early. A little girl it was. Miss Maggie sew that little baby a doll. Then she took a trip with my Zeb and she come home without the baby. Thet's alls I know, Massah, honest it is!"

Another bullet slid easily into the gun. "What about all the valuables? I suppose you know nothing about them either?"

"She take all them things into town and come home without them. But I don't know what she done with them! And that's the Lawd's truth!"

He leveled the gun and squinted down the barrel just to keep the woman talking.

Like a mother hen trying to protect a chick she spread herself over the man. "She weren't expectin' you home. Not this soon, Suh. She wrote you a note! Left it on the mantle for you to find, she did."

He strode to the fireplace, leaving her to do what she would with the dying buck.

The note had been simple. *Good bye, Simon. Your wicked deeds have folded back upon you. May God have mercy on your soul, for I cannot. Margaret….*

…He rubbed his sweaty palms down the front of his pants. This would be the telling moment. Had he figured things out correctly? Or had he spent years of his life on a desperate search for something that didn't exist? That would certainly give Mags the last laugh.

Two steps and he had the doll in his hands. He squeezed and

felt nothing hard on the inside. He cursed. If all these years he'd been searching for a phantom…. He started with each leg and methodically squeezed and bent them. Nothing. The main part of the body, stuffed with something soft, held no hard objects. Nothing in the arms. That left the head. He compressed it. It was hard. Filled with sand? He grinned. "Ah Mags. You really were a smart one. Some days I miss you."

The seam in the head was mostly covered by yarn, but a small section of it became visible at the doll's neck. He should just take the whole doll and work on it in his room at the boarding house. But by the way they'd looked at the picnic, he had plenty of time before they came home and he didn't want anyone to notice anything amiss. He just needed to find her sewing basket and a pair of scissors. After a few moments he would return the doll looking as if it had never been touched and slip away totally undetected.

★

CHAPTER TWENTY

"**M**ay I have everyone's attention!" Mr. Reed stood at the top of the hill and clapped his hands. Silence settled across the hillside and Victoria focused her attention on the man. "The board members and I have been talking. This turnout has been such a success, and we know we owe a lot to our special school teacher, a woman who grew up attending our fine school, Miss Sharyah Jordan." He held a hand out in Sharyah's direction and everyone applauded and several whistles pierced the air.

Victoria frowned. Where had Cade gone? He'd been by Sharyah's side only a moment earlier, but now she seemed to be alone and her face held all the color of bread dough.

Sharyah smiled, however, and waved her thanks. Perhaps Cade had just wandered off for a moment.

"But that's not all we talked about," Mr. Reed continued. "As you all know, every year the children participate in the three-legged-penny races and the winners receive half the pot for that race. Those races will start in a moment—"

A cheer rose up from the cluster of children by the creek but Mr. Reed held up his hands for silence. "But first, this year, we've decided to give the opportunity for parents and children to enter the race as teams!"

A murmur of excitement rippled over the hillside, but Victoria noticed several of the orphans on Hannah's blanket squirm uncomfortably. She closed her eyes, her heart going out to them.

"Now, listen!" Mr. Reed had to yell now to be heard over the growing tumult. "There are several children in our midst who do not have parents. So we'd like to ask any of you who don't have children of your own to race with, to partner up with one of the orphans and let's make this a day of fun and celebration for all!"

The little faces on the blanket next to theirs brightened considerably and Victoria eased out a slow breath of relief.

"Can we enter the race?" Jimmy blurted as he, ChristyAnne and Damera suddenly appeared back at the blanket with expectant looks of anticipation. They glanced first at Rocky then her, bouncing from one foot to the other.

"Well, I don't know…" Rocky glanced over at her a twinkle in his eyes, and it was almost more than she could do to keep a somber expression as, in unison, the children's countenances fell. "…why we wouldn't."

It took a moment for his last words to register. Then…

"Yes!" Jimmy spun in a circle.

"Oh Goody!" ChristyAnne clapped her hands.

"Hooway!" Damera jumped up and down, kicking her legs like a spring calf.

Victoria grinned at their delight in something so simple.

Rocky chuckled and stood to his feet, dusting his pants and settling his hat on his head before he reached down to help Victoria up. Once she was standing, she started to pull away, but he tightened his grip on her hand and stepped closer. "There's three of them!" he whispered in her ear, near panic lacing his voice.

She chuckled and whispered back, "You have two legs, make it a four-legged race!" She stepped back and this time he allowed it.

"Ah!" A light of understanding dawned on his face as he turned to look at the children. "Okay, here's how we are going to do this. ChristyAnne, you pair up with Victoria. Jimmy and Damera you're with me."

ChristyAnne hopped over to her side and Victoria draped an arm around the girl's shoulders as they made their way to the starting line.

"I've never been in a three-legged race before. Some children back home went to a picnic one time and ran in one and they told me about it later, but Mama…." The little girl's voice trailed off and Victoria gave her a gentle squeeze, sensing she needed to say whatever it was she'd been about to say.

"Mama, what?"

"Well," ChristyAnne bent down and plucked a blade of grass, shredding it with her thumbnail as she talked, "my daddy used to work in a factory. But one day one of the machines caught his leg and crushed it and they had to take his whole leg off."

"Oh honey, I'm so sorry." Victoria rubbed her palm up and down her arm.

ChristyAnne sighed. "Daddy couldn't work after that and he changed a lot. Got mad real easy."

Victoria's heart weighed down, at that revelation. How much these girls must have gone through! She wanted to speak soothing words of comfort, but held her peace, knowing that often simple silence and a listening ear was more comfort than anything.

"Our church back home was going to have a picnic with three-legged races, but Mama wouldn't let us go to church that day. I think she was worried about how Daddy would feel, seeing all those people pretending at something that he had to live with everyday."

"Does it make you sad to be in the race? Because we don't have to do it if you don't want to," Victoria reassured.

"No. I want to. Somehow I don't think Daddy would mind. After all, he's in heaven now, so he doesn't have to worry none about a missing leg anymore. Leastwise, not if what the pastor says, is true."

Victoria gave her a squeeze. "That's right, honey. Do you mind my asking… what happened to your mama and daddy?"

The little girl stiffened and gave a small sigh. "Our neighbor lady said it was cholera. It took Daddy first. Then Mama." She looked ahead to where Damera hopped along by Rocky's side, seemingly without a care in the world. "Mama made me promise, before she passed, that I would take good care of Damera." She swallowed and bent to pluck another blade. "There were so many times when I was so scared they were going to separate us! I prayed hard every day that God would keep us together and let me keep my promise to Mama." She looked up and the pain in her expression was almost more than Victoria's heart could take. "You have no idea how happy I was to hear you say you wanted to take us both. I know God used you to answer my prayers, and I'll forever be indebted to you, even though you and Mr. Jordan can't keep us."

"Oh, honey!" Victoria pulled her close and laid her head against the little girl's. "I'm so glad Rocky and I were there to take you! God often works for us in ways we can't see until we travel ahead a bit and can look back with a little perspective. Rocky just reminded me the other day about the verses in Psalm 23 that talk about God preparing a table for us even in the presence of our enemies. I wonder sometimes if we even recognize when we are sitting at a table God prepared especially for us. I'm sure there have been times when I haven't realized it. And it is so good that you are wise enough to recognize that God had a lot to do with keeping you two together." She squeezed the little girl again. "And I, for one, am so glad that God let me be part of your answer."

"Me too." ChristyAnne hugged her back.

They had arrived at the starting line now, so further conversation would have to wait. Standing side by side, they placed their feet next to each other, slipped the loop Mr. Reed handed them around their ankles, and cinched it down tight.

Victoria noticed that Mama and Doc had both partnered up with an orphan, as had Sharyah, Sky and Brooke. Rachel Jordan stood on the sidelines holding baby Sierra, but Sean was also on the starting line with an orphan by his side. And even Hannah grinned at her from down the line, one sturdy leg being tied to the leg of a little girl less than half her size. When Victoria returned her grin, Hannah lifted her palms as if to say, "What else was I to do?"

Rocky paid the nickel entry fee for the five of them. There was much guffawing and laughter as Rocky had both his legs tied, one to Jimmy and the other to Damera.

"Hey that's not fair," Doc joked. "They're going to have a distinct advantage! They've got four legs instead of three!"

Mr. Reed grinned as he wrapped an arm around each of his girls. "Well he won't have an advantage over us, will he girls?" Elsa and Daria giggled and shook their heads as Mrs. Halvorson cinched down the last knot tying them to their father.

Mr. Halvorson stepped up to the end of the line and raised his arms above his head.

"You need a pistol!" someone shouted.

There was a pause as Mr. Halvorson waited for someone to bring him a gun.

Beside her, Victoria felt ChristyAnne tremble and she wrapped her arm around her and bent down. "Okay, now listen. To win a three-legged race we have to work together. We both start with our middle legs and then our outside ones. We need to go slow at first until we get our rhythm, then we can start moving a little faster, okay? Just listen to me and do what I say and whatever we do, let's not let Rocky, Jimmy and Damera beat us!"

Gun in hand, Mr. Halvorson raised his arms above his head once more. "Ya'll take your marks now!"

The little girl giggled. "We definitely can't let Jimmy beat us! We'll never hear the end of it!"

"Get set!"

"Okay, then. It's a pact." Victoria grinned, amazed at the swell of love that surged through her, not only for ChristyAnne, but for Damera and Jimmy, too. In that moment she knew she would do anything for these children.

Even allow yourself to have a complete relationship with Rocky?

The thought so flustered her, when Mr. Halvorson's gun went off, she started on the wrong leg and she and ChristyAnne tumbled into the grass.

"I thought you said to start with the middle leg?" ChristyAnne giggled.

Victoria fought her skirts and ChristyAnne's weight as she fumbled back to her feet. "I did!" She laughed. "Okay, this time, ready? Middle leg. Go!"

They started off in unison this time and quickly passed up,

Rocky, Damera and Jimmy who had fallen in a tangled heap next to a similar mound formed by Mr. Reed and his two girls.

"Damera! Get up!" Jimmy's tone held the epitome of frustration.

"I'm twying, but yo' sitting on my dwess!"

ChristyAnne giggled and glanced back to see if they were making any progress, which turned her body into Victoria.

"Oh!" Victoria lost her balance and tumbled forward, her ribs connecting solidly with ChristyAnne's shoulder as she landed on her and rolled over the top of her.

They both lay still in a stunned, frozen state for a split second then ChristyAnne said, "Ow!" She spit out a clump of grass that had somehow found its way into her mouth during the tumble. "Ew!" With swift fingers, she swiped at her tongue trying to remove the last vestiges of grass bits.

Victoria tried to stand but, when she couldn't move her free leg, realized her foot was in a partially caved-in rabbit hole. "Ah!" She collapsed back to the ground and grunted when she landed on ChristyAnne's hand.

"Sorry!" ChristyAnne jerked her hand free and shook the smashed appendage. "Ow again!" With a grunt she tried to get back to her feet but was jerked back down because Victoria's derriere firmly pinned her skirt to the ground. With a huff, she gave up and sat still.

They looked at each other in befuddlement for a long moment. ChristyAnne's mouth quirked up at one corner and Victoria felt her own humor mounting. All at once, they both burst out laughing.

"Ow!" Victoria put one hand to her ribs and tried to stifle her laughter to keep the pain to a minimum.

But ChristyAnne pointed a finger at her and flopped over backwards, her little shoulders heaving with convulsive giggles. "You… have… grass… *everywhere*!"

Victoria took one look at the grass covering ChristyAnne and knew she must look a sight and couldn't help the mirth that shook her, even while she pressed one hand to her throbbing ribs.

Down at the end of the field, where the finish line stretched, Brooke Jordan and the little orphan girl, Daisy, broke the ribbon.

"And we have the winners!" Mr. Halvorson held Brooke's and Daisy's hands high in the air.

Beside her, ChristyAnne pulled in a long breath and managed to say. "Well at least we didn't get beat by Jimmy and Damera!"

Victoria wiped her eyes and turned to look behind them. Rocky had just finished untying the knots and stood to his feet. He helped Damera up and dusted her off, then handed Jimmy, who'd already leapt to his feet, the sections of rope and gestured that he should take them back to the basket at the starting line. Glancing around, his eyes met hers, decided humor in their dark depths.

"Care to help a couple of damsels in distress, kind sir?" she asked.

"Sure! Where are they?" He pretended to diligently search the field, which sent ChristyAnne into another fit of paralyzing giggles.

Victoria chuckled too, then winced and clutched her ribs again.

Rocky's joviality turned to concern and he strode over, kneeling down in front of them. "Are you okay?" He frowned as he began to work at the knot in the rope.

"I'm fine. Just… my ribs met with ChristyAnne's shoulder and apparently her shoulder and my ribs don't get along so well."

ChristyAnne pointed toward Victoria's foot and another spasm of laughter shook her. "Her feet don't get along with rabbit holes too well, either!"

"You two are a mess." The ropes untied, Rocky started to pull away some of the dirt that had collapsed on top of Victoria's foot, burying it up to the ankle. "Is your ankle twisted?"

She shrugged and pulled her foot loose from the hole. "I don't think so." She held her leg out and rotated her ankle "It doesn't hurt."

Rocky nodded with satisfaction. "Good. Let me help you up."

Doc and Mama approached, eyeing her with concern.

"You okay?" Doc questioned.

Victoria started to wave away his concern, but Rocky said, "Her ribs will need looked at, Doc. She and ChrisAnne, took quite a tumble."

Still seated on the ground, ChristyAnne sucked in a sharp breath.

"And what about you, young lady," Rocky held out a hand to help her up, "are you hurt anywhere?"

ChristyAnne shook her head no, but the stricken look on her face concerned Victoria.

"What's the matter?" She pressed.

"Nothing."

Victoria narrowed her eyes.

"It's just. My Daddy used to call me that…ChrisAnne… before."

Rocky tilted his head. "Does it bother you if I call you that?"

She shook her head. "No." A crimson hue tinted her cheeks. "I kinda like it."

"Well then…," Rocky mussed her hair, "ChrisAnne it is!" He pulled her into a quick hug and turned to meet Victoria's gaze over her head.

Jimmy and Damera bounded up jabbering about the hilarity of trying to get back on their feet after they'd fallen and Victoria's heart literally pained her as she looked around at the small group. Her gaze settled on Rocky. He still studied her over the top of ChristyAnne's head, a soft gleam in his eyes.

She swallowed. *Lord, I don't want to give this up. Please, help.*

ChristyAnne pulled back from Rocky but his gaze lingered, warm and soft. Could he be feeling the same longing she was?

He stepped toward her and started to say something, but just then Cade thundered down the hill on a horse that had clearly been ridden hard all the way to town. "Doc! Doc, it's Ma!"

CHAPTER TWENTY-ONE

Doc dashed toward his buggy, gesturing from Rocky to Mama in indication that Rocky should see her home. Rocky nodded and waved his assurance.

Rachel rushed to Cade's side and laid a hand on his leg.

Victoria swallowed. Rachel and Brenda had been friends for a long time. That's how Cade and Rocky became such good friends. She couldn't hear Cade's words, but he was as pale as fresh-laid snow, and Rachel took a step back, turned, and buried her face against Sean's chest.

Beside her Rocky whispered, "Dear Lord, no."

As Cade and Doc rode away, he placed a hand to her back and guided her over by his parents. Sky and Brooke arrived from the other direction at the same time they did.

"Ma?" Sky questioned.

"The pain medication that Doc gave her doesn't seem to be helping. She collapsed again this afternoon." She glanced up at Sean. "I should go out and be with them."

He nodded and rubbed his hand down the back of her head. "I'll take you." He swallowed, his gaze tender on Rachel's face, and Victoria could see the fear in his eyes and knew he was wondering how he would be feeling if it were his own wife.

She fiddled with her locket and glanced over at Rocky. What would she do if it were Rocky?

Zing. Zing. Zing.

"I'll watch the jail for you," Sky said to Sean.

"And I'll make sure all the ladies get home," Rocky offered.

"Thanks boys." Sean placed a hand on his wife's shoulder and directed her up the hill to their buggy.

The picnic dismissed early, no one feeling much like celebrating in light of the dim news. But by the time they'd gathered all the children and headed the wagons down the road toward Mama's place, Victoria's worry about Brenda's condition had her hands jittery.

Rocky escorted Clarice to her front door and waited while she fumbled with the key. "Do you need me to get you anything?"

"No. No. I'll be fine. Thank you." She gave him a wan smile.

"Alright. Ah…" He rubbed the back of his neck. "I'd appreciate it if you'd send the Cox boy over with any news when Doc gets home."

She laid her hand on his arm. "I will. Try not to worry."

He nodded but as he made his way back to the wagon, settling his hat onto his head, he couldn't help but wonder how he'd be feeling were he in Cade's position. *Lord, give him strength.*

Sharyah stared silently across the horses' backs as he drove her toward Ma and Pa's place. She'd been unusually quiet all afternoon, shoulders stiff, back ramrod straight. Something had obviously happened between her and Cade at lunch. And the news about Brenda had to be affecting her grievously. Their families had been close since all of them were babies.

Beside him, Victoria fiddled with her fingers, rubbing, twisting, folding and unfolding them.

He covered her hands with one of his own.

She jolted and looked at him.

"Worrying won't change anything."

She made no comment but hooked one finger around his, keeping his hand close for a moment longer.

He pulled the wagon to a stop outside of the white farm house he'd grown up in. The wraparound porch with the bench swing on one end gave the place a welcoming feel. That and the flowers Ma had planted around the place.

He swung Sharyah down from the seat, but held her steady by her shoulders for a moment. "You going to be alright?"

"Yeah."

But she blinked back tears. He pulled her into an embrace.

He wanted to offer assurances, but had none to give. Finally he set her away. "Do you want to come to our place?"

"No. No. I'll be fine, really." She offered a tremulous smile, an attempt to reassure him.

"Come on over if you need anything."

Sharyah nodded. "Okay."

The wagon seat creaked as he climbed back aboard.

Victoria's fingers were fiddling again. Covering her hand, he gave her what he hoped was an encouraging smile. A long night stretched out before them all.

Victoria sighed as they arrived back at the house. Both of the girls had fallen fast asleep. Rocky scooped up ChristyAnne, and Victoria followed suit with Damera and they carried them into the house. As they came out of the girls' room, Jimmy was setting up the chess board with a hopeful look on his face.

Rocky grinned and clapped a hand onto his shoulder. "Chores first, Jim, then we can play a game of chess."

Jimmy sighed in defeat and, with great exaggeration, slumped out the door after Rocky.

Victoria grinned even as she realized that exhaustion pulled at every muscle in her body. The news about Brenda had sapped all her strength.

She put away the leftovers from the picnic and cleaned the kitchen from top to bottom, then went to her room and sank down on the edge of her bed. She would read for a bit and then retire early tonight.

As she lit the lamp a warm glow filtered throughout the room and she reached for *Little Women*.

She blinked.

The doll that her birth mother had left with her at the Foundling Hospital lay slumped sideways and the book had toppled over. The doll's head was misshapen and limp.

Picking it up, she gasped at a prick to her finger. "Ow!" She tucked her finger tip into her mouth.

There was sand all over the table, and a needle poked through the head of the doll! Someone had torn the stitching on the doll's head and had attempted to sew it back together.

She sighed. One of the girls, no doubt. Why would they have done something like this?

The sound of Rocky and Jimmy chatting easily out at the chess board filtered into the room. Maybe one of them would know who had played with it.

Carefully holding it so that no more sand would spill out she stepped out into the living room. "May I ask? Did either of you see one of the girls playing with this doll earlier?"

Both of them looked up.

Jimmy eyed the doll for a moment, then shook his head, his expression clear and honest.

Rocky frowned slightly. "No. I didn't. Why?"

"Someone tore it and apparently attempted to fix it. I found it just now. That doll was with me when the nun found me at the Foundling Hospital."

"I'm sorry they got into it."

She waved a hand. "No harm done really. I'll talk to the girls about it in the morning. 'Night."

"'Night."

Back in her room, she scooped the rest of the sand back into the doll's head, stitched the small hole shut and set it back into its place.

She would have to let the girls know how precious this doll was to her.

★

Chapter Twenty-Two

Night still cloaked the yard as Cade led Doc's horse and buggy out of the barn and slung the reins around the corral pole. He leaned his arms against the top rail and stared off into black nothingness. Everything around him seemed bleak, undefined, unimportant.

Wind touched the maple tree across the way and brought it into focus as the monochromatic leaves whispered sadly, matching the desolation of his heart.

He closed his eyes, settled his face into his palms and suppressed a groan. Wishing he could wake up from this nightmare, yet knowing all too well it was reality slashing at his soul. He blinked away the dampness from his eyes and scraped one hand over his jaw.

The first rays of the sun rose past the horizon and pierced the darkness, turning the leaves from black and gray shadows to green twirling wraiths shot through with blinding shafts of light.

It didn't seem right that the sun should rise on a day like today. He winced and looked toward the ground, still dark and crawling with dawn's shade. Pushing his hat back on his head, he allowed his focus to blur.

His stallion trotted over, whuffed and jostled his arm.

"Go." He pressed the animal away without ever looking at it.

He hadn't expected the numbness.

Behind him, he heard Doc settle his bag into his buggy and then come to stand close by.

"I'm sorry, Son. I wish there was something more I could have done."

Cade nodded, his back still to the man.

"I'll go on home now. I'll let Pastor Hollybough know. I'm sure he'll be out later today."

He gave another nod.

Doc's feet shuffled. "Your Dad... He's going to need you to be strong, Son."

Cade dropped his head and massaged the muscles along the back of his neck. How was he supposed to be the strong one when he only felt numbing emptiness?

How could she be gone? She was in the prime of her life. Only last month she'd helped him birth two late calves. Just a few days ago she'd teased him about the fact that he hadn't yet made her a grandmother.

And now... he never would.

"Son?" Doc laid a gentle hand on his shoulder.

Cade flinched, stepped away, and waved a dismissive hand. "I'll be fine, Doc. Thanks." He glanced over at the house. "Are Rachel and Sean still in there with him?"

"Yes. They said they would stay until arrangements have been decided."

Cade settled his hands at his belt and kicked a rock watching it jounce across the yard. So many things to think about. So many things he had never even considered. He stretched his neck from side to side. How were they going to get along without her?

Doc cleared his throat. "I don't mean to be telling you your business, but I think you need to get inside and talk to your father. He sorta fell apart after you came out to get my buggy."

For the first time since he'd come outside, Cade met Doc's gaze and read the worry there. His brow lowered. His father had always been strong. He was going to be just fine. Still... He nodded, "Alright. I'll go check on him. Thanks, Doc."

With heavy steps he pushed through the back door as Doc drove the buggy out of the yard. Rachel Jordan stood at the stove stirring a pan of scrambled eggs. His mind revolted at the thought of eating, yet his stomach turned traitor and rumbled as the smell registered. He hadn't eaten since the picnic lunch yesterday. Come to think of it, none of them had.

Rachel left the stove and pulled him into a warm embrace. "Cade, Honey, I'm sorry." A sob caught in her throat. "So sorry."

Cade blinked, refusing to give in to tears. He patted her back, as much the comforter as the comforted.

Ma's scent still lingered here. Cinnamon, sugar, vanilla and her distinct lilac toilet water swirled tauntingly. The mixture of pie dough she'd started before her headache got so bad yesterday still sat on the counter, the wooden spoon jutting out of the bowl as though she would walk back into the kitchen at any moment and resume where she'd left off.

His stomach clenched. He needed to get out of here. Stepping back, he held Rachel's shoulders and looked into her face. "It's going to be alright. We're all going to make it. Ma wouldn't let us handle this any other way, if she were here."

Rachel chuckled even as she swiped tears off her cheeks. "Isn't that the truth?"

He glanced toward the front room. "Where's Pa?"

She spun around and concentrated on stirring the eggs with seemingly more than necessary focus. "Uh. He's in the parlor with Sean. They were talking through some things."

"Doc said I should come in and talk to him?"

"He's just grieving, Honey. He said a few things that… were not like him."

Cade frowned. "He didn't insult Doc, did he?"

"No. No." She shook her head. "Nothing like that." She pierced him with a look. "You should probably just go in and see for yourself. I'll bring in a tray with some food in a few minutes."

Cade stopped just outside the parlor door and swept his hat from his head. He swallowed. The last time he'd been in the room had been to check on Ma the day before yesterday. She'd been lying on the settee with her feet up, another of her headaches pinching her brow. But she'd smiled at him and held out one hand, giving him a squeeze when he'd taken it. She'd asked him then to help her upstairs to her room.

"Ma." He choked on the breathy word and blinked back tears, looking toward the stairs, twisting his hat and crimping the brim all the way around it.

"I just don't know if I can do this, Sean!" His father's cry from inside the parlor brought Cade back to the present.

"I know, Smith. It's going to be hard. But the Lord doesn't ever give us more than we can bear."

"This place… I won't be able to stay here without her. She was everything to me!"

"I know she was. But you have Cade to think of, too."

Pa sniffed. "Cade's a grown man. He doesn't need me."

"He owns half this place."

Cade felt suddenly light headed. He should walk into the room and let them know he was there. But he couldn't make himself move just yet. Surely, Pa wasn't thinking what it sounded like he was thinking.

"I'll give him the first shot to buy my half."

Cade's knees lost their strength, but somehow he stayed on his feet. This ranch was Pa's dream. Every day that Cade could remember he'd spent improving it, changing procedures to ensure some little glitch wouldn't happen again, growing some of the best cattle and breeding the best horses in the entire state. What would Pa do, if not that?

"All I'm saying is that I think you should give yourself a couple weeks before deciding. You just lost your wife this morning. You are in no condition to be making a decision like this right now."

"That *is* the reason I'm making this decision right now. I won't live here for even one day without her. We built this place the first spring after we crossed the Cascades. Cade was just a tyke. All but a couple years of our life together has been here. You know that. It just doesn't feel right to go on as though nothing happened."

They should be talking about funeral arrangements and here Pa was—

Rachel stepped up behind him with a tray.

He glanced at her and she must have seen something on his face because she smiled encouragement. "Let's go in and eat something. We'll all feel better after we get some food into us."

He nodded and pushed the door open holding it wide for

her, then followed her into the room and tossed his hat onto an end table. Sinking down wearily on the settee, he scrubbed his face with his hands. Mechanically, he ate the eggs and oatmeal Rachel placed before him, but no taste registered.

After a few moments Pa cleared his throat and looked over at him. "Cade, we need to talk about a few things now."

Cade sighed. Yes. They did.

A loud banging on the kitchen door jolted Rocky awake the next morning. Who would be knocking on their door at this hour? He snatched up his pants and thrust his legs into them, then snagged his gun belt and swung it around his hips. Boots in one hand and socks in the other, he padded toward the kitchen in his bare feet, tossed them down in a pile on the kitchen floor, and stepped over to open the door.

The Cox boy stood on the other side. "Sorry to disturb you so early, Mr. Jordan. But Doc Martin said it was real important that I bring you this message right away."

Rocky's heart sank in his chest. "Come on in, Son."

"Uh, I still need to go to your brother Sky's place, Sir. So I won't come in."

"Alright." Rocky gripped the frame on either side of the doorway and waited in silence.

The boy shuffled his feet for a moment, causing Rocky's heart to sink even further.

"Uh, it's Mrs. Bennett, Sir. She passed on early this morning. Just a bit ago, Doc said. He said it might be good for you to go out and see Mr. Cade."

Rocky closed his eyes and tightened his grip on the door frame. He pulled in a deep breath and then turned to study the pale gray of the sky. After a moment he realized the boy was still there. "Was that everything he asked you to tell me?"

"Yes, Sir."

"Alright. Thank you. I appreciate you coming out to let us know."

"Yes, Sir." The boy started to turn away, then paused and looked back at him. "Do you believe in heaven, Sir?"

"Yes I do, Son. And if anyone is there, Mrs. Bennett surely is. I've known her since I was just a little boy and she definitely loved the Lord. She's not in pain any longer. It's us who will experience some pain now for awhile."

Danny Cox swallowed. "Yes, Sir. She surely was a kind lady. Last spring when Ma was so sick after Ida was born, Mrs. Bennett, she came over once a week and helped us clean up the place and brought us food."

Rocky smiled softly. "That sounds exactly like something she would have done."

"Yes, Sir." The boy shoved his hands into his pockets. "Well… best I be getting on to your brother's place."

Rocky nodded. He watched the boy for a few seconds, then closed the door, leaned his forehead into it and just stood there staring numbly at the floor. Brenda gone. It was just so hard to fathom.

He lifted his head and forced himself to move. He needed to tell Ria. They would want to go out and express their condolences. He rubbed the muscles at the base of his neck as he made his way back through the kitchen and living room and tapped softly on her door.

For a long moment there was no sound. He tapped again. "Ria?" He kept his voice low, hoping not to disturb the children just yet.

He heard movement inside then, and after a moment the door eased open a few inches. Her hair tangled in a mass of red curls about her face. Blue eyes rounded in sleepy confusion, and face flushed with the brush of sleep, she looked innocent and vulnerable.

And suddenly he ached to hold her. Smith had had so few years with the woman he loved.

He smiled instead, rested one arm against the lintel and reached out to wrap one of the curls around his finger. *Lord, thank you for this wonderful, amazing woman.*

A furrow formed on her brow and she angled her head in question.

The locket that she always wore lay skewed to one side and shimmered in bright contrast against the white fabric at her throat.

"Rocky? What is it?"

He couldn't find his voice just yet. Carefully, though his hand trembled noticeably, he lifted the locket and studied the intricate pattern in the dim morning light, putting off his reply. It didn't look like a cheap trinket. Baxter Cane had said something about this locket. He'd also mentioned the doll. Maybe the man was Victoria's real father, after all. How else would he know about the locket and the doll? Unease pricked at the back of his mind and he stilled. What? A fleeting impression he couldn't pin down discomfited him.

The locket and the doll. Victoria's only possessions from her birth parents.

Victoria's breathing grew shallow. "Something's wrong. What's happened?"

He turned to look at the doll where it still lay on the bedside table. Victoria had said somehow the head had been torn and someone had left a needle in it, as though they'd been trying to sew it back together.

Surely—

Victoria stirred and stepped closer, blocking his vision of the doll as she laid a hand on his cheek. "Just tell me."

He didn't know how to say it other than to just say it. "It's Mrs. Bennett." He swallowed. "She's gone."

"Oh, no! Why she was just… We just…" She gestured to the kitchen where Brenda's empty pie tin still sat on the counter, and tears spilled down her cheeks.

"I know." He felt a sting in his own eyes as he pulled her into his arms. "Cade's going to need someone to talk to this morning. I have to go in to work later, but I'd like for us to swing by there. I imagine Sharyah will cancel classes. The service will probably be this afternoon."

Victoria pulled back and swiped her face with the flats of her fingers. "Okay. I'll get the children up and make a quick breakfast. Then we can head out there."

He nodded, "I'll get the wagon." As Rocky walked toward the barn, his emotions ran the gamut. From love for Victoria, to sorrow for Cade and Smith's loss, to worry for Cade, Smith, Ma, Sharyah and everyone who would be deeply affected by Brenda's death.

And then his thoughts turned back to Baxter Cane, the locket, and the doll.

He needed to do some checking on that man today.

CHAPTER TWENTY-THREE

C ade looked terrible. There was no other way to describe it. Rocky fiddled with his hat as he studied him across the yard, unsure how to talk to the man who'd been his best friend for as long as he could remember.

Ria had gone inside to help Ma prepare Brenda for burial. Sharyah had taken the children into town for a bit.

But Cade hadn't moved from his spot at the corral since they'd pulled into the yard. Actually he'd barely glanced up when they drove in before he'd gone back to staring listlessly toward the horizon, his arms draped across the top rail.

Rocky dusted his hat against his jeans and then headed towards Cade.

He cleared his throat as he stepped up beside him and dropped his hat over the post to their right. He clapped a hand on Cade's shoulder. "I'm so sorry."

Cade acknowledged the gesture with a dip of his chin, then quiet settled between them.

Rocky waited him out, knowing Cade would eventually start talking. He was never one to let silence stretch long unless it was absolutely necessary.

After several moments, Cade's stallion trotted towards them, stopped a few paces off, stretched out its neck and gave a soft whicker. A light breeze lifted the animal's dark mane and ruffled its tail. Rocky never ceased to be amazed by the beautiful creature with its intelligent brown eyes. When Cade made no response, it shook its great head, mane flopping, then backed up a few paces and blew a great gust of air through its nose. Lifting its head, it froze and studied them.

Sighing, Cade rubbed the back of his neck, then stretched his hand out toward the animal. "He knows something isn't right."

Rocky nodded silently as the horse trotted over to receive a good ear scratch from Cade's hand. Cade attentively petted and rubbed, allowing the silence to linger. Finally, he gave the stallion a lump of sugar from his pocket and then slapped it on the neck, sending it loping across the paddock once more.

Angling Rocky a look, Cade rested his head against one hand. "I don't know what we're going to do without her." His voice was low and husky.

"It'll take time, but you'll get it figured out." Rocky watched him closely, willing him to believe the words.

Cade picked at a splinter on the corral rail. "Pa's falling apart…." He swallowed. "He plans to sell the place."

Rocky blinked in surprise. "Really?" Smith's plan was obviously born of grief. The man had poured his life into the Bar B.

Giving a nod, Cade eased out a long breath. "He said he'd sell out to me. But for him to get a fair price, I'd have to take out a loan. I could do that, but I just," he shrugged, "I don't think he should be making these kinds of decisions right now." Methodically, he broke the splinter he'd loosened from the pole into tiny bits. "But he went into town to have Reed write up the paperwork this morning. He says he won't spend even one more night here without Ma."

Rocky scuffed one toe in the soft dirt by his feet. That was rough.

"I'm torn." Cade glanced up at him. "I don't know whether to put my part up for sale, too, and go with Pa to… wherever he's going, or stay here and just let Pa have some time to himself."

"He didn't say where he planned to go?"

He shook his head. "He said he just needed to drift for a while. Clear his head before he decided on the next phase of his life."

Rocky worked his upper lip with his teeth. "When's the service?"

Cade turned his back toward the corral and leaned against the rails, shoulders slumping at the heaviness of the decisions before him. "This afternoon. One o'clock. Pastor Hollybough was by just a bit ago. He tried to talk Pa into staying put and giving himself some time, but Pa wouldn't hear of it."

"Want my opinion?"

Lifting his hat, Cade scrubbed one hand through his hair, and then settled it firmly on his head once more. "Sure." He rested his elbows on a rail and propped one heel on the bottom rung as he leaned back.

"Smith's obviously not thinking straight, right now. It would be a shame for you to sell out, because I think he's going to regret leaving one day. Maybe he does just need a little time to think. If you keep the place, at least he'll have it to come back to when he's ready."

Methodically, Cade scanned each building on their spread. The silence stretched. Then finally, he sighed. "Yeah, I think you're right. I should stay." His throat worked. "Ma would have wanted me to stay. I'll talk to Reed about a loan this afternoon."

Rocky rubbed one hand over his cheek and considered…. He'd never find a better partner than Cade. Still, to offer partnership to him in this hour seemed so… crass. Yet… it would be helping him out. Finally, he said, "I've been saving up, hoping to get a place of my own. How about if I buy out your Dad's half?"

The look of sheer relief that crossed Cade's face set Rocky's hesitation over the offer to rest. "Would you? Dad does so much around here. I'd have to hire someone to help with the work. But if you bought in, well… I know you'd carry your weight."

"It would be an honor to partner with you, but I'd like to talk it over with Victoria before I give you a final decision."

Cade nodded. "Sure. You've no idea how that eases my mind." He held out one hand.

Rocky clasped it. "I'll let you know as soon as I get a chance to talk it over with her."

Victoria stepped out onto the back porch then. She looked their way, defeat cloaking her countenance and Rocky knew that Brenda must be ready for burial. Beside him Cade shifted.

Rocky squeezed his shoulder. "Why don't you ride into town with us?"

Cade nodded. "I'll just tie him," he gestured over his shoulder toward his horse, "to your wagon so you don't have to bring me back out."

"Alright," Rocky agreed, "why don't you get him saddled and I'll get… the wagon ready." It would be better if Cade didn't have to watch them carry Brenda out of the house.

Cade swallowed, blinked hard, and dipped his chin as he dropped one hand on Rocky's shoulder. "Thanks," he said, his voice barely audible. With one last glance at the house, he headed into the barn.

Sky had spent the morning fashioning a casket and Rocky helped him lift it into the back of the wagon and then lay Brenda inside. Smith nailed the lid down, himself, his hands trembling so badly that Rocky feared he would smash his thumb. But he got the task done without incident and then mounted up and reined his horse toward town after Sky.

Rocky's tears nearly overflowed as Cade tied his horse to the tail gate and then crawled into the bed of the wagon and sat down right next to the coffin.

Quietly, he helped Victoria up to the seat and then climbed up to take the reins. The group was very silent as they drove toward the church.

Simon Saunders' stomach growled as he lay on his bed at the boarding house and looked at the key he'd removed from the doll's head. Holding the ends between thumb and forefinger, he studied both sides of it. The head of the key, quite ornate with intricate scroll work, had no distinctive markings of any kind. Nothing to tell him what the key *unlocked*.

With a disgusted grunt, he tossed it down on the table by the bed.

He should be thankful that he was here to look at the key at all, but he worried that he hadn't had time to finish sewing the doll's head back together. He'd almost been finished when he'd heard their buggy pull into the yard and he'd had to leave the doll lying there half-sewn.

He sighed. With any luck, they'd assume one of the children had gotten into it. He'd been careful other than that. He'd hidden behind the house until the husband had gone inside from the barn, then he'd rushed over to return the crow-bar to the tack room and nearly been caught when the man came back out to the stable with the boy to do chores. Thankfully, they hadn't come into the tack room and he'd made his escape once darkness had completely fallen.

Simon tucked his hands behind his head and studied the water stain on the ceiling. He needed to know what this key was to. He had no doubt what he would find once he figured that out. There would be money, and lots of it. But he needed more information. What were his other options?

Mags wouldn't have gone to all the trouble of stripping him of everything that was worth anything, only to throw it all away. No… He knew her. She'd hidden it away so that their daughter would find it one day. And she would have left clues. Clues she would assume he'd never find.

The locket. There had to be more information in the locket.

He needed to figure out a way to get his hands on it.

But first he needed some dinner. He lumbered to his feet. It had been a long time since the measly meal he'd eaten yesterday just before he'd walked out to their farm.

A little stop at the diner, and then he would decide what his next move ought to be.

Hannah squirmed restlessly on the pew, something she would have sharply rebuked one of her young charges for, were they here. *Lawd Jesus*… She hated funerals. The little church was full to overflowing with people from Shiloh and the surrounding community, most of them here because Brenda Bennett had meant so much to them.

Beside her Clarice reached out and gave her a one-armed hug, sniffing back tears.

Hannah sighed. How many quilting bees had they all been

to together? How many church pot-lucks? None of them had thought that Brenda would beat them home to Glory.

Pastor Hollybough closed his encouraging message with prayer and announced that the burying would follow in a few moments outside in the church cemetery.

Her heart clinched as the images of other gaping holes in the ground, ones dug by her own hands, paraded across her memory.

As they waited for Pastor to come back and let them know all was in readiness, everyone sat quietly visiting in the church.

But Hannah couldn't suppress her worry over Cade. Word had spread quickly around town that his Daddy had gone off half-cocked, and she knew that boy would be trying to take on more than he could handle, right now. He needed to give himself some time to grieve.

She lifted her chin to see Cade and Smith over the heads of the crowd.

Just as she'd assumed, Smith was still sitting on the front pew, elbows planted on his knees and hands hanging limply between his legs, staring listlessly at the bouquet of flowers she'd brought from her garden, and Cade was on his feet, shaking people's hands and thanking them for coming. He tried to smile, but she recognized the dazed look on his face. Knew that in the years to come he probably wouldn't remember much of this day other than the numbness.

Pastor Hollybough stepped to the front and gestured the room to silence. "We're ready outside now. I know there are so many of you here who want to pay your last respects to a woman you dearly loved, so I would ask that you all make room for each other out there. It will be a little crowded, but," he smiled softly, "I know it means a lot to Smith and Cade that so many of you came today."

Cade nodded. Smith didn't seem to register the comment.

"After the ceremony outside, there will be some food and refreshments served across the street in the community hall. Smith and Cade have asked me to convey that all are welcome."

With that Pastor stepped down from the pulpit and preceded everyone outside.

As the crowd surged to their feet, Hannah leaned over to whisper in Clarice's ear. "I'll just head over to the hall and make sure all is ready."

"Do you need some help?"

"No." She shook her head. "You go on now, I'll be jus' fine. Won't take me a minute to make sure things is all set over there."

Rocky and Victoria moved down the aisle ahead of her, with the three orphan children just in front of them. Rocky and Victoria appeared to be deep in conversation, and by the way Rocky had one arm wrapped around her shoulders and the way Victoria gazed into his face as she gave her quiet reply, it looked like they may have worked a few things out.

Hannah smiled and angled a glance toward the heavens whispering, "Lawd, You surely is good. Yes, suh, You surely is."

At the back of the church, she parted from the crowd and headed across the street instead of around the back of the building. She couldn't suppress the sigh of relief as she left the cemetery, and the gaping hole now exposed at its center behind.

Ever since that day when she'd had to dig two graves and bury the two people who'd meant the most to her in this life, putting people in the ground was something she tried to avoid if at all possible.

She hurried down the boardwalk, her boots clicking out a hollow rhythm. It wouldn't be long before everyone would be over. She mentally ticked off the things she would need to do as she fumbled for the center's key in her reticule. "Where *is* that key?" She peered into the dark depths of the bag.

Just ahead of her the café door opened and she collided with a man coming out.

"Oh, I'm so sor—" She felt all the blood drain from her face. The man before her was one she'd hoped to never see again, one she'd prayed to exorcise from her dreams at night, one who could only bode ill will wherever he went.

"Huh." He grunted. "Watch where you're going, darkie."

And with that he gave her a wide birth and strode away.

For one long moment Hannah simply stood there, frozen, staring after him. He hadn't recognized her? The man turned right and disappeared from sight around the corner of the mercantile without so much as a backward glance, but there was no doubt in her mind that he was indeed Simon Saunders.

Hannah's heart gave one giant thud. And then another. Her breaths came in short gasps. Dark spots swirled in her vision. The *thwack* of her reticule hitting the boardwalk jolted her back to her senses. "Oh Lawd Jesus!" she whispered, "He done found her!" Bending, she snatched up the bag and hurried off down the boardwalk.

CHAPTER TWENTY-FOUR

Simon rounded the corner of the mercantile and burst into a sprint, his heart hammering like a judge's gavel in an unruly court. She had recognized him. Her jaw had dropped and a look of shock had etched her features for just a split second. It had taken him several moments to realize who the black woman he'd just bumped into was, and then it had been all he could do to walk casually down the street as though he hadn't a care in the world.

Turning onto Second Street, he bolted up the boardinghouse steps to his room. He needed to gather his things and quickly. He only had moments to come up with a plan and it would now have to be bold and daring or all his years of hunting and searching would come to naught.

Snatching up his valise, he jerked open the dresser drawers and tossed his clothes inside. From under the bed he pulled his gun-belt and slung it around his waist. He wouldn't need his disguise now. With luck he'd be out of town by dusk. Pulling the clerical collar from around his neck he threw it into the suit case and undid the top button on his shirt splaying the buttons and feeling like he could finally breathe for the first time in days.

He picked up the key on the nightstand and shoved it in his pocket as he glanced around the room and then snatched up his bag. Giving a low snort, he turned and stalked down the hall without a backward glance.

One valise, all he had to his name, seemed a paltry amount of possessions for a man of his age.

But if things went as planned, that was about to change. A jolt of sheer excitement surged through him. After all these years... today, today was *the* day.

As the members of Brenda's family approached the grave to sprinkle dirt on her coffin Rocky squeezed the back of Victoria's neck with one hand and leaned over to whisper in her ear. "I'm going to slip away to the office. Could you please go talk to Sharyah? I know she is taking this hard."

Victoria nodded, her fingers fiddling with the pendant at her throat as she stared down at the coffin in the earth.

He gave her another gentle squeeze. "She's in a better place."

She swallowed. "I know."

"When you get done at the hall have Jimmy drive to the office. I should be able to get away a little early tonight so we can all go home together."

"Okay." She gave him a tremulous smile, tears welling up in her eyes.

He sighed, knowing how she felt. He glanced at Cade and Smith, once more. *Lord, see them through.*

Jimmy peered around Victoria. "Can't I come with you?" Pleading eyes begged not to be left with the women folk.

But someone needed to be there to drive Victoria and the girls when the time came.

Rocky opened his mouth to protest but Victoria laid a hand on his arm. "He could walk back over to the hall to get us a little later. Why don't you let him come with you for a few minutes?"

Rocky settled his gaze on the boy and made a split-second decision. "Alright." He glanced back at Victoria. "See you tonight." Resettling his hat, he gestured for Jimmy to follow him as he headed into town.

"Yes!" he heard Jimmy's characteristic exclamation of happiness and allowed a grin to tug at the corners of his mouth. Jimmy stretched his stride out to match his own longer one and Rocky subtly slowed his gait to allow the boy to keep up without getting winded.

"Pa and Sky have been keeping the jailhouse running all week while I took some time to get to know you all, so today it's my turn." He gave the boy a sideways glance. "You any good at scrubbing out jail cells?"

Jimmy's features tightened and by the look on his face Rocky could tell he hadn't counted on being put to work. He held back a chuckle. A little hard work never hurt a boy, but...

"Tell you what," he dropped one hand onto Jimmy's shoulder and held out a nickel, "why don't you take this over to the mercantile and get yourself a piece of hard candy from the jar on the front counter. Grab a couple for the girls too. Then meet me back at the jail ready to work, alright?"

"Yes, Sir!" Jimmy snatched the coin and darted off across the street.

Rocky resettled his hat as he watched the boy's departure. Jimmy leapt from the road to the boardwalk without touching a single step and Rocky grinned. Wasn't so long ago that he and Cade would have responded just the same way had someone done something similar for them.

Just as Jimmy disappeared inside the mercantile, Rocky felt the cold press of metal against the back of his neck. He froze in his tracks, his hands lifting to shoulder height by instinct.

"Good thinking. Now lower your hands nice and slow and undo your gun." The voice was all too familiar. *Baxter Cane.*

Rocky complied and Baxter, or whatever his name was, took the belt from him when he held it off to one side.

"Good. Quickly, now. Into the alley."

Rocky's eyes dropped shut for just a breath, and then he studied the length of the town. The street was deserted with everyone still at the funeral. But if he stepped into the alley he'd have absolutely no chance at anyone seeing him. He remained where he stood.

Baxter jabbed the gun again. "I said move!" His voice, while low, held a note of desperation.

"I think I'll stay out in the open. You're less likely to try and kill me out here where there could be people watching us from any one of those windows." Rocky flicked his fingers in the direction of the buildings across the street, but was careful to keep his hands raised.

"Fine you want to do this your way? That your boy who just went into the mercantile? Be a shame if something were to happen to him the moment he came out. Something like having a bullet split open his skull."

Rocky clenched his teeth, the muscle in his jaw working in and out, even as he turned toward the alley in compliance.

"I thought you might see things my way. Now we are going down the alley all the way to the end. And no sudden moves or your brain will no longer be able to communicate with the rest of you." The last statement was emphasized with a sharp jab of the pistol.

As Baxter prodded him along, Rocky was careful to keep his hands plainly visible. He wracked his mind for a way of escape, but Baxter kept the pistol pressed firmly to the back of his neck. His knife was in his boot, but there was no way to get it just yet. He'd have to bide his time.

"You'll never get away with this, Cane." He needed to keep the man talking. That would be his best shot at catching him off guard.

"Shut your trap." Baxter peered out onto the street and glanced both ways.

Rocky grimaced at this bad luck. Not a soul in sight.

But just then a shout rose from just behind. "Hey!"

That was Jimmy. Rocky felt his first jolt of terror since this ordeal began even as both he and Cane spun around as one. *No no no no.*

Jimmy's arms arched in mid-swing with a thick stout stick, but Baxter, surprisingly quick on his feet for a man of his size, stepped inside the swing and jammed the barrel of his pistol up under Jimmy's chin. "Drop it!" He glanced over his shoulder. "Jordan, one move and the kid loses his head."

Jimmy went wide-eyed and slowly dropped the stick.

Rocky's breath came in short spurts. His hands were still up near his shoulders. Everything had happened in a split second.

His knees went weak with thankfulness that Jimmy was alright. *For now.* "I'm not moving, Cane." He assessed Jimmy. Except for the terror radiating from his face, he appeared fine. "We're going to be alright, Jim. Just do what he says."

Jimmy gave a barely perceptible nod.

"Good, now let's go." Baxter turned them once more toward the street and their wagon hitched just behind the livery a few buildings down from the office.

Victoria forced herself to sit next to ChristyAnne and Damera and not pace the room. Where could Jimmy be? Surely Rocky would have sent him over to get them by now. Everyone had left the hall but Pastor and Mrs. Hollybough, who were only waiting around out of politeness, and it was getting a little embarrassing.

Hannah had been strangely absent from the after-funeral gathering and Victoria wondered what had happened to keep her away. When everyone had arrived from the graveside, the door to the hall had been propped open and the coffee had been made, so she knew Hannah had been here for at least a little while. But it wasn't like her to disappear without telling anyone where she was going.

ChristyAnne shifted on her chair and Damera's head nodded off to one side for the third time.

Finally, Victoria stood. "You know what? We'll just walk on over to the Sheriff's office. It's only a couple of blocks. I'm sure Rocky has Jimmy doing a chore for him and they've both simply lost track of the time." She bent and gathered Damera into her arms.

The little girl sighed, wrapped her arms around Victoria, pillowed her head on one shoulder, and promptly started snoring in her ear.

Victoria grinned and settled her into a more comfortable position. "ChristyAnne, get the pot of soup, would you?" She turned to the Hollyboughs. "I'm so sorry to have kept you. I know you've had a very long day helping the Bennetts."

Mrs. Hollybough waved a hand and rubbed circles on Damera's back. "Don't you worry about a thing, dear. You were a big help with the clean up, here."

"Glad to help." Victoria smiled. "I guess we'll see you in church on Sunday. And please let me know if there is any other way we can be of assistance to the Bennetts."

She hurried the girls to where they had left the wagon before the funeral. She would just drive it over to the Sheriff's office so that when Rocky was ready they could all get right home. But when she rounded the corner of the livery their wagon wasn't there. "Strange." Something wasn't right. An uneasiness settled in the pit of her stomach.

ChristyAnne looked at her with a worried little frown.

She smiled and hoped it didn't look as stiff as it felt. "Don't worry, honey. I'm sure everything is fine."

By the time they arrived at the sheriff's office, she was ready to hand Damera's dead-asleep-weight off to Rocky, but she only found Hannah, pacing the walk in front of the locked door.

"Hannah? I wondered where you were. Have you seen Rocky or Jimmy?"

"Oh, Lawd Almighty!" Hannah exclaimed. "He ain't with you? I was hopin' he was with you. I been lookin' all over town and when I couldn't find him I came and have been waitin' here for him. I put the coffee on over at the hall and then I set straight to lookin' for him. I arrived here jus' a few moments after I left the funeral and Rocky never—he never come. When's the last time you seen him?"

Uneasiness gripped Victoria. She bent and eased Damera down onto the bench to one side of the office door. "Just after the burial. He said he was coming to the office. I don't know where he could be. Jimmy was with him. He said he'd send Jimmy over to get us from the hall, but he never arrived."

Hannah stepped closer to the wall behind her, darting a look up and down the street and seeming to study every shadow.

The taste of metallic fear prickled Victoria's tongue. "What's going on, Hannah?" She swallowed.

Without answering Hannah bent, lifted Damera into her ample arms, and marched off down the boardwalk.

"Hannah!?" Victoria trotted after her, ChristyAnne on her heels. "You are scaring me witless. What is the matter?"

Hannah paused in front of the bakery and jerked open the door. "Inside, hurry now! Won't do if he sees me talkin' to you."

"What are you—"

"Inside!" She flapped her hand as best she could with the child in her arms and tossed a glance over her shoulder, scanning the street once more.

Victoria had never seen Hannah like this. Her fear radiated like heat waves. The fact that it was level-headed, calm, ever-in-control, Hannah acting this way…. Victoria swallowed and pushed past her, pulling ChristyAnne through the door behind her.

Mr. Jonas looked up from the table behind the counter where he was wrist deep in a batch of bread dough. "Hello, ladies. Victoria, with the funeral and all I didn't expect you'd be bringing your rolls today, so I'm making some of my own."

His words barely registered, so deep was her concern over Hannah's strange behavior. "Oh, I didn't bring any bread, Mr. Jonas. We're just," she glanced over her shoulder at Hannah and then out the window before turning to face him again, "stepping in from outside to visit for a few moments. I hope that's alright?"

"Certainly! Certainly." He gestured with the ball of dough to indicate they had the place to themselves and then went back to kneading.

Lowering her voice, Victoria turned back to Hannah. "So, what is it? Why weren't you over at the hall for the gathering?"

Hannah waved away the question. "I need to talk to Rocky. Do you have any idea where he could be?"

"No." Victoria pressed a hand to her chest. "What did you need to talk to him about?"

Hannah pinched the bridge of her nose and let out a long breath of air. And when she opened her eyes they were full of so much pain, Victoria took a step back.

"You listen now, and you listen good. I cain't tell you the whole story right now. And I only gots time to say this but once." She bent forward and peered emphatically into Victoria's face. "I think you might be in danger. Maybe Rocky and Jimmy too, and we gots to get some help."

The room turned dark around the edges and started to swirl, but Victoria gave her head a little shake and pulled in a long breath.

Rocky in danger? Not now. Not again. Just when she'd decided to try to trust again. Just when Rocky had convinced her that maybe God didn't have it out for her, but had good in mind for her…. She pressed her fingers to her temples, and sighed. "I'm listening."

"There's a man in town. A bad man that I used to know and I got reason to believe he might want to hurt you."

"Me?!" Victoria clutched the pendant at her throat, her gaze darting to ChristyAnne and Damera still in Hannah's arms. "Why would someone want to hurt me?"

Would they hurt the children too? Where would the children end up if something were to happen to her?

Hannah dismissed the shock in Victoria's tone with a wave of her hand as she bent closer. "Listen now. We gots to get to Sean's house and give him a message. Simon Saunders is in town. We'll just tell him that and tell him to come to the office and look through his wanted posters." Reaching out one hand, Hannah gave her shoulder a jolting shake. "Come on, now. Don't you pass out on ol' Hannah."

Victoria *zinged* the pendant on its chain, irritation tightening her shoulders. "I'm not going to pass out."

"Good." Reaching over, Hannah pressed one hand to ChristyAnne's back and guided her to the door, but her gaze never left Victoria. "Let's go then. My buggy is next to the church. We'll talk to Sean and get this all sorted out."

"Okay." Victoria stared out the window. Her feet felt rooted to the floor.

Impatiently, Hannah nudged her to the door.

Dust from a passing wagon tickled her nose as she stepped out after Hannah and scanned in both directions. She didn't even know who she was looking for!

Her head lolling on Hannah's shoulder, Damera had not a care in the world. Victoria envied her that.

Hannah bustled as fast as she could, carrying the sound-asleep child.

Victoria kept one hand to ChristyAnne's back, her gaze roving the town. The lid on the soup pot gave a clank every once in a while when the girl was jolted by an uneven place in the boardwalk. The only other sound that broke the late afternoon stillness was the hollow *thunk* of their shoes and the creaking of Hannah's buggy as they all climbed aboard and headed it down the road to Sean and Rachel's place.

Rachel answered the door within moments of their fervent knock and after one glance took a step back, one hand going to her throat. "Oh my. What is it?"

Hannah tossed a look over her shoulder. "Can we come in?"

"Certainly." Rachel stepped back out of the way, gesturing them inside.

Hannah didn't waste any time. She pushed the door shut and said, "We needs to speak to Sean, please."

Rachel fidgeted. "He's not here. He and Sky stayed after the funeral to help finish the burying and then planned to ride out to the Bennett place to check on Cade. Smith rode out of town as soon as the service finished."

Hannah pushed Damera into Rachel's arms. "Can Victoria and the girls stay here with you a while?"

Rachel blinked and took the little girl purely by instinct. "Of course."

Victoria was already shaking her head before Hannah even turned around. She willed strength into her weak knees and stood her ground. "I'm not staying here. Not when Rocky might be in danger! And certainly not when you haven't even told me what this is all about!"

"Rocky's in danger?" Rachel gasped.

Hannah gave Rachel a quick side-arm hug of assurance then stepped up in front of Victoria and framed her face with her large palms. "Chil', I promised your Mama, the one what give birth to you, thet I'd take care o' you. And I' done my bes'. But I cain't do that with this man around. He after you. You gots to stay safe!"

Victoria felt the shock wash over her, even as she searched Hannah's face trying to reassure herself of what she'd just heard. "You knew my mother? My real mother?"

Hannah's dark eyes softened as she nodded. "I did. And I'm gonna tell you all about her, just as soon as ever I can. But right now, I need you to stay here." She stepped back and gave Victoria the look that meant she would brook no nonsense, the same look she'd used on Victoria countless times when she was a little girl.

But this time there were bigger stakes on the line. "Jimmy and Rocky are—" Victoria threw her hands up in the air, "who knows where! I can't stand by while Jimmy and the man I love most in the world are in danger!" Realizing what she'd just said, her face flamed and she peered over at Rachel.

Rachel only adjusted Damera in her arms and gave her a gentle smile. "I know just how you feel, dear. But I really think it's better that we let the men handle these things. Let Hannah go find Sean and Sky, and you stay here with me." Without waiting for Victoria's reply she turned to ChristyAnne. "Would you like to help me lay Damera down and then we can make dinner?"

ChristyAnne nodded but no one moved.

Defeat washed over Victoria, yet she couldn't help but admire Rachel's calm demeanor. How could she remain so self-assured when her husband would be headed off into a dangerous situation? She studied the woman for a moment and Rachel seemed to read her mind.

"I learned a long time ago, honey, to put Sean, and the boys, in God's hands. His Word says He loves them even more than I ever could and I have to trust that God knows what He's doing. I'd hate to walk through this life without Sean. But if God asked me to, I know He'd give me the strength to make it through."

With that she walked down the hall, head held serenely,

ChristyAnne trailing after her. Realizing that Hannah was headed down the steps, Victoria scrambled out the door and trotted after her.

"Hannah, please, let me come with you. I just want to know Rocky is safe."

"Listen now," Hannah spun towards her and held out one finger. "You stay here and do what your mother-in-law says. Jus' pray and put thet boy and thet man o' yours in the Lawd's hands. I promise to let you know what's happening just as soon as I find out. Meantime, you'll be much safer here with Rachel and the girls. I'm going straight to get Sean and Sky. They some of the best trackers this side o' the Mississippi and they gonna find Rocky. Jimmy, too."

Shoulders slumped, Victoria stood at the bottom of the steps for a long time, watching until Hannah's buggy disappeared at the far end of town.

Finally, she tilted her face toward the sky and allowed the sun to warm her face. *Lord, everyone keeps telling me just to put this in Your hands. Rocky said I should look at what you've done for me, and not what you've done to me, but I have to confess, I'm having a hard time doing that. At the same time, I keep realizing, I have no one else to turn to. Who else is there to help me? Only You can do that. Help me to see that table you've prepared before me in this instance.*

Lifting her skirts, she turned to mount the steps. That's when she heard the distinct cock of a pistol.

★

CHAPTER TWENTY-FIVE

Victoria stiffened and turned to see Baxter Cane leaning against the corner of the house at the end of the porch, his gun trained on her and one finger pressed over his lips. She couldn't help the small gasp that escaped as her heart jolted into a rapid rhythm.

He grinned and whispered, "Hello there darlin'! Why don't you join me over this way." The gun never wavered as he gestured her toward him.

Victoria darted a glance toward the open door into the house. Rachel had taken Damera to the back to lay her down and ChristyAnne had followed her, but surely they would be back at any moment. If she could stall him for a bit, maybe they would see her out here and notice something amiss. Then again, if that happened someone was likely to get hurt. Without another thought she lifted her skirts and stepped toward him.

His clerical suit had been replaced with denim pants and a greasy flannel shirt that buttoned over his bulging middle. Thick black suspenders cut a wide swath across each shoulder. And his hair, which had before been so carefully combed, now stood in wild disarray around his head.

The distance between them was only a few paces, and the moment she got close, he grabbed her arm and thrust the point of the gun into her ribs.

"Not a word now. I'll shoot the first person that comes out after us!"

He hustled her down the side of the house and within a few steps they were behind the chicken coop and hidden from view of the house. A long bushy hedge fenced the yard from the back of the chicken coop keeping them hidden, and as they came out at the corner, she saw the missing wagon. Giving her a rough shove, Baxter forced her toward the wagon bed. "Get in."

She scrabbled over the wheel well, fighting her skirts and trembling legs until she finally made it up into the bed. A canvas tarp covered two odd lumps, one large and one smaller, on the wagon floor. She gasped, eyes widening in fear as she immediately realized it must be Rocky and Jimmy, and started to turn. But Baxter clamped a damp rag over her mouth and nose and pinned her roughly to his chest.

A sickly sweet stench filled her nostrils. She struggled, clutching at his smothering hand, his arm, trying to throw her elbow into his ribs, but to no avail.

Beneath them the wagon shifted as the horses, agitated by the kafuffle, shied and snorted.

As he lost his balance Baxter cursed and they both fell. Victoria's head smashed into the wagon seat, but, oddly, she felt nothing.

"Lie still you little—"

She made one more effort to push the man away, but her limbs would not respond. They were weighted – heavy and sluggish. The heaviness grew, until the leaden leaching even pulled at her vision and all went black.

Rocky came to with a groan. He rolled his head from side to side assessing the pain that pulsed in his temples.

He'd had worse, he decided. Where was he?

Slitting his eyes, he winced at the invasion of light, closed them for a moment, then tried again. His vision blurred, but he blinked hard and forced himself to focus. His head was hanging and the plank floor beneath his boots was the first thing he saw.

In a house.

Pain rippled through him. He tried to move his legs, but realized they were tied to the chair legs, likewise his wrists to the armrests, and his chest to the backrest. A rope, wrapped around his head, bit into the corners of his mouth and effectively gagged him.

Jimmy lay in a heap on the floor to his right, hands and feet bound and a similar gag between his teeth. But his chest rose and fell rhythmically and he appeared otherwise unhurt.

Slowly, Rocky lifted his head, every muscle in his neck and back protesting at the movement. He must have sat there unconscious for quite some time. He scanned the room and realized he was in a small cabin of some sort. The room was dim, its only light filtering through a dirty windowpane just above him and to his right.

Baxter Cane sat across from him, tilted back against the wall, the front two legs of his chair a good six inches off the ground. His Colt lay across his lap and a smirk flattened his lips. "Not so tough now, are you?" He blew a ring of smoke toward the ceiling and crushed the butt on the arm of the chair tossing it onto the floor by Jimmy's head.

Rocky tilted his head and looked away, trying to push back a throbbing headache and remember what had happened.

Town.

Baxter taking him at gunpoint.

Jimmy trying to rescue him with a stick wielded as a club.

The wagon behind the livery.

The drive out behind Ma and Dad's house.

He remembered pulling the wagon to a stop, but nothing after that.

Cane must have knocked him out and tied him to this chair.

What did the man want with him?

Cane's chair thumped to the floor and he stood. "Bet you're wondering why you're here. You didn't believe me the other day, but your wife really is my daughter. And she's got something I need. So…," Cane grinned at him, "now we wait for her to regain consciousness and tell me what I need to know." He flipped a gesture just to Rocky's left and he glanced over.

His stomach pitched.

Victoria, tied to a chair in much the same manner he was except for the gag, sat with her head canted off to one side her mouth hanging open slightly and a trickle of blood oozing down her cheek from a nasty gaping gash above one eye. Her mass of curls had come loose from their pins and cascaded around her in tangled disarray.

Realizing how vulnerable she was, Rocky's pulse spiked. His jaw clenched and he strained against his bonds.

Cane chuckled at his helplessness and lit another cigarette. "Oh, she'll be fine. She'll come around in a few minutes. And if she gives me what I want, I might even walk away and let you all live. Course, you'll only live if someone shows up to find you." He winked and pulled in a long drag, the tip of his cigarette glowing red. "From what I can tell this old place has been abandoned for quite some time."

They must be in the old Chauvers' place a few miles out of town. Chauvers had given up after only one winter and gone back east. Coming here was a mistake on Cane's part. Old abandoned buildings would be some of the first places Pa, Sky, and Cade would look for them. Still, he had to keep them all alive until then.

Rocky bit down hard on the rope and gripped the arms of the chair, fury trembling through him as he watched the man pace the room. Taking a calming breath, he tried to assess his options. Earlier, with Cane on the alert and his gun pointed at him, he hadn't had a chance at escape. But now that he was tied up, Cane would let down his guard. He just needed to put himself in the position to take advantage of the inattention when it came.

So help him, if the man so much as laid one hand on Victoria! He jolted, thumping the chair on the floor in frustration.

"Hey!" Cane leveled the revolver at him. "Sit still!"

Victoria moaned and her eyes fluttered open. For a moment she held his gaze without recognition. Then she blinked and jerked her head upright. Her eyes widened before she gasped and snapped them shut against apparent pain.

Helplessness washed over Rocky. *God, get us through this*!

"Well! See there? I told you she'd come around." Baxter lifted her chin and slapped her cheeks. "Come on. Wake up."

Victoria winced, trying to pull away from the man to no avail and Rocky growled, straining at his bonds, once more.

Baxter chuckled and tisked, shaking a finger at Rocky. "Don't get yourself too worked up, now. The fun's just about to begin."

Hannah found Sky and Sean out at the Bennett place helping Cade do his evening chores and as soon as she told them that Rocky and Jimmy were missing all three men quickly accompanied her back to town. On the way she told them about Simon Saunders and what he'd done to her mistress years ago. They looked grim at that news.

Cade was the one to find Rocky's footprints in the alley first. And when they followed the trail to the back of the livery and realized Jimmy had apparently confronted them and also been taken, a chill raced down Hannah's spine.

They followed the trail toward the edge of town, but it wasn't until they saw Rachel running toward them down the road that Hannah felt her skin prickle with a dreaded premonition.

She leapt from the wagon and raced to meet her.

"Victoria's gone!" Rachel pushed her palm to her forehead. "I took the girls upstairs to lay Damera down and when I got back the front door was open and Victoria was nowhere to be found!"

"Oh, Lawd Jesus!" Hannah's arms trembled even as she pulled Rachel into an embrace. "Oh, Lawd. Oh, Lawd."

The men all looked at each other.

"He had to have been at the house," Sky said.

The other two nodded.

Sean turned to the women. "You two go back to the house and be with the girls. We'll look around the yard and see what we can find."

Victoria had never felt so terrified in all her life. She watched as Baxter Cane sauntered toward a table that held an array of knives, set his gun down, and selected one with a six inch blade. Scraping his thumb across the sharp edge, he eyed her.

She swallowed and darted a glance toward Rocky. Real fear tightened his face and that scared her even more.

They had to get away! But how?

She tested the strength of the ropes tying her to the chair, but there was no give. One of the ropes around her ankle was so tight she couldn't feel her foot.

"Now. Here's what's going to happen."

Victoria was surprised when Baxter stepped over beside Rocky, instead of coming toward her with the knife. But at the look of relief that crossed Rocky's face, she felt the first stirrings of despair. The man clearly thought she had some information he needed and planned to torture Rocky until she told him what it was. "I'll tell you whatever you need to know. Just, please, put the knife down." Her mouth felt thick and dry, like it was packed with cotton. She pleaded with her eyes.

He chuckled. "You are so much like your mother was."

So her mother was dead? While that felt like a mule kick to the stomach, it did not surprise her. She had assumed as much from what Hannah had said. The next thought that registered was the fact that her own father was torturing them. A man whose blood flowed in her own veins! And yet somehow it didn't matter anymore. Rocky was right. She was nothing like this man. Just because he was her father didn't mean she was a bad person. She had her own choices to make. The relief of that realization brought a smile to her face. "That sounds like a compliment. At least I'm not like you."

He took two swift strides and backhanded her, knocking her over, chair and all. Her head bounced off the floor with a painful thud and the room went black for a moment. From far away she heard Rocky roar and at the same moment she realized one of her ankle ties had slipped over the end of the chair's leg, and her ankle, while it still had the piece of rope around it, was now free.

Baxter leaned over her, jowls jiggling and eyes wild with rage. Grabbing the rope that wrapped around her chest with one hand, he hauled her upright again and pressed the tip of the blade under her chin as he glowered into her face. "Don't you *ever* speak to me that way again." His breath, hot and fetid, made her want to gag.

She turned her face away and tucked her foot back under her skirts where he wouldn't be able to see it. She wondered about her mother. What had the woman seen in this man? "What is it you want, exactly?" At least he was near her now and not near Rocky who she could see just past the man's side. Jimmy had come to and scooted closer to Rocky. His hands were tied in front of him and his feet were bound together but he was blessedly alive.

Baxter stepped back and wiped the corner of his mouth with the back of one hand. "When she gave you away your mother gave you a locket. Hand it here." He held out a meaty palm.

"It's around my neck. You'll have to untie my hands."

He snorted. "Not likely." He reached one hand under her hair and to the back of her neck where he found the chain and gave it a jerk.

She felt a sharp pain as the chain snapped and pressed back the threatening tears. She'd worn that locket every day of her life since she could remember. The one thing beautiful about her past.

Baxter turned and paced past Jimmy and Rocky. He didn't even glance their way. He took the locket to a table against the far wall and laid it out, opening the pendant and examining it carefully.

Jimmy bent his feet up by his side and eased over onto his knees. His gaze fixed on Baxter Cane's back, he worked his hands around until he could slip the fingers of one into his pocket. A grin lit his face as he pulled free his pocket knife.

Victoria felt her heart rate climb on the wings of hope even as it hammered with fear. If Baxter caught him with that he would kill him. She shook her head at him, but Jimmy ignored her and pulled open the blade.

She turned her attention back to their captor, lest she draw his attention to the boy.

Baxter used the tip of one of his knives to pry the daguerreotype of her mother out of the locket and gave a grunt of satisfaction as a small square of paper fluttered to the floor. He laid aside his knife and unfolded the small square, smoothing the wrinkles with a few swipes against the corner of the table. While it wasn't very big, both sides of the thin onion skin paper were filled with a flowing scrawl.

Victoria blinked at it. All these years she'd had that in the locket and she'd never even thought to lift the picture and look behind it.

Baxter scanned the words and then slammed it against the table's surface with his palm. "This tells me nothing!" he ground out. He stormed toward her and bent down until they were at eye level. "Where's the money!?"

Victoria frowned. "What money?"

He shook the paper in her face. "The money!" Stomping back to the table he snatched up something and then marched back to pause before her. Between his thumb and forefinger he held aloft a key. "This key was in that doll's head. It goes to something! What does it go to?"

She gasped. "You were the one who— You? The doll?" She darted a glance at Rocky but he was distracted with Jimmy, who had slipped his knife under one of the ropes around Rocky's ankles and was working to cut through it. She immediately looked away so as not to draw Baxter's attention to them. "I—I don't know anything about any money."

He cursed and backhanded her again.

This time she saw the blow coming and was able to move her head enough that it glanced off her cheek and she didn't crash to the floor. But the pain made her gasp and for a moment she saw double.

"I guess you need a little more persuading." Baxter started to turn around.

He was going to see Rocky and Jimmy! "Wait."

He froze studying her, and she swallowed away the coppery taste of blood, taking her time, yet trying to think quickly, but to no avail, the room gyrated in an uneven dance and she couldn't seem to focus on any one spot.

"Well?"

"If I tell you where the money is, do you promise to walk away and leave us alone?" Dare she lie to the man? If she could just get them out of this situation surely Rocky, Sean, Cade and Sky could track him down and arrest him. But where should she say the money was? She had no idea what type of lock that key went to.

But in that moment Jimmy dropped back to the floor and Rocky stood, lifting the chair by the one hand that was still strapped to its arm. Baxter heard the sound and started to turn, but Rocky only had to take one long stride before he swung the chair with all his might. It crashed across Baxter's shoulders and upper back, splintering into pieces that flew in every direction.

Baxter merely grunted and turned to face Rocky, fists raised. Quickly he stepped in and thrust a punch to Rocky's injured shoulder.

Rocky hissed in pain and dodged back. He was free from the burden of most of the chair's weight, now. But the arm rest and two splintered spindles still dangled from his right wrist. He flipped it up into his hand like a club, leapt forward, and jabbed the end of it into Cane's solar plexus then followed that up with a left jab to his face and danced back out of his reach before the man could retaliate.

Cane gasped for air, but kept his hands up and at the ready.

They circled in the middle of the room, eyeing each other warily.

And then, Baxter Cane dodged in and swung an uppercut toward Rocky's chin.

Rocky feinted left, and Cane's punch skimmed harmlessly by his face. Rocky took advantage of the man's now unprotected torso and jabbed him with the armrest twice in quick succession.

Baxter stumbled back, gasping for air, and Victoria, seeing him coming, extended her foot into his path. He tripped over it with a cry of surprise and fell flat on his back. He groaned audibly and then his head slumped over to one side.

For a heartbeat, no one moved as they all stared at the man

on the floor. Then Rocky, still breathing heavily from the fight, surged forward, and bent over the man to feel for a pulse.

As soon as Rocky's fingers touched Cane's throat, the man's eyes snapped open. With lightening speed his fists smashed into both sides of Rocky's momentarily unprotected face.

Victoria gasped. "Rocky!"

Rocky shook his head and stumbled sideways.

Cane's knees curled in towards his chest and with a hard kick to the middle of Rocky's torso, he launched him backwards across the room.

The entire frame of the little cabin shook violently as Rocky crashed into the log wall and slid toward the floor.

Cane was on top of him in a heartbeat, fists pummeling mercilessly.

Rocky's head snapped back and forth like a flag in a strong wind.

"Rocky!" Victoria screamed again. And that's when she saw Jimmy. He had managed to cut himself free and now ran across the room with a leg from Rocky's broken chair above his head.

Cane was too busy with Rocky to notice the boy.

With a scream of wild cougar proportions, Jimmy brought the wooden leg down over Cane's back. The wood splintered into a blur of shattered pieces, but Cane only grunted and spun away from Rocky to focus on the boy.

The distraction was all Rocky needed. With Cane's attention on Jimmy, Rocky gripped the broken armrest still strapped to his wrist and swung at Cane's head with all his might.

There was a hollow thunk, as the rounded end connected with his temple, and then the man slumped over onto the floor.

Scrambling to his feet, Rocky rolled the man onto his stomach and pinned him down with one knee. For a moment he shook his head and pressed his fingers and thumb against his eyes, blinking as though to shake off a fog. Then he fumbled with the rope still keeping the armrest tied around his wrist, keeping a wary eye on Cane. But the man showed no signs of having any fight remaining.

Victoria slumped in relief.

It took Rocky only a few seconds to free himself and he didn't waste any time using his own ropes to bind the man's hands and feet.

Just as he was finishing that task there came a call from outside. "Hello the house!"

Rocky chuckled and glanced at Jimmy. "Get the door, would you son?"

Jimmy jogged across the room and jerked open the door.

Sean, Sky and Cade stepped inside, guns drawn and wary.

With Cane tied up, Rocky sank back onto the floor. "Nice timing fellas." A weary grin stretched his lips as he leaned his back against the wall. "You arrive just when Jimmy and I finally have things under control." He met Victoria's gaze across the room and slowly his smile faded. Lurching to his feet, he crossed to her.

At the sight of everyone okay and the unconscious man on the floor, Sky, Sean, and Cade holstered their guns. Sky squatted down in front of Jimmy checking him over, and Sean and Cade hauled Baxter up between them and began to drag him out the door, but Victoria never took her focus off Rocky.

He scanned the plains of her face, then reached out and ever so gently, like the brush of a butterfly wing, skimmed his fingers over her swollen cheek bone. "You okay?"

She nodded, studying his left eye which was swelling so that he wouldn't be able to see out of it soon.

His fingers slid back into her hair. "I'm so sorry."

Her breath escaped on a huff. "I'm the one that should be sorry."

He shook his head and touched her chin. "This is not your fault."

A dark stain spread across his shoulder. His wound must have opened up. "Your shoulder is bleeding."

His attention never left her face as he nodded. "I'll be fine."

She wanted nothing more than to be in his arms. "Can you untie me?"

In a flash he was down on his knees and working on the knots. "Of course. Sorry." And when he had her free he pulled her into a gentle embrace.

She sank into his strength with a sigh. Then reached out an arm to gather Jimmy, who was hovering nearby, close. *Thank you, Lord.*

CHAPTER TWENTY-SIX

Later that evening, with Baxter Cane safely behind bars, everyone gathered around the table at Sean and Rachel's place. Mama and Doc were there and ChristyAnne had shyly inserted herself between them. Damera sat on Rocky's lap, her tousled head resting back against his shoulder. Sky was down at the jail, but Brooke sat to Victoria's right and Sharyah, a little more quiet than usual, sat at the end of the table talking in low tones with Jimmy.

Hannah had left one of her older girls in charge at the orphanage and had shared dinner with them. She'd promised Victoria the story of how she happened to know Baxter Cane and now with dinner done and coffee before all the adults, everyone settled in to listen to her story.

Hannah twisted her mug on the table, then glanced up and met Victoria's gaze. "Long time ago, I used to be a slave to a rich family back east. The man what owned that plantation was your grand-daddy."

Victoria felt her jaw go slack.

Hannah waved a hand. "I know. I know. I shoulda tol' you a long time ago. But there's so much pain there that I thought it best to leave you think what you may for a few more years. But today...well, when I saw the man who, well the man who should have been a daddy to you. Your father." Hannah sighed. "I knew nothin' good could come from him bein' here."

Mama moved uneasily and Victoria glanced at her before fixing her attention back on Hannah.

"Why?"

Shifting to a more comfortable position, Hannah sighed. "Massah Ewan, your granddaddy, he done freed all us slaves the year yo mama turned twelve. But we all stayed with him on account o' he was so good to us. Miss Maggie – thet's your Mama – when she was just eighteen, she up an' married Simon Saunders. Oh he seemed slick to her 'fore she took the plunge, but the rest o' us, we seen the signs." Hannah shivered. "A few months after the weddin', Massah Ewan took sick. We done everythin' we knew how to do, but he went to a Senatorial ball one night and never made it home. And thet very night, everyone o' the hands left. Right in the middle o' the night. Everyone 'cept my Zeb and I. We tried to talk some o' them into staying and helpin' but Massah Simon.... Well...no one wanted to be around if he was gonna be in charge. Zeb and I, though, we couldn't see leavin' Miss Maggie all alone with her new husband."

She swallowed and stared into the black depths of her mug, her gaze unfocused and Victoria knew she wasn't really seeing, but was lost someplace back in time.

"After that, Massah Simon…"

Hannah's voice trailed off and she remained silent so long that Victoria finally prompted, "After that, Master Simon, what?"

Hannah sighed. "He never beat her 'fore that. But after her daddy was gone, thet's when he started into the beatin's."

Tears pooled in Hannah's eyes.

"I know'd thet girl from the time she was in wetpants and many's the time I wanted to offer thet man a passel o' his own medicine. Zeb did, too. But neither of us ever spoke up in her defense. We jus' helped doctor her the next day and prayed he'd leave, or thet she'd be able to figure out what it was thet set him off so."

Hannah swiped at her cheeks and blinked back the tears.

"Then she was with child." Hannah met her gaze directly. "For awhile he left off the beatin's but then toward the end he started in again. Thet's when she decided she'd leave him. But she knew she couldn't leave with you. The chances were too high he'd find her – an' you with her. So she waited until he was gone on one o' his trips. Was the Lord's own providence thet you came a few days early. You and your curly red hair and balled up fists, just a screamin' at the world."

Hannah smiled softly then, a sad longing in her expression and Victoria fidgeted. Rocky reached one hand to rub her back and she scooted closer to him, pulling Damera up onto her lap.

"I handed you off to Zeb to hold whilst I helped clean up your Mama and he just laughed and laughed about how cute you was, hollerin' like you could do somethin' about everyone's troubles. Your Mama and I, we could hear him out in the hallway trying to shush you and him makin' almost as much racket with his shushin'as you were." She cleared her throat. "I think thet's when your Mama decided for sure to give you up. When I put you back in her arms, she took one look at you and busted up cryin'. It weren't a light decision she made to give you up. She done it because she loved you so much."

Victoria heard the words as though they were coming to her from a far distance. Pressing her lips to the top of Damera's head, she let her eyes drop shut. All these years, she'd thought her parents had given her away because they didn't want her. "So my mother's still alive?"

Hannah fussed with stirring another teaspoon of sugar into her cup, her lips trembling and tears finally spilling over to course down her cheeks. "Thet very afternoon, after she dropped you at the Foundling Hospital, when she got home, Massah Simon he was there and already half way to drunk, as was his way. You see, when your Mama gave you away, she not only took you from him, but she done sold anything what was worth somethin'. I never did know what she did with all the money, but she spent several days just before you were born and had me and Zeb help her in emptyin' thet ol' house of every valuable. She and my Zeb they took four or five trips into town with wagon loads of things from side rooms in the house. Everytime Massah Simon took a day trip somewhere, Miss Maggie, she'd have us empty another room and she and Zeb would come home empty handed. Zeb, he wouldn't tell me what she done with it. He said it was better that I didn't know nothin' in case somethin' ever happened. Well, then Massah Simon, one day he discovered thet his silver cigar snips was missin'. Thankfully he didn't look for it hisself, or he'd have discovered the other things she'd sold. As it was, he gave her a bad beatin' and she went into labor and had you early in the morning on July twenty-first."

Victoria frowned. "The twenty first? You mean the twelfth, right?"

"No," Hannah shook her head. "In order to protect you when they sent you away, they changed your birthday to the twelfth, but really you was born on the twenty-first."

Victoria felt numb. Her birthday wasn't even her own, and yet all these years she'd had the wrong impression of why she'd been given up for adoption. What would it be like to have to give your child away in order to protect it? She pinched her lips together and brushed at her skirt. She still had so many questions. "So where was my father that day?"

"He was gone on a business trip. He was supposed to be gone for neigh onto a week, but he come home three days early. Your Mama was just walking in the door from the trip where she left you at the Foundling Hospital." She blinked hard. "The minute he seen thet you'd been born, he flew into a rage. By thet time he'd also discovered all them missin' things and he set to chokin' Miss Maggie because she wouldn't tell 'im where you was." Hannah's hand trembled as she took a sip of coffee. "I broke a vase over 'is head, then I opened the door and hollered for Zeb to come quick. But Zeb, he tried to talk to him instead of jus' knockin' him out like he should have. Massah Simon, he shot Zeb in the leg and then Miss Maggie she tried to stop him and he pushed her and she hit her head on the arm o' the settee and—" she glanced at Damera, "well, she didn't make it and neither did my Zeb."

Victoria handed Damera to Rocky and stepped over to pull Hannah into a firm embrace. "I'm so sorry, Hannah. And here all these years, I've been thinking that my parents gave me up because they didn't want me. My mother made a huge sacrifice to protect me, but so did you. Thank you." She set Hannah at arm's length. "How did you get away from Bax—Simon after...?"

"When he seen what he'd done to your Mama he sorta went into a trance. He didn't care none about Zeb, but I think he mighta been sorry 'bout what happened to your Mama. I hurried out the door and hid in the fields whilst he was still dazed. About an hour later he rode off and never come back. I, well, I laid them to rest the next day myself."

"How did you find me?"

"I followed you from the Foundling Hospital. When you lived in Nebraska I lived there, too. You was just too little to remember. Your Mama and Daddy…" Hannah cleared her throat and looked over at Mama.

Mama's eyes softened and she nodded for Hannah to continue.

"I went an' tol' them my story not too many days after you was adopted. They agreed to let me stay around so's I could keep an eye on you like I promised your Mama I would. But I never tol' them yo Daddy might come lookin' for you. I guess I jus' hoped he'd never find you." Hannah swiped at her cheeks and pushed back. "Now where's this letter you said Simon found in the locket?"

Victoria pulled it out of her pocket and smoothed it out on the table.

"Well I'll be…. Go on and read it to us."

Victoria cleared her throat and began….

My Dearest Girl and the God Blessed Family who took you in,

I set down today and put my pen to paper with the heaviest of hearts and great trepidation. For I ken not another way to solve this problem but to give my child into the hands of God for her own safety. Though it breaks my heart to undertake this forfeiture, I canna in good conscience keep her in this house of danger for even another day.

Even as I set pen to page, my trusted servant stands guard at the door and the babe sleeps by my side. I can see that twill be my own red hair she'll be having.

For her sake, when she comes of an age to understand, I want her to have the story from me own hand of why this lot fell to her.

I am of the house of McKenna. My father is the right honorable senator Ewan McKenna from New York.

A year and a half past, I met a man who presented himself as a gentleman visiting the continent from England. The Good Lord in heaven help me, I fell for his silver tongue and fabrications and married we were, Simon Saunders and I, ten months past.

It took me naught but a week to realize that I'd fallen prey to one of the lowest pretenses of humanity on the face of the earth. And me body bears the scars to prove it.

Yet from one of the most awful nights of me life sprang one of me greatest blessings, and she sleeps in quiet peace next to my side at this very moment.

One month past Da, God rest his soul, expired while at a senatorial banquet. While he ate nothing but what those around him ate, I know in me heart that Simon had something to do with his passing. Yet the doctors could prove nothing and came to the conclusion that his heart simply gave out. If that be the case, it is still the fault of Simon, who had tormented Da quietly for those many months previous.

With Da now out of his way, I and me precious one are the only two people standing between Simon and that which he most covets, our family money. For me father (perhaps in wisdom, perhaps in an unwitting stroke that brought about his death) when he discovered that Simon was frittering away money at the gaming tables, cut him off. What me father didn't consider, (Lord help us, what none of us considered) was what the case would be if Da died. Having spoken at length with me trusted attorney I am assured that the courts will uphold the despot's claim to the finances, since it couldn't be proven there was foul play at work in Da's death.

I have lived every day with the fear of even eating in me own home and the worry of what might happen to this wee child once it emerged into this cruel world.

Yet God, in his mercy, granted a boon. While Simon was called out of town on a special business meeting, I went into labor and delivered from the depths of myself this child so beautiful as to rend me heart asunder.

The plan I hereby set into motion came to me in the midst of me birth pains and I dare not hesitate another day for two reasons thus.

One being that with each beat of me heart I grow to love this child of hope endless measure upon measure more than I could have ever imagined.

And the second that Simon could arrive home any day and I dare not risk her life at his hand.

I take the time to set down these words, only that she may someday know the great pain her departure causes me and the unfathomable depth of me love for her.

Like the mother of Moses, I set this child of my heart into the hands of the Living God and pray He guides her to ones who will love her as much as I ever could and who will point her to the only One who gives Life.

I made her a doll. Some small token that one day she may caress and wonder what the woman who stitched it looked like. In it lies her key to Great Happiness. Please keep it with the child.

Penned this twenty-first day of July in the year of our Lord 1870,

Maggie McKenna Saunders.

Hannah snatched the letter from her grasp almost before she had time to finish the last line. "What did thet last paragraph say?" she asked.

"Great Happiness!?" Rocky snapped his fingers and arched his brows at Hannah.

She scanned the page, running her finger down until it paused near the bottom. "In it lies her key to Great Happiness...." She glanced up, a dazed look on her face. "Well, if thet don't beat all." A wide white smile splitting her face, she leapt to her feet. "Ya'll stay here. I'll be back just as soon as ever I can." And with that she bustled out the door muttering excitedly to herself.

Everyone glanced at each other questioningly. Everyone seemed bewildered but Rocky. "This is going to be good," he declared.

"What is?" Victoria tipped her head to one side.

He just grinned and winked. "My lips are sealed."

Victoria frowned, but then decided to drop it until Hannah returned.

By the time they'd tucked the girls into Rocky's old bed upstairs and were coming back down, Hannah had arrived. Under her arm she carried a small wooden ship. She set it down in the middle of the dining table with a flourish and stepped back settling her hands on her hips.

"My Zeb he give this to me just two weeks before he was killed. He worked on this every chance he got, night and day for nigh onto a month. I thought he'd done taken leave of 'is senses. But when he got it all built he give it to me. I teased him somethin' fierce about the name he give it. But he said I was his great happiness." She turned the boat so everyone in the room could read the name painted in a gently sloping scrawl across the stern of the ship. *Great Happiness.*

Victoria gasped. *In it lies her key to Great Happiness.*

Hannah gently laid the ship on its side. "See here? He done carved each o' these tiny little round windows in the side toward the front, jus' like on a real ship. Only one day I noticed thet it looked like he made a mistake on one. See this one right here?" Hannah pointed to a port hole that had a small rectangular hole perpendicular to the circular one.

Victoria touched it. "A key hole."

Hannah nodded. "Least wise we'll soon find out if it is. Now where's thet key?"

Rocky patted his front shirt pocket and then pulled out the small silver-gray key.

The room seemed to still as he inserted the key into the hole and turned it. There was a faint click and then the top half of the ship separated from the bottom. A canvas sack filled the narrow cavity. Rocky lifted it out and dumped the contents onto the table.

A smaller bag, heavy and bulging, thunked to the table followed by two inch thick stacks of hundred dollar United States Treasury bank notes each wrapped with a band of paper, and two folded squares of paper.

Victoria gasped in unison with everyone else. Her legs lost their strength and she plunked down into the chair that thankfully was directly behind her. *Thousands of dollars.*

Rocky glanced at her with a grin. "You okay?"

She nodded, one hand at the base of her throat.

One of the notes was to Hannah from her husband. The other was addressed to "My Dear Daughter." The bag was full of gold coins each individually wrapped in squares of cotton presumably to keep them from jangling together and drawing premature attention to the treasure in the ship's belly.

"Hannah you read your note first."

Hannah folded open the paper with her name on it, her hands trembling so badly, she could barely smooth out the paper.

My dearest Hannah,

You readin' this, it means I've done gone on to my reward. I wish thet weren't so, cause I wanted to stay around and grow old with you, darlin'.

Hannah's voice wavered and she paused to clear her throat.

But we cain't always have things our way. The Good Lawd, He asks us to do hard things sometimes and I hope, if I'm done gone on, He helped me make a God fearin' decision there at my end.

Miss Maggie and I talked. I wanted to include you on what we was doin' but Miss Maggie, she didn't want no harm to come to you on account o' her bad choices. She figured the less you knew the better.

We both decided thet if something were to happen to us, you would follow that cute little red-headed snippet of a gal to the ends o' the earth, 'fore you'd let her outta your sight.

And we also knew you wouldn't allow yourself to be parted from this, my last gift to you. An' I recon if you's readin' this thet we was right.

Keep the faith, darlin'. One o' these days we's gonna see each other again.

All my love is ever yours,
Zeb.

Hannah clutched the letter to her breast, closed her eyes and tipped her face toward the ceiling, tears leaving glistening tracks on her dark cheeks.

Victoria stood, wrapped one arm around her and rested her head on Hannah's ample shoulder. "I'm so sorry, Hannah"

Hannah patted her and dashed the tears from her face. "None o' this is your fault. Don't you worry none about ol' Hannah. Now, what's thet other letter say?"

Pressing her lips together, Victoria slowly opened the second square of paper and smoothed it flat against the table.

It wasn't a letter but a signed statement of Maggie's wishes.

I suppose since I did marry him, this money legally belongs to one Simon Saunders. I can only hope that by the time this money is found, he has either repented of his ways, or gone on to his eternal destiny. Yet if this money is found and he is still alive, I do hereby declare that it is my wish that all this money go to my daughter. I do not know what her name may be at the finding of this letter, but she has a small red birthmark in the shape of a heart on the back of her right shoulder. Simon deserves none of it, for he is a cruel man who will only use it for evil.

Penned this twenty-first day of July in the year of our Lord 1870,

Maggie McKenna Saunders.

Victoria met Rocky's gaze. "Will that hold up in court?"

He settled one hand at the base of her neck. "I don't know, but it will help."

"An' I'll certainly be happy to testify to the fact that he shot my Zeb and thet it was his push thet caused Miss Maggie's passin.'"

Sean stood and stretched his hands above his head. "Judge Bowman is a good man. I think we have enough evidence that Simon will probably face a trial before the week is out. Until then, I'll have to keep all this," he waved his hand toward the scattered items on the table, "in the safe down at the jail until the trial is over."

Victoria suddenly felt weak with relief. So many things had happened in the last few hours. She turned to Rocky, "Let's go home."

He pulled her to him for a moment. "Sounds good. Sounds mighty good."

★

CHAPTER TWENTY-SEVEN

Victoria sat on her bed, alternately clenching her hands in her lap and plucking at the quilt beside her as she stared at the inside of her bedroom door. Rocky had gone out to take care of the stock and he would be coming back any minute.

She closed her eyes and pressed her lips together, willing away the trembling in her limbs and praying for the strength to do what she wanted to do, but was terrified to do all at the same time.

Since the girls had already been asleep, Sean and Rachel had insisted that they leave them be and let them sleep. And at the crestfallen look on Jimmy's face, Sean had said he needed a man's help around the place and asked Jimmy if he'd be willing to stay over and help him with a project in the barn the next day.

Victoria and Rocky were alone in the house, or would be when he got back inside.

She remembered Hannah's words from just a few mornings ago about keeping Rocky happy in the bedroom and heat surged into her cheeks. She leapt to her feet, jerked open her door and marched out into the kitchen, her heels clicking loudly on the plank floor. She would need some warm water to clean Rocky's shoulder again.

She worked the pump handle until the kettle had enough water, set it on the stove, and added pine kindling to the fire so it would burn rapid and hot. Rocky hadn't come in yet, so she grabbed the broom from the corner and swept the already clean floor, then wiped down the sideboard and the table, even though she knew she'd already done it earlier, and straightened the chairs. Still no Rocky.

With a little groan of impatience she stomped over to the sink and pulled back a corner of the curtain to peek out into the darkness. "I don't know the first thing about keeping a man happy in the bedroom!"

A soft chuckle echoed from behind her.

With a gasp she spun around.

Rocky grinned at her and pushed his hat back on his head. Leaning against the closed door, arms folded across his chest, he raked her with an assessing gaze.

"How did you—" She clutched the material at the throat of her dress.

He shrugged. "You were walking towards the window when I opened the door."

Her face flamed and she looked at the floor then back at his shoulder. "We need to get that cleaned up and bandaged again."

He nodded.

"Ria." He stepped over and stopped in front of her.

She closed her eyes and her shoulders relaxed of their own free will. Today when he'd been pinned to the floor and nearly beaten unconscious by Baxter Cane she'd suddenly realized that what her mother had been telling her all along was true. She loved Rocky, and keeping him at arm's length, wouldn't make it hurt any less if he were killed. And all she'd been able to think about was all the opportunities she'd missed to share a bit of joy, laughter, or happiness with him, because she'd been too afraid to let him into her heart. Well no more. That ended tonight. She opened her eyes and studied him.

His left eye was swollen shut and black and blue, and a cut puckered the corner of his upper lip, but he was the most handsome man she'd ever seen. Standing on tiptoes she grasped a double handful of his shirt and softly pressed her lips to his. Her eyes fell shut with a sigh of satisfaction as she dropped back down to her normal height. "I love you, Rocky Jordan."

Then she brushed past him and gestured for him to take a seat in one of the chairs. She sloshed some of the warm water into the waiting bowl and dropped a clean rag in, too. But when she turned for the table, she gasped and almost spilled all the water on the floor. Rocky hadn't taken a seat as directed, but stood close behind her.

He took the bowl from her and set it on the sideboard. Then slipped his fingers back into her hair and rested his forehead against hers.

Heaven help her she was having a hard time thinking.

He studied her, working one corner of his lower lip with his teeth. "You gonna be okay?"

About the incident today? Yes. About the fact that she was trying to find a way to invite him into her bedroom? *Never in a million years....* She scrambled for a reply that was honest and settled for a change of subject that she hoped would be safe. "Let's look at your shoulder."

He shook his head, his hands still cupping her face. "Say it again, Ria."

She smiled faintly, "Let's look at your shoulder."

He chuckled.

But then she dropped the act and looked at him, wanting with all her heart for him to see the truth in her face. "I love you, Rocky Jordan. More than you will ever know."

His lips grazed across hers. "I love you, too. I'm so glad you are safe." And with a sigh of satisfaction he stepped back and gestured to his shoulder. "It was hurting quite a bit after chores but it feels better now." His gaze never left hers as he took off his Stetson and hooked it over the post of one of the chairs. He reached into his pocket, pulled out a fresh bandage and set it on the table, then started to unbutton his shirt.

Have mercy! "Good." The word came out on a tiny squeak as she darted a look towards the corner of the ceiling. She swallowed, her hands fluttering and finding no place to rest. *Safe, indeed!* "That's good."

She heard the fabric's soft caress as he draped the shirt over the back of a chair. He unbuckled his ever-present gun belt and hung it on its hook by the door. The chair scraped across the floor as he pulled it out and sat down. And still she did not look at him.

He waited quietly, the heat of his gaze warming her neck.

She took a fortifying breath. *I can do this.* Deliberately she dropped her gaze to his.

Amusement danced in the depths of his dark eyes.

Irritation rising, her brows peaked. He seemed to be quite entertained by this whole ordeal. She pressed her lips together and lowered her study still further.

Taut muscles filled out the expanse of his chest, the clean perimeter of the bandage on his shoulder standing in stark contrast to sun-browned skin.

She must have stared for a long time, because suddenly he was grinning at her and holding out the round roll of clean white bandages.

She cleared her throat, stepped closer, and took the roll in trembling fingers. Carefully she examined the wound. She dipped the cloth from the warm water and wet down the bandage so she could pull it loose without causing more damage.

As she worked she tried to ignore the intensity in his expression as he studied her face.

She sponged the dried blood from his shoulder and pressed gently. There appeared to be no infection and the bleeding had stopped. The memory of the fact that she could have lost him today sizzled through her, and her fingers trembled to the point of uselessness. "Today when Bax—Simon…when he was…" She blinked tears away. "I thought you were…going to die. And all I could think about was how sorry I was that I'd never let myself fully love you."

All amusement left his face. "Ria." The word was a hoarse whisper. His hands settled softly around her waist

She jumped and rested her hands on his shoulders, dropping the new bandage. It rolled across the room, but when she started after it he tightened his grip. She looked down into his face, holding her breath.

Why have I been fighting this? She didn't want to fight it anymore. Hadn't wanted to fight it for several days now. "I'm sorry, Rocky. I love you so much."

His lips were just below hers and his gaze darted across her features hungrily. He swallowed. "Just say the word and I'll stop." His thumbs rubbed up and down in short strokes against her side. And his breath dusted warmth across her lips as he slowly leaned toward her.

She closed her eyes and curled her mouth into a flat line, but pushed back the familiar lie that wanted to crawl from her throat. She was letting go. Letting go of fear and worry. All she had was today and she was going to live it to the fullest.

She tilted her face down until her lips pressed, gently coaxing, against the line of his mouth. As he responded to her kiss, her stomach rode a wave of pure pleasure and she relaxed into him, her fingers sliding of their own will into the hair at the back of his head.

With a low groan, he stood and pulled her against him. His breath came short and fast as his mouth slanted over hers.

Desire prickled her skin and she pressed herself closer to him.

His lips trailed a searing path across her jaw to the soft skin just below her ear. He splayed his fingers against her neck and pushed her a fraction of an inch back, his thumbs caressing the rapid pulse beating at the hollow of her throat.

She'd never seen such heat in his eyes.

He swallowed, his gaze roving over her face. "Tell me now if you don't want this."

"I can't," she whispered. All the air had seemingly been sucked out of the room. She was finding it hard to pull in a breath. "I do want this. You. Me. Forever."

"You're sure?"

She nodded, took his hand, and led him to her room. And as his head tilted toward her once more, she silently uttered a fleeting prayer. *Lord, please don't ever take this man from me.*

CHAPTER TWENTY-EIGHT

The faint hint of approaching dawn had barely penetrated the darkness of their room the next morning when Victoria woke to find Rocky studying her intently, one of her curls wrapped around his finger. His eye was swollen completely shut, his lip had doubled in size, and the whole left side of his face was oddly discolored, even in this light. Never had she seen a more welcome site.

She smiled softly. From the pain pulsing through her cheek, she probably didn't look much better. "Good morning."

He tilted forward and brushed a soft kiss against her lips. "Morning." Resting his head against his bent arm he worried his upper lip for a moment then said, "I realized in all that happened yesterday, I forgot to talk to you about something."

Her heart thudded. "Oh?"

"Smith is selling his half of the Bar B."

She relaxed. "Of course you should buy it."

His teeth flashed white. "Good, because I already told Cade I wanted to, but I'd need to talk to you first."

"I have one condition." She laid a hand ever so softly against his cheek.

A frown flitted across his face. "Oh?" Then realization dawned and he chuckled. "Of course we should keep the children."

She felt a jolt of joy and…rightness. "Let's go tell them!"

One of his eyebrows quirked, "The sun's barely up."

"I know."

He laughed. "Alright."

Thirty minutes later, at their knock, Sean answered the door in his bare feet. At the sight of them standing on his porch with sloppy grins on their faces, Sean rubbed his jaw and glanced back and forth between them, a frown of befuddlement on his face. "You two do know what time it is, don't you?"

Victoria felt a stab of consternation. "This was my idea, I'm sorry we woke you. We just—"

Rocky laid a hand against her shoulder and brushed past his father. "He's teasing, Ria. He's probably been up for at least an hour already."

She looked at Sean who grinned with an unrepentant shrug and motioned her inside.

"Pa, I'm buying in with Cade."

Sean nodded. "Figured you would."

"And we're going to keep the children."

He grinned at that. "I'm glad."

"We'd like to take them out to the ranch, let them know our decision and show them around the place a bit."

Sean gestured up the stairs without a word, but a glimmer of moisture shone in his eyes.

Rocky started up the stairs, but when Victoria started to follow, Sean laid a hand on her arm. "Young lady, I don't believe I've told you yet…" he pulled her into a warm fatherly embrace, "but welcome to the family."

She hugged him back, feeling a little overwhelmed by the roil of excitement and joy welling through her. "Thank you."

A few moments later, Rocky handed a sleepy Damera up to her on the wagon seat and Victoria snuggled the little girl into her lap. She rested her chin on the top of the mop of dark curls and closed her eyes, love and thankfulness rolling over her. Rocky boosted ChristyAnne up to sit beside her and Victoria wrapped one arm around her, pulling her up tight against her side as Jimmy climbed into the back.

"Where are we going?" There was a hint of trepidation in ChristyAnne's question.

"Just a few minutes and we'll show you," Rocky said. He clicked to the horses and set them into motion with a snap of the reins.

The children settled into silence, Damera's soft little snores, the musical notes of the birds, and the jangling of the trace chains, the only sounds marring the morning stillness. A few minutes later Rocky pulled the team to a stop at the top of a hill overlooking the Bar B spread.

Victoria scooted nearer to Rocky and pulled ChristyAnne even closer to her side, making room for Jimmy on the seat beside her.

"Jimmy, come on up here and sit next to your sister." She met Rocky's gaze and he gave her a wink and a smile.

"She ain't my sister," Jimmy grumbled even as he complied and climbed over the back of the seat to plunk down beside ChristyAnne.

Rocky set the brake and looped the reins around the brake handle. "Oh yes she is." He grinned at the family seated beside him.

ChristyAnne's head popped up. "I am?"

Victoria and Rocky answered together. "Yes. You are."

"Wait, so you're saying...?" Undisguised hope tinged the edges of Jimmy's question.

"We're saying," emotion clogged Rocky's voice and he cleared his throat looking to Victoria for help.

Victoria put one hand on his forearm. "We're saying you're home to stay."

ChristyAnne squealed in glee and threw her arms around Victoria, startling a sleepy Damera into wakefulness.

A grin the size of a half moon spread across Jimmy's face and he reached out and tweaked ChristyAnne's hair. "Guess that means I can tease you for real now."

Damera pushed ChristyAnne away. "I'm twying to sweep. Pwease be quiet."

ChristyAnne pulled away from Damera and folded her arms with a disgusted glare in Jimmy's direction. "What it means, Jimmy, is that you have to stick up for me now instead of helping all the boys tease me!"

Jimmy chuckled and looked down at the spread below them. "What's this place?"

"This is the Bar B, our new home."

"Really?!"

"Wow!" Jimmy leapt to his feet. "Can we go down and look around?"

Rocky chuckled. "We sure can." With a flip of the reins he set the team in motion again. After several hours of exploration looking around the ranch and showing the children the horses, including the mare Rocky hoped would be the start of a great herd, they trooped back to the wagon in happy spirits.

"When do we get to move in?" ChristyAnne asked. "I've never had my own room before!"

Victoria smiled. "Well, we need to give Cade some time to decide what he wants to do with the things in the house. It won't be easy for him so it might be a few weeks before we actually move." She squeezed the girl in a sideways hug. "The most important thing is that we're all together."

ChristyAnne nodded with a happy sigh and Victoria couldn't remember the last time she'd felt this joyful. But a few moments later when they pulled into their yard, the sight of a man waiting in a buggy, set her pulse racing.

"Whoa." Rocky pulled the team to a stop by the front porch.

"Who's that?" Victoria couldn't disguise the tremor in her voice.

"I don't know." Rocky leapt to the ground and reached up to help her and the girls from the seat, then approached the man. "Hello. Name's Rocky Jordan. What can I do for you?"

"Good to meet you." The man shook Rocky's hand eyeing first his battered face and then Victoria's with a frown of concern. Finally, he pushed his round spectacles up on his nose. "I'm Roger Evans, here on behalf of The Children's Aid Society."

ChristyAnne's hand slipped into Victoria's and held on tight.

"Would you like to come in?" Rocky stretched his hand toward the house.

"No. No. That won't be necessary. I need to be on my way, but wanted to drop in and check to see if there was anything you needed with regard to the children."

Rocky didn't hesitate. "We've decided we'd like to adopt all three children. Can you help us with that?"

The man blinked and pursed his lips. A flick of his wrist and a pistol appeared in his hand. A pistol aimed directly at Rocky. The man glanced over at Victoria calmly. "Does your husband beat you ma'am?"

Victoria gasped in shock, wondering where in the world he'd gotten that idea, then suddenly she remembered her face. "Oh! No! This wasn't him. Another man did this to me, and Rocky got that," she gestured to his face, "when he came to my rescue. The other man is now in jail. It's a long story."

Roger seemed to ponder that, then a huge smile split his face as he holstered his gun. "Sorry. I've seen a lot of strange things in this job and one can never be too careful. As to your question, Sir, certainly! This is just what we like to see happen. Our goal at the Society is to try and find new families for children, not just places for them to stay. I have to admit, that I had my reservations based on the information I received from Miss Nickerson, but I've done some checking on you two in town. You both come highly recommended by your friends and neighbors. So I don't see any reason to delay adoption at all so long as the story you've told me here today turns out to be true."

Rocky grinned and Victoria realized she and the children were all doing the same. "It's true. You can check in at the Sheriff's office in town. They'll confirm what happened."

Roger settled his top hat more firmly. "I will. And if all is as it seems I'll bring by the paper work next week. Does that sound alright?"

"Yes!" Victoria couldn't help the outburst. "Yes, it does!"

Everyone laughed.

"Well, alright then. I will see all of you next Tuesday. Say three o'clock?"

"That should be fine," Rocky affirmed.

Later that night after they'd tucked three very excited children into bed Victoria collapsed onto the settee in the parlor. Rocky came in a moment later and eased down beside her. Leaning forward he rested his elbows on his knees, clasped his hands together and looked over at her.

She couldn't stop the tears that sprang to her eyes.

"Hey." Scooting closer, he wrapped one hand around the back of her neck and pulled her head down onto his chest. "Shhhhhh. Everything's alright, now. Everything's alright."

She dashed the moisture from her cheeks. "All these years I've been so sure about the reasons I was given up for adoption. But then when I heard the story of why my mother gave me away, I realized how wrong I've been. I'm so ashamed."

Rocky brushed her hair back from her face and dropped a kiss on her temple. "You have nothing to be ashamed of."

She ignored his reassurance. "All these years, I've thought God must not really think I'm special because he allowed me to be born to parents who just tossed me away like so much garbage. Yet that wasn't the case at all." Awe seeped into her voice. "She loved me. She really loved me."

"Yes, she did." He nuzzled her temple again.

"I feel like the Psalmist when he said God prepared a table for him in the presence of his enemies. God watched over me and gave me refuge from what could have been a horrible life." At the thought of growing up with Simon Saunders for a father instead of her own dear Papa, she shuddered.

"Yes, He did." His arms tightened around her. "I'm sorry I couldn't stop him from hurting you the other day. I've never felt so powerless."

She lifted her head and looked deep into his eyes, then leaned forward and pressed her mouth to his briefly. "I felt the same way. I don't want to hold back anymore Rocky, but it still scares me. I don't think I could handle it if anything happened to you."

Softly, his fingers skimmed over the swollen cut on her cheek and she felt a tremor race through him. "And I don't think I could handle it if anything happened to you. So what are we going to do with each other?"

She gave a little chuckle and snuggled even closer. "Well, maybe we should just never leave the house again."

He cocked an eyebrow. "In case you've forgotten, we've got children. I don't think the never-leaving-the-house idea is going to work so well."

"Well maybe just for tonight then." She tilted her head up and gave him a lingering kiss. "After all each day has enough trouble of its own."

"Now you're talking." He cupped the back of her head and pulled her firmly toward him, slanting his mouth over hers.

Distinct snickering emanated from the hallway.

Rocky jerked his head up and met her gaze, a twinkle glittering in his eyes as he dropped one lid in a quick wink. "Seems like the mice in this house must be getting bigger," he said loudly. "Sure hope I don't have to stomp a couple of them!"

There was the sound of scrambling feet and then silence.

"Now where were we?" he asked.

She grinned. "Oh, I remember, but perhaps we'd like to continue this in another room?"

He pumped his eyebrows twice. "Why yes, I think we just might."

He stood and reached down a hand to help her up and as Victoria followed him down the hallway, she praised God for helping her to recognize the refuge He'd placed her in and for blessing her with such a wonderful family.

Don't Miss…

THE SHEPHERD'S HEART - BOOK 1

ROCKY MOUNTAIN
Oasis

He's different from any man she's ever known.
However, she's sworn never to risk her heart again.

Idaho Territory,

Brooke Baker, sold as a mail-order bride, looks to her future with dread but firm resolve. If she survived Uncle Jackson, she can survive anyone.

When Sky Jordan hears that his nefarious cousin has sent for a mail-order bride, he knows he has to prevent the marriage. No woman deserves to be left to that fate. Still, he's as surprised as anyone to find himself standing next to her before the minister.

Brooke's new husband turns out to be kinder than any man has ever been. But then the unthinkable happens and she holds the key that might save innocent lives but destroy Sky all in one fell swoop. It's a choice too unbearable to contemplate…but a choice that must be made.

A thirsty soul. Alluring hope. An Oasis of love.
Step into a day when outlaws ran free, the land was wild, and guns blazed at the drop of a hat.

Find out more at: www.lynnettebonner.com

Also Available…

THE SHEPHERD'S HEART - BOOK 2

HIGH DESERT Haven

Is Jason Jordan really who he says he is?
Everything in Nicki's life depends on the answer.

Oregon Territory, 1887

When her husband dies in a mysterious riding accident, Nicki Trent is left with a toddler and a rundown ranch. Determined to bring her ranch back from the brink of death, Nicki hires handsome Jason Jordan to help. But when William, her neighbor, starts pressing for her hand in marriage, the bank calls in a loan she didn't even know about, bullets start flying, and a burlap dummy with a knife in its chest shows up on her doorstep, Nicki wonders if this ranch is worth all the trouble.

To make matters worse, terrible things keep happening to her neighbors. When her friend's homestead is burned to the ground and William lays the blame at Jason's feet, Nicki wonders how well she knows her new hand…and her own heart.

A desperate need. Malicious adversaries. Enticing love.
Step into a day when outlaws ran free, the land was wild, and
guns blazed at the drop of a hat.

Also Available…

THE SHEPHERD'S HEART - BOOK 4

SPRING ★ MEADOW

Sanctuary

He broke her heart.
Now he's back to ask for a second chance.

Heart pounding in shock, Sharyah Jordan gapes at the outlaw staring down the barrel of his gun at her. Cascade Bennett shattered her dreams only last summer, and now he plans to kidnap her and haul her into the wilderness with a bunch of outlaws…for her own protection? She'd rather be locked in her classroom for a whole week with Brandon McBride and his arsenal of tricks, and that was saying something.

Cade Bennett's heart nearly drops to his toes when he sees Sharyah standing by the desk. Sharyah Jordan was not supposed to be here. Blast if he didn't hate complications, and Sharyah with her alluring brown eyes and silky blond hair was a walking, talking personification of complication.

Now was probably not the time to tell her he'd made a huge mistake last summer.…

Two broken hearts. Dangerous Outlaws. One last chance at love.
Step into a day when outlaws ran free, the land was wild, and
guns blazed at the drop of a hat.

AN EXCERPT
Spring Meadow Sanctuary

PROLOGUE.

Shiloh, Oregon.
September, 1887

Cade Bennett massaged one hand over the muscles of his neck as he stepped out of the bank. He'd just returned from a long trail drive and weariness weighed heavy.

"Cade Bennett! How've you been?"

Cade blinked. Sam Perry was a long ways from home. "Sam! Good to see you." Cade shook his friend's hand, even as a leery uneasiness narrowed his gaze.

The short greenhorn stood in the center of the boardwalk blocking Cade's progress, and his presence here could only mean one thing, more work. And likely the work revolved around some trouble with Sam's conniving sister, Katrina.

He rolled his head stretching tired muscles. "Walk with me, would you?" he said, as he pushed by and headed toward the mercantile. "What can I do for you, Sam?"

Even as Cade asked the question, he dreaded the answer. All he wanted was to drop into a chair out at the ranch, drink a hot cup of coffee, and catch up with Rocky and his wife, Victoria. He hadn't spoken with Rocky, his best friend and partner, for several months, and it would sure be nice to sleep in a real bed for a change. Maybe find out a little information about Rocky's sister, Sharyah. Was she still teaching here in town?

Sam snatched his bowler from his head and hustled to catch up, his snakeskin boots beating a tattoo on the boardwalk and the gold chain from his pocket watch clinking against the buttons of his vest. "Now Cade don't brush me off so fast. You know I wouldn't be here unless I really needed your help."

Cade kept walking. Whatever had brought Sam here, especially if it did revolve around Katrina, smelled like trouble. And trouble he could do without. Perry, an eastern banker who'd only moved west a few years ago, owned a ranch near Beth Haven where he lived with his sister. Cade had sold Perry horses on a number of occasions, but the man had never come to him – he'd always summoned Cade to his lavish spread, always too busy to leave home. So whatever had broken his pattern must be important. Still… he rolled his shoulders wishing away some of the weariness… the last thing he wanted right now was another cross-country trip.

Knowing Sam would get to the point soon enough, Cade stepped down into the dust of the street, crossing just in front of an oncoming buckboard.

The little man darted after him. "I asked around. And I'm still hearing that if I want to hire an honest hombre to do some lawmen's work, you're the one to talk to."

Hombre pronounced with his Yankee twang, was quite the thing to hear. Cade suppressed a grin. "Sam, my friend, I'd like to help, but you're catching me at a bad time. I'm not interested. Sorry." Cade pushed into Halvorson's Mercantile, the bell jangling above his head. He couldn't go out to the ranch without some candy for the three kids Rocky and Victoria had adopted.

Seemingly undeterred Sam darted in front of him and put one hand on his chest.

Cade released a breath of frustration and stopped next to the sacks of chicken feed. Maybe if he just talked to the man for a few minutes he'd go away. "Did Katrina sell another herd of your cattle to that *caballero* for five dollars a head?"

Sam didn't look happy to be reminded of that little incident. "You're just in from a cattle run, correct?" He apparently wasn't going to rise to Cade's bait.

Cade nodded.

"I'm willing to pay you three times what you just made if

you'll come to Beth Haven and help me track down some cattle rustlers. They've been plaguing me for months and with my work at the bank, I simply haven't had time to deal with it." The little man folded his arms, his bowler poking out to one side.

Cade arched a brow. Sam could always come up with an elaborate plan, but generally the plan called for someone else to execute it. "I made good money on this run, Sam."

A gleam leapt into Sam's eyes as though he knew he had Cade's attention. "Whatever you made, I'll pay you triple. These rustlers have caused me enough trouble and money. And now Katrina's with them!"

Just as he'd assumed. Cade settled his hands on his hips. Sam's sister had always been peril-in-a-skirt. "Sounds like a job for your local law enforcement."

Sam snorted. "You know old Sheriff Collier would rather fish than track down a clue any day of the week."

Rubbing one hand across his prickly jaw, Cade studied the stack of feed sacks to his right. He didn't have another job lined up yet. And triple what he'd made on this run was certainly good money.

Rocky and Victoria were doing a fine job of running the ranch while he was away. And he hadn't been looking forward to seeing Victoria working in Ma's kitchen, anyhow. With Pa off to who knows where, maybe… His thoughts turned to Sharyah Jordan. If he had any reason to stick around town, she was it. Would sure be nice to see her again. It was certainly time to explain the disaster he'd made of things last summer. Maybe he could make up for it somehow.

Just then Mrs. Halvorson stepped into the aisle. "Why Cade Bennett! It's so good to see you home! When did you get back?"

Cade snatched his hat from his head and nodded. "Mrs. Halvorson." The woman must have heard the bell a moment earlier. She had ears like a fox when it came to her bell and local gossip – but didn't hear much else most of the time. "Good to be home, ma'am. I just rode into town this afternoon. How has everything been around here since I've been gone?"

She cupped one hand to her ear. "What was that?!"

Cade leaned toward her and raised his voice. "I said, 'How has everything been?'"

"Well, it's been downright... different over the last few months what with the Jordans adopting those three children and moving out to your place after the passing of your—oh listen to me go on, I'm sorry to bring that up. How is your father, dear?"

A wave of sorrow washed over him even as he suppressed a roll of his eyes. The woman could at least try to be subtle as she pried for information to hand on to the next customers to walk through her doors.

He clenched his jaw. Yes, life certainly wouldn't be the same in town for him, now. He had no idea where Pa was, or how he was doing, or if he was even alive. But Mrs. Halvorson waited for an answer so he searched for something truthful to say. "He's fair to middling, ma'am. Getting along as well as can be expected, I suppose." Pa had pulled up every stake he'd ever put down and taken for the hills the very day Ma had passed on. Cade hadn't seen him since and the roll of anger the surged through him threatened to upset his stomach. He swallowed away the bitter taste at the back of his throat, and suddenly realized that Mrs. Halvorson was looking from him to Sam Perry an expectant arc in her brows. "Oh, ah... Mrs. Halvorson," he gestured to Sam with his hat, "Sam Perry. Mr. Perry, meet Mrs. Halvorson."

Sam bowed over her hand. "It's a pleasure to make your acquaintance, ma'am."

"And where do you hail from, Mr. Berry?"

"Uh, Perry, ma'am. I'm from over east of the mountains, a little settlement near Farewell Bend."

"Where was that?"

"Farewell Bend, ma'am." Perry spoke a little louder.

"Really? Well! Our school teacher recently moved east of the mountains to take a school. A town called Madras. Also not too far from Farewell Bend, I believe. I hear tell that it's hot over there this time of year. And the way ol' Mr. Crockett tells it, the outlaws are thick as morning cream out that way." She tsked. "I do hope our young Sharyah makes it back home alive."

Cade's heart tripped over itself. So Sharyah was out of town.

Decision suddenly made, Cade turned to Sam. "Have you had dinner yet, Sam?" He smiled and tipped his head at Mrs. Halvorson, taking Sam's arm and pulling him toward the candy display.

The man blinked, a little startled. "No. No I haven't." His mouth stretched as he took in the three sticks of peppermint Cade picked up. "Are we having that for dinner?"

Cade grinned and headed for the front. "Why don't you come out to my ranch with me and we can discuss the details of the job you're talking about."

Perry trotted after him. "Certainly. Certainly. Yes, that would be fine. I knew you wouldn't turn me down."

Cade heaved a breath of relief as he placed the sticks of candy on the counter. He hadn't realized until now how much he'd been dreading the thought of living out at the ranch, once again. A few more months on the road wouldn't hurt any. Rocky could certainly be trusted to keep things running smoothly, and the money he'd make on this job would be a nice cushion against any unforeseen expenses in the future.

A certain blonde woman came to mind, but he pushed the thought away. Still, Madras was only a crow's hop from Beth Haven....

CHAPTER ONE

Sharyah had just bent over the papers she needed to grade when the small rock landed on her desk with a soft thud. The titter of laugher ceased as she snapped her head up to study her students. Everyone seemed to be in deep concentration and intent on their lessons. She focused her gaze on Brandon McBride, but he looked as innocent as an angel and sat attentively reading his history lesson, just as he should be. Sonja and Sally Weaver both gave her sympathetic glances, from the last row of desks where they were working on their math lesson together.

Sharyah sighed, knowing from past experience that asking the class who had done the deed would prove futile. She'd been here two weeks, now. Two weeks in the God-forsaken little back-water town of Beth Haven and for a solid week-and-a-half she'd been longing to pack her bags and return home.

She had been approached about teaching in Madras, but upon arriving learned that the former teacher had decided to stay on for another year. Disappointed, she'd been all set to go back home when the head of the board told her that Beth Haven had been having trouble keeping a teacher and he thought they might be searching for one again. When she'd arrived and informed the Beth Haven board of her interest in the teaching position, they'd been ecstatic. She could see why, now. No teacher in their right mind would want to stay and deal with this, but she was determined to make it work.

The first week, she'd spent countless hours grilling the students both collectively and individually as to the identity of the trickster, but whoever the little devil was, he had a fierce grip on the loyalty of everyone else in the class. No one would give him up.

For the last several weeks, she'd tried to ignore the incidents in hopes that the prankster would give up out of sheer boredom.

Never one to be squeamish, when she'd found the snake in her top desk drawer she'd calmly picked it up and tossed it out the window. A few of the boys had gaped in disappointment, but the next day a tack had appeared on her chair. She'd noticed it before she sat on it, thankfully, and had whisked it out of sight and plunked herself down on the chair with zest. But, even though she'd been watching their faces carefully as she dropped into the seat, she hadn't been able to determine which child was the most disappointed when she didn't cry out in pain.

A couple days ago, she'd actually almost laughed when she'd discovered that all the chalk had been replaced with garden carrots, fuzzy green tops and all. Thankfully she'd had an extra piece in her satchel.

Today however, the large spider in her lunch pail had been almost more than she could bear. She shuddered at the memory and thanked her lucky stars that Papa had never allowed her to luxuriate in a fit of the vapors – because if ever there was a moment when she'd been tempted to, that had been it. The thing had been so large she could see its beady eyes looking right at her! And fuzzy! She rubbed at the goose-flesh on her arms. All afternoon her stomach had been grumbling its complaint. The thought of eating her sandwich and the apple that a spider crawled all over had been more than her fortitude could handle.

Yes, packing up and returning to home would be heaven. But, in a way that would be just like succumbing to the vapors, and she wouldn't allow herself the weakness of retreat. She would get a much-needed break in the spring, just a few short months away, when her entire family came over for Jason and Nicki's March wedding. Tears pressed at the backs of her eyes as longing to see them all welled up inside her. But she blinked hard and reined in her emotions. Until then, she would simply have to forge ahead.

All her life she'd wanted only one thing.

Well, two things if she were honest, but she wasn't going to think about Cascade Bennett today. She sighed and glanced out the window. If she was smart she wouldn't ever again waste another moment of time pondering the way he'd broken her heart. God promised in his Word that goodness and mercy would follow her all the days of her life, so obviously the good things God had for her didn't include Cade Bennett.

Samuel Perry - that's who she should be thinking on. Yes, Sam. If he ever got around to asking her, he would make a very… suitable husband. She could learn to be happy and satisfied with a man like Sam.

Giving herself a shake, she returned her focus to her students. The one thing she'd wanted ever since she could remember was to be a teacher. She loved children, loved to see their eyes light up when understanding dawned. Loved their frank outlook on life and their quickness to forgive and move on. Loved to help them make something of themselves. That love was the reason she was here, and she had to figure out a way to get these children to accept her, or at least respect her.

She glanced at the clock and stood from her desk. "Alright, children. It's time to head home for the day." She gave them all her sunniest smile. "See you bright and early in the morning, and don't forget tomorrow is our day to go leaf collecting, so bring a sack or pillowslip from home to carry with you." She pinned Brandon with a look. "Brandon, if I could have a moment of your time up by my desk, please? Everyone else, you're dismissed."

Purposely she turned her back and began to erase the chalk board, but inwardly she cringed, waiting for some missile or projectile to bombard her. With a determined clench of her jaw, she threw back her shoulders. *Show no fear!*

Amazingly enough nothing happened and soon, other than Brandon shuffling his feet as he waited for her to finish, the room filled with silence.

Finally, she hung the rag on its hook by the board and turned to face her little nemesis. My, but he had the most alluring big chocolate eyes. And right at the moment they were dripping with innocence. *Future women beware! Brandon McBride cometh!* She bit off a grin and folded her hands carefully in front of her.

"Did you need my help, Miss Jordan?" He looked around as though expecting her to ask him to carry something for her.

"No, Brandon. But I want you to know that I'm not going anywhere."

He seemed puzzled. "Not going anywhere, ma'am?"

"No matter the number of tricks played on me, I will finish out the school year. Now," she held up a hand to still his protest, "it can be a good year for both of us, or it can be a miserable year. Your choice."

"But ma'am, I don't...." Suddenly his eyes widened. "You think I'm the one that's been playin' tricks on you?" He shook his head, dark eyes wide and gleaming with sincerity. "It ain't me, ma'am. Honest it's not."

"Isn't. 'It isn't me, ma'am,'" she corrected automatically, then sighed. "You are dismissed, Brandon. See you tomorrow."

"Yes'm." He turned to fetch his lunch pail and slate.

Was that an impish gleam in his eyes? Or simply relief at not being in too much trouble?

She watched him dash out the door, his ever-present slingshot cocked at an angle in the waistband of his pants, and then sighed as she sank down onto her chair.

Wasp-venom-pain stabbed into her backside. With a yelp, she leapt to her feet. And pulled the offending stick pin from her posterior.

Her eyes narrowed. "Why that little—"

The back door crashed in, startling the rest of the thought from her mind.

A man tromped in, black bowler pulled low over his brow, red bandana covering his nose and mouth and a gun leveled at her chest.

Cade Bennett stood in the alley, his heart beating a competition with the tinny piano playing inside the saloon. Judd Rodale and his younger brother Mick had gone in only moments ago. He took a calming breath and checked his weapon one more time, then stepped around the corner and pushed through the bat-wing doors of The Golden Pearl.

The room looked the same as it had the night before when he'd scouted it with Rocky and Sky. Upright piano in the back right corner. Bar along the wall to his left. Stairs leading up to the second floor along the rear wall. And six round tables scattered throughout the room. Judd and Mick sat at a table close to the bar. They'd already been dealt in to the perpetual poker game The Pearl kept running. The dealer wore a white shirt with black armbands and a visor cap, and looked a little nervous as he dealt out a card to Judd. *The other two men in the game must be locals.* Cade didn't recognize them.

He sidled up to the bar and rested his forearms there, lifting a finger to the barkeep.

"What'll it be?" The man wiped his hands on a rag that looked like it would leave more behind than it would clean off.

"Whiskey. Make it a double."

The bartender sloshed the liquid into a glass and slid it his way.

Cade lifted it in a gesture of thanks and turned to face the room, propping his elbows on the bar and one boot on the rail below. He sniffed the whiskey but didn't taste it. He would need all his senses to pull this off.

The poker hand came to an end and Rodale raked in his winnings.

Time to turn on the charm. *Lord, a little help here.* "You gentlemen care to let a weary traveler in on a bit of the fun?"

Judd Rodale didn't even look at him. "You gonna drink that whiskey, kid? Or just look at it?"

Mick snickered and organized his stacks of coins, taking his brother's lead in not even glancing Cade's way.

Cade chuckled. "Well, I need all my wits about me if I'm going to go up against you Rodales in a poker game. I've heard you're the best."

Judd looked up then, scanning him from head to toe.

Good. He had the man's attention.

"I'm sorry, kid, but I can't say your reputation has spread as far as mine. I have no idea who you are."

Cade grabbed a chair and circled around so that his back would be to the wall when he sat. He turned the chair backwards and straddled it, setting his whiskey on the card table. "Well now, I'm going to ignore the fact that you called me kid in that tone, because basically I'm nobody." He stretched his hand across the table giving Rodale what he hoped was an irritated smile. "Name's Schilling. Cade Schilling."

The dealer fumbled the cards he was shuffling.

Judd's eyes widened a bit as he studied Cade, ignoring his proffered hand.

Cade felt his first moment of ease. So their planning ahead on this one had paid off. These men had definitely heard of Cade Schilling.

One of the locals gathered up his money and stood. "Time for me to call it a night, fellas. Catch you another time."

No one seemed to notice his departure. All attention at the table was fixed on Cade.

Mick cursed. "*You* are Cade Schilling? The Cade Schilling who—"

Judd cleared his throat loudly.

Mick caught himself. "—well, *the* Cade Schilling?"

Cade grinned. "Never met another one of me. So what do you say? We playing cards, or not?" Casually he removed a stack of gold eagles from his jacket pocket and laid them on the table.

Judd flicked a gesture to the dealer. "Deal him in."

"Now you're talking." Cade stood, flipped his chair around the right way, removed his jacket and hung it over the back. He rolled up his sleeves as he sat down again, and grinned at the men who were all staring at him in question. "Had a friend get shot once. Someone thought he had a card up his sleeve. I watched him die, choking on his own blood." He shrugged. "I've made it a point to roll my sleeves up for every poker game since then."

Mick chuckled and picked up his hand of cards.

The kid would be easier to win over than Judd. But if he could get Judd to like him, the rest of the Rodale Gang would fall in line.

Cade let the first two hands go, cringing inwardly at the amount of money Judd was taking off him. He reminded himself that the money was Sam's anyway – all part of the ruse.

They were halfway into the third round when Rocky and his brother Sky pushed through the doors, their badges plainly visible. Sky sauntered to a table and Rocky eased up to the bar. Cade's heart rate kicked up a notch. The other local folded, snatched his hat from the back of his chair and quickly strode from the room. The only other patron in the room hurriedly followed him out the doors.

Smart men. A little more of the tenseness eased from Cade's shoulders. Less potential for casualties. Less witnesses. The bartender, piano player, and dealer were the only others left now, and they would be easily convinced to keep quiet about the events that were about to unfold.

Cade thought through the plan one more time, making sure he had every detail of what was to happen figured out. Jason had wanted to be here too, but Nicki, the widow Jason had fallen in love with, was due to have her baby any day now and they'd all convinced him they could pull this off without him.

Lord I hope we were right on that count.

He laid a card aside and took another from the dealer. It was time to put everything into play. He lowered his voice and kept his perusal on his cards as he said, "Judd, unless I miss my guess, your dandy of a brother here has been sneaking down to town and has caused a little ruckus. Two lawmen just came in. One at the bar, one at the table near the door." He He

Judd's voice was just as low, barely audible over the plinking of the piano. "I see 'em. We don't have anything to worry about. Sheriff Collier wouldn't know an outlaw from a bread roll. This is his town."

Pretending great interest in his cards, Cade lifted one shoulder. "The barber said they brought in a couple new men. This must be them."

"Well, we ain't done nothing to warrant their attention. They mostly leave us alone so long as we keep to ourselves. I'll handle this." Judd swilled his whiskey and took a gulp then started to stand.

Cade flicked the corner of one of his cards. "I hear tell Judge Green's daughter is sure a pretty little thing."

Mick shifted uncomfortably in his chair.

Judd cursed softly and sank back down. "Mick?"

Mick couldn't seem to meet his brother's gaze.

Judd swore again. "I ought to shoot you, myself! We are just about—" he cut off, tossing Cade a glance before he returned his attention to Mick. "Now I have to figure out a way to get us out of here."

Cade leaned forward. "Maybe I can help you with that."

Judd glowered at him.

Cade pressed on. "I've been needing a place to … hang my hat, for a bit. I get you out of here and …?" He shrugged. Their whole plan hinged on the decision Judd would make right here.

Mick nodded at Cade. "You get us out of here and you can stay with us for as long as you want."

Judd wasn't so quick to take the bait. He lowered his brow. "Why would you do us any favors?"

Cade pushed out his lower lip and eased into a comfortable posture. "Suit yourself. Like I said, I've been needing a place to lie low. Word hereabouts is you have the best hide-out around, and …" He lifted his shoulders and resettled his hat, once again leaving the decision in Judd's hands.

Rocky and Sky stood erect and turned to face their table.

"Judd, just let him help us." Desperation tinged the edges of Mick's tone.

Judd glanced toward the slowly approaching lawmen. Then gave Cade a barely perceptible nod.

Cade suppressed a sigh of relief as he stood and swung his jacket over his shoulder. "Gentlemen," he said loudly, "the game has been fun, but I sense it is time to move on." He tipped his hat to Sky and Rocky as he stepped past them. They were already drawing their guns, right on cue.

"Mick Rodale, you are under arrest for the molestation of Missy Green."

Cade palmed his gun, spun around and swung his coat over Rocky's Colt knocking the aim down and away. He pressed the muzzle of his pistol to Sky's chest. Sky only had enough time to let loose a surprised cry before Cade pulled the trigger.

The report was a little loud, but about right.

Sky flew backward and crashed over a table, sliding across the surface and disappearing over the other side as the table toppled onto its edge. His body was concealed, only his legs protruded from one end.

Too bad about that. He couldn't see if the blood packet they'd rigged had worked.

Rocky had recovered from his pretended surprise by this time and had his Colt leveled at Judd's head. "Drop your gun! I will kill him!"

Calmly Cade turned and pressed the muzzle of his pistol under Rocky's chin. "Your friend over there is lying in a pool of his own blood. Do you think I'd hesitate to kill you too? You have five seconds to drop that gun."

Rocky's eyes narrowed.

"Four… three…"

"Alright! Alright!" Rocky's gun thumped onto the table and he raised his hands above his head.

This was the critical moment. Now he had to keep Judd and Mick from shooting Rocky themselves.

He kept his pistol aimed directly at Rocky and his body between him and the Rodales. "Have a seat in that chair behind you. Judd, Mick. I got this. I'll meet you outside of town."

Mick shucked his gun and pushed Cade aside. He stood trembling in excitement before Rocky. "Let me kill this one."

Dear God, give me wisdom. He hoped his breathing sounded normal to the others in the room. It rasped ragged and thready in his own ears. He made a quick decision, met Rocky's gaze and then thunked him a good one with the butt of his pistol. Not hard enough to actually knock him out, but Rocky took the cue and slumped over, toppling to the floor with a low moan.

Cade pierced Mick with a look. "You kill a lawman and it will follow you to your grave. Trust me, I know."

Judd had his pistol free now. He gestured the bartender, piano player, and dealer toward the back wall and they stumbled over themselves to comply. Cade made swift work of tying up Rocky and the bartender while Mick grumbled his way through binding the other two.

Judd stepped over and eyed Sky, then turned to Cade and nodded. "Thanks. We owe you one."

Cade smoothed down his sleeves, buttoned the cuffs, and swung his jacket on. "Best we make ourselves scarce." He wanted to get these two out of here before one of them decided to put an extra bullet into either Sky or Rocky.

Judd snapped his fingers at Mick. "Let's go."

With a sigh of frustration Mick followed them out the doors. They mounted up and galloped toward the foothills.

A tremor of sheer relief coursed through Cade. *First step down. Thank you, Lord.*

CHAPTER TWO

S haryah blinked at the bandit, her hand still holding the stickpin, frozen in mid air.

It only took her a moment to recognize him.

"Samuel Perry! You nearly startled me right through the Pearly Gates!" She slumped into her chair, resisting the urge to rub her posterior once more, and dropped the tack into her desk drawer. No need for Sam to know the problems she currently faced at the school.

Sam laughed and holstered his pistol. "Aw! You ruined my fun." He pulled the bandana down and winked at her. "I was hoping to rustle me a kiss from the prettiest school teacher ever."

Sharyah knew she should feel flattered by that. Instead her irritation rose. "And what if the gun had accidentally gone off?" Her father would have whipped her brothers good if any of them had ever tried a stunt like that.

Sam lifted his bowler and scooped his fingers through his straight sandy hair. "You're right. I'm sorry." He grinned then. "You should have seen the look on your face, though, Darling."

The "darling" grated. Especially since she knew he didn't really mean it. Sam might find her a passing fancy, but his affections belonged to someone else. The signs of a broken heart were all there. *I should know them well enough.* She just hadn't figured out who the woman was yet. But she had no doubt Sam dallied with her in an attempt to forget someone.

Who was she to talk? Wasn't that the same reason she allowed him to call? So she could forget Cade? She sighed and set to gathering the materials she would need at home tonight. "I'm glad I could be your entertainment for the day, Sam."

He turned serious in an instant. "I'm honestly sorry, Sharyah." He cocked his head to one side. "Is everything alright?"

She shook herself from her melancholy and forced a smile. "Yes, I'm fine. Just tired, I suppose."

"Children giving you trouble?"

"All's well," she quickly assured. Sam was the head of the school board. It wouldn't do for him to think she couldn't handle the children. "The students and I are just… learning to adjust to one another."

"Good." He clasped his hands behind his back and gave her a petulantly pleading look. "Let me take you to dinner, then. You won't have to cook and I'll be able to make up for my little bandito faux pas."

She carefully checked the first window to make sure the lock was secure. "You know my contract stipulates that I can't fraternize with men." Crossing to the other window, she checked it, too.

"Well," he stuck his lower lip out, "I happen to know the banker who is the head of the school board pretty intimately. I know he won't mind. And the other members are eating from the palm of his hand. They won't make a fuss. If they do he'll just call in their loans."

She grinned and slung her satchel over her shoulder. "This head of the school board seems a little arrogant and callous, don't you think?"

He laughed outright at that and reached to take the stack of books from her hands. "It's only arrogant if it isn't true. As for callous…," he shrugged, "maybe a little." With a grin, he held the door for her. "Mrs. Dougherty down at the boarding house makes a mean pot-roast, what do you say? I'll be a perfect gentleman the whole night. Besides, I have a surprise for you."

A surprise? Surely he wasn't planning to… No. It couldn't be. Sharyah lifted one eyebrow as she pulled the door to and latched it. "Something tells me you aren't used to being told no."

He shrugged. "True. So let's not start now, shall we?" He peered at her over top the stack of books, pleading with his dark eyes.

How could she say no to that? But what if he was planning—

she cut herself off from that thought and picked up the pace toward home. It was too soon. Even though she didn't have that to fear, she really should say no. But she simply didn't want to spend the evening alone. Her little cabin on the edge of town was very nice, but also … solitary. "Well, I would hate to be the one to introduce you to the word no, I suppose."

He grinned. "I was counting on that. How about I pick you up at seven then?"

"Seven sounds fine."

They had arrived at the cut-off she needed to take to get home.

Sam deposited the heavy books back into her arms. One toppled off and sprawled in the dirt. "I'll get it." He picked it up, brushed at the cover and then set it atop the stack and stepped to one side. "Very well, then. I'll be back this evening." He tipped his hat. "I'm very much looking forward to it, Sharyah. Good afternoon." And with that he hurried off toward the livery.

Sharyah rolled her eyes and readjusted her load. Pa would have tanned his hide for leaving her with a pile of books to carry, too.

As she started on toward home she mumbled, "But no man is perfect, right?" A dark-haired visage with alluring blue eyes immediately popped into her mind and she shook it away. "Oh stop it, Sharyah! Not even *he* was perfect." *I'm pathetic.* Still pining for a man who'd made it very clear he was only interested in friendship. But if she didn't find someone to marry soon, she would end up a genuine old maid. God had good in store for her. His Word said so. Obviously the time had come to stop being so picky and accept that she needed to readjust her wants. She would be nineteen on her next birthday.

She had nearly reached her front door when a loud shot rang out from somewhere in town. She paused to listen but there were no responding reports.

Strange. Perhaps someone scaring off a stray dog? Not likely. She wondered what that could have been about? With the Rodale Gang hanging around, who knew what could be happening. That thought brought Missy to mind and she made a mental note to stop by and see her on the way home tonight. It was a terrible thing to have happened to such a nice girl. Worse yet she felt sure, Missy had been subtly snubbed at church for the past two weeks by the other girls in town. As if the girl was somehow at fault for the monstrous thing that had befallen her. Sometimes society was simply ridiculous!

Smith Bennett squinted his eyes against the Oregon dust filtering over him from the churning of hundreds of hooves. He'd been riding drag for the past hour. Give him lead or flank any day of the week. The constant eating of dust that came with bringing up the rear wore thin, and quick.

He adjusted his bandana and checked the angle of the sun.

Another forty-five minutes and they'd circle up. Tomorrow they'd reach Portland and payday would follow a couple days after that. His boss on these runs had been fair, but this one would be his last. It was time to go back home.

He snapped his whip to the outside of a wandering cow, scaring her back into line.

What would Cade be up to these days? Had he sold the ranch?

Smith's jaw clenched. Doubtful he'd sold out. But whether his son would welcome his return, was another thing altogether.

Couldn't say as he blamed him, either. Running off the way he'd done after Brenda's passing wasn't something he was proud of. But time had given him a little distance and a clearer focus. Family ought to stick together. And he aimed to do his part to make that happen.

What Cade decided when he showed up... well, that would be up to him.

Sam arrived at Sharyah's door promptly at seven o'clock wearing a black suit and pulling at his collar. As he helped her up to the wagon seat, she glanced around. Seeing nothing remotely resembling his promised surprise, she teased, "I don't see my *surprise.*"

His brown eyes twinkled. "Patience is a virtue, Miss Jordan."

She smoothed the skirt of her best blue serge and adjusted her gloves as he strode around and hopped up in the driver's seat beside her. She tilted him a smirk. "A virtue best left for times when surprises are not pending."

He guffawed and slapped the reins down. "So patience isn't your strong suit, I see." The team settled into an easy gait and Sam rested his elbows on his knees and looked over at her. "I promise, Miss Impatient, that the surprise will be plainly evident the moment we arrive at the boarding house."

He was good on his word, for when they were still a block from Miss Dougherty's Boarding House Sharyah noticed the two men standing on the porch. "Sky! Rocky! Oh, thank you!" Before she thought better of it, she reached over and squeezed Sam's arm. "Thank you, so much!"

He reined the team to a stop and she didn't even wait for him to come around and help her down but jumped immediately to the ground and rushed up onto the porch. "It's so good to see you!" She pulled first Sky and then Rocky into an embrace. "I've missed you so mu—" She frowned, only at that moment realizing that Sky had winced when she hugged him and a distinct lump bulged on the side of Rocky's head. "—Are you two okay? Rocky what happened?" She reached toward his head.

He jerked away before her fingers could connect with the lump. "We're just fine." He met Sky's gaze briefly. "Nothing a little time won't ease. Now, how about you?" He offered her his arm and indicated the diner. "Shall we?"

"Yeah," Sky chimed in, "how are you liking your new job?"

Sharyah ignored their attempts to change the subject and stood her ground. "That shot I heard earlier? That had something to do with you two, didn't it?"

Both of her brothers looked guilty, but her focus zoomed in on Sam, who was just joining them. "And you? How do you know my brothers?"

Sam's feet shuffled. "Well… they were doing a little work for me today. I've known Cade for years – bought stock from him on a number of occasions, and he introduced me to Rocky and Sky not too long ago. I needed a little job done, so I went and hired them. And Ca—"

"—let's go into dinner."

"—that roast sure smells good."

"Cade? He's here?" Sharyah glanced around. A surge of joy pumped through her, yet a hint of unease at Sky and Rocky's rush to stop Sam from saying his name also niggled at the back of her mind.

Sam's brow furrowed speculatively. He settled his hands into his suit coat pockets, studying Sharyah with a curious lift of his brow.

Sky sighed and folded his arms over his chest, piercing Sam with a glare.

And Rocky attempted to pull her toward the diner's entryway. "Let's go eat, shall we?"

"He wasn't k-killed, was he?" Sharyah couldn't move. The sudden thought had frozen her to the boardwalk, and a wave of light-headedness washed over her.

Sky huffed, rubbed a hand over his chest, and winced. "Cade will most likely outlive us all."

Rocky touched the lump on his head. "Isn't that the truth." He looked at her. "He's not here, Shar. But he's fine."

The relief nearly took the strength from her legs. "O-okay. Let's go in and eat." She needed to change the subject. "How are Brooke and Sierra, Sky?"

The mention of his wife and daughter brought a smile to Sky's face as he held the door for them all to enter. "They're fine. Sierra's crawling all over the place now. And talk about a chatter box." He whistled. "Can't hardly get her to be quiet now that she's discovered she has a voice."

Sharyah chuckled and sat in the chair Sam held out for her. "I miss her so much." She glanced at Rocky as she settled the blue-and-white-checked napkin in her lap. "And Victoria and the kids? How's everyone?"

"They're good." Rocky's countenance softened. "They miss having you as their teacher, but they like Miss Cooper well enough. Especially Jimmy." He chuckled. "That boy's been studying his lessons like there is no tomorrow."

Sharyah laughed. "Oh good. He's so bright. Well, so are Damera and ChristyAnne."

"Yes, they all are."

The evening passed too quickly and Sharyah was soon blinking away tears as she hugged her brothers goodbye. Their work done, they would be heading home in the early hours of the morning. "Give my love to Ma and Pa."

Sky stepped back from the hug. "We'll do that. You take care of yourself now." His attention paused on Sam and held a hint of appraisal. "Be careful with my little sister."

Sam tipped his hat. "I wouldn't dream of being anything else." He touched Sharyah's elbow, escorting her out onto the boardwalk as Sky and Rocky headed up the stairs to their room.

They rode in silence for a time, the only sounds the soothing rustle of the wind through the junipers, the occasional squeak of wagon wheels, and the jangling of trace chains. The moon, hanging low and perfectly round, highlighted the road with a wash of milky light. She angled her head and studied the sky. Strips of clouds scuttled across the surface alternately concealing and then revealing the pinprick glimmer of the stars. Off to their right a whoosh of wings drew Sharyah's attention to an owl swooping through the moonlight to snatch up a poor, helpless critter.

Sam broke the silence with a soft cough. "So… This Cade… He mean something to you?"

Sharyah felt the heat that climbed into her face, and smoothed an invisible wrinkle in her skirt, thankful for the concealing darkness. "N-no. Not really. Just a childhood friend."

He turned and pierced her with an assessing gaze, the reins draped casually between his knees. "I see."

She couldn't meet his eyes. "I'd like to stop by the Green's if you don't mind."

"The G-Green's?" He returned his attention to the road. "Certainly."

Curiosity brought her focus to his face. Surely he wasn't like others in town who didn't want anything to do with the poor girl now, just because of the terrible thing that had happened to her? But Sam's face remained composed. Perhaps she'd only *thought* the name had startled him.

"I'll only be a moment," she said when he pulled to a stop outside the Green's small farmhouse just a short ways out of town.

"Hold on, I'll come with you."

Was that a cold determination she detected in his tone?

Missy herself answered the door and Sharyah gave her a quick hug.

"Miss Green." Sam tipped his hat and shifted from one foot to the other.

"Sam!" Missy's eyes widened and she paled slightly, but she quickly regained her composure. "How is Kat?"

Sam's mouth quirked up. "The same as ever, I'm sorry she hasn't been by to see you. She's... out of town."

Curiosity piqued at Sam's and Missy's reaction to each other. So it was Missy who'd broken Sam's heart? Or maybe this Kat? Sharyah brushed her inquisitiveness away. She could ponder more on that later. "How are you?" She tilted her head, really trying to assess if Missy was alright.

Missy shrugged, then looked down at the floor. "I've had better days."

"I know. I'm so sorry. I brought you something." Sharyah dug through her satchel and pulled out *The Black Arrow* pressing it into her friend's hands. "This is a brand new book. I just finished reading it to the children this week and I thought you might enjoy it. Maybe it will help take your mind off of... things for a few minutes."

Missy took the book without a word. She rubbed her hand across the cover and tears sprang to her eyes.

"Oh Missy, I'm sorry. You don't have to read it. I just thought—"

"No. It's not that." Missy's gaze darted to Sam, before she met Sharyah's eyes, her tears spilling over to course down her cheeks. "The book is wonderful. Very thoughtful. Thank you." She smiled. It looked forced but it was a smile none the less. "You have no idea how much this means to me, Sharyah. Really. You are the only—" She pressed her lips together. "Well," she lifted the book, "thank you. Would you like to come in?"

"I'm sorry I can't. Mr. Perry needs to get me home. My contract stipulates that I must be home by eight thirty. My brothers were in town and he drove me in to have dinner with them. But maybe later this week?"

"Sure. That would be fine."

"Good." Sharyah pulled her into another embrace. *Lord, give her comfort in this trial.* "I'll see you later then."

Sam was silent on the drive home and Sharyah didn't press him for details about the woman who'd obviously broken his heart. Whatever strain lay between him and Missy was really none of her business.

Sam reined the team to a stop outside the teacherage, walked her to the door, and tipped his hat. "Goodnight, Sharyah." He started away.

She touched his arm. "Thank you for dinner with my brothers."

He smiled. "Anytime. My pleasure."

She made herself a cup of tea and looked over her lessons for the next day. Then as she banked the fire and prepared for bed she thought over how truly wonderful it had been to see Sky and Rocky. She missed home so much. She would be teaching there still if she hadn't made the fateful mistake of slapping Cade Bennett that day in Victoria's sitting room.

He never would have realized she had feelings for him, if it wasn't for that. But he had figured it out, and he made it more than clear that he thought of her only as a little sister and nothing more.

And since she hadn't been able to stand the sympathetic looks she kept getting from everyone around town, here she was. Far, far away from Cade Bennett and his brotherly affection.

Sam was a good man. She would be happy with him. If he ever decided he could be happy with her too.

With a sigh, she crawled under the covers and blew out the lamp. She had nearly drifted off to sleep when a thought struck her and she bolted upright. Sam had said he'd hired Cade, too. Could Cade be working somewhere in the vicinity?

With a little groan of helplessness she flopped back against the pillows. Why couldn't she simply forget about that man? With a frustrated huff, she flipped over onto one side, mashed her pillow into a compliant lump, and forced herself to close her eyes and breathe normally.

She wouldn't give the man another thought.

If you would like to keep reading you can purchase Spring Meadow Sanctuary here: www.lynnettebonner.com/books/historical-fiction/the-shepherds-heart-series/.

Want a FREE Story?

If you enjoyed this book...

...sign up for Lynnette's Gazette below! Subscribers get exclusive deals, sneak peeks, and lots of other fun content.

(The gazette is only sent out about once a month or when there's a new release to announce, so you won't be getting a lot of spam messages, and your email is never shared with anyone else.)

Sign up link: https://www.lynnettebonner.com/newsletter/

ABOUT THE AUTHOR

Born and raised in Malawi, Africa. Lynnette Bonner spent the first years of her life reveling in warm equatorial sunshine and the late evening duets of cicadas and hyenas. The year she turned eight she was off to Rift Valley Academy, a boarding school in Kenya where she spent many joy-filled years, and graduated in 1990.

That fall, she traded to a new duet—one of traffic and rain—when she moved to Kirkland, Washington to attend Northwest University. It was there that she met her husband and a few years later they moved to the small town of Pierce, Idaho.

During the time they lived in Idaho, while studying the history of their little town, Lynnette was inspired to begin the Shepherd's Heart Series with Rocky Mountain Oasis.

Marty and Lynnette have four children, and currently live in Washington where Marty pastors a church.